Joseph Roth (1894–1939) was the great elegist of the cosmopolitan, tolerant and doomed Central European culture that flourished in the dying days of the Austro-Hungarian Empire. Born into a Jewish family in Galicia, on the eastern edge of the empire, he was a prolific political journalist and novelist. On Hitler's assumption of power, he was obliged to leave Germany and he died in poverty in Paris.

Michael Hofmann is a poet. His most recent collection, *Approximately Nowhere*, was published in 1999. He is the translator of six previous books by Joseph Roth.

Also by Joseph Roth

COLLECTED SHORTER FICTION OF JOSEPH ROTH

Translated by Michael Hofmann

Granta Books
London

Granta Publications, 2/3 Hanover Yard, Noel Road, London N1 8BE

First published in Great Britain by Granta Books 2001
This edition published by Granta Books 2002

A CIP catalogue record for this book
is available from the British Library.

3 5 7 9 10 8 6 4 2

Typeset by M Rules

Printed and bound in Great Britain by
Mackays of Chatham PLC

CONTENTS

INTRODUCTION

There seem to be two sorts of novelist, those – think of Kafka or Lawrence or Hemingway or Scott Fitzgerald or Thomas Mann or Jean Rhys or Paul Bowles – who made a particular study of short fiction, took a particular technical interest in it, achieved a particular expertise in it; and those others – Dickens, Flaubert, Turgenev, Woolf, even Joyce – who also wrote it, but more occasionally, more casually – or more deliberately – as a sideline, a by-product, or part of their apprenticeship. With the former, it would be perfectly sensible and worthwhile just to read their shorter works; with the latter, it would be rather peculiar and self-denying. It is not that they are necessarily less good or less distinctive, merely that their achievement doesn't form a kind of twin peak, but remains part of the central *massif* of their life's work.

Joseph Roth is of the second group. Even though the number of his stories has been bumped up over the past couple of decades from eight to eighteen in the German edition – the seventeen pieces presented here, plus *The Legend of the Holy Drinker*, which has already appeared separately – there are still not substantially more of them than there are novels – fifteen. And that's without getting into questions of classification. Three of the pieces here (four, with *Die*

Legende vom heiligen Trinker) were called novellas, and published between their own covers; two more, "Strawberries" and "This morning, a letter arrived . . .", are the beginnings of novels – or perhaps the same novel – and I'm sure further disqualifications could be devised. It is true to say, therefore, that the "short story" in the American sense of the term, the *Saturday Evening Post* or *New Yorker* sense, was not a regular arena for Joseph Roth.

One can think of two principal reasons why this should have been so. First, Roth was all his life a hard-working and self-motivating journalist in the wonderful Viennese line of Karl Kraus and Alfred Polgar. What he wrote was allowed to be unclassifiable, and to be justified by its beauty and distinctness. It had manifest literary pretensions, and irresistible literary qualities. This was the so-called "feuilleton", which partook of essay, article, travel piece, opinion, and, why not, short story. If therefore something short – something less than a novella – proposed itself to Roth, it seems likely it would have taken that particular gracious and elusive and accommodating form. There is a story about Roth on his 1927 visit to Albania, giving himself airs to the other journalists, swanning around, seemingly under no pressure to "produce", claiming in fact that he wrote "for posterity". They were accordingly gleeful when a telegram arrived impatiently soliciting Roth's copy ("Who's that? Posterity?!"), and he quickly sat down and knocked off one of his jewel-like pieces. – Still, it's easy to see that these are no conditions in which to write short fiction.

The second reason – or counter – might be to protest that Roth's novels are like strings of stories anyway, unpredictable, precipitate movements from tableau to tableau: this is certainly one's experience of reading them. (It's not irrelevant at this point to remark that many, perhaps even most of Roth's novels first appeared serialized in newspapers; some, even, in what one might call classic serial mode, with the novel unfinished and the serialization underway! Installment or miniature is therefore already in him.) To imagine Roth's speed, his fatalistic interest in the overthrow of a character, his huge appetite for catastrophe, all condensed down to ten or twenty or thirty pages, one might well conclude that a short story by the same hand would be quite an alarming prospect. And so they are.

The contents of this book break down as follows: the first seven pieces are early, preceding or barely contemporaneous with his first novels (*The Spider's Web* was serialized in 1923, *Hotel Savoy* and *Rebellion* in 1924). Some of them only came to light fairly recently, and are among his earliest surviving writings. Then come "April" and "The Blind Mirror", two novellas in widely differing styles, both published separately in 1925. "Strawberries", from 1929, marks an important turning-point in Roth's career, the turning away from contemporary observation and satirical realism towards the irretrievable, mica-shining past; it is Roth's first attempt to write his *Brody Roman*, a novel revolving around his childhood in Galicia. This is the shtetl he described in *The Wandering Jews*, the little border town in *Job* and *The Radetzky March* and *Weights and Measures*, and the first pages of it – deft, curt, beautiful, provocative, witty – are on a level with anything he ever wrote, I would say. (I wanted to have this volume called *Strawberries*.)

The woodpeckers were already hammering at the trees. It rained a lot. The rains were soft, water in its most velvety form. It might rain for a day, two days, a week. A wind blew, but the clouds didn't budge, they stood in the sky, immovable, like fixed stars. It rained diligently and thoroughly. The paths softened. The swamps encroached into the forests, frogs swam in the underbrush. The wheels of the peasants' carts no longer crunched. All vehicles moved as though on rubber tires. The hooves of the horses were silent. Everybody took off their boots, hung them over their shoulders, and waded barefoot.

It cleared overnight. One morning, the rain stopped. The sun came out, as though back from holiday.

That was the day we had been waiting for. On that day
the strawberries had to be ripe.

The last four pieces – and the absent "Holy Drinker" – need no
justifying or extenuating. They are among Roth's great achieve-
ments. "Stationmaster Fallmerayer", published in the first Nazi year,
1933, in an anthology of writers who had fled Germany, is, I think,
one of the great *coup de foudre* stories, or simply one of the great
stories on any subject; as good as Chekhov's "Lady with Lapdog",
or a story by a Soviet writer, Konstantin Paustovsky, which also left
an indelible impression on me (night, rain, Volga steamers, an officer bearing bad tidings, a widow), and that may, come to think of
it, owe something to Roth. (I've lost it, and the title.) "The
Triumph of Beauty", a cynical story about the loss of a woman, and
"The Bust of the Emperor", a lyrical one about the loss of a country, manage between them to synthesize Roth's 1938 novel, *The
Emperor's Tomb*. "The Leviathan" and "The Legend of the Holy
Drinker" are neither of them quite of this world. In them, Roth's
fabulism encompasses contraries as never before: both lean heavily
towards death, but are full of joy and serenity; magic and money;
irony and lyricism; naivety and wisdom; the structures and freedoms
of oral storytelling, and a penetrating but purely decorative psy-
chological insight, that's quite deliberately restricted to amusing
matters of detail.

Where does this latest book take us with Roth? It shows us a cen-
trifugal, kaleidoscopic creator. The first two stories set the pattern,
by offering us complete human destinies. (This remains typical for
Roth: he whirs through a life like a chainsaw – it sometimes seems
difficult for him to do anything less, to work by implication, to
show just a crisis or microcosm.) Roth does precocious small boys,
old women, men returning from wars, and, time and again, women
who have wasted their lives and their tenderness ("Barbara",
"April", "The Blind Mirror"). In the stories, we re-experience his

discoveries as a novelist of his subjects and settings: the small town and the transient visitor; the men struggling to make something of themselves ("Rare and ever rarer . . .", "Strawberries", "The Grand House Opposite"); the man in uniform and the calamity of love ("Fallmerayer", "The Triumph of Beauty"); what the fall of a man looks like, and the fall of a woman ("Career", "Fallmerayer", "The Honors Student", "April", "The Blind Mirror"); the moment in which a character is psychologically – chemically would be a better word – transformed for all time, as in this one exuberant instance from "The Leviathan": "Oh yes, this wasn't the old terrestrial Nissen Piczenik who was addressing an armed sailor, it wasn't Nissen Piczenik from landlocked Progrody, this was somebody else, a man transformed, a man whose insides were now proudly on the outside, an oceanic Nissen Piczenik." What some writers do by means of a gunshot, Roth does by a letter (as in *The Radetzky March* or *The Tale of the 1002nd Night*, but here in "The Honors Student", "Barbara", "Fallmerayer", "The Grand House Opposite", or even the boisterous but faintly embarrassing "Cartel" – which stands in relation to the rest of Roth's work a little as *Old Possum's Book of Practical Cats* does to the rest of T. S. Eliot's).

In fact, it seems to me that by stripping out and simplifying and merely sketching the outlines, these stories offer us a peculiar insight into Roth. They are something like his most autobiographical writing. Things are not embellished or complicated or dissembled as they are in the novels, but left more or less as they are. For a fabulist like Roth, an inventor, a liar, this is not necessarily an advantage, but it is certainly fascinating to the reader in its revelation of, shall we say, "a probable truth". For instance, the type of the boy in "The Honors Student" and the alarmingly analytical fragment, "Youth" – we see him later, for instance in Paul Bernheim in *Right and Left* – is surely a self-loathing bit of self-portraiture, I would guess. The narrator, barely sketched in, of "The place I want to tell you about . . .", who misses school, hangs around with an older friend in the cemetery (Regimental Doctor Demant in *The*

Radetzky March is another devotee of cemeteries), as he does again in "Strawberries" or "This morning, a letter arrived . . .", smokes and drinks, goes to the school of life – or perhaps the school of death – that surely is Roth. Then, there is the small, somewhat rascally town, with its park, its monument (or lack of monument), its soda pavilion (as in *The Radetzky March* again), all of it knocked all of a heap by the stranger, the visitor that Roth was later to become. These characters, tropes, emblems, call them what you will, as they come to be repeated in the purer, simpler contexts of these stories, lose their quality of invention and acquire some of the hardness of fact. Where everything else in Roth is phantasmagoria and variorum, this is an unexpected and somewhat endearing attribute.

I have translated, I think, getting on for thirty books, but never yet a collection of stories. It surprised me how demanding I found translating these. The absence of any sort of base or tone or constant meant that I was continually having to begin again. It seems an obvious point, but I was unprepared for it. That brought home to me – if I didn't know it already – what an incredibly varied writer Roth is. It begins with the well-upholstered satire of "The Honors Student", goes through the brusque minimal sentences of "April" to the somewhat fluffy sensitivity of "The Blind Mirror", to an increasingly resourceful and intelligent simplicity in "Fallmerayer" and "Strawberries". Some of these modes were more easily accessible to me than others, but I felt, obviously, that I had to learn them all. The last and not the least thing these stories provide is a swift index of the range of styles that Joseph Roth mastered over a writing career that spanned less than twenty-five years. To read them is to get some sense of the accelerated development otherwise known as genius.

Michael Hofmann
February 2001

THE HONORS STUDENT

Anton, the son of the postman Andreas Wanzl, was the oddest child you ever saw. His thin, pale little face, with its sharply etched features, emphasized by a grave beak of a nose, was surmounted by an extremely sparse tuft of white blond hair. A lofty brow lorded it over a practically non-existent pair of eyebrows, below which two pale blue deepset eyes peered earnestly and precociously into the world. A certain stubbornness showed in the narrow, bloodless lips, clamped tight. A fine, regular chin brought the ensemble to an unexpectedly imposing finale. The head was perched on a scrawny neck, the whole body was thin and frail. Altogether incongruous on such a frame were the powerful red hands that looked as though they had been glued on at the delicate wrists. Anton Wanzl was always neatly dressed and in clean clothes. Not a speck of dust on his jacket, no hole, however tiny, in his stockings, no mark or scar on his smooth pallid little face. Anton Wanzl rarely played, he never got into fights, and he never stole red apples from the neighbor's garden. All Anton Wanzl did was study. He studied from morning till late at night. His textbooks and exercise books were nicely wrapped in crinkly white greaseproof paper, all bearing his name on the cover, written in an oddly small, pleasing hand for

1

a child. His glowing reports, ceremonially folded, were kept in a large brick-red envelope next to the album of specially beautiful stamps, for which Anton was even more envied than for his reports.

Anton Wanzl was the quietest boy in the whole town. At school, he sat still, with his arms folded in the approved fashion, always keeping his precocious little eyes fixed on the teacher's mouth. He was top of the class, naturally. He was always held up to the others as an example, never was there any red ink in his books, with the exception of the mighty A that regularly graced all his work. Anton gave calm, factual answers, he was always there, always prepared, never sick. He sat on his bench at school as though nailed there. The most disagreeable thing for him were the breaks. Then everyone was made to go outside while the classroom was aired, and only the monitor stayed behind. Anton went out in the yard, hugged the wall fearfully, and didn't dare to take a single step, afraid he might get knocked to the ground by one of the noisy, rowdy boys. When the bell rang for resumption of class, Anton breathed a huge sigh of relief. Calmly, headmaster-like, he strode along behind the surging rabble of boys, calmly he took his place beside his bench, didn't say a word to anyone, stood there bolt upright, and sat down mechanically only once the teacher had given the command.

Anton Wanzl was not a happy child. He was consumed by a burning ambition. An iron desire to shine, to outdo all his comrades, almost destroyed his puny constitution. To begin with, Anton had only one end in mind. He wanted to be a monitor. At that time, this post was occupied by someone else, obviously not such an outstanding pupil, merely the oldest boy in the class, whose venerable years had sufficed to make him, in the eyes of the master, trustworthy. The monitor was a sort of stand-in for the master. He had to watch over his peers, take the names of boys who misbehaved, and pass them to the master. He was, further, responsible for the state of the blackboard, for the presence of damp sponge and sharp chalk, and he collected the money for exercise books, inkwells, and repairs to cracked plaster and broken windowpanes.

Such an office was vastly impressive to little Anton. He spent sleepless nights brooding determined, vengeful plans, he plotted endlessly how he might bring down the monitor, and take over the position himself. One day he thought he had found a way.

The monitor had a weakness for colored pens and pencils, for canaries, doves and little cakes. Such presents were acceptable bribes, and the giver could go on to make as much noise as he pleased. This was where Anton could take a hand. He never brought presents himself. But there was another boy who also didn't pay tribute. Since the monitor couldn't denounce Anton, because he was so obviously above suspicion, this other little boy, poor fellow, was the daily victim of his monitorial denunciations. Anton saw a wonderful opportunity. No one would guess that he wanted to be monitor. So, if he took the poor, beaten boy under his wing, and informed the teacher of the shameful venality of the young tyrant, that could only be termed just, fair and courageous. And there was no other candidate for the monitor's post than – Anton. So, one day, he plucked up courage and denounced the monitor. The boy was immediately stripped of his office, given a few blows of the cane, and Anton Wanzl was solemnly appointed in his place. He had made it.

Anton Wanzl loved sitting on the raised dais at the front. It was such a blissful feeling to look down on the classroom from a dignified height, to wave his pencil self-importantly, to issue warnings in some cases, and to play god in others, writing down the names of the oblivious noisemakers, thus delivering them to a condign punishment, knowing in advance the form an implacable fate would take. One was taken into the master's confidence, was permitted to carry exercise books, could appear important, enjoyed the awe of one's fellows. But Anton Wanzl's ambition was not satisfied. He always had a fresh goal in mind. And it was towards this that he set himself to work as hard as he could.

He was by no means a "crawler". He kept a veneer of dignity, each one of his little actions was carefully considered, he liked to

3

pay little acts of courtesy to the teachers, but never obsequiously, helping them into their coats, say, but always with a stern expression on his face. Each one of his flatteries was unobtrusive and had something of the character of an official act.

At home he was called "Tonerl", and was a figure of some standing. His father was the typical small town postman, half public official, half private secretary, in on all kinds of family secrets, a little bit dignified, a little bit submissive, a little bit proud and a little bit wanting a tip. He had the typical stooped walk of the postman, he scuffed his feet, he was small and thin like a little tailor, his cap was slightly too big for him, and his trousers slightly too long, but all in all he was a "decent fellow", and enjoyed the good opinion of his superiors and the citizens of the town.

But to his one and only son, Herr Wanzl accorded a degree of respect that he otherwise felt only for the mayor and the Director of the Postal Service. Yes, Herr Wanzl would often think to himself on his Sunday afternoons off: the Director is the Director. But think of what my Anton might one day become! Mayor, secondary school headmaster, alderman, and – at this point Herr Wanzl took a huge leap of faith and imagination – perhaps even Minister? When he expressed such thoughts to his wife, she would dab her eyes with the corners of her blue apron, sigh, and go "Ah. Ah." For Frau Margarethe Wanzl had an enormous respect for husband and son, and if she set a postman above all others, what could she do with a minister?

Little Anton paid his parents back for their loving care by being mightily obedient. Admittedly, it wasn't that difficult for him, because, as his parents didn't give many orders, Anton didn't have much obeying to do. But just as it was his ambition to be an outstanding pupil, so he desired to be thought of as a "good son". When his mother sang his praises to the assembled neighborhood women on the egg-yellow wooden bench outside the door in summer, Anton could feel his heart burst with pride, as he sat out in the hencoop with a book. He took care that his expression remained quite impassive, buried in his book, as though he didn't hear a word of their women's talk. For Anton Wanzl was a diplomat to his fingertips. He was too calculating to be good.

No, Anton Wanzl was not good. He lacked love, he lacked heart. He did only what he thought was clever and sensible. He gave no love, and asked for none. He never needed any affection, any tenderness, he wasn't given to feeling sorry for himself, he never cried. Anton Wanzl didn't even have tears. A good boy wasn't allowed to cry.

And so Anton Wanzl grew older. Or rather: he grew. Because Anton had never been young.

Nor did Anton Wanzl change when he got to the Gymnasium. He only became still more careful. He continued to be the scholarship boy, the model pupil, industrious, well-behaved and virtuous, he was equally good at all subjects, he had no so-called "favorites", because there was nothing in him that was to do with affect or taste anyway. He declaimed Schiller's ballads with verve and pathos, took part in various school productions, and spoke sagely and precociously about love – though he was careful never to fall in love himself, and with girls played the boring role of confidant and pedagogue. But he was an excellent dancer, a sought-after partner at dances and hops, his manners and his boots were exquisitely lacquered, both his trousers and bearing were nicely starched, and his shirt front supplied the purity that was lacking in his character. He always helped his peers, not because he wanted to, but because he was afraid he might one day need something from them. He continued to help his teachers into their coats, was always discreetly available when needed, and, in spite of his sickly appearance, he was never ill.

After sailing through his final exams, and the usual round of congratulations and good wishes, the embraces and kisses from his parents, Anton Wanzl paused to think about the direction his future studies should take. Theology! That would have been perfect for him, with his pallid sanctimoniousness. But then again – theology!

How easily one might come a cropper there! So not that. He didn't like his fellow-humans enough to be a doctor. He wouldn't have minded becoming a lawyer, especially a prosecutor – but law was vulgar and unidealistic. Philosophy was idealistic. And especially: literature. Even if, as people said, there was "nothing you could do with it". But if one went about it the right way, surely it was possible to make one's fortune and one's name. And going about things the right way – that was Anton's specialty.

So Anton became a student. The world had never seen such a "proper" student. Anton Wanzl didn't smoke, didn't drink, didn't brawl. Of course, he had to belong to a fraternity, that was deeply ingrained in his nature. He needed to have peers whom he could put in the shade, he needed to shine, have a position, hold forth. And even if the other members of the fraternity laughed openly at Anton, called him a lag and a stay-at-home, they were actually rather intimidated by the young person who was only just beginning his studies, but already displayed such astonishing learning.

Anton won respect from the professors as well. That he was clever, they could tell at a glance. He was moreover an extremely useful reference work, a walking encyclopedia, he knew all the books, authors, publication dates, bookshops, he knew all the latest, improved editions, he was an indefatigable browser and bookworm. Besides, he had a sharp logical gift, he was a bit of a swot, but the trait of his that the professors most welcomed was a truly delicious natural gift. He was able to nod for hours on end without getting tired. He was always in agreement. Never did he contradict a professor. And so it came about that Anton Wanzl was a significant presence in seminars and lectures. He was always agreeable, always quiet and conscientious, he tracked down the most obscure tomes, wrote out notes and announcements of lecture dates, and he also continued to hold coats, he was a Swiss guard to the professors, a doorman, an accompanist and a page-turner.

There was only one field in which Anton Wanzl had yet to make a showing: and that was love. He didn't need love. But then again, when he turned it over quietly in his mind, he was forced to agree that only the possession of a woman would assure him of the completest respect of friends and colleagues. Only then would the mockery come to an end, and then he would stand there, Anton, impressive, respected, untouchable, the very quintessence of a man.

Also, his immeasurable overbearingness cried out for a creature wholly devoted to him, that he could knead and shape as he pleased. Thus far, Anton Wanzl had obeyed. Now he wanted to command. Only a loving woman would obey him in everything. But it needed to be gone about the right way. And going about something the right way, that was something that Anton knew a thing or two about. –

Little Mizzi Schinagl worked in the corsetry department of Popper, Eibenschütz & Co. She was a dark, pretty little thing with two large brown doelike eyes, a pert nose, and a slightly short upper lip, exposing a set of shimmering little mouse teeth. She was, also, however, "as good as engaged" to one Julius Reiner, traveling sales-man specializing in ties and handkerchiefs, also in the employ of Popper, Eibenschütz & Co. Mizzi was fond of her clean-cut young man, but neither her little head nor her heart quite saw in Julius Reiner a husband for Mizzi Schinagl. No, she couldn't possibly give herself in marriage to the young man who just two years previously had been given a couple of resounding slaps by Herr Markus Popper. Mizzi wanted to have a husband to look up to, a gentle-man, a social superior. A real woman, endowed with that innate sense and discretion that a man can only ever hope to learn, she found certain aspects of the specialist in ties and handkerchiefs not to her liking. Mizzi Schinagl would have preferred a student, one of the swarm of young fellows in colored caps that waited outside for the female staff at the end of business hours. Mizzi would have loved to be spoken to by a gentleman like that on the street, only Julius Reiner always kept such an annoyingly close watch on her.

But just then, her aunt, Frau Marianne Wontek, took in a nice new lodger in her apartment in the Josefstadt. Herr Anton Wanzl was very learned and serious-looking, but he was wonderfully polite and attentive, especially towards Fräulein Mizzi Schinagl. On Sundays, she would take him his afternoon coffee in his room, and the young gentleman always thanked her with a friendly word and a smile. Once, he even asked her to sit with him a moment, but Mizzi mumbled something about not wanting to bother him, blushed, and slipped off to her aunt's room in some confusion. But when Herr Anton bumped into her on the street, then Mizzi was only too glad of his company, even taking a slightly roundabout route. She arranged to meet the student of philosophy, Herr Anton Wanzl, the following Sunday, and the next day quarreled with Julius Reiner.

Anton Wanzl duly appeared, simply but elegantly clad, his colorless, pale hair was more carefully parted than ever, but some little excitement did seem to be perceptible on his cold, white, marmoreal face. He sat in the park next to Mizzi Schinagl, thinking hard about what he should say. He had never been in this awful situation before. But Mizzi knew how to chatter. She talked about this and that, the evening came along, the perfumed lilac breathed, the blackbirds sang, the month of May came giggling out of the undergrowth, and Mizzi Schinagl forgot herself and said out of the blue: "Oh, Anton, I love you." Herr Anton Wanzl was somewhat taken aback, Mizzi Schinagl more than somewhat herself, she needed to bury her burning little face somewhere, and could think of no better hiding place than in the lapels of Herr Anton Wanzl's jacket. This had never happened to Herr Anton Wanzl, his starched shirt front crackled audibly, but he mastered himself – after all, it was bound to happen sooner or later!

When he had calmed down, he had an inspired idea. "I am thine, be Thou mine," he quoted half aloud. And he followed that up with a little lecture on the troubadours, he discoursed with feeling about Walther von der Vogelweide, got on to the first and second consonantal shift, and from there on to the beauty of our German mother tongue, and from there, a little unexpectedly, to the faithfulness of German womankind. Mizzi listened as hard as she could, she barely understood a word of it, but that was because he was a scholar, that was just how someone like Herr Anton Wanzl would express himself. She thought his lecture was every bit as lovely as the warbling of the blackbird and the fluting of the nightingale. But, herself bursting with love and springtime, she couldn't take any more, and she interrupted Anton's impressive lecture by planting a distinctly pleasant kiss on Wanzl's thin, pale lips, which he found it just as pleasant to return. Before long, kisses were raining down on him, that Herr Wanzl neither could resist nor wanted to. Finally they walked home in complete silence, Mizzi with too much on her mind, and Anton, for all his pondering, unable to find a single word to say. He was relieved when, after another dozen heated kisses and hugs, Mizzi finally let him go.

Ever since that memorable day, the two of them were "lovers".

Herr Anton Wanzl found his feet pretty quickly. He did his studying on weekdays and his courting on Sundays. It tickled his pride to be seen out with Mizzi by various fraternity pals, and to be greeted by them with winks and grins. He continued to display industry and stamina, and before long, Master Anton had become Dr. Wanzl.

He entered the Gymnasium as a "candidate", acclaimed and congratulated by letter from his parents, "most warmly" commended by his professors, and cordially received by the headmaster.

The head of the Second K. and K. National Gymnasium was Court Councilor Sabbaeus Kreitmeyr, a celebrated philologist, with many so-called ins, popular with the students, held in high regard by his superiors, and moving in the best society. Cecile, his wife, was adept at the management of a "big household", and put on soirées and balls with the purpose of getting the Director's little daughter, Lavinia – as he had rather unaptly named her – married off. Like many old-fashioned scholars, Court Councilor Sabbaeus Kreitmeyr was somewhat hen-pecked, he agreed with everything his redoubtable spouse decreed, and he believed in her as much as he did in the uniquely beatific qualities of Latin grammar. His Lavinia was a highly obedient child, who didn't read novels, was only interested in Classical mythology, and still managed to fall in love with her young piano teacher, the virtuoso Hans Pauli.

Hans Pauli had the true artistic temperament. Lavinia's girlish being had taken its toll on him. He was as yet inexperienced in love, Lavinia was the first female with whom he had spent any time alone, and he had never received as much admiring attention as he had from her; and even though the Court Councilor's daughter was no beauty – she had a very wide forehead, and watery, colorless eyes – she wasn't exactly plain either, and had a striking enough figure. Hans Pauli's dream was of a "German" wife, he put a high price on faithfulness, and, like most artists, he wanted a feminine wife, with whom he could indulge his moods, but also find comfort and relaxation. Fräulein Lavinia seemed an excellent prospect, and since she was in the bloom of youth, the artistic imagination of Master Hans outdid itself, and the aspiring virtuoso promptly fell in love with Fräulein Lavinia Kreitmeyr.

None of this escaped Herr Anton Wanzl on the very first evening he spent in the Kreitmeyr home. Lavinia Kreitmeyr didn't do anything for him. But the instinct with which life's honors students are kitted out told him that Lavinia would be a suitable spouse for himself, and Court Councilor Sabbaeus the ideal father-in-law. It should be easy enough to see off the infantile artist Pauli. One just needed to go about it in the right way. And going about something the right way – that was something Anton knew a thing or two about.

It took no more than half an hour for Herr Anton Wanzl to discover that the dominant personality in the household was Frau Cecile. To win the hand of Fräulein Lavinia, he would have to win the heart of her mother. And since he was rather better at entertaining elderly matrons than young girls, he combined in classic fashion the pleasant and the useful – *dulce* and *utile* – and set about courting the headmaster's wife. He offered her the kind of compliments that a fool like Pauli would have wasted on Fräulein Lavinia.

And it didn't take long before Frau Cecile Kreitmeyr was won over by Herr Anton Wanzl. Anton treated his rival Hans Pauli with polite condescension. The musician's sensitivity told him what he was up against. Foolish youth that he was, he could see through Herr Anton Wanzl more than any of the wise men and professors could. But Hans Pauli was no diplomat. He always told Anton Wanzl exactly what he thought of him. Anton remained calm and objective, Pauli lost his temper, Anton advanced the heavy weapons of his erudition against him, in the face of which Hans Pauli was helpless, like many musicians he wasn't a man of any particular learning, his slow-witted dreaminess didn't leave much room for "intellect", and he was forced to withdraw in confusion.

Fräulein Lavinia Kreitmeyr adored Bach and Beethoven and Mozart, but as the true daughter of a distinguished philologist, she had an equal reverence for learning. Hans Pauli was a sort of Orpheus figure to her, capable of charming even the plants and animals. But now a Prometheus had come on the scene, bringing the sacred fire of Olympus directly into the drawing room of Court Councilor Kreitmeyr. Hans Pauli had made an exhibition of himself several times lately, he barely figured in society any more. And Anton Wanzl was a man whom the Court Councilor held in very high regard, and whom Mama also praised. Lavinia was a dutiful daughter. And when Herr Kreitmeyr one day urged her to link hands with Dr. Wanzl in a partnership for life, she said: "Yes." The delighted Anton got to hear the same affirmative when he made his modest proposal to Fräulein Lavinia. A day was set for the engagement, it was to be on Lavinia's birthday. Hans Pauli grasped his tragic destiny as an artist. He found it unbearable that an Anton Wanzl had been preferred to himself, he hated the world and god and men. He bought a ticket, sailed to America, played in cinemas and night clubs, became a dissipated genius, and finally starved to death on the street. The engagement was celebrated on a gorgeous June evening in the Court Councilor's house. Frau Cecile rustled about in gray silk, the Court Councilor felt ill at ease in his badly fitting tails, alternately tugging at his skewed tie and his spanking clean cuffs. Herr Anton beamed next to his white-clad, rather earnest-looking bride, toasts were proposed and reciprocated, champagne bumpers clashed, huzzahs rang out through the open window into the tooting of the horns.

Outside, the waves of the Danube sang their ancient song of becoming and fading away. They transported the stars with them and the little white clouds, the blue heavens and the moon. Night lay in the fragrant jasmine bushes, and held the wind in her soft arms, so that not the quietest breath moved through the steamy world.

Mizzi Schinagl stood on the bank. She wasn't scared of the deep dark waters below. It must be lovely and soft in there, you wouldn't bump against corners and edges the way you did up on the stupid earth, down there, there were only fishes, mute creatures who didn't lie to you as wickedly as the horrible people did. Silent fishes! Silent! Her little baby had been born silent, been born dead. "It's better this way," Aunt Marianne had said. Yes, it probably really was better that way. And life was so wonderful! A year ago today. Yes, if the baby had lived, then she, the mother would have had to live as well. But now! Her baby was dead, her life was dead –

The silence was broken by low bass singing. Fraternity songs, old songs – they had to be students. Were all students like that? No! Wanzl wasn't! He wasn't even a real student! Oh, she knew him well! A coward he was, a smooth, sanctimonious hypocrite! Oh, how she loathed him!

The singing came ever closer. She heard the tramp of feet as well.

Anton's fraternity brothers were returning from their summer party. Xandl Hummer, student of laws, in his late thirties and his eighteenth semester, "Beer Barrel" to his friends, didn't easily get drunk but had made stupendous efforts now. His little eyes discerned the outline of a woman over on the bank. "Ho, brothers, there is a life to be saved!" he said.

"Hold on, miss!" he cried, "I'm just coming!"

Mizzi Schinagl stared dully up at Xandl's puffy red face. A thought abruptly flashed through her brain. What about — Yes, she wanted vengeance! Vengeance on the world, on society!

Mizzi Schinagl laughed. A metallic, cackling laugh. The laugh of a — she thought. She took one last look at the water. Then she stared into space.

She didn't listen to the student's crude remarks. But he took her arm. She was led in triumph back to Xandl's "digs".

The following morning, "Beer Barrel" delivered her to "Auntie" Waclawa Jancic's "Pension" by the Spittel.

Herr Anton Wanzl returned from honeymoon with his young wife. He was a strict, fair, conscientious teacher. He grew in the eyes of his superiors, moved in society, and embarked on a learned work. His salary went up and up as he moved through the various pay-scales. His parents had considerately died, one after the other, soon after his wedding. Now Herr Anton Wanzl astounded everyone by asking to be transferred back to his birthplace.

The little Gymnasium there was run by an elderly director, a rather slapdash fellow, a childless bachelor who lived in the past and let his duties take care of themselves. In spite of that, he had grown fond of his work, had grown used to seeing laughing young faces about him, to tending his trees in the big park, to being respectfully greeted by the burghers of the small town. The administrators in the regional educational secretariat felt sorry for the old man, and were merely waiting for him to retire.

Anton Wanzl arrived and took over the running of the school. As a senior master, he soon became deputy head, he compiled reports to the school inspector, took charge of the funds, kept an eye on the tuition and maintenance, in a word, established order. He still managed to get to Vienna from time to time, and at the soirées his mother-in-law continued to put on, albeit less frequently, he took the opportunity to give a gentleman from the Ministry a verbal report. He was a past master at putting his own role in the limelight, speaking about the headmaster with a persistent undertone of sympathy in his voice, and accompanying his words with an occasional, eloquent shrug. Frau Cecile Kreitmeyr did the rest.

One day, the old Head was taking a turn in the beautiful Gymnasium grounds with his deputy, Dr. Wanzl. The old fellow delighted in so much green, occasionally interspersed with a flash of pink-faced boy. It warmed the old heart of the Director.

Just then the school porter appeared in the avenue, bowed, and presented a mighty envelope to him. The Director thoughtfully cut it open, pulled out a piece of paper with a great official seal on it, and began to peruse it. Suddenly an expression of terror animated his old, slack face. He clutched at his heart, staggered and collapsed. After a few seconds, he had died in the arms of his deputy.

Headmaster Dr. Wanzl was content. His ambition was satisfied. From time to time he couldn't help thinking of the university professorship he could probably have made his own, but the thought never detained him very long. He was very pleased with himself. And still more with people in general. Sometimes in the furthest recesses of his heart he laughed at their credulity. But his pallid lips remained shut. Even when he was alone within his own four walls, he didn't laugh. He was afraid that walls might have eyes as well as ears, and could therefore betray him.

He had no children and didn't miss them either. At home he lorded it, his wife gazed up at him in awe, his pupils worshipped him. Only he hadn't been to Vienna, not for several years now. The last time, something very upsetting had happened to him. On his way home from the opera with his wife, he was accosted by a gaudily painted woman who took a look at his wife Lavinia beside him and cackled shrilly at him. That wild laughter rang in the ears of Herr Anton Wanzl for a long time.

Director Wanzl carried on living contentedly with his wife. But his constitution gradually weakened. His overstrained organism was getting its own back. His underlying weakness, so long suppressed by sheer force of will, suddenly manifested itself. Anton Wanzl was laid low by pneumonia. He took to his bed, never to get up. He died after weeks of terrible suffering.

All the pupils turned up, all the citizens of the little town, wreaths trailing long black ribbons covered the coffin, eulogies were given, farewells were taken.

But Herr Anton Wanzl lay in the depths of the black coffin and laughed. For the first time, Anton Wanzl was laughing. He laughed at the credulity of people, at the foolishness of the world. Here he could dare to laugh. The walls of his black box couldn't betray him. And Anton Wanzl laughed. Laughed long and heartily.

His pupils insisted on putting up a marble tombstone to their dearly loved and respected headmaster. On it, under the name of the deceased, were these words:

> Aye practice truth and honesty
> Until thy cool grave!

BARBARA

She was called Barbara. Didn't the name sound like hard labor? She had one of those faces of women that look as though they'd never been young. Nor is it possible to tell how old they are. Her rumpled face lay on the white pillows, and could only be distinguished from them by its yellow-gray sandstone coloration. The gray eyes fluttered to and fro, like birds that had gotten lost in the mass of bedding; but periodically they stopped to dwell on a dark fleck somewhere on the white ceiling, a hole or a sluggish fly. And then Barbara thought back over her life.

Barbara was just ten when her mother died. Her father had been a wealthy tradesman, who had started to gamble and had lost his money and his shop in short order; but he was back in the pub, gambling. He was tall and thin, and kept his hands buried in his trouser pockets. You weren't quite sure: was it his way of hanging on to what money he still had, or was it to prevent anyone else from reaching into them to see what they contained – if anything? He loved to surprise people. Even when his partners at cards, say, thought he had lost everything, he would still manage to nonplus everyone by pulling out some ring or trinket from his pocket, and carrying on playing. He finally died one night, quite suddenly and without warning, as though to deliver one final surprise. He keeled over like a sack and was dead on the floor. His hands were still in his pockets, and it was difficult to get them out. Only then did people see that his pockets were empty, and that he had presumably died because he had nothing left to lose . . .

Barbara was sixteen. She was put with her uncle, a fat pig-dealer, whose hands resembled the little cushions embroidered with "rest easy" or "forty-one winks", that were dotted about his living-room. He patted Barbara's cheeks, and it felt to her like five little piglets scrabbling over her face. Her aunt was a tall woman, lean and scrawny as a piano teacher. She had big, rolling eyes that protruded from their sockets, as though they didn't want to stay in her head, but wanted to get about and see the world for themselves. They were the pale greenish color of the cheapest kind of wine glasses. With those eyes, she saw everything that went on in the house, and right inside the heart of the pig-dealer, over whom she had extraordinary authority. She put Barbara to work, "to the best of her ability", but it didn't always come off. Barbara had to be terribly careful not to break anything, because then her aunt's green eyes would come rolling up like great waves breaking icily over her blushing face.

When Barbara was twenty, her uncle got her engaged to one of his friends, a rawboned carpenter with broad callused hands that were as massive and heavy as planes. He crushed her hand at their engagement so that the bones cracked, and she retrieved a bundle of lifeless fingers from his mighty fist. Then he gave her a powerful kiss on the mouth. And with that they were engaged.

The wedding that followed soon after passed off conventionally, with white dress and green myrtles, a brief, ingratiating address from the clergyman, and a wheezing toast from the pig-dealer. The happy carpenter broke a couple of the precious wine glasses, and the eyes of the pig-dealer's wife rolled over his strong bones without affecting him in the least. Barbara sat there, like a guest at someone else's wedding. She couldn't get it into her head that she was now a wife. Finally she did. When she became a mother, she gave much more attention to her son than to the carpenter to whom she brought lunch in his workshop every day. That aside, the man with the mighty fists was little trouble. He seemed to have an oaken constitution, always smelled of fresh wood shavings, and was as conversational as a bench by the stove. One day in his workshop, a heavy beam hit him on the head, and killed him on the spot.

Barbara was just twenty-two, not unattractive, the manageress of the business, and there was the odd journeyman who wouldn't have minded slipping into the carpenter's shoes. The pig-dealer came and trailed his five little piglets across Barbara's cheeks to comfort her. He was all in favor of Barbara marrying again. But instead, she took advantage of a decent offer for the workshop and thenceforth took in work at home. She darned stockings and knitted scarves, and so earned a keep for herself and her child.

She was almost consumed by love for her boy. He was a strapping little fellow, having inherited his father's raw bones, but given to tears and tantrums, and he thrashed so hard with his limbs that Barbara, watching him, could have sworn he had at least a dozen fat little arms and legs. He was an unprepossessing child, of a positively robust ugliness. For her part, Barbara could see nothing unpleasing in him. She was proud and content and praised his qualities of heart and mind to all her neighbors. She sewed little bonnets and colored ribbons for her son, and spent whole Sundays decking him out. In time, her earnings became inadequate, and she had to look for other sources of income. Her apartment seemed to be bigger than she needed, and she put up a sign outside the building, in funny, clumsy lettering that looked as though it might slip off the board at any moment and shatter on the hard paving stones, that there was a room for let. Lodgers came, strangers bringing a cold whiff of themselves into her apartment, stayed awhile, and drifted off somewhere else, only to be replaced by others.

But one day, it was the end of March, the eaves were dripping, he arrived. Peter Wendelin was his name, he was a clerk at a law-firm, and there was a shimmer of decency and trustworthiness in his golden-brown eyes. He made no fuss of any kind, unpacked his things, and stayed.

He stayed into April. He went out in the morning, and came back at night. Then one day he didn't go out. His door remained shut. Barbara knocked and went in, and there was Herr Wendelin, lying in bed. He was ill. Barbara brought him a glass of hot milk, and a warm and sunny gleam came into his golden-brown eyes.

In time, a kind of intimacy developed between the two. Barbara's son was an inexhaustible subject of conversation. Of course, they spoke about other things as well. About the weather and current events. But it was as though there was something quite different behind the unexceptional conversations, as though the ordinary words were containers for something quite exceptional and miraculous.

It seemed that Herr Wendelin must be fit and healthy and able to work again, as though he were just loafing in bed for his own private amusement. Eventually he did get up. The day was warm and sunny. There was a little neighborhood park, a rather grubby and dusty place, with gray walls all round it, but the trees there were already showing their first green. And if you forgot about the buildings enclosing it, you could think, briefly, that you were sitting in a proper, beautiful park. Sometimes Barbara went there with her little boy. That day, Herr Wendelin accompanied them. It was afternoon, the young sun kissed the dusty bench with its beams, and they spoke. But once again, their words were no more than containers, and when they fell off, there was naked silence around them, and in the silence was the trembling spring.

One day, it happened that Barbara had to turn to Herr Wendelin for a favor. A little repair was needed to the hook of the old hanging lamp, and Herr Wendelin set a chair up on top of the wobbly table, and mounted the unconfidence-inspiring structure. Barbara stood and held the table. When Herr Wendelin was finished, he happened to prop himself on Barbara's shoulder as he jumped down. But he had been back on the ground for some time, and had solid ground underfoot, and still he was grasping Barbara's shoulder. They didn't realize what was happening, as they stood there and didn't move and gazed at each other. For some seconds they remained like that. Both wanted to speak, but their throats were too tight to let a single word out, and it was like a dream in which you want to shout and can't. They were both pale. Finally, Wendelin took heart. He took Barbara's hand and gasped: "You!" "Yes!" she replied, and it was as though they had only just recognized one another, as if they had been casually adrift at a masked ball, and had only just taken off their masks.

And now a feeling of release came over the two of them. "Is it really? Barbara? You?" stammered Wendelin. She was opening her mouth to reply "Yes," when little Philip tumbled off a chair and raised a piteous wailing. Barbara had to leave Wendelin as she ran to comfort her child. Wendelin went after her. When the boy had quietened down, and there was just the occasional gurgle of a sob to be heard in the room, Wendelin said: "I'll come for her tomorrow! Goodbye!" He took his hat, and walked out, but it was as though there was a nimbus of sunlight all round him as he stood in the doorway and looked back at Barbara once more.

When she was alone, she burst out into loud crying. The tears gave her relief, she had the sensation of lying pillowed on a warm bosom. She allowed herself to be caressed by the pity she felt for herself. She hadn't felt this well for a long time, she felt like a child that had gotten lost in a forest, and after much wandering, had finally managed to reach home.

She had wandered about in the forest of life for a long time, and now she had gotten home. Darkness crept forth from a corner of the room, weaving veil after veil over all the objects in it. Evening was abroad on the street, and peeped in at the window with its single star. Barbara was still sitting there, sighing quietly to herself. The boy had gone to sleep in an old rocking chair. Suddenly he stirred in his sleep, and that reminded Barbara. She lit a lamp, put him to bed, and sat down at the table. The clear and sensible light of the lamp helped her to think calmly and clearly. She considered everything, her whole life to date, she saw her mother, her father, lying prone on the floor, her husband, the crude carpenter, she thought of her uncle, and she could feel his five piglets on her again.

But again and again, Peter Wendelin appeared too, with the sunny glimmer in his kind eyes. Tomorrow she was certainly going to say "Yes" to him, the sweet man, how much she loved him. Why hadn't she already said "Yes" to him tonight? Of course! The boy! Suddenly she felt a kind of rancor surge up within her. It lasted only for a fraction of a second, but by the end of it she still had the sense that she'd murdered her baby. She raced over to his cot, to assure herself that the child hadn't come to any harm. She leaned over him and kissed him and with despair in her eyes, begged him for forgiveness. Then she thought how everything was about to change. What would happen to the child? He would get a different father, and would he be able to love the boy? What about her, herself? Other children would come along, whom she would love more. – Was that possible? More? No, she would remain true to him, her poor little boy. Suddenly she felt as though she was about to leave the poor, helpless child tomorrow, to go into a different world. And he would be left behind. – No, she's not going anywhere, and it'll all be fine, she tries to comfort herself. But the fear keeps coming back. She can see it, she can see herself, leaving the little boy unprotected while she herself left with a stranger. But he wasn't really a stranger at all!

Suddenly the little boy cries out in his sleep. "Mama! Mama!" he goes; she bends over him, and he puts out his little hands towards her. Mama! Mama! It sounds like a cry for help. Her baby! – He's crying like that, because he can sense her leaving him. No! No! She will remain with him for ever and ever.

Her mind is made up. From a drawer she pulls out some paper and something to write with, and she marks the laborious, limping

21

letters on the page. She isn't excited, she's perfectly calm, she's even at pains to make her writing as nice as possible. Then she holds the letter in front of her and reads it back to herself.

"It cannot be. On account of the child!" She puts the paper in an envelope, and sneaks out into the passage to the door of his room. He'll find it tomorrow.

She returns, blows out the lamp, but she can find no rest, and all night she gazes out of the window.

The next day, Peter Wendelin moved out. He was tired and broken, as though he'd lugged all his bags himself, and there was no more shine in his brown eyes. Barbara stayed in her room all day. Before Peter Wendelin finally left, he came in with a little bunch of wild flowers and laid them silently on Barbara's table. There were tears in her voice, and when she held out her hand to say goodbye, it trembled slightly. Wendelin looked around the room for a moment, and again the golden gleam came into his eye, and then he went. Over in the little park there was a blackbird singing, Barbara sat quietly and listened to it. Outside the front door, the room for rent notice was once more fluttering in the spring wind.

The lodgers and the months came and went. Philip had grown, and was going to school. He came home with good reports, and Barbara was proud of him. She had the idea her son had some special destiny, and she was determined to do all she could so that he could study. In another year, it would be decided whether he would be apprenticed to a trade, or enter the Gymnasium. Barbara had great ambitions for her son. She didn't want all her sacrifices to have been in vain.

Sometimes she thought of Peter Wendelin. She had his yellowed calling card that he'd left behind on his door, and the flowers he had brought her when he came to say goodbye, both carefully pressed between the leaves of her prayer book. She didn't pray very often, but on Sundays she opened it to the place where the card and the flowers were, and she sat for a long time over her memories.

Her income didn't suffice, and she began to draw on the little capital that she had left from the sale of the workshop. But she couldn't go on doing that for ever, and she looked around for other possibilities of making money. She took in laundry. Early in the morning she went out, and at noon she dragged home a heavy bundle of dirty washing. She spent many hours in the fug of the laundry room, and it felt as though the steam condensed on her face and left the dirt behind.

Her face grew pallid and sandstone-colored, and round her eyes trembled a delicate net of fine fissures. The work deformed her body, her hands were cracked, and the skin bunched on her finger-tips from so much hot water. She walked with a stoop, even when she didn't have a bundle to carry. The work weighed heavily on her. But a smile played round her bitter mouth each time she saw her son.

She had succeeded in getting him into the Gymnasium. He didn't find it easy, but his memory retained everything he had heard once, and his teachers were happy with that. Every report he took home was a cause for celebration for Barbara, and she was always glad to buy him little treats. Extras that she had to economize for. Philip had no idea about anything, he was thick-skinned. He cried rarely, set out towards an objective and did what he had to do with a kind of bodily force, as if it were a matter of planing down an oak plank. He was his father's son, and he didn't understand his mother. He saw her working, but that seemed perfectly natural to him, he didn't have the fineness of perception required to discern the sorrow that was in his mother's heart, and that was in every one of the sacrifices she made for him.

And so the years swam by in the steam of dirty laundry. Gradually, Barbara's soul was touched by indifference, a dull exhaustion. Her heart kept only a few of its old silent rejoicings, among them the memory of Wendelin and a report card of Philip's. Her health suffered, sometimes she had to take a break from work because her back was in too much pain. But no complaints ever passed her lips. Even if they had, they would have been deflected by Philip's elephant skin.

23

It was now time for him to think of a profession. There wasn't the money for further study, nor the patronage for a place at the university. Philip had no particular desire for a profession, he didn't have any particular desires for anything. The most congenial area was theology. There were places available in the seminary, and it set you up for a comfortable and independent living. So, once he had finished school, he slipped on the robes of divinity. He packed his few belongings in a little wooden case and moved out into the narrow chambers of his future.

His rare letters were as dry as wood shavings. Barbara read them with difficulty and reverence. She started going to church more often, not because she felt any spiritual promptings, but to get a sight of the priest, and, in her mind's eye, to replace him with her son. She was still working very hard, even though she no longer needed to, but she was like a wound-up watch that can't stop as long as the little cogs are turning. But things were going perceptibly downhill with her. On occasion, she had to take to her bed and stay there for days at a time. Her back hurt her, and a dry cough racked her shriveled body. One day, the cough was joined by an incapacitating fever.

She lay there for a week, for two. A neighbor came by to do what she could. Finally, Barbara took the decision to write to her son. She could no longer hold the pen herself, she had to dictate. She hurriedly kissed the letter when she handed it over to be posted. After eight long days, Philip arrived. He was healthy but dirty, and wearing blue robes. He had what looked like a top hat on his head. He set it down on the bed very gently, kissed his mother's hand, and appeared not in the least put out by her condition. He talked about his doctorate, produced his diploma, and as he did so, stood so stiffly that he resembled the scroll of parchment, with his robes and hat as the tin roll. He talked about his work, even though Barbara didn't understand the first thing about it. At times, he lapsed into the complacent drawl he had heard from his professors, and had begun to affect himself. When the bells started ringing, he crossed himself, pulled out a prayer book, and spent a long time whispering with a reverent expression on his face.

Barbara lay there in astonishment. She had pictured it all so differently to herself. She began to tell him of her yearning to see him once more before her death. No sooner did he hear the word "death", than he began to talk about the hereafter, and the reward that awaited the faithful in Heaven. There was no grief in his voice, only a kind of self-complacency, and pleasure at being able to show his mother on her death bed what he had learned.

The sick woman felt a violent need to summon a little love from her son. She felt it was the last time she could speak, and, somehow automatically, as though receiving dictation from some spirit, she began, slowly and hesitatingly, to speak of the only love of her life, and the sacrifice she had made for her son. When she had finished, she lapsed into an exhausted silence, trembling with expectation. Her son did not speak. He didn't understand. He wasn't moved. He remained dull and stiff and silent. Then he stifled a yawn and said he had to go out for a while to get a breath of air.

Barbara lay there, not understanding. Deep melancholy throbbed in her and a grief for her life. She thought about Peter Wendelin, and smiled sadly. Even in the hour of her death, the shine of his golden-brown eyes was still enough to make her feel warm. A fit of coughing shook her. When it was over, she lay there unconscious. Philip came back, saw his mother's condition, and began frantically to pray. He sent for the doctor and the priest. Both came; the room filled with the sounds of weeping neighbors. But by then, uncomprehending, ununderstood, Barbara was stumbling towards Eternity.

CAREER

For twenty-three years, he had been assistant bookkeeper with Reckzügel & Co., saddle and leather goods exporters, and he earned three hundred and fifty crowns per month.

Gabriel Stieglecker was his name.

In order to keep body and soul together, he had been forced to look to other sources of employment – and with some success. Towards the end of each month, he helped out at Pollacek & Co., with Simon Silberstein and Bros. and with Rosalie Funkel. All told, then, Gabriel Stieglecker earned six hundred and seventy-five crowns per month. And at such a rate he had been dying now for the past three years and five months.

He was an excellent bookkeeper, reliable and prompt. Thanks to his services, Pollacek & Co., Simon Silberstein and Bros. and Rosalie Funkel all managed to do without a fulltime bookkeeper. He kept their accounts in order, knew what couldn't be told to the police and the tax authorities, and was as discreet as a hole in the ground.

Gabriel Stieglecker loved his work. He preferred green ink to blue, and red to green. But his favorite color of all was violet. All the bookkeepers in the world write numbers in black imperial ink.

But Gabriel Stieglecker, on principle, wrote his numbers in violet. He claimed to have it on good authority that violet ink was more durable than any other, and that it allowed itself to be absorbed with an unrivaled intensity by the paper. Yes, it was even safe to assume that figures written in violet ink would continue to exist – like luminescent ghosts – long after the paper itself had rotted away.

As far as Gabriel Stieglecker's figures are concerned, it should be said that they could not possibly have been taken for those of any other bookkeeper. They had a unique quality, specific to themselves, they were individuals, characters in both senses of the word. His 3s didn't have a belly, his 2s didn't have a hunchback, his 7s no tail. All these figures had "contour", they were as slim and delicate as modern girls, and in point of artistic elan, could only be outdone by the models in the newest fashion magazines.

For Gabriel Stieglecker loved the figures that were his creations. He gave them the breath from his own body, so to speak, and that may be why they looked so undernourished. He played with them, the way a boy might play with tin soldiers, he had them march past in double rows, and he marked the edge of their parade-ground with a grass green line. Or, with the red he caused a bloodbath among them, albeit one that never spilled messily over the field, but was drawn off with a ruler into tidy runnels. Come what may, order had to be maintained.

Otherwise, it wouldn't be possible to understand how, since the sixth month of the fourth year, Gabriel Stieglecker had been dying on six hundred and seventy-five crowns per month. And when I say "dying", that isn't a slip of the pen, or a figure of speech, it's what I mean to say. Because this is a true story, I have changed the name to Gabriel Stieglecker, but he is a real person. In any case, the story is too extraordinary to have been made up by anyone but life itself. As may be seen from what follows.

Gabriel Stieglecker was still a guest at the regulars' table at the Café Aspern, where he took his black coffee with saccharine every Sunday. And every Sunday, just as he was thinking about the strange sheen of his newly bought violet ink, he was forced to listen to reproaches. Why hadn't he asked for a raise yet? Didn't he see he was being exploited in the most shameful way? in these times? by that firm? by society?

In order to put these reproaches thoroughly behind him, Gabriel Stieglecker went to the office after each of these Sunday rounds to copy figures. He got through all his work for Monday morning, and he would have gone to bed a happy man, if he hadn't worried instead – worried that he might not have left himself anything to do the following morning.

Gabriel Stieglecker's Sunday nights were full of torments and anxieties.

In fact, Gabriel Stieglecker could have done without Sundays altogether.

Then, all on one day, the following things occurred:

The laundrywoman announced a ten percent rise in her charges;

the electric tram introduced a two crown fare;

and his landlady quoted "the rise in electricity prices" as a reason to hike up the rent by thirty crowns.

(The fact that Gabriel Stieglecker still had no electric light in his room I simply take as read, and only mention it now lest some readers decide to take the landlady's part.)

This threefold calamity prompted the assistant bookkeeper Gabriel Stieglecker to have a word with the principal bookkeeper.

The principal bookkeeper took off the spectacles that he wore to work in, and put on his golden pince-nez; which was something he usually only did when the head clerk sent for him.

Whereupon the principal bookkeeper did not look at Gabriel Stieglecker, as might have been expected, through the middle of his lenses, but rather over their gold rims. At the same time, he inclined his head down on to his chest, as though planning to charge Gabriel with some invisible horns.

"Wasn't your twenty percent raise enough for you then?" said the principal bookkeeper, who was only the principal bookkeeper by virtue of the fact that he had been copying figures in the firm for thirty-two years now; and, needless to say, only ever in imperial ink.

The question was whispered, but it bore the same unambiguous message, say, as a rumble of thunder emerging from the midst of a bank of fleecy clouds.

"I never had a twenty percent raise!" groaned Gabriel in reply.

"Then you'd better ask for it, hadn't you," the principal book-keeper said aloud, whereupon he took off his pince-nez, and put his spectacles back on.

That was the signal for Gabriel Stieglecker to go away.

He went back to his desk and thought things over. Of course one couldn't go and ask for a twenty percent raise, just like that. But by carefully making mention of the recent raise kindly afforded to all employees, and with special reference to the rising cost of living, one might ask, in all humility, for a raise of, say, fifty crowns.

Gabriel Stieglecker dipped a new pen in the violet ink with the strange sheen, and addressed a letter to his boss. He asked for fifty crowns and signed himself "Your humble servant", right in the bottom right hand corner. So far down that his surname almost slipped off the table.

The following morning, Gabriel Stieglecker found a letter on his desk, in which the firm informed him that, as of the fifteenth inst., his monthly salary would be raised by twenty-five crowns.

At home, to his great surprise, Gabriel Stieglecker found another letter. This one was from the firm of Simon Silberstein and Bros., where Gabriel regularly helped out with the bookkeeping. God forbid, could they be about to tell him they had no further need of his services? Then he would be done for.

But what Silberstein and Bros. had to say to the bookkeeper Gabriel Stieglecker was that they had considerably expanded their business, and wanted to hire him as their principal bookkeeper on a starting salary of one thousand crowns per month. Would Gabriel Stieglecker be so kind as to write promptly to let them know whether "he might be in a position" to accept their offer.

First, Gabriel Stieglecker assured himself that the signature was genuine, and then he sat down at his desk to express his willingness to join Simon Silberstein and Bros. on the conditions listed in theirs of the ——th inst. Then he remembered that he didn't have any violet ink at home. And of course he couldn't write a letter of such decisive importance in imperial black.

While he ate his mashed potatoes and gravy, he started to have doubts. Of course he would have to give in his notice. Only how? Just by writing a letter to the company? Was that really all it took? He had been with them for twenty-three years now. Two more years, and he would be up for an award. The boss would come in person and give him a present, maybe some extraordinary attention, and the head clerk might make a little speech, and the principal bookkeeper would wear his golden pince-nez. Was it possible, under these circumstances, simply to give in one's notice?

And even then! The notice was really the least of it! Because of course the boss, or at the very least, Herr Reckzügel junior, would call him in to the executive office. And the office, yes, that's what Gabriel was really afraid of.

There was a double door. The outer door was wood, the inner one was padded. It was not unlike the door of a safe, it was so quiet and distinguished. If you so much as looked at the door, you felt a little bit tired. Sitting on the upholstered leather chairs, you were in the sort of pre-hypnotic condition that you found yourself in when Herr Reckzügel addressed you. The office had wide, comfortable leather sofas round a nut brown table. In the left hand corner there was a massive writing desk, and on the left wall slept the brown fire-safe, with the closed metal shutters over its combination locks. Meanwhile, the air was full of an intoxicating scent of Havanas, pineapples and wax polish.

Gabriel had such a distinct sense of the room that he fell into a kind of lethargy. And it was in that state that he wrote his reply to the firm of Simon Silberstein and Bros., in which he stressed that, while he felt greatly honored by their offer, in view of his long association with his present employers, for whom he had now been working for twenty-three years, he felt obliged to ask for a week in which to consider the position.

That week was the most disagreeable in Gabriel's entire less-than-agreeable life.

Gabriel Stieglecker had even forgotten his figures. He wasn't really thinking about them, and on occasion – just imagine! – he even filled up a whole row on the debit side with black imperial ink. From time to time, his 2s had a hunchback, and his 7s a little tail. It was awful.

Gabriel had to make his mind up by Monday. On Sunday he didn't go to his regular café. He didn't go in to the office either.

Instead, in view of the mild, springlike weather, Gabriel took a walk in the park. And there he met the firm of Simon Silberstein and Bros.

The firm of Silberstein and Bros. treated Gabriel with extraordinary consideration. They seemed to take it for granted that he would be joining them as bookkeeper, and that it was just a question of dotting the i's and crossing the t's. By way of conclusion, they went on to invite him to a modest supper in the park restaurant. –

When Gabriel got back on Sunday night, he had decided that he would join the firm of Silberstein and Bros. as a bookkeeper.

He got up at five a.m., shaved, and did his exercises with a chair. He breathed in, held his breath, and behaved, all in all, exceedingly strangely. The exercises were a form of Swedish courage.

Then he took the tram to work – for the first time since the introduction of the new two-crown fare.

Swiftly and almost youthfully, he sat down at his desk, dipped a fresh pen into the violet ink with the strange sheen, and wrote out his notice.

Just as he was about to sign himself "Your humble servant", the office boy came up to him. Gabriel was wanted by the boss.

Not since the first of January, the day on which, as tradition required, Gabriel Stieglecker had wished his boss the best of luck for the year just beginning, had Gabriel Stieglecker been inside the perilous, hypnotizing room. What did the boss want with him? Maybe he had gotten wind of Gabriel's intention, and wanted to head him off? Well, so much the better!

In the boss's office, there was the emphatic smell of cigars, pineapples and Perolin.

Herr Reckzügel senior was standing in the middle of the room, under the chandelier, handily reflecting its lowest brass ball on his shiny pate, holding a dark blue jacket over his arm.

Gabriel stopped right by the padded inner door. He felt quite stunned. As through a very thick wall he heard his boss say:

"Herr Stieglecker, I just wanted to say that I've turned up this in and of itself" – Herr Reckzügel was rather given to the expression "in and of itself" – "very serviceable jacket in my wardrobe. I have formed the impression that your current circumstances left something to be desired. Well, I just wanted to let you know that in and of itself I would have nothing against it. I hope you take my meaning, and so on and so forth." Herr Reckzügel always put in "and so on and so forth" when he couldn't think of the exact words.

Gabriel Stieglecker staggered out with the jacket, and tottered back to his desk. There he collapsed. He ripped up his resignation letter in tiny pieces. And all the while imagined that he was ripping up the jacket.

How, under these circumstances, could you still resign? The jacket, the jacket! How could he be so ungrateful! He had been presented with a jacket, and now he wanted to resign?! Not he, not Gabriel Stieglecker.

Instead he did as follows: Once again he dipped a fresh pen in the violet ink with the strange sheen and wrote to the firm of Simon Silberstein and Bros. to say that, while properly grateful for yesterday's kind invitation, he saw himself compelled, in view of certain very particular developments that had only occurred within the last hour, regretfully to inform, etc.

Then, with the selfsame pen and in the violet ink with the strange sheen, Gabriel proceeded to draw slim flawless figures on the credit side.

They were quite the most majestic figures that Gabriel Stieglecker had ever drawn.

THE PLACE I WANT TO
TELL YOU ABOUT . . .

The place I want to tell you about would probably once have been described as being some way out of town. No one would think of saying so today. It is still, admittedly, bordered by open fields and boggy meadows, but the crumbling walls that surround it are encrusted with poor hovels, like eaves with the nests of house-martins. Women stand in front of their dirty yellow doors chatting, and children tumble in the dirt and scrap. In the springtime, the cuckoo calls there, interrupting the chitchat of the women, the blackbird whistles, and in the evening, an attentive listener will catch the sheerest nightingale gold pouring from the tiny throats.

The place whose situation I was describing to you is the old cemetery of my native town. The weathered inscription over the boarded-up entrance bears the date 1470. The cemetery has been closed for at least fifteen years now by the praiseworthy magistrate of my birthplace. "As a danger to public health", as was said in the announcement. The people of my native place often enjoyed long lives – it was not unknown for them to live to the age of a hundred, or even longer. So the little old cemetery only rarely acquired new inhabitants. But one fine day – or rather, one fine year – all that was to change. My respected fellow-citizens seemed no longer to care for this earth, and they went, before their allotted span, on that journey to the unknown land, from whose bourn no traveler returns. Their mortal remains were, however, no longer laid to rest in the old cemetery as before, but were taken a little further afield. A new burial-place was opened in the vicinity of the so-called frontier woods; and the old cemetery was closed.

But of course there had to be a warden in place, to show the grandchildren and great-grandchildren the resting-places of their grandfathers and -mothers, should they ever be minded to visit them, whether they wanted to have a good cry and go away comforted, or whether they wanted to ask the departed, who could be expected to be on a good footing with the Almighty, to intercede for them in some greater or lesser matter. It was strange, then, that no one wanted to take on this wardenship. Finally a former usher agreed to do it, a well-known atheist from a nearby German settlement, a misanthrope who barely spoke to anyone, took huge quantities of snuff, and seemed very much at home in this gloomy setting. He had known many of the dead when they had been alive, and could give information on them to whatever inquisitive grandchildren or great-grandchildren might present themselves. There was also a little patch of untenanted ground, where Martin Schwab — for that was his name — could grow potatoes and beets. He moved into a little room in the warden's cottage, which was also the side-entrance to the cemetery, and there he took snuff, roasted potatoes, and generally kept himself to himself.

When I was a student at the Gymnasium, I used to spend many hours in that cemetery. If I knocked on old Martin's door, the beaked nose of my friend would show in a grille, and a cavernous voice would inquire: "Did you bring any baccy?" And if I held a little package up to Martin's nostrils, he would sniff at it for ever, it seemed to me, maybe five minutes, as though he wanted, elephant-like, to snuff it up through the grille. Then, finally, he would draw back the heavy bolt, make a grab for the package, let me in, and push the bolt again. I would make my stumbling way through

Martin's poky room, over broken chairlegs and vast, lumpy potatoes, and out the other door into the cemetery. I lit a cigarette to put off the wasps and the insects, and spent hours wandering among the graves, reading their various inscriptions, sitting on stones that had been half swallowed up by the earth, communing with bygone times and long-forgotten families.

Among the newer gravestones was one that bore the legend: Markus Möllner, d. 15 June 1901.

I remembered old Markus. He had often been a guest in my grandfather's house, and I vividly remembered the extraordinary stories he used to tell. Wanting to learn a little more about him, I decided I would ask around among the town's older inhabitants. The first one I turned to was, not unnaturally, Martin. He claimed not to know anything about him. I held out the prospect of some tobacco – and that did the trick. Martin told me his story.

Towards the end of the nineteenth century, the people of my native place were of two sorts: they were either very poor or very rich. To put it another way, there were masters and servants. The Almighty, who always takes the side of the rich, seemed to have created the poor for the exclusive purpose of making life pleasanter for the rich. There were patricians and plebeians. The latter either worked for the former directly, as coachmen, cooks, servants and lackeys, or indirectly, i.e. by supplying domestics, as agents, dealers, suppliers of butter, eggs and poultry to the houses of the rich, they were sent out for hot meals, they baked and washed and lived for and from the rich. The rich, of course, had a monopoly of all the public offices of the town. Parish-councillors came from their ranks, they made up the boards of public institutions, they were the ones who managed the orphanages and inspected the schools. They were always dressed in formal dark suits, shiny top hats, gleaming boots, they kept their little pot bellies under flowered waistcoats and golden watch-chains, and on formal occasions, it was their breasts that sparkled with various medals and orders. They sent their sons to the Gymnasium.

And once they had dodged past the simultaneous equations and irregular verbs to their final examinations, they either took on some public or private office, or followed the well-trodden path to the capital, to return having completed their degrees, as qualified doctors, lawyers, Gymnasium teachers, etc. Admittedly, there were also instances of one or other of them being so degenerate that he forgot to return to his birthplace, and vanished without trace in the wonderful world of the Almighty's creating. But that only happened in a small minority of cases, and all in all, life in my hometown followed the same slow immemorial trot.

But then someone came along – and the son of the burgomaster at that – who shook the little town right out of its customary sleepiness, and made the good souls of his fellow-citizens go all of a tizz.

Even in his Gymnasium days, young Markus had been a case apart. He turned the girls' heads, had colorful adventures, got into slanging matches with the teachers, and – worst of all, and sufficient on its own to instill panic fear in the bosom of the burgomaster and his bosomy wife – Markus wrote verses. Nothing would deter him: neither punishment nor blows nor threats to send him home had the slightest effect. Markus wrote verses.

He hated the Gymnasium, he hated the rules, he hated the whole narrow-minded small town world he had been condemned to live in. So it was a huge relief to him, once he had scraped through his final exams, when he could finally spread his wings. In the end, with bags packed with necessary and unnecessary things, sent on his way by fatherly advice and bedewed by motherly tears, he trundled towards the capital city, the site of his aspirations. There he registered in the law faculty, and found himself a student.

Laws and decrees – nothing could have been more calculated to rub the young Markus up the wrong way. He cut his lectures, had no interest in his studies, lived the life of Riley, drank and lost vast sums at cards. When his Papa, "the old geezer" as Markus privately referred to him, urged him in his short and rather infrequent but far from vacuous letters to go on and take his exams, Markus replied that he was fully prepared, and the exams would be a breeze, and if it was anyone's fault that he hadn't done them yet, it was his father's. For, as Markus went on to explain, the university proceeded alphabetically, and seeing as his name was Zwerdling,* and he was the last on the list, with some nine thousand students ahead of him, he had no option but to be patient. The good burgomaster had run a business all his life, and his ideas about universities and studying were accordingly vague. When he went to one of the local schoolmasters to ask if things really were like that at universities, the man crinkled up his eyes, thought to himself that the rich young man might as well have himself a few jolly years, and replied that it was quite possible that there was a new disposition that did indeed run along alphabetical lines. And so the burgomaster calmed himself, and with exemplary punctuality sent his son the required sum on the first of every month. But then, as demands for larger and larger sums continued to be heard from the capital, the burgomaster one day packed his bag, remembering the umbrella with the ivory handle, and set off for Vienna to see for himself.

He went to his son's digs, and found him in the midst of a most lively, mixed company. His Papa was the last person Markus had expected to see. He needed to come up with a story, and pretty quickly. A hoary old student was put forward as a professor, whose birthday it happened to be that day, and who was celebrating it in the home of his favorite student. It would have worked too, only the burgomaster couldn't help wondering what women were doing at a professor's birthday celebrations. He thought about it briefly, then asked his son to step into the hall, where he gave him two resounding slaps in the face. This shocked the company to such an extent that, perhaps fearing a similar fate themselves, they hurriedly

---

* Either absent-mindedly or to make this point Roth has changed the character's name

left the field, taking the "professor" with them. Nor was that the end of it. A terrible scene ensued, in which Herr Zwerdling swore on his chain of office that he would wash his hands of his only child, and he got on the train, and rode home. Neither the pleas of his friends nor the tears of his wife made any difference. Markus, for his part, disappeared.

Years passed. The burgomaster and his wife were dead and buried in the cool earth. Their house had been acquired by a doughty butcher who had red lamps in front of the door to light up the juicy cuts of meat in the window. There was a new spirit abroad in the little town. It was the spirit of electricity and democracy, factories sprang up out of the ground overnight, strangers were for ever coming and going, a splendid hotel was put up, and a burgomaster of quite another type than the worshipful Herr Zwerdling now occupied the curule chair in the town hall. Then one day Markus came home. He was sporting a wild gray beard and a floppy hat, an artist's cravat and a long tailcoat and gaping shoes. He went to the man who now owned the house his parents had once occupied. No one ever learned what was said between them. But that same day, Markus moved into a little bow-windowed first floor room in the butcher's house, bought himself a shiny, if resolutely old-fashioned bowler hat, a black coat, and boots of the same color. Thereupon, he called on all the rich people in the town. Everywhere, they asked to hear his story. Markus told it. But he had the savvy always to conclude his absorbing narrative with a request that couldn't be refused. They were always for little things: a razor, a tie, a tie-pin. He was given them, and other things besides. Every day, he took his lunch somewhere else. The people who had known the old burgomaster presumably felt honored to have young Zwerdling in their homes. The rich were happy to have him. But in time the guest became a kind of domestic appliance. Markus was a kind of superior servant, who performed all the tasks that were entrusted to him to the satisfaction of his taskmasters.

Markus had a great aptitude for domestic tasks. To him, the most impossible things became possible. He could repair broken oil-lamps flawlessly, knot rope-ladders, prepare cunning mousetraps, mix rat-poison, sharpen knives to hair-sharpness, and block up mouseholes. And there was much, much more besides. He was especially good with children, and he knew wonderful stories to tell them. He could spin anecdotes, make fireworks, carve puppets and perform little playlets. But even his personality gave the children something to entertain them. He had a stooped gait, sharply etched features, small, watery blue eyes, a curved beak of a nose, a hairless skull on which the inevitable topper shimmered formally, the long skirts of his tailcoat flapped round his trembling knees, his yellow trousers were tucked into boots polished to a mirroring shine, his left hand was always in a canary-yellow leather glove, which Markus only ever took off – with a formal gesture – to work. In short: Markus could do everything. If something was needed in the household – Markus would fetch it. Admittedly, it often transpired that some essential tool, such as an ax or a saw had gone astray somewhere. And old Markus would have taken it somewhere where it was required. In this way, he set up an informal circulation of property among the various houses, so that oftentimes a citizen would be astounded to notice something of his in his all-unknowing neighbor's house. But no one really minded old Markus. He was a useful pet and an "honest soul".

Yes, above all, Markus was honest. Perhaps even too honest for his own good. A remarkable transformation had taken place in him. The youthful rebel and romantic and sworn enemy of all human laws had turned into a dusty pedant, a stern "moralist", stiffly pressed into his bourgeois straitjacket, a walking book of laws. Infinitely proud of his patrician forefathers, he still didn't find it beneath him to serve others. Besides, he was more of a tutelary spirit to the houses where he went, than a servant. Yes, he discharged his tasks as though doing condescending little favors, accepted small presents with the air of an Eastern potentate being given honorary payments by his subjects. There was never any idea of thanking them, it was enough acknowledgment if he agreed to accept gifts at their hands.

Over time, he had become a little eccentric. He was convinced that he was the sole proprietor of the house, where he was merely suffered to stay in it, and often he gave the impression that the good butcher only owed it to his, Markus's, charity, that he was permitted to stay at his house. And the house – that was his holy of holies. His bad conscience at perhaps having driven his parents into a premature death, his remorse at a botched life, might have driven him completely mad, if his imagination hadn't been able to persuade him that he was a solid, respectable citizen, a chip off the old block [. . .]

SICK PEOPLE

It was a quiet street, like a street somewhere in the sticks. The sounds of the city only reached it in the form of a harmless, diminished humming and jingling. It was lined with small cottages and postage stamp gardens. The day was autumnally mild and clement. A day one ought to enjoy with calm and equanimity.

If you carried on down the street, and just walked on and on, you would presumably eventually reach open country, where the little houses were no longer holding on to one another but standing apart, where there were meadows and brush, tempting dark hills and woods stretching to the horizon; where couples went walking, ate plums from paper bags, and held hands, to show their love quite openly by strong or subtle pressure; where the houses had poles with ugly straw weavings in front of them, to announce that another autumn was at hand, with another season of new wine to bring merriment and, oh, forgetting.

But the few people who passed along the street on that day had no time for hastening towards the woods and meadows, or for giving themselves over to love or to wine. They were going the other way, towards the city, towards their daily grind: men in blue, oil-stained overalls, men in bowler hats, women in dresses as bright and colorful as the day; carrying large bags easily and lightly – even the awkward weight of their burdens could not take away the delicacy and beauty of their stride, which is such a distinguishing feature of the women of this city.

There was one among them who did not appear to be typical of the people of this street, who somehow gave the impression of being a stranger, who, unlike them, seemed to have no errand or mission. A big man in plain dark clothes, bareheaded, slightly stooped, walking with a slightly vague, swaying stride, and favoring his right foot. He scrutinized the people he passed in the street, and the women were a little startled by his look, by the large dark eyes that seemed to stare out from his pallid face. He looked at the houses, one after the other, and it seemed that he was looking for one of them in particular. Evidently, though, he was in no hurry; he walked very slowly, almost as though afraid to find whatever it was he was looking for. A man can get to where he is going even with slow, swaying strides: among the small, low houses there was one that was large and stately, not magnificent but pleasing and inviting like a country house that in long ago days had served to relax some great man from the strains of exercising power. On closer inspection, however, the superscription over the big gate was anything but pleasing and inviting; "Hospital Entrance" it said, in large letters.

When he reached the house and read the inscription, the stranger in the quiet street gave a start. And then he carried on walking, but a little faster, the way he was dragging his right foot becoming immediately more noticeable. He walked past the house, and carried on down the quiet street, in the direction of the meadows and the woods. But the man couldn't go into the peaceful rolling expanse of the woods; he couldn't yesterday, and he couldn't today or tomorrow either.

He obeyed the instructions that were invisibly within him and around him, and returned to the house that looked like an old and amiable country seat, and that bore the superscription "Hospital Entrance".

A blonde girl came charging out of the door, followed by a grinning youth. She squealed and ran out with reckless impetuosity. And so collided with the man walking down the street. He staggered, caught himself on a fence rail, then looked into her hot young face. The girl's laughter died. Then the youth caught up with her, took her forcibly by the arm, and marched her up the street in the direction of the meadows and bushes. The girl's laughter filled the street once more, and was heard by the man, who was still standing by the fence, watching the easy carelessness of youth, its hurry to get out of his sight. The young couple's laughter rang in his ears a while longer before becoming harsh, discordant and finally leaving him.

Then he was once again standing in front of the friendly-sober country house. He took a long look at it, as though to pierce the walls with his eye and find its secrets.

He saw a board with an announcement that visiting hours for first- and second-class patients were every day between nine in the morning and nine at night, and for third-class patients between two and four in the afternoon on weekdays, except Friday. That told him: they had their way of doing things behind the brown gate. He rejoiced to see that people have a sense of order, and apply it wherever they can and wherever they deem it necessary. Only the wide world where everyone, brothers and sisters, the masses and the races and the peoples all have to live together, still has a little disorder in it. There, not even the board separating the first- and second-class people from the third-class, is enough. But one day, eventually, people's beautiful, ever-alert, ever-vigilant love of order will establish order everywhere, in the cities, in the countries, throughout the whole big wide beautiful world. For today, he had to content himself with the knowledge that there was order behind the stately brown gates.

And the stranger in the quiet street tried to smile, but all that he produced was a skewed grin, with the right corner of his mouth a little above the left.

Then a little door opened next to the big brown gate, and a fat little man with a cap on his head emerged and busily, amiably said: "Good morning, sir, were you thinking of coming in to see us? Please step inside!" And his hand politely ushered him the way.

A shudder ran through the man's long, thin frame, but he had his instructions within him and around him, the instructions that had often accompanied him in quiet lanes and in wide, busy streets and squares. And he walked through the little doorway, bowing his head slightly, because of the low lintel.

Carefully, the friendly porter shut the little door of the mental hospital, and quietly and politely, escorted the stranger like a guest. He led him to a large bright waiting-room, where people were sitting on chairs and benches and in little wheelchairs. Heinrich Reinegg joined them, and began waiting with them. It doesn't matter where I wait, he thought. Somehow, somewhere, we're always waiting.

They looked at the newcomer with curiosity, even benevolence. They whispered. A woman came in wearing a blue sister's uniform, tall and serious, and helped a girl to get up out of a wheelchair. The girl's face was delicate and fine and smiling. But there seemed to be a struggle in her between cheerfulness and pain. She propped herself on two rubber-tipped sticks. Just as she put her weight on them, one of them skittered across the smooth floor, and the girl fell to the ground with a quiet wail. Heinrich Reinegg, who was sitting closest to her, helped the sister get the girl back on her feet. It wasn't difficult; her body was incredibly light. The girl looked up gratefully into the large, dark, staring eyes of the stranger; she didn't scare, as the women outside the brown gates had done; she was smiling again; cheerfully and a little sorrowfully.

Then the girl was back on her slender feet, and she had to walk. Hesitantly, she slid her left foot forward, then her right jerked up into the air, forward a little, and down. That was two steps. The sister led the girl gently and patiently towards one of the white doors. Heinrich Reinegg thought briefly of the dainty, confident, light tread of the girls and women in the lane outside.

"Her dancing days are over," said a man with a black patch over his left eye that darkened his bony face.

No one replied.

An old woman shook her little gray head. It was the slightest movement of disapproval. It recurred at short, regular intervals. Why shouldn't she shake her head, thought Heinrich Reinegg, it's a perfectly natural thing to do.

The old woman looked disapprovingly at the man with the eye-patch. She leaned down to the indifferent young man who was sitting at her side, and whispered something. The young man countered quite calmly: "Don't get all het up, mother, what's there to get het up about? There's no need." Apathetically, his eyes passed over the room, and the things and the people in it.

For a second or two, they rested on the hands of a little girl with black hair, who was leafing in a book incessantly. But when the girl felt it and looked back at him, he turned away indifferently.

The man with the eyepatch was suffering from the malicious silence. He didn't understand why no one replied. There was a little crack in his voice when he said: "She's a dancer, you know. A professional dancer." And his right eye wandered over to the door behind which she had disappeared.

Then, a little guiltily, everyone looked across with him. And everyone looked at the white door. The old woman started shaking her head again, gently and disapprovingly. Her son looked apathetically at the clock. The black-haired girl went back to leafing in her book.

Suddenly, the girl put her book down on the table with a little bang, turned her little girl's face towards the man with the eyepatch and said, quite emphatically: "Six weeks ago, I wasn't able to walk either. Now I can walk again. Soon I'll be able to go home. Maybe as soon as next week. I'm just about to be told when I'll be able to go home." She looked out the window, and then at the white door again. "Yes. And the dancer's going to be able to walk again. And dance, yes, maybe she'll even be able to dance and all." And with that she stopped. And everyone knew that she was thinking to herself: And so what if she can't dance – ! The dancer!

The old woman forgot to shake her head; there was a slight, joyful sheen on her gray face. "Quiet, mother," her son murmured with equanimity, "be quiet, there's no need." And with that, he cut her off before she could speak.

The man with the eyepatch looked crossly out of his right eye at the black haired girl. "You've got something different the matter with you," he said, "what's the matter with you? It's something different to what she's got. What are you trying to say? Sure you'll walk again. But that woman – she'll never dance again." His voice was a little more cracked than before. He had said too much and talked for too long. He was silent. He adjusted his eyepatch. The tall, sober sister opened the white door, and led the dancer back into the room. Carefully, the dancer slid her left foot forward, then her right jerked up into the air, forward a little, and down. And her light dancer's body moved strangely after. And so skipping and dancing, she made her way to her little wheelchair. She smiled at Heinrich Reinegg, who sat in a stupor.

The one-eyed man, who wanted to be the helpless dancer's chevalier, offered to escort her. But there already was a fellow in white overalls, who pushed him aside, saying: "Get out the road! That's my job." He was a hospital porter, and he didn't care whether his loads were alive or insentient or dead.

A sunbeam fell into the room, and stayed in the dancer's red hair. Her hair shone. But the wheelchair trundled on, and the sunbeam fell on the floor, where it made a hot white splash of light.

Once again, the earnest sister opened the door. This time, Heinrich Reinegg went in. He was a little reluctant, but he had to go in. Any number of white and gray and black doors had opened in front of him. Any number of times he had hesitated, but he had gone in, because he had had to.

A woman seated at a desk looked up, calmly and questioningly, at Heinrich Reinegg. Why a woman? he asked himself. What does a man do when he's confronted by a woman? He bows to her, a little more awkwardly and clumsily than he would to a man, and then he might look, a little furtively, to see if she's young and pretty, and what color hair she has. It might take him a while, to his delight or detriment, to discover the human being.

Now was it going to be easier or harder for him, because there was a woman sitting there? The woman wore a lab coat. That masked her figure, and spread a kind of neuter quality; it was the lab coat that was decisive here.

There is always some mystery in a doctor's surgery. There's a bed in it that isn't for sleeping, there are glass-fronted cabinets full of glittery things that look at you with evident malice. There's someone with special qualifications to discover whatever in your head or chest or belly is different from the way it is meant to be, according to the laws he is familiar with. Heinrich Reinegg was put in mind of a watchmender, shaking a watch beside his ear and scrutinizing its works for a long time through a magnifying glass before he goes to work; or of a mechanic, starting a motorcycle engine and listening hard for any knocking or unusual sounds. But weren't those mistaken thoughts? People aren't the same as watches or motorcycles, and doctors can't be watchmakers or mechanics.

A doctor, still young but already bald, walked into the room. He looked fleetingly, indifferently, at Heinrich Reinegg. Then he looked away. He had a brief discussion with the woman in the lab coat about a "case". A few technical terms, as menacing to the healthy as to the infirm, buzzed through the room. Then the doctor left.

The woman wrote Heinrich Reinegg's name and age on a yellow form. Then her eyes, hiding behind a plain pair of spectacles, settled on his face.

"Tell me," she said, "why were you sent to us?"

Heinrich Reinegg thought that her voice sounded kindly and warm and sincere, and that her question wasn't put in the routine manner of a watchmaker. But it wasn't enough to overcome his suspicion, which was always vigilant.

He sat there stolidly.

"Why?" he said, "I didn't have any say in the matter."

She didn't become impatient. Not right away. She asked another question: "Were you sick?" It's nice of her, he thought, to put that in the past tense, and not in the present. His lips twitched ironically, barely perceptibly.

Sick? Yes, of course he'd been sick. A lot of people had been at the time he was laid low. And not all of those who were sick were laid low. Quite the opposite: they were all very active and believed in their sound health. Then it occurred to him that it might be a symptom of disease if you thought other people were sicker than you. And so he kept his thought to himself.

Sick? Yes, he would tell her about it. He didn't want to be rude. Not because she was a woman. That made it, if anything, even harder to talk. But maybe because she didn't ask questions like a watchmaker.

He spoke slowly and haltingly. And much of what went through his head he didn't say.

Sick? There were – had always been – dictators who were sick, and who had become dictators because they were sick.

Was the whole world not sick? Its economy, its structure? Hadn't mankind been shaken with fever for the past twenty years and more? Were its nerves not painfully inflamed and overstimulated? Hadn't a sick brain overriden all inhibitions, so that dangerous madness stalked abroad, and children's cribs afforded them no protection? There were doctors, who, like wounded surgeons, suffered from the illnesses they wanted to cure. There were others who wanted to multiply the number of boards giving the visiting hours for first- and second-class patients, and third-class patients, and who saw those boards as somehow therapeutic. There were charlatans who got into colored robes, and stood out in town squares touting their wares, claiming like quacks ancient and modern that just one little phial of a certain liquid was sufficient to detect and heal the illness; they had huge crowds around them. And there were serious doctors who saw symptoms and wanted to fight the illness, but couldn't or wouldn't find its cause, because they were afraid to make a diagnosis, and to recommend a course of treatment.

Heinrich Reinegg was tempted to ask the woman in front of him, the woman in the lab coat, whether medical science believed that it could effectively combat an illness by temporarily relieving its symptoms. He didn't. Had he done so, maybe she would have viewed it as a further symptom of illness. He had better get around at last to talking about the progress of his own illness.

Heinrich Reinegg looked past the woman. Images came into the little surgery and vanished again. Images from the diseased world that began at the little door of the institution which he had had to stoop to enter. A cell. A couple of iron beds with straw mattresses that were black, with blankets that were stiff with dirt. A stove in the corner, cold. A rickety table. A bucket that stank. A wooden partition that had been put up round the bucket fell crashing to the floor. Heinrich Reinegg picked it up again, and read the graffiti that had been scratched into it. They cursed, they proclaimed their innocence, they complained. They praised freedom. And love. Their praise of love came complete with illustrations. Men had praised love in a similar way in primordial times, in their caves.

A man lay on a straw mattress, wailing: "I'm turning into a criminal. You're driving me to crime."

A lock crashed. An iron bolt rattled back. A door creaked. A uniform walked in and screamed at the man on the straw mattress: "Take off your shoes!"

Heinrich Reinegg grinned. Heinrich Reinegg hobbled across the room. His right foot failed, agony. A doctor came, shook his head and left.

A lock crashed. An iron bolt rattled back.

A loudspeaker was playing. A man stood up on the mattress to listen. A woman's voice was heard quietly and faintly from the distance. A woman's voice.

Two men were lying on black straw mattresses. Spoke. Were silent. Wondered: How much longer? Hoped. Saw their hopes dashed. Smoked. Smoked all the time. Shared cigarettes. Were friends and comrades. Cellmates.

"There are people who always make sure they come out on top," spat Heinrich Reinegg, "they never spend time behind bars."

"Yes," groaned his friend on his straw mattress, "yes, and tomorrow – I'm going to ask the jailer to get me some work. I'm suffocating. It'll make me into a criminal yet."

"Nah, it won't. – Isn't slopping out enough for you?" It's funny, you remember every word you said in the cells, and every word that was said to you, thought Heinrich Reinegg as he sat in the bright little room in front of the woman in the lab coat.

Images came. Vanished.

A lock crashed. A hinge squeaked. There was a car outside. Heinrich Reinegg hobbled across to it. Under armed guard. A car drove off. Down roads that were beautifully snowed under, through villages he knew, and forests that he loved.

Then there was a cell, a judge, a doctor. Hours passed, and whole nights, each one an eternity.

And finally, finally, there was a day. Heinrich Reinegg stood on the noisy city street, leaning heavily on a stick. Cars passed. Pedestrians. Women smiled. Men worked. For them it was just another day.

Freedom! Freedom?

The woman at the desk stared in front of her and listened, from time to time she wrote down a couple of sentences on her yellow pad.

"What's that you're writing?" asked Heinrich Reinegg rudely.

She smiled. "Nothing much. Just a few notes on the state of your right leg. It's better now, isn't it? What about your head?"

The head? A tricky business. The more skewed someone's head, the more convinced its owner that it's all the others that are skewed, and his own is straight as a die.

Images came.

Someone was standing in the fog of a sick world. Felt abysses. Could go neither forward nor back. Was beaten and humiliated. Starving. Thought about his life, and grinned into the fog with rage and bitterness. Because there was always one thing, it was always the same, you couldn't avoid it: the abyss, a wall in front of you to scale, and you lost your footing. A childhood without laughter, an adored mother who died, because mothers who go hungry and suffer are doomed to tuberculosis. A laborious climb. He took others by the hand and helped them up. Helped them! Helped them! In every woman who trudged along in a headscarf, he saw his mother. And he helped! Was glad. For moments at a time. Climbed. Slid. Climbed.

Slid!

Stood in the fog. There were many standing in the fog and calling. He didn't hear them, didn't see them. But he suffered with them, and they with him.

And so his own destiny was amplified by the sufferings of many who wandered about in the fog, and he felt oppressed by so much suffering, so that he fell to the wet earth at the very bottom of the fog.

Images came.

A man lay in bed. Objects were waving around him: the table, pictures. A plant on the bedside table. Two plants that were one. A doubled plant. When the man shut one eye, he saw a plant rise up. When he opened them both, there were two, widely separated. A man came in. He had two heads and two ties. A doctor held his thumb in the air. "Are there one or two?" There were two. But the invalid thought hard, and said: "There's one." His hand reached for a glass, for a spoon, and missed.

Heinrich Reinegg vomited. It made him a little happy; that was something natural and sensible.

A doctor cried out in alarm: "No smoking! He mustn't smoke! That could be the end." Heinrich Reinegg heard him indistinctly; he liked the word "end".

Then another doctor came along, who said: "Give him whatever he wants!" He was annoyed because the torch he wanted to shine into the sick man's eyes wasn't working. He ordered: "Say: 'glacial moraine!'"

Heinrich Reinegg was determined to say it. Another order: "Stick out your tongue!" Heinrich Reinegg duly did so; and why shouldn't he stick his tongue out at the world? It slid off to the right.

A priest came, all friendly solicitude, and said: "The Church isn't to blame for anything."

And there were hours that were nothing but fog and a dull astonishment in Heinrich Reinegg about the persistence of his flickering life.

People came and prayed. Peasants had Masses read. Women complained, even though they were old and warm. Men walked for hour upon hour over streets and flights of stairs, for the sake of a greeting. And there were others, not many, that expressed pleasure at the proximity of the "end".

Heinrich Reinegg, however, girded his fearful body and got up off the wet earth. Stood once more in the foggy deep. And slowly, groping and stumbling, tried to walk.

The woman at the desk said something, and the images were dispelled.

"Will you go next door, and strip to your underwear. Then come back."

He wasn't sure whether this was natural or not. But it was the lab coat that gave the orders in this room. He went out and came back in undershirt and shorts. Lay down on the narrow little bed that wasn't for sleeping in. The woman stuck a thin needle in his head, left side and right side, like one of the Fates, and asked him if it felt any different. She asked him to shut his eyes and stretch out his hands. She asked him to squeeze her hand. He asked her mockingly, how many hands she had to squeeze in a day. On her instruction, he took a few steps back and forth. In his undershirt and shorts. His right foot dragged. Charming, thought Heinrich Reinegg, a man parading around in front of a woman in his underwear. But then she was wearing the lab coat, which disguised the woman. For her, a man in shorts was neither a pleasing nor an unpleasing thing, it went with the room, just as a stripped-down watch went with the watchmaker's workshop. But no. There were differences. For instance: The watchmaker strips the watch there and then, whereas the man was told to go next door and do it. Heinrich Reinegg's face was as grim and sunken as ever, but he felt the gentle mockery he often applied to himself, that he cherished in both bad and seemingly good times like a protection; or maybe that was self-deception.

When the man was back in his street clothes, the woman asked: "And what about your lung?"

He produced a piece of paper with a doctor's report on it. At that moment, the bald young doctor came in, looked at the report and observed: "We're not a sanatorium, there must be some mistake."

"No, no," said the woman doctor, "there's no mistake. He's one of ours all right."

Well, that's nice, thought Heinrich Reinegg, it seems I've finally found the place where I belong.

RARE AND EVER RARER
IN THIS WORLD OF
EMPIRICAL FACTS . . .

Rare and ever rarer in this world of empirical facts and predictable consequences are those bizarre destinies that, if one can believe what people say, one used not long ago to encounter at every turn. And yet, even today, the diligent seeker after remarkable persons and destinies cannot fail to be struck by certain events that seem not to have been formed by sheer randomness, but by a positively literary force that on occasion seems to direct the world.

Of all the people in my immediate circle, probably no one has had such an arresting, tragicomic, surprising-inevitable fate as the man to whom the following pages are devoted, and whose second name I will not divulge, not only because I still count him among my friends today, but also because I am convinced that some extraordinary, unexpected, unpredictable fate still awaits him, which I am afraid of forestalling by baldly stating some bald fact.

On 3 November 1918, Heinrich P. determined that he would earn his daily bread as a writer.

It was on one of the first days of the Revolution, when people believed that while an individual had no way of influencing historical events, he was still required to place himself in a certain distinct relationship to them. Like many millions, Heinrich P. had gone to the War, and like only a few, he had returned from it hale and hearty. An officer in the Austrian Army, at the outset, he suddenly found himself a civilian and a citizen of the newly created Czech Republic.

On 1 November, he had returned to his native Brünn. What he saw there – the Revolution in the little capital of the erstwhile Crown Land, the procession of the army band dressed in its old imperial uniforms and playing a new Nationalist anthem, the Czech soldiers who went about plucking the old cockades from the officers' hats, the whole foolish glee of the liberated nation – struck my friend Heinrich P. as crying out for literary expression, and hence for a man to give it such expression. Being of a passive disposition, Heinrich P. was experiencing the Revolution in a kind of long, historical perspective. He conceived of himself as a "student of events", and the speed and the sheer color of events left him no time to consider his own immediate future. One morning, merely because it was what other returning officers were also doing, he went along to the army headquarters, where everyone was already conversing in Czech, the erstwhile second language in which most of them were almost as fluent as German, their mother-tongue. He was told that the newly formed government offered him a place in the new army, for which officers were needed. He replied that he wanted time to think it over, was paid his last month's salary, and asked for an itinerary to Prague. Then he went to the station, boarded the train, quite automatically looking for a second-class carriage until he realized that the whole train consisted only of third-class carriages, and finally found a place on one of the hard yellow wooden benches that were for the most part occupied by the rank and file.

En route, he encountered one of those impromptu examining committees that, in the first flush of revolutionary enthusiasm, not knowing what else to do with themselves, used to stop perfectly innocent trains, looking for God knows what. It was as though it had taken the sight of the examining committee in their Czech

Sokol uniforms to alert Heinrich P. to the new state of the world; a clear and unambiguous change in the external world to draw his attention to the change in his personal situation; and now at long last, Heinrich P. began to think of his immediate future, and to consider practical worries that would before long imperil his existence.

He still had some money. He had been able to save a couple of thousand marks from his officer's salary, and now he began reproaching himself for not having accepted the offer to join the new army. What else could a person of his undoubted passivity do with himself in these evidently rather active times? He could feel himself drifting around the periphery of events, not at their center, and he was as far from affecting them as they were from influencing him. Now, assuming he had the talent to write about them, he would try to tackle them with that perspective that is the exclusive domain of the writer, but – did he know that he could write? He thought of the headmaster of his Gymnasium, who used to write theater reviews for the local paper. Was old von Hauer still alive? Heinrich P. arrived at the station in Prague, fell into the arms of a soldiers' committee, showed them his papers, and was delighted to recognize in their commander the janitor of his old school. He went to his aunt's apartment.

She was one of the type of female relative in whom a reunion with a male relative gave rise, in equal quantity, to joyful celebrations and to moaning about these terrible times. Heinrich P. gave her the money she claimed to be desperately in need of, and went into the city. He went to old Hauer's apartment, had a conversation with him in which sentimentality tried to assert itself against the drama and unexpectedness of recent events, and was given the name of an editor on the paper. And to him Heinrich handed in his account of his revolutionary experiences. The following day, his article appeared, and as he read it, Heinrich had the sensation that he had made up the Revolution, his homecoming, and his experiences at the station. He distrusted himself. It seemed to him that he had exaggerated the enthusiasm and the confusion, and that there was at least as much difference between the truth of the Revolution and his version of it, as between the Revolution and the War. He had written about people reeling and intoxicated, but in truth there had been no more reeling and intoxicated people than on an average Sunday afternoon in peacetime.

He was still reflecting on his article when a man called on him, identified himself as a detective, and claimed to have orders to take him to one Herr Dr. Slama in the police headquarters. Dr. Slama was the new government's censor. It turned out that all he wanted was to meet Heinrich P., and maybe try to win him over – he was obviously impressed by the article – for the Czech government, just as he himself, an erstwhile official of the Monarchy, had been won over.

The attempt to win over Heinrich P. for the new, so-called autonomous Czech people remained fruitless; not because Heinrich P. was any sort of German nationalist, but because, in obedience to the laws of his character, he was determined to avoid anything that would commit him to any future course of action. In fact, if he had been able to think at all about the current plight of the German part of the population, he would have had to come to the conclusion that siding with them would have been more in keeping with his innate passivity. But at that time, Heinrich P. wasn't thinking all that much. The situation – both of the generality, and of his own person – was much too tangled for him. And, creature of convenience that he was, he decided to go to one of those peaceable countries where political conflicts had seemed resolved for hundreds of years, and where perpetual peace was assured to the individuals happy enough to live in them.

And so, with the rest of his money, he went to Switzerland, settled initially in Zürich, and, merely because of the ethical imperative to do something, he began to write articles for the German-language newspapers. His earnings remained small, his expenditures ate into his capital to the point that one day, in June 1919, he found himself unable to pay the rent.

But evidently, there is a merciful-unmerciful Providence that watches over certain young men, and, however banal its expedients, it does at least enable its favorites to make a little further headway, saving them from the sort of premature catastrophe that would make it impossible for us to tell certain stories. Banal as these destinies generally are, so too was the circumstance that brings to the house of Heinrich P.'s landlady one of her young nieces, and causes the old lady to promote a relationship between this niece and her one and only tenant. The reader doubtless knows how easily such a banal situation may become fateful for the man in question, and therefore we are absolved of having to describe Heinrich P. duped into love by a shallow affect, and prompted by a profound instinct to flee bourgeois existence. Instead, we content ourselves with relating the sudden arrival of a letter addressed to Heinrich, a letter that read as follows:

Dear Friend,
Not long ago, my eye was caught by your name in a newspaper, and that took me back to the weeks and months we spent together in the field. Following the collapse of the Monarchy, I moved to Germany, am living in Berlin as a lawyer, have married (and married well), am on the board of my father-in-law's firm, and learn to my surprise that you are living in Zürich. What prompts me to write now is a feeling of nostalgia that may well strike you as absurd. My wife and I are going to Marseilles next week, and we would like to take you with us. Please, should you be able to meet us at the station in Basel next Tuesday, 28 July, at 2 in the afternoon, will you notify us by wire?
Your friend
Otto Reichhardt

THE CARTEL

On 12 November, the Boston *Aurora* printed the following bulletin in large type on the front page of its eight-page edition:

The renowned suffragette leader Miss Sylvia Punkerfield has been missing since yesterday. Mass demonstrations had been planned for today outside the government building, to which suffragette leaders from Chicago and New York had been invited. As we reported yesterday, the police had even heard of plans to bomb the government building, which they have taken steps to foil. In addition to being at the forefront of the women's movement, Miss Sylvia Punkerfield was said to have been masterminding the demonstration. Her sudden disappearance only hours before it was due to begin seems quite inexplicable. Foul play cannot be ruled out – Miss Punkerfield of course had numerous rivals. In spite of their best endeavors, the police have so far failed to trace the missing Suffragette leader.

Of course, all Massachusetts knew Miss Punkerfield. Sylvia Punkerfield, the wasp-waisted suffragette with the Eton crop, the sheer black jersey dress that looked as smooth and as plausible as a political program, with those astoundingly plain wooden buttons covered in black corduroy, like points in that program. But for all that, there was a measure of sophistication in that plainness. Or did anyone really believe that Miss Sylvia wore her hair short because it was practical and masculine? There was no better hairstyle for Miss Sylvia's youthful face and boyish features. Miss Sylvia had blue eyes. Blue, you say, and you think of the sky or some other fixture of similar hue. But the blue of that girl's eyes had something of the cool violet of late autumn clouds, and nothing of the spring sky. There was the chilly glitter of damascened steel blades in those eyes, when Miss Sylvia addressed a meeting. She spoke in the rasping, but not disagreeable tones of a bareback rider or a lion-tamer at a circus. When Miss Sylvia shouted a slogan into a crowd, her slender body stretched up on the stage, and she clenched her elegant fingers as though to grip an invisible whip. Her boyish, sinewy arm described a curve through the air, and it looked as though Sylvia had hurled the slogan into the crowd, like a rubber ball. And her voice acquired a metallic timbre, like a saber smiting brass. Such was Miss Punkerfield.

No wonder that the whole of Massachusetts knew her. The elderly Miss Lawrence, who was as flat as a board, could be as ruthlessly logical and consequent as an algebra primer. No one dared to tangle with her. With her hairfine logic, she divided every opponent in two perfectly equal halves. – The young, but already leathery Miss Esther Smith knew the thinkers of three centuries by heart, and emptied vats of their thinkings over the heads of her enemies till they sank to their knees and begged for mercy. – Miss Ethel Fisher, the daughter of "Sausages" Fisher, was feared for her more than manly coarseness. Her words were as heavy and crude as the hammers with which her father's employees mashed the horseskins to sausages. But what were any or all of them, compared to the supernatural qualities of Miss Sylvia! Miss Sylvia was surrounded by an aura of victory. She radiated victory. Victory was her element. It's because she's so smart, said the women of Massachusetts. It's because she's so cute, said the men of Massachusetts. And if Miss Sylvia hadn't so suddenly disappeared, we would have faced the extraordinary prospect of all the women quitting Amazonism, and all the men becoming suffragettes. Already a few Boston professors had given her their support, the three youngest of the forty state senators of Massachusetts made no secret of their sympathy with the suffragettes, and young Pedro dal Costo-Caval, the world famous bullfighter who three months before had arrived from his Portuguese home, in that time had attended every meeting that Miss Sylvia Punkerfield had addressed, and clapped his torero's hands whenever she made a peroration, or settled the hash of some opponent.

And now Miss Sylvia had disappeared! Nothing was known about her beyond what had appeared in the columns of the *Aurora*.

In the Chesterton café, in the corner on the left by the window, sat the three gentlemen who were known to all Boston and all Massachusetts: they were Messrs. Washer, Pumper and Klingson.

Mr. Washer was a reporter on the *Little Times*. He wore a large brown hat and tall hip-boots. The actual Mr. Washer was located somewhere in the middle, and there was precious little of him. Mr. Washer was short and ugly. His head was a small oval. His face was like a crumpled piece of paper. His nose was jammed between two fleshy creases in his face, as though buried in a pillow. It was one of those noses that are unable to support a pince-nez, and therefore Mr. Washer wore a pair of spectacles in front of his sharp green eyes. These spectacles were the only impressive aspect of Mr. Washer. They were burnished and glittering, and in stark contrast to his yellow-brown complexion. When Mr. Washer took off his hat and spectacles, his head, with its numerous indurated wrinkles, resembled a walnut. Anyone who had clapped eyes on Mr. Washer tended to remember three things about him: the brown hat, the tinted spectacles and the enormous boots. Take them together, and you got "Mr. Washer", whereas the actual Mr. Washer quite disappeared. But the actual Mr. Washer was nonetheless an interesting figure. He was a crime reporter of distinction. His paper, the *Little Times*, had the most detailed information about the parentage, lives and family circumstances of anyone who was involved with the law in any capacity. If the corpse of a factory worker was fished out of the river somewhere, it was Mr. Washer who knew that she had been going out with such and such a laborer at the cotton mill. Mr. Washer interviewed the laborer, found out what he made, knew that he was illegitimate, that his great-grandmother was a Negress, and turned all this information into an artful construction all his own. He dealt lovingly with his knowledge, and played with his reports the way a child might play with its building bricks. Occasionally, a finished building might lack a little gable, a little turret, a little crenellation. Mr. Washer would append a delicious little interview – a tender, careful interview full of grace and delicacy – with the laborer's bit on the side. Mr. Washer then thought of himself as a master baker, putting a raisin on a finished cake, a few almond slivers, a little stiff eggwhite. Everything was neat and tidy and faultless, and still there was something racy about it as well. These crime stories had made Mr. Washer famous.

Mr. Pumper was the direct opposite. Big and strong and coarse. In recent years he had begun to go to fat and breathlessness. He wore a suit of manifestly crude elegance. His hands were hairy, between a couple of diamond rings on his right index finger three pert little hairs made a stubborn point of being there. Across the smooth curve of his waistcoat, the links in his gold watch-chain jingled in time to his breathing. His legs were short and knock-kneed. His little mustache was black and shiny with pomade. Occasionally there was a green speck of brilliantine caught between the hairs. His hairless skull was smooth as a billiard ball. There was a great bulge of neck that rolled over the collar of his coat. That was Mr. Pumper.

He wasn't one to chisel or file away, he wasn't a man for delicacy and sentiments like his colleague Mr. Washer. He did an express service in murders and assaults, specializing in hacked up bodies and other gruesomenesses. He knew the all-night bars like his waistcoat pockets. He was on first name terms with murderers and drank with police spies. He knew about murders that hadn't yet happened, and gave nothing away until the day dawned, when he described the act as precisely as if he'd seen it with his own eyes. Everyone was amazed by the reporting of Mr. Pumper, and the *Boston Kiker* paid him a thousand dollars a month.

The third was Mr. Klingson. Long and thin like one of the cheap cigars that were never out of his mouth. His blond hair was smoothly parted, falling in a heavy mass over the left half of his face, and hiding a defect: Mr. Klingson was without his left ear. During a ride he had once undertaken on behalf of his paper, the *Bloody Tomahawk*, it had been shot off. Mr. Klingson had one inestimable quality: he was as discreet as the grave. If you asked him what was going on, he would simply reply: Nothing. And all along he would have the latest robberies in his left breast-pocket, in printer-ready copy. He was a leak-proof container for sensations. You poured the headiest news items into him, and none of it got out. He was like a well-corked, opaque, dark green bottle.

This trio of reporters made up the Massachusetts "cartel". They always knew what was going on. On other matters, the *Aurora* was well informed, but they were always behind on crime. The *Aurora*'s editor was livid. The *Aurora*'s reporters ran all over Massachusetts like frightened rabbits. Their tongues hung down to the ground. They never picked up any information. In the Chesterton café, news and current events were created and blazoned out into the world. Immured in the Chesterton café, the cartel seemed impregnable. Whoever went in there to try an attack would be put to flight by Mr. Klingson's terrible, lethal "Nothing!" There was nothing to be done about the cartel.

God only knows where the three of them got their fresh news from all the time. Even if there wasn't any, they still seemed to have it. If there hadn't been any robberies of late, then the cartel put their heads together and discussed the possibility of there being a robbery. Or Mr. Washer would come forward with one of his infinitely subtle, delicate interviews, and bring out a story about the past of Tommy, the great sex-attacker. Or Mr. Klingson might write: "It has been brought to our attention that the inquiry into the arson attack on the property of Tompson the oil magnate has so far come up with nothing. Our readers may, however, remember the name of 'long Jimmy', who had sworn vengeance on Mr. Tompson. The said Jimmy traveled to Australia as the stoker on a ship, and there put himself at the head of a band of robbers. Four months ago – we have it from his immediate circle – he was seen back in Massachusetts." There followed an extraordinarily sensitive, subtle interview that Mr. Washer conducted with "long Jimmy's" latest "squeeze".

One day, a new reporter suddenly turned up: Mr. John Baker from Chicago. He was as long and lean as a greyhound. His nose had left his face, practically declared independence from it. It could steer to the left and right, up and down, without Mr. Baker having to move a muscle in his face. This nose was an autonomous independent creature, positively skittish in its vivacity. It was never dormant. It sniffed out events. It attracted sensations the way a magnet attracts iron filings. It could smell out human flesh, scalpings, sex attacks, robberies. It was a very distinguished nose.

Mr. Baker went straight from the station to the offices of the *Aurora*.

"What can you do?" asked the editor. "Everything," said Mr. Baker.

He was given eight hundred dollars, and became a reporter on the *Aurora*.

Mr. Baker was keenly interested in the suffragettes. He and the Portuguese bullfighter Pedro dal Costo-Caval became best buddies.

He attended all the meetings and applauded loudly. He won the trust of the leathery Miss Esther Smith by placing an article in the *Aurora* in which he took the part of the suffragettes.

The news of the sudden disappearance of the celebrated Miss Punkerfield was broken by Mr. Baker in the *Aurora*. It was terrible.

Mr. Pumper, Mr. Washer and Mr. Klingson were in session. Today, the world wouldn't be fobbed off with the arson attack in the prairie, or with long Jimmy, or Jenkins who cut off schoolgirls' pigtails, or Tommy the sex attacker. What was all that compared to the disappearance of Miss Sylvia Punkerfield? You had to give the what, where, how and why of that. Mr. Washer went to see Miss Lawrence, to ask her for an interview, but she had lost her marbles. She gave him no information.

The police had let their best-trained sniffer dogs off the leash. Mr. Washer gave one of them a race, to see who would find Miss Sylvia first. He found nothing.

The cartel sought out Mr. Shelly, the chief of police. "Mr. Shelly," began Pumper, "I've got a hunch!" "Well, spit it out!"

"I suspect our colleague Baker on the *Aurora* of the kidnapping of the suffragette. That man will stop at nothing! He's capable of committing a murder, purely to get a scoop."

Mr. Washer nodded sternly in agreement. He was so exhausted from his race with the police-dog that he couldn't speak. Mr. Klingson was stiff and silent and sucked on his cold cigar-end as though that could produce a breakthrough in the grim affair.

The chief of police decided to take in the *Aurora* reporter for questioning.

But when the men in blue turned up at the *Aurora* offices, they heard that Mr. Baker had taken the early train to look for Miss Sylvia.

All the while, Mr. Baker was in his room, reading a letter and smiling a contented smile. For the first time in his life, his nose was perfectly still. It didn't even twitch. The letter was dated 11 November, and was headed: On board the *Atlantis*. It was from the Portuguese bullfighter, Pedro dal Costo-Caval, and it read as follows:

Dear Friend,
Now I know the extent of my debt to you and your news-hound's ambition. Your idea of getting me to fall in love with Miss Sylvia was inspired. Your suggestion that I kidnap her was even better. In any case, it all passed off with her consent. She was fed up with chucking bombs. All a woman really wants from life is a bullfighter anyway. Everything else – the politics and the bombs – is just a poor substitute. I'm kidnapping her with her enthusiastic approval. We're very happy together.

When my son is born, I want you to be his godfather. I'll write.
Cheers,
Your Pedro

Mr. Baker reached for his pad, and addressed a telegram to the *Aurora*, date-lined 12 November, New York.

The next morning, the Boston *Aurora* printed the following bulletin in large type on the front page of its eight-page edition:

New York, 12 November.
(From our special correspondent)
The mystery surrounding Miss Sylvia Punkerfield has been solved. Miss Sylvia has eloped with Pedro dal Costo-Caval, the Portuguese bullfighter. The two of them have for some time been romantically linked. The couple are presently on the *Atlantis*, en route for Portugal.

There was great excitement in the Chesterton café. Mr. Pumper read the bulletin and sank lifeless to the floor. Mr. Washer came down with a high temperature, conducted interviews in his ravings, and died a week later from the bronchial infection he had caught as a result of his race with the police-dog. Mr. Klingson was fired over the phone. You can still see him today, sitting in the Chesterton, waiting for the elopement story to be denied, so he can be the first to break it.

APRIL

The story of a love affair

The April night on which I arrived was heavy with clouds and pregnant with rain. The silver silhouettes of the town rose soft out of the fog and bold and almost singing into the sky. A frail coltish gothic spire clambered up into the clouds. The egg-yellow face of the illuminated townhall clock seemed to be suspended in the air on an invisible thread. Around the station, there was a sweet dry waft of anthracite, jasmine and fragrant meadows.

The town's only hackney cab was waiting, all dusty and apathetic, outside the station. It must be a very small town. It obviously had one church, one fountain, one burgomaster, one cab. The horse was chestnut, with broad hooves, reddish cuffs over its fetlocks, and no blinders. Its eyes glooped large and benevolently over the square. When it whinnied, it tipped its head to the side, like a man about to sneeze.

I climbed into the cab, and soon left all the bouncing hat-boxes and swaying suitcases and the people hanging on to them behind me on the road. I heard what the people were saying to each other, and I felt the poverty of their destinies, the smallness of their experience, the tininess and weightlessness of their sufferings. Like molten lead, the fog poured over the fields on both sides, creating a semblance of sea and limitless expanse. That was what made the hat-boxes and the people and their talk and the cab so ridiculous and small. I really believed it was the sea on both sides of me, and I was surprised at its quiet. A dead sea, I thought. A factory chimney, alarming in spite of its slimness, suddenly loomed up next to a white block of houses, like a defunct lighthouse.

A few stray people were encamped by the side of the road: a sort of advance guard of the town. They were trusting and honest, I could see what they were up to. There was a mother washing a child in a barrel. The barrel had a shiny, cruel tin belt, and the child screamed. – A man sat on his bed, while a boy pulled his boot off for him. The boy's face was red, puffy and contorted, and the boot was caked with dirt. – An old woman was sweeping the floorboards with a twig broom, and I knew what she was going to do next: she would take up her red-and-blue tablecloth, and go over to the door or the window and shake it out into the little garden. I felt for the child in the barrel, the boy pulling at the boot, the crumbs on the tablecloth. Old women who tidy up at night are always wicked. My grandmother, who looked like a dog, always used to sweep her floorboards at night with a twig broom. I was very small, I hated my grandmother and her broom, and I loved scraps of paper, cigarette ends and rubbish of all sorts. I picked up everything that lay on the floor and stuffed it in my pockets, to save it from my grandmother. I especially loved straws. Of all things, they were the most alive. Sometimes, when it rained, I would look out the window. Bobbing and twisting and dancing blithely and coquettishly along on the waves of one of the innumerable streams, was a little straw, never guessing it was moving towards the drain where it would disappear. I ran on to the street, the rain was lashing down furiously, but I chased after the straw and caught it just before it reached the drain.

I saw lots of people out at night. Was it that the people of the town went to bed very late, or was it April and the expectancy in the air, that kept all the living from their beds? All those I saw had some significance. They carried destinies, or were themselves destinies; they were happy or unhappy, in no case by chance or indifferently met; at the very least, they were drunk. In small towns, there are no chance people abroad on the streets. All are lovers or prostitutes or nightwatchmen or poets or lunatics. Chance and indifferent persons are safely at home.

In the middle of the market place, as though on guard, stood the founder of the town, a stone bishop. So central and substantial. I think the people thought he was a dead irrelevance. They walked past him without a greeting; they would have thought nothing of spilling their secrets in front of him, or even of committing a crime. What did they want to hang on to him for?

I felt sorry for the bishop, who must have gone to a lot of trouble to found the town. He had a grim set to his mouth and looked distinctly like someone who has come up against the ingratitude of the world. That night, I promised I would read up all I could on him. In the end, I never got around to it. Because even in this small town, the living had stories that collided with me, surrounded me and diverted me. Besides, it was spring, and in springtime I don't care for any bishops or founders.

The very next morning, I had my first couple of stories.

I knew that the postman had only been limping for a matter of days, and not at all from birth. He drank rarely, only twice a year: on his birthday, which was 15 April, and on the day of the death of his son, who had committed suicide in the big city. His inebriation was protracted, and the postman spent three days reeling around within the walls of the little town, before he sobered up. On those three days, the people of the town got no mail. Communications with the outside world came to a halt.

A week before, on 15 April, the postman in his drunkenness had had a fall, and twisted his leg. Hence his limp.

That wasn't the only story.

The hotel I slept in smelled of naphtha, musk and old wreaths. The big dining-hall past the bar had a low vaulted ceiling, and the walls were adorned with little brown wood plaques with proverbs and sayings on them. Anna, the barmaid, propped her right arm on the windowsill, and made sure the glasses were never empty. They never were, either. Because people didn't drink a lot of wine here, and they tapped their glasses if Anna happened not to be paying attention.

Anna was then twenty-seven years old, and had smooth fair hair. She always looked as though she'd just climbed out of the water. That's how taut and fresh her face was, and how newly the damp blonde strands of her hair looked to have been scraped back from her forehead.

She had slender, strong but shy hands that I always thought were somehow ashamed of themselves.

Anna came from Bohemia, and she was in love with an engineer there. The engineer was the manager of the factory where Anna's father worked. Anna had had a child by the engineer.

The engineer had married someone else, and had given Anna some money for the baby and the journey. And so Anna had ended up as a waitress in the small town.

I once happened to walk into Anna's room and I saw a photo of her baby. It was a pretty thing, grabbing the air with plump fists and drinking in the world with big eyes. Anna was taciturn, and told her story in few words.

I don't like engineers like that, and I fell in love with Anna.

"Do you still love him?" I asked Anna.

"Yes!" she replied. She said it as matter-of-factly and unhesitatingly as if it was some piece of information she had been asked for.

In the town there was a little cinema. The owner was a Jewish draper. He had started the cinema because he was energetic and enterprising, and it irked him not to have anything to do with his Sundays. Therefore, he sold his cloth on weekdays, and showed films on Sundays.

I took Anna to the cinema.

There was a library in the little town. The young man who looked after the visitors, and did the dusting when there weren't any, was pale, of a romantic pallor, and as thin as the ghost of a poet. His yellow blond crest of hair flickered up from his head towards the ceiling. He was always standing on a stepladder, he wandered around behind his counter with the stepladder, he was terribly good at it, better than any housepainter. It was as though he had learned to walk on stepladders. The library had some good old books as well, and I took Anna to the library.

Anna was very happy.

Sometimes I knew that Anna could be tender. I loved women in whom goodness, like a buried spring – invisible, unavailing, but indefatigable – keeps pushing up towards the surface, and because there is nowhere there for it to emerge, is forced back down, digs hidden channels for itself, digs and digs until it exhausts itself. I loved Anna. I couldn't leave her riches alone. She didn't know what she was missing as she walked on, living in the past, tending only her desire for the past, extinguishing every other desire.

I haven't yet said anything about the park where love flourished in this town. Laburnum throve madly and untidily in amongst chestnuts and lindens. The benches were not, as they normally are, on the paths and walks, but in the middle of the flowerbeds. I thought these benches must have been planted in the earth by the bishop when they were very young, and every year they grew a little bit wider. Their feet had surely taken root in the loose earth.

On Sunday, after the film, I took Anna to the park.

We watched a couple kissing, and Anna laughed.

"Anna," I said, "it's not good to laugh at love. I don't like people who are capable of betraying themselves to that degree."

Whereupon Anna stopped laughing.

When we got back to the hotel, it turned out that the manager had been looking for Anna, because a guest had arrived. He had a squeaky, new leather suitcase covered with red and green stickers. He had dark curls and blazing eyes. He could probably play the mandolin, and certainly he knew how to seduce girls. If I had been able to sneak a look in his wallet, I would have found an entire collection of colored ribbons and blonde ringlets and pink love-letters. I wasn't able to look, but I still knew.

He was drinking beer in the bar. Beer didn't go with him, he would have done better to drink wine. He let Anna wait on him, and he was very polite. It was all no-please-after-you rigmarole. I expect his signature is just as ornate as his speech, I thought.

That night, I noticed my light was gone. I opened the door and went into Anna's room. Anna was sitting there in her nightie, weeping. She stayed sitting on her bed, and wasn't at all put out by me, she just went on weeping, calmly and abundantly.

Finally she said: "He looks exactly like that!"

The new arrival looked just like Anna's engineer.

"It's terrible!" said Anna.

Ever since that time we were in love, and we didn't hide it from one another. Anna could be very tender and also jealous. But I didn't care about other women. I didn't like the women in this town.

Only when I saw them wandering out into the fields on gilt-framed spring evenings, one pair after another, did they move me. They were there to renew the world. They grew and then they loved and then they gave birth. They began their maternal work in the springtime, and ended it years later. I saw them swarming out into the woods, like mayflies, intoxicated and delirious, harmless and eager to fulfill God's instruction.

Late at night, they were still standing in dark entryways, glued to the lips and mustaches of their men, giggling and humbly grateful for every kind word that was tossed to them. They were beautiful nights, full of the twittering of crickets and girls.

And so were the rainy days beautiful too.

The girls stood in the windows, reading books from the lending library and eating bread and butter. An umbrella swayed down the lane, shielding the frail figure of the notary clerk. He looked like a grasshopper on two legs.

Straws danced, whirled and spun coquettishly, bobbing along ignorantly towards the drain and doom. I no longer chased after them to catch them. I kept thinking I ought to. The rain, the innocence of the straw, the drain and I, we all belonged together. Maybe the notary clerk as well. The rainy day was a crosshatched gray, the straw drowned, the drain swallowed it up, the notary clerk stalked down the lane under his umbrella. And I should have come to the rescue of the straw. Everything in the world has its allotted task.

Every morning, I got up very early. Anna was still asleep, and the hotel manager and the other guest. The boots of the people in the hotel stood outside their doors, not yet cleaned, a piece of yesterday. In the courtyard, the poodle wandered about, yawned and looked for old bones under the hotel carriage, which, unyoked, with its shafts unemployed, stood outside the stable as though it had already been dug up. Jakob, the coachman, was snoring loudly and fervently in the stables; he was snoring his hymn to nature and health. His snoring was anything but ridiculous. It sounded assertive and masterful; something in nature, a muffled roll of thunder, or the belling of a stag. At five o'clock, the wailing toot of the steam mill rose distantly, as from some alien sphere, and swelled to wake Jakob the coachman. He must have been sleeping in his clothes, because he came out at the same time as the last trembly echo of the siren, in his checked long-sleeved waistcoat, trousered and booted, bareheaded, with a wrinkled parchmenty face, spraying water from his mouth into his cupped hands, and splashing it over eyes and brow. Then, heavily and effortfully, as though each of his legs was a tree that he first had to uproot, he crossed the yard into the house.

On the corner, Käthe opened her window, and looked down into the town. I always greeted Käthe. I had never spoken to her, I didn't have anything to say to her, all I did was greet her, because she was looking out of her window, and because at that time in the morning, the world was not yet conventional, but simple as in the earliest days of its infancy, a year or two after the Creation, when there were a score or so of people alive, and all twenty of them were polite and considerate to one another. By the time I returned, it was already noon, the world was several thousand years older, and I no longer offered a greeting, because in such an advanced world it wasn't done to greet a girl one had never spoken to.

A round-bellied water-wagon crunched its way through the park, sprinkling the lawns and beds. A blackbird bounced along beside it, with wide-boy gestures, batting away the droplets with its wing. There was the celestial racket of an invisible school of larks that had been packed off on holiday. All round the benches planted in the middle of the flowerbeds, the grass looked tired and a little ravaged by the nocturnal amours that had been enacted on it. And heading straight for me was the long tall assistant railwayman, striding through the park on his way to work.

I hated the assistant railwayman. He was freckled and unbelievably tall and erect. Every time I saw him, I thought of writing to the Railway Minister. I wanted to suggest he use the ugly assistant railwayman as a telegraph pole somewhere between two little stations. The Railway Minister would never have done me the favor.

I couldn't explain my hatred for this official. He was exceptionally tall, but I don't have a principled hatred for anything exceptional. It seemed to me that the assistant railwayman had shot up so much on purpose, and that riled me. It seemed to me that he had done nothing else since his youth but acquire freckles and grow. On top of everything else, he had red hair.

Also, he invariably went around in his uniform and red cap. He took short, slow strides, even though, with his long legs, he could quite easily have walked fast. But he walked slowly, and grew, grew, grew.

To this day, I don't know much about the railway official. But even then I could have sworn that he had secretly committed lots of skullduggeries.

An assistant railwayman like him could quite easily, for instance, cause a train that had an enemy of his on it to crash, and get the locomotive driver blamed for it. It made taking a train anywhere at all a big risk.

An assistant railwayman like him, I thought, would be incapable of dispensing with his red cap for the sake of a woman. If he was ever in love, he would definitely lay his cap carefully on a chair, upside down. He didn't forget to hitch up his trousers when he sat down, and he was certainly unacquainted with the pleasure of being in a woman's debt. He was capable of getting his way with a woman by cunning. And he was jealous too.

Each time I saw him, I thought about writing a letter to all the women in the world: Women! Beware of the assistant railwayman!

Anna didn't like the assistant railwayman either. She asked me: "Why do I hate him?"

I didn't know what to say in reply, and so I told her the story of my friend Abel, and the woman in his life.

My friend Abel yearned for New York.

Abel was a painter and caricaturist. Even before he could hold a pencil, he was already a caricaturist. He had a low opinion of beauty and he loved crippledom and distortion. He couldn't draw a straight line.

Abel had a low opinion of women. What men love in a woman is the perfection they think they see in her. Abel, though, had no use for perfection.

He himself was ugly, so that women fell in love with him. Women suppose that male ugliness hides perfection or greatness.

Once, he was able to travel to New York. On the boat he saw, for the first time in his life, a beautiful woman.

When he reached port, the beautiful woman vanished from his sight. He took the next ship back to Europe.

Anna didn't grasp the connection between my friend Abel and the lanky assistant railwayman.

"What are you telling me about Abel for?" she asked.

"Anna," I explained, "all stories are related. Either they resemble one another, or else one proves the opposite of the other. There is a difference between my friend Abel and the lanky railwayman. A very banal difference: my friend Abel is doomed, whereas the railwayman will prosper and in time be promoted to stationmaster. My friend Abel has yearnings. The assistant railwayman will never have any yearning save to become stationmaster. My friend Abel left New York because the woman of his life had vanished from his sight. The assistant railwayman would never leave New York because of any woman."

I was sure that Anna now understood the connection. But she embraced me and asked: "Would you leave New York on my account?"

That night, I loved Anna very much because I knew I would never leave New York on her account. I was afraid to tell her so, and I loved her for it. I was a coward and behaved in a terribly manly way. Anna, however, understood, and she wept. I must look like the engineer, I thought to myself.

In the morning, Anna was asleep when I left. She sensed that I'd got up, and, still asleep, she put out her arms where I'd been lying.

It was raining, so I went to the café.

The waiter wore a crumpled set of tails and he had a heavy leather purse on his right hip. Ignatz was his name, and that was what everyone called him. He didn't have any other name. Only I said: Waiter!

Ignatz was on duty day and night. He slept on a couple of chairs in the café, hence the crumpled condition of his tails. He never unbuckled his purse. He was slightly squashed down the sides, like a fish. His arms dangled, like disguised dorsal fins. Also, he had bulging gray-green fishy eyes and cold damp hands that he kept wiping on his leather purse. I didn't care for Ignatz, because he didn't really want to be a waiter at all. He read all the newspapers and discussed politics with the customers. He wanted to be a politician.

But a waiter was what he was, and so he was a malcontent.

He always looked as though he blamed the customers for his bungled career.

He said a rather graceless thank-you for tips.

Once, I took Anna to the café, and Ignatz asked: "How are you, Fräulein Anna?" and he wiped his hand on his leather purse to greet her with a dry hand. "How are you, Ignatz?" Anna replied and shook his hand.

Because Ignatz kept hold of her hand for too long, I said: "Waiter!" Then Ignatz bowed and went.

There was a big calendar hanging on the wall of the café.

Every morning at eight o'clock the Postmaster came along, an old gentleman with white side whiskers. The Postmaster had a very upright gait, and wore trousers that were too long for him, and spurs on his boot-heels, maybe to keep his trouser bottoms from brushing the ground. He was unquestionably ex-artillery.

The Postmaster had such improbably blue kindly eyes, that I suspected him of having had them made specially by an optician. His side whiskers were of a fairytale whiteness, too. Perhaps he powdered them every morning, or before going to bed.

Every morning, the Postmaster tore off a leaf of the calendar hanging on the café wall. If it had been left to Ignatz, 1 January would have stayed up all year. The Postmaster saw to it that every day had its own name and number.

I loved the Postmaster.

The park where love flourished was not in the center of town, but at one end of it, where it frayed into footpaths and meadows. At its entrance was an inn where I ate my supper. The post office was directly opposite. It was a new building, with snow-white white-wash; it had a crest on its brow, and a curved post-horn over its green double gate. The post office was the town's only two storey building.

The Postmaster lived in the second storey.

There was always a window open in the second storey. I thought: Up there is where the Postmaster lives. It's always looking up at the sky that keeps his eyes so blue. The Postmaster is a childless old man, I thought, and he will have an old wife with a white bun. They only talk to each other in the evenings, the Postmaster and his wife.

I always sat in the inn in such a way that I could see the open window. Maybe the Postmaster will appear and look at the sky – I hoped. One day a beautiful girl sat in the window and looked at the sky.

I was taken aback by her beauty and stared up at her so intently out of the inn window that she couldn't help notice it, and looked back at me. Feeling embarrassed, I greeted her. She greeted me back. From then on, she was at the window every day.

I plant my experiences like wild vines, and watch them grow. I'm a lazy fellow, and my passion is Nothing. Even so, from the moment I first saw the girl in the window, I've been living in a constant tension that I haven't felt since I was a boy. Back then I was still part of the world, a straw in the whirlpool of events, afloat, swept away. I used to cry over the loss of a paper bag, over nothing at all. Ever since I've gotten to be old, I've stopped crying and stopped laughing. No one can hurt me. I've outgrown sorrow and joy.

But now I was living in sorrow and joy, and I wallowed in trivia.

The girl was looking out of the window every day when I passed. Every day I greeted her. On the third day, she smiled.

Her smile taught me that there is nothing trivial under the sun. Her smile on the third day was a great event.

Her face was small and pale. Her black eyes gleamed as though polished. Her smooth hair was brushed back. Her shoulders bony and apprehensive.

Even when it was raining she looked out the window, and had the window open. I was sitting in the inn, where the windows were misted over from the cold and damp. I had to keep wiping the glass. The girl smiled at me every time.

Once, a couple of men were sitting at the table by the window, and I didn't eat, I went out and walked up and down in front of the inn, and behaved as preposterously as a nightwatchman. I put up my coat collar and walked slowly, with big steps. My clothes were dripping. People huddled in the gateway of the post office building or at the pub door, waiting for it to stop raining. Each time there was a flash of lightning, they flinched and stopped talking. Sometimes they looked at me. A young peasant woman, in wooden clogs and with large full breasts that were trembling with cold and arousal under a wet blouse, moved to one side on the doorstep, plucked at my sleeve, and pointed to an empty space next to her. I walked on, and above me the girl smiled.

The people looked up at the window and laughed. The young woman laughed, too. I looked around, and they all looked sheepish; maybe they thought I was crazy.

That incident kept me going for a whole week. I told Anna about the girl, and Anna laughed at me. "Don't laugh," I said. "I'm in love with the girl in the window."

"Why don't you go up and see her, then?"

"I intend to!"

"No, don't," Anna begged me. "Perhaps you really will fall in love with her."

I'll never forget the day I saw the Postmaster standing in the window beside the girl. I greeted him, and he greeted me back. As naturally as if I'd been a good friend of his.

The girl was his niece, Anna said to me.

I decided to go and see the Postmaster.

But two weeks passed, and I still hadn't gone. I wanted to say: Respected Postmaster, I like your eyes and your spurs and even your overlong trousers. But I love that girl. I think she is the love of my life. I don't want to lose her, as happened once with my friend Abel.

And then I would tell him the story of my friend Abel.

The Postmaster would smile and get to his feet, and his spurs would jingle softly like adolescent cymbals that haven't quite learned how to sound.

The girl would understand my story, and not have to ask questions, the way Anna did.

She's a very different girl altogether.

I would know how to talk to her, too.

I traveled to the big city to send some money to myself, and I spelled my surname wrong, and used only an initial for my first name. Then I returned and waited for my money to arrive.

The postman came in a state of high excitement, because it was two years since he'd last had to deliver money to anyone. That was a long time ago now, and he quickly went through the formalities and asked to see my papers. He kept his cap on in my room, because he was on duty.

He was on the point of giving me the money, but I said:

"Look, my name is spelled differently."

"That doesn't make any difference," said the postman.

"You can't say that!" I said. "Let's take the money to the Postmaster, and ask him if you're allowed to give it to me."

Then I spent ten or fifteen minutes sitting with the Postmaster. But all we talked about was my money, and he said he didn't have the slightest doubt about me being the rightful recipient. No one in the town had ever had my name, or anything resembling it.

"Yes, this is a very quiet little town," said the Postmaster, and he was actually trying to compliment me. It was as though he was saying: Come off it! No one here has such a fine and sonorous name as you.

His spurs jingled like adolescent cymbals, and everything was exactly the way I had imagined it would be. Only there was no mention of the girl in the window.

When I was outside, I looked up to the window. There was the Postmaster standing in the window. I greeted him once more, and he nodded. I thought it would have been the perfect opportunity to go back up and talk about the girl, but I've never been any good at taking advantage of the perfect opportunity.

Everything in life gets to be old and worn, the words, the situations. All the perfect opportunities have already happened. I can't bear to repeat words and situations. It would be like always wearing discarded clothes.

That evening, the girl wasn't in the window. I decided I would leave.

I went back to the hotel and packed my suitcase. Anna came and asked: "How long are you going for?"

It would never have occurred to her that I might leave for good.

"Two days!" I said, and felt no compunction about my lie. What was a lie to Anna? The girl in the window wasn't there any more, and I'd failed to take advantage of the perfect opportunity with the Postmaster.

"Have you been to see the Postmaster?" asked Anna.

"Yes!" I said. "But I didn't see the girl in the window today."

"I expect she's sick!" said Anna.

"Sick? – What makes you say that?"

"She's sick! Don't you know? She's sick anyway! She's got TB, and she's lame. That's why she never goes out on the street. She's going to die soon!"

Anna said all that very fast. Her words tumbled over themselves. Even so, I heard every syllable, crisp and dry. Those syllables imprinted themselves in my brain like coins in a sheet of soft wax. I saw Anna standing there, with her hair scraped back, shiny wet, as though she'd just come out of the water. Anna's not going to die! I thought.

The girl in the window is going to die! is going to die! is going to die!

I'll never speak to her. That's why I failed to take advantage of the perfect opportunity. Not because I don't like perfect opportunities, but because the girl is sick.

"Anna!" I said: "Now I'm going to go away for ever."

"Because she's sick?" laughed Anna.

"Yes!"

"But I'm healthy!" said Anna.

Just then, there was something triumphant in her face. It was pale and cold.

"I'll go with you to the station!" said Anna.

Anna went with me to the station.

A train pulled in, and I was just on my way to the ticket office. Just then the traveler came by, and greeted me. He had his squeaky leather suitcase, and he smelled of hair oil.

Anna clutched my arm, and I stopped.

"Please don't go!" she said.

She wasn't triumphant any more. She looked like a poor, disturbed animal, like a squirrel at bay, in an open treeless field.

The traveler came up to me and said: "At your service!" and "Good evening!" and "You just got in as well? Or are you on your way somewhere?"

"No!" I said. "Just arrived!" – and I went back into town with Anna.

I couldn't sleep all night, because I was thinking of the dying girl. Ever since I'd known she would soon be dead, I felt confident of my power over her. I had her in my grip, I could hold her hands. She was mine.

It didn't even occur to me to think that she'd been sick already. For me, it was as though she'd just become sick. She will die, I thought, and I felt like someone who knows that people will come in an hour to confiscate some object that he cherishes.

I spent the whole of the next morning walking up and down in front of the post office. The Postmaster stood in the window every hour, saw me and felt some perplexity, I'm sure. At lunchtime, he walked out, I greeted him, he replied, and felt perplexed. Then, at three in the afternoon, he returned, and I was still walking up and down in front of the building. I walked unthinkingly to and fro, a clock weight driven by unknown gears.

That evening, I took my seat in the inn, and looked up: the post office window opened, and there she was.

She greeted me first, a little hurriedly, I thought. She probably thought I wouldn't be waiting for her today, because she'd been sick the day before. I glanced up, and there was a whole long speech in my glance.

If I'd spoken for three days, I couldn't have said as much.

I was in a state of stupid and boyish excitement. It seemed to me, she understood what I had said. Then she closed the window as it grew dark, the room was suddenly full of light, and the curtains were drawn. Suddenly the shadow of a big man fell across the soft, bright expanse of the curtains. It wasn't the Postmaster's shadow, because that would have had side whiskers. It was that of a beardless man. Her brother's, perhaps.

I walked in the park for another hour. People were still in one another's arms on the benches and in the flowerbeds. I met women wandering around, apparently aimlessly, on the gravel paths, with loose hair and the strange exhilaration of intoxication and loss. They seemed to stagger, and yet be full of feeling and life. They were like spinning tops that had been set in motion by some unknown force whose effect was presently wearing off, but left them still in a state of giddiness, turning their last few circles and vainly seeking some point of stability or balance, inside or outside them.

All these, I thought, are healthy and not about to die.

I saw Anna in her room, sitting on the side of her bed and crying. She didn't hold her face in her hands the way people usually do when they cry. It seemed that her tireless, even, rain-like crying didn't come from her soul, but somehow from outside; something alien, sudden and catastrophic that she was unable to oppose, and that it was pointless to conceal.

That night, I loved Anna as I had the very first time, with the tenderness and joy that you lavish on a new possession.

The next morning, I experienced the last story of this little town.

The traveler was sitting in the café very early, eating cake. He didn't eat with his fingers, but rather elaborately with a teaspoon and a knife, because the traveler was a gentleman, and he knew how to behave. He spent a long time over his cake. Then he stood up, went over to the calendar on the wall, and tore off yesterday's date, decisively, as though he were responsible for the new day, as proud as a god in the plenitude of his power. I dreaded the arrival of the Postmaster.

For decades it had been the Postmaster who tore off the old days and revealed the new, humbly and carefully, not like a god but like the servant of a god. Today he would look at the calendar in shock, get all confused over the dates and the days of the week, and not know what was happening any more.

Therefore, I picked up the crumpled piece of paper, smoothed it down, and re-attached it to the calendar as well as I could.

The traveler looked at me and said: "Sir, today is 28 May!" I was taken aback, by the loud voice in which he said the date, and even though it was a very simple thing, and the whole world must know it, it seemed to me as though the traveler had bellowed a shy secret out into the world.

The 28 May!

Just then, the clock struck half past seven, and the Postmaster walked in, his spurs set up a quiet and exuberant jingle, they giggled, and the Postmaster went ceremonially up to the calendar and revealed the new day. Now it was 28 May!

That 28 May became one of the most important days of my life, because that was the day I decided to leave.

What else was there for me to do in the little town? The girl in the window was going to die, Anna hurt me, the sight of her injured me, and I couldn't help her. I knew the postman inside out, and the silvery spurs of the Postmaster too. Käthe, I thought, will open her window at the same time every day, and it will hardly matter that I won't be there any more to say good morning. And it was already 28 May.

On 28 May, I couldn't possibly stay any longer. Almost without my noticing it, the wheat in the fields had grown head-high and more. If half a dozen rabbits piled on top of each other had careered through the fields, you wouldn't even see the tips of the ears of the one on top. It was a blessed year, and in the orchards the blossoms were piled so thick that you could have walked there bare-footed and only felt the earth as a distant reality.

Also, you could see it in the clouds that were no longer lounging around in the sky youthfully and insouciantly, but were pitched there heavily and thoughtfully, or they were rolling their swollen, fertile bodies around, in the performance of a duty. By 28 May, you know what you want.

It is so ridiculous, I thought, for me to hang around night after night in front of the windows of a girl who's about to die, and whom I won't ever be able to kiss. I'm not that young any more, I thought. Every day is a task, and each one of my hours was a sin against life.

Once, I had a dream of a great port. I heard the colossal rattle of twenty thousand ships' chains and the shouts of busy sailors. I saw heavy cranes go up and down, smoothly and easily and without strain, as though steered not by men, but working by their own will, and by God's. It wasn't the tenacity of iron, but the supple ease of natural powers.

Sometimes I dreamed of a great city, maybe it was New York. I inhaled the clattering tempo of its life. Its big, wide, unstoppable streets flowed with people and cars and paving stones, and lamp posts, and billboards, I don't know where or why. The city didn't stand, it ran. Nothing stood. Giant factories sent their smoke up into the sky through huge chimneys. For seconds at a time, I would close my eyes to listen to the melodies of that life. It was a hideous music; it sounded like the melody of a huge, demented hurdy-gurdy whose rolls had all gotten mixed up. But the music stimulated me. The notes were ugly, but not false. For a while I screamed along to the rhythm; then I woke up.

When I awoke, I was surprised to find myself not a part of the city, but someone detached from it, a ridiculous inhabitant of a ridiculous small town. Who was I really? The man outside the window. Chum, I said to myself, bury that girl, who's barely alive any more anyway, and deal with life. Life is what matters. It might have been better (by the rules that people make for themselves anyway, it might have been better) to go up to the girl and sit on her bed in the daytime, and be at the window with her in the evening, and bring her something of the gigantic chaotic rattle and red blood that flows through the veins of the world.

But more important is life.

Being so ruthless to myself was an attempt to bury my pain. I buried it under a landslide of ruthlessness.

I left in the town's one and only hackney cab, the same one I'd come in. I hadn't said anything to Anna.

It was late in the afternoon. The sun poured down in broad, gold streams. The station lay curled in the sun like a big yellow cat. The rails ran out into the world, they girdled the planet in iron.

By the time I was sitting in the train, looking out of the window, I was already separated from the town, and from the last few weeks, by ruthlessness, joy and strength.

Let the postman get drunk, the Postmaster jingle his cymbals, the traveler reek of hair oil. Ignatz the waiter have clammy hands. Anna become his lover.

And the girl at the window? . . .

She can die! I said, and am not ashamed to admit that I rejoiced in my own good health.

What was this condition in which I'd spent the last few weeks? What kind of sentimental fool was my friend Abel? Never ever ever would I leave New York for the sake of a girl.

In fact, I want to go to New York. America is a wonderful country. It wasn't founded by any stone bishop.

While I was thinking that, the train whistled and gave a jerk. At that instant, the lanky assistant railwayman with the red cap stepped out of his office on to the platform. He left the door ajar behind him.

And trailing after the assistant railwayman came the most beautiful girl in the world. It was, it was the girl at the window.

"Stay, won't you!" I heard the railway employee say to her. "I'm almost finished!"

But the girl didn't listen to him. She looked at me. We looked at each other. She stood upright, and she was wearing a white dress, and she was healthy, and not at all lame, and not at all tubercular. Obviously, she was the assistant railwayman's fiancée or his wife.

Then, when the train gave another start and slowly began to move away, I waved, and I looked the girl in the eye. I wrote this story just because of that look.

In my compartment, I felt I was expected to cry, but instead I laughed. I saw a shepherd whipping his dog, I saw a line-keeper stand to attention beside his signal, while his wife hung up the laundry, and a little cart wobbled along a country lane.

"Life is very important!" I laughed. "Very important!" and I went to New York.

THE BLIND MIRROR

I

Little Fini was sitting on a bench in the Prater, in the warmth of the first mild day in April. She felt herself yielding, as to a melody, to a strange faintness that she had never known before. The blood beat fast against the thin skin at her wrists and temples. The pale green of the trees and meadows spread out to cover everything, even such things as prams and gravel and benches. Everything she could see ran together, it was like looking out from a very fast train into a very green world.

It took a moment, or an eternity. Then the people and things around her returned to their original limits, their shapes and their lives, their gait and their stance, distinguishing characteristics and familiar aspects. But the faintness remained with her, like a voice in her blood, moving within it, filling her entire body as a chorale fills a cathedral. It was a singing emptiness, her limbs were heavy, but life was light and ethereal, her heart had wings as if it had just overcome death. The black fears settled far off, there was no threat from darkness, no power was waiting, no fear lurked anywhere on the whole wide, happy horizon of a wonderful day. Fini could hear the slow throb of her heart, she felt the comforting presence of her own warm being, it was a surprise, the first time that she had been alone with her heart and so conscious of it, and its beat was like the slow drip of a reassuring reply to anxiously repressed questions. It felt like the aftermath of grief, a happy melancholy, as if she'd been crying, as if, after years of pain and constriction, fetters had been taken off her — at last, at last.

Fini, little Fini, got up and stretched out her arms, like a young bird attempting to fly, and as she took the first step, her thoughts came back. They had been somewhere lurking around, and now they descended like a swarm of flies; the little alarms, the swift black worries, the hateful scuttling cares, the threats of tomorrow and the day after, grisly images of grisly days, and down came fear like a curved yoke on a trembling neck. Gone was the sweet music of unconsciousness, the kind, sleepy song of oblivion, dimmed all the shining distance of the untroubled Void, and a chill came over the mild spring day. Fini shivered in the April evening as she got up to deliver the letters to the firm of Mendel & Co., to the First and Second Provincial Courts, to the co-plaintiff Wolff & Sons, all the letters contained in her green-bound book, the strange letters to be delivered to strange anterooms, the light and demanding load she had to carry to earn the postage, from four in the afternoon to seven at night.

She walked through the big streets, a tiny, lost figure, and it wasn't until she was in the next antechamber that she noticed that the letter, the important letter to the First Provincial Court, wasn't there any more. In the column of brisk signatures there was one missing, there was one empty line that when you fixed it turned into a staring hole, a white hollow eye-socket. Then a great trembling came over the little shivering girl, and she felt a cold that she could hardly bear, in the middle of a spring evening in April that she knew must be warm. Fini wanted to draw down the warmth of the evening, and wrap it over her thin shoulders. Just as the evening swathed the city, so she wanted it to protect her as well, who was lost in the immeasurable street.

Oh! if you're so light and frail, then it's a good thing to have some shelter in the noisy desert of the city. Life is an iron vault over our tiny heads, and we're helpless and lost, at the mercy of the barking dog and the gleaming policeman, and the lustful eye of the man and the shrill cry of the tough woman, when we happen to cross their paths, these powers that live in the public squares and lurk in dark corners. Now it would be good to know of a house one could go to, a safe house with a wide doorway, to take us in like a mother and feed us and comfort us and expel the great fear from our hearts, like a mighty porter an unauthorized vagrant; now that we have felt the pitilessness of the outside, a big and sheltering house would do us good. We wouldn't have to worry there about the lost letter and about our dread of what the morrow might bring.

When the man in the white overalls came and lit the lamp with his long pole, a little warmth hurried through the shivering girl, and the faint but welcome consolation that there was still a long night to come between today and tomorrow. Between the misfortune and its dire consequences there were ten or twelve hours, a sleep and perhaps a saving dream – time enough for a miracle that surely must come once in our lives. Perhaps, if no dream came and the wonder let us down, we might still be able to speak to Dr. Blum the partner in the morning, who was better because he was younger and wore his hair in a fringe, like a student.

If only it wasn't for the hallway we have to pass through every evening, the hallway that was worse than the street, with its stench of the excrement of young cats and its lurking concierge, and the stairs with their broken balustrade like a set of teeth full of gaps, and miserable Mother with her inevitable inquisitiveness and her ear cocked in suspicion – if it wasn't for all that, then we might have been able to leave tomorrow to God, to the Almighty, and enjoy today in a soft bed, with a book and picture postcards on the ceiling.

II

Mother wasn't back yet. – It's a good thing when our Mothers aren't there, our Mothers with their probing, unbelieving eyes that are sad and must cry, terrifying and stern but still sad, our poor Mothers, who don't understand anything and scold and make us lie to them. Then we don't need to report to anyone, and there is no fear in us of the consequences of what we say, no fear of the need to lie and none of its discovery. Slowly Fini undressed; she felt a warm trickle down her thigh, it had to be blood, she was alarmed. Something had happened to her, and she racked her forgetful brain for some sin that she had committed, gray days ago.

It's nice to be able to undress alone in our room in front of the mirror – all alone, the door locked, as if we had a room of our own, like Tilly, our older friend – and see how our breasts are growing, round and white and crowned by pink tips, though they're still not as big and well-defined under our clothes as Tilly's, who has a boyfriend and is allowed to kiss.

Entranced as though petting a small animal, Fini felt her body, stroked the aspiring curve of her hips and the coolly rounded knee, and saw the blood marking its narrow red path down her bare leg.

Little girls are afraid when they see the red blood and they don't know where it's come from, and they are all alone and naked, without the protective covering of a dress, in a locked room with a living mirror, and when they see the mysterious blood, flowing for mysterious reasons, then their fear is three times as great. Wonders have their cause and their being in our selves, and we are frightened to find them so near when we had supposed them to be distant things, and remote from our bodies. Fini held her breath and suddenly heard the great emptiness in the room, felt the deadness of all the dead things, saw the lamp burning in a fog, a white fog that took on the likeness of a face, a ghostly face with a core of light. An infinity away, Fini heard voices on the street and the squealing of a tram, the melody of an everlasting violin, and a consoling hiss of silence as from a large seashell. The endless silence flooded in cool and soft, an ocean rising from her ankles – already it was round her knees, and the blue stillness washed around her hips and rose menacingly towards her heart.

A merciful darkness came and covered her up. She lapsed into unconsciousness, a soft, welcoming cloak of tender velvet.

III

And that was how her Mother found her, her perpetually busy, graying, worried Mother, on her return from her installment selling round in Purkersdorf with the suburban train.

She tossed her hat – skewed, beaten up from the trip, indispensable for the collecting of installment payments – on to the sofa. Eggs cracked abjectly in her handbag. She had opened her mouth to swear, already her lip was curled for a bad word when she gave a start, she thought about suicide and dreadful reports in the paper, and she leaned down over Fini.

The girl woke and she saw her Mother's broad face above her, and she looked into the anxious eyes, and saw in them an unfamiliar kindness, comfort and unwonted hesitation. Swiftly her Mother picked her up in her strong arms and carried her to the soft, white, broad bed, brought her cold milk, and kissed her forehead, mouth, and eyes as not for a long time. The touch of her Mother's lips was familiar, long absent and like the return of a half-forgotten childhood. "My darling," said Mother and she said it again, and her voice was different, it was the voice of an old, former, gone and now returned Mother. "You're poorly," said her Mother, and: "Now you're a woman." And Fini understood what Tilly, her grownup friend, had always used to ask her: if she'd been poorly yet. A quiet rejoicing set up within her, a secret celebration, as though she were wearing a white dress for her confirmation.

"Stay in tomorrow," said her Mother, "don't go to work." Her voice wafted over Fini's face, soft and warm as a small friendly wind. How strangely changed everything was; her usually rampaging brother was quiet, Mother was humming in the kitchen, and the night wind rattled a loose windowpane next door. Everything was calm and white where she was, the cozy warmth of a newly regained home, limitless home, goodness without end, and the shared bonds of adulthood and womanhood connecting her to her mother. She was no longer the punishing Mother, but a woman and a sister.

Later on, the doorbell rang. It was the neighbor come round for a chat; her keys jangled softly, and Fini could hear her talking. She listened. The two women were talking about the war; they'd read about the battle of Sadowa in the evening paper, and now they were talking about their menfolk, who hadn't written for some time. The smell of baking potatoes spread through the apartment. The women ate and giggled. Then Mother was talking about Fini, and the old woman's giggling became unpleasant, and her whispers were an incomprehensible and disquieting hissing from the kitchen.

The coziness of her white homey bed was too lovely, and it was too exhausting to try and listen. It was better to lie down and not have any thoughts.

Suddenly Fini remembered the terrible lost letter, and she called her Mother and told her about it, and she wasn't panicked and didn't swear, but instead became still kinder and still softer, and promised comfort and intercession, and smoothed the sheets with both hands. Such a different world, gratitude comes gushing from a thousand streams, and from the buried depths of childhood, we fetch our old, heartfelt little prayers and cry a little to the resurrected God, and then we fall asleep.

IV

At eight o'clock, they were woken by a loud ring, betokening either a field postcard from Father, or else the news of his death; it had to be one or the other. Day after day, hour after hour, they'd been waiting for the card, the notification from the regiment, and they trembled at the short shrill of the bell, having previously ached to hear it. Fini heard her Mother's customary groan on getting up, the shuffle of her slippers across to the door and back, the good morning of the postman, and the rattle of the wooden blinds being pulled up. Minutes passed, minutes of sweet uncertainty and apprehension that we love, tense minutes of not daring to breathe in the face of great surprises that we always long for, even if they turn out to be terrible.

Mother's happy exclamation sounded from the kitchen, she hurried over to the bed and sat down and announced that Father was coming home, would soon be here, he'd escaped with his life, but he was hurt and might be returned to them now for good.

With trembling fingers she crumpled up the red card, she quickly looked crestfallen, and the poor soul forgot Josef's sandwiches, and the other tasks of the morning hours. She sat on the side of the bed with her thin pigtail wound round her head, dreaming of giving up some of her territories, the pointless ones at least, and of buying up others from Uncle Arnold that would be safe and profitable, around the munitions factory, where the workers drew steady wages and paid off their installments dependably.

Life displayed a strange bounty, God poured out His mercy, He transformed Mother, the foul-mouthed, the judge, the avenger, into a kind and joyful woman. It was hard to credit. Oftentimes that morning, Fini wondered, had she woken into the actual day, or was she drifting along in a continuation of her dream? Everything seemed improbable, the sun and the twittering sparrow on the tin windowsill, the shaft of sunlight gilding the dust in the corner by the stove, the return of Father and the peace in her own heart.

Mother gave off the sultry aroma of her warm body and the warm bed, she smelled as familiar as warm milk, and made Fini want to throw her arms around her neck, to feel the yielding softness of her Mother's breasts, and to weep happily. If it wasn't that the thought of the lost letter was still with her in its full terror, what a wonderful and serene morning this would have been, if it wasn't that the very next hour she would have to be in the office, explaining everything to Dr. Finkelstein.

"I'll go and talk to him," said Mother. And then Fini remembered her school years, and her Mother's efforts on her behalf and the clumsy excuses and the embarrassing scenes between Mother and teacher, and she resolved to go herself. If God really had come back, and wanted to help, then surely He would help little girls in their difficulties, and, as always when we are practically at our wits' ends, a story slowly ripens in our minds, and becomes a plausible account that we end up believing ourselves. Couldn't we turn up with the field postcard in our hands, and use our excitement over that news as an excuse for the lost letter, which surely they would accept, whereas a common or garden fainting-fit would merely make them smirk? Plenty of miraculous things had happened since yesterday, today was bound to bring many more. – And so little Fini walked down the streets she had been so afraid of yesterday, and she wasn't tiny and lost any more, but proud and upright, grownup and mature in the sultry, rainy air of the gray day. The clouds hung ready to drop their burdens. The infinite atmosphere seemed somehow smaller and closer to the world; and the heavens lay above the earth, ready to embrace and to fertilize it.

V

The miracles didn't cease, the kindness of God was never ending. A quarter of an hour before Dr. Finkelstein arrived, a man came in bearing the lost letter. Fini gave him the last of her tram money. She looked closely at the man, and kept a memory of his face, his clothes, his mustache. Years afterwards, she knew that gray tufts of hair sprouted from his ears. Admittedly, Blum, the partner, walked in the moment the man had left, tall, powerful, scented and beaming, a god to humble secretaries. Carefully and paternally he grasped Fini's arm, there was mildness and clemency in his voice, as he urged her to be more careful in future. She felt the insistent pressure of his fingers on her upper arm, looked up at him, and saw his smiling mouth and the studiedly unruly wave of hair over his left eye.

Later, the miraculous yielded to the normal tedium of an irritating day. Fini sat in front of the brown telephone switchboard with the tangle of jacks and the jungle of wires, green striped or red striped or blue, and the unoccupied sockets, before which the strange shutters strangely fell away with a soft click, like leathery old eyelids. The telephone yelped, an imperious female voice demanded to speak to Dr. Blum; a plug flew into a random socket, and Fini waited for it to work. She straightway guessed it was the wrong connection, and she waited apprehensively as she had at school, when she'd done a sum wrong, and she felt the awkward silence of the rest of the class behind her back, and the gleeful breath of the teacher at her shoulder. How, among all the possible connections, was it possible to know the right one on this machine, without some miracle coming to one's aid?

But it didn't come, alas. Instead Dr. Finkelstein came. Headlong, with his briefcase, he plunged in, always avid, always plunging, quarrelsome behind his glittering spectacles; because the call had gone through to him, and not his partner, the Honorable Helena had no business with him – "no business, I say" – that snake would ruin the pair of them. "I don't do litigation, you really ought to know that, after all you've been sitting here for ten years!" Noise preceded him, Dr. Finkelstein, he lived in a cloud of noise, and he started to dictate. "Leave that machine, you'll never get the hang of it anyway, and take a letter!" – And he softly repeated to himself:

"Been sitting here for ten years" – until he shot a glance over at Fini, and a dim memory awoke in him of something Dr. Blum had said about some new secretary being hired.

How your heart fluttered while he gave dictation, the long, strange, never heard of words bubbled out, streams of extraordinary syntax, fantastic exoticisms, Latin terms, sentences of labyrinthine construction, with cunningly hidden predicates that sometimes inexplicably went missing altogether. As Fini took it down, she missed out a word, she misheard a name, and the pencil, in her cramped grip, began to skitter wildly across the rustling paper, the sound of a word suggested another that was similar to it, and at the end of the dictation loomed the inevitable reading back from the shorthand, which was a prospect that distracted Fini even while she was writing. The next half hour loomed, in which it would be revealed how pitifully she had performed, the disastrous sentences full of mutilated names, missing paragraphs and transferred predicates. It was like being given a crazy whirling wheel to transcribe; large colorful wheels revolved, spiraled with red and purple rims out of her paper.

And the inevitable upshot was that she would be given her notice, perhaps even dismissed on the spot. Sent back with hanging head to looking in the small ads of the morning paper. To waiting in anterooms and careful noting down of identical terms and conditions. "Period. Finished!" shouted Dr. Finkelstein, "Read it back to me, quickly!" But on that wonderful day, rescue – sudden and gratefully received – streamed from every door. There was a ring, and the Honorable Helena entered, her bright voice rang out like a fanfare, she swept in in a light dress and a boldly undulating hat laden with youthful cornflowers. She came from a strange grown-up world, the world of an aristocratic clientèle; she was surrounded by empty space that permitted of no typists or office boys, her glance pierced through clothes and bodies, people were invisible to her, glass. Dr. Finkelstein's wild rage was over. He stammered courtesies and left, promising to find his partner.

There was a file to be found, a missing file. The Honorable Helena versus her spouse. They sought it under H, quickly and desperately. Five times Fini went through H, until Dr. Blum impatiently shouted out Tuschak, the Honorable Helena Tuschak. The file duly turned up under T. Meantime, Tilly kept her head down, shuffling papers, sharpening pencils, arranging erasers, trimming blotting paper, counting stamps; in vain did Fini seek to catch her eye, her friendly eye promising help – naughty Tilly, pretending to be busy, and leaving her in the lurch. It was hurtful and upsetting. Her cheeks flushed, Fini could feel a garter was coming loose, but she couldn't put her hand to her knee to fix it, it would have looked like scratching an itch, the loose garter and the sliding stocking robbed her of whatever composure she had left, papers flew everywhere.

There followed a curative silence without any more ringing. Fini looked out the window, saw the slowly moving clock, the red brick nunnery with the nuns promenading in the park, coming and going in their black and white, alien beings in the beyond behind the red walls, in the garden, in the outer court of eternal bliss. Her awe of the brides of Christ disappeared, and the cloister gardens seemed a wonderful place. The golden hands slid slowly round, the Honorable Helena went away. For a moment Dr. Finkelstein stood in front of her with his glittering spectacles, and then he clattered off with his black briefcase and bouncing hat brim.

It was spring on the streets, it had been raining, and the big paving slabs shone in red and blue, as if reflecting a rainbow. The grass on the lawn beds was freshly rinsed, the blackbirds stood out on the middle of the road, Fini strolled along with Tilly, feeling newly grown up, and unwell and a woman. "I look pale," said Fini, "can't you tell? I'm poorly," said Fini casually, and she gauged Tilly's breasts trembling under her sheer blouse. The men smiled at them, the young men prowling through the streets.

Trilby's beckoned with yellow icecream, served with crisp wafers in cut glass bowls, one scoop or two on the little marble tables outside, and the deep basket chairs. Half her hard-earned stamp money went on an icecream, the waitress got a tip too, and then, just as a one-year volunteer was about to walk over to their table from his corner, the girls quickly got up and stalked off into the sunset, feeling pleasantly strengthened.

At home, there's a smell of sweet things being prepared against Father's return, her brother Josef is rampaging around — it's as though hundreds of years have passed since yesterday. The building is full of unappeasable grayness, the staircase, Mother. The warm coziness of yesterday abed is gone, Mother comes questing out of the kitchen, insatiable, wanting to hear about her day. The sighs of her dissatisfaction cut Fini to the quick. Night comes along and with it the mean oil lamp with its grayish-blue mantle, from which the neighbor predicts rain for tomorrow.

VI

It did rain, and Father came, gray at the temples, inexplicably shrunken and redolent of iodine, soap, Red Cross and railways.

A shell-burst had buried him alive, thanks be to God; and now he was restored to them, perhaps for good, baffled to be in the midst of his own intact family, numb from his arrival in his own apartment, feeling alien at home and conspicuous in the midst of the ordinary, his eyes probing, slipping away and returning to a distance, a remote distance whose outline we could barely guess at, and whose reality was never discernible to us.

To Fini, he was the big strong man who had taken her in his arms when he left, only now he was small and hunched, and Fini took him in her arms. "Speak up," he said, explaining that he had become hard of hearing. They spoke up, they yelled, and still he didn't understand, he was as deaf as a post, and two days later he turned up with a black ear-trumpet, that weirdly and shockingly craned its long neck and wide funnel mouth from the top pocket of his uniform jacket. He was a changed man when he didn't have it, and still more when he pressed it to his ear. Every day he hobbled off to hospital with his stick, and he came back with the smell of medicine on him, and sometimes a great long loaf of bread that you couldn't get at the baker's. The relatives came to see him, they shouted zestfully, delighted in his misunderstandings, and sniggered at him. Uncle Arnold was adamant that he wouldn't sell them his best territories, and they discussed making a fresh start instead.

Then the noisy days of company were over, and once there was an argument about a box of matches that Father had left behind in hospital – or was it in the pub, who could say? He drank a little, and then he quietened down, and sometimes he stole little things from home. Mother yelled, she was the only one he could understand, and he wasn't slow to reply either. But if she spoke quietly, he had no idea what she was saying, and she was able to eff and blind, and words that she would have bitten back if he had been able to hear, now tripped off her lips, and didn't affect him, so that he still smiled when she said, "Bastard".

At night, though, if Fini happened to wake, she could hear them exchanging whispered tendernesses in bed; way past midnight, the heady whispers could be heard in the bedroom. His hearing probably improved at night, because they were talking about love. Strange that they could forget about their wrangles when they laid their bodies together; the warm milky smell that emanated from Mother must help to soothe him, Fini thought.

The night was warm, and warmth came from the bed; Fini got up and went over to the open window, while Father and Mother, both giggling, lit a candle in the bedroom.

Night is full of feeling and surprise, out of the blue, longings come to us, when the distant whistle of a locomotive catches in the window, when a cat slinks along the pavement opposite, hungry for love, and disappears into a basement window where the tom waits. There is a big starry sky above us, too remote to be kind, too beautiful not to harbor a God. There are the little things close at hand and there is a remote eternity, and some relation between them that escapes our understanding. Maybe we would understand it, if love were to visit us; love relates the stars and the slinking cat, the lonesome whistle and the vastness of the heavens.

Two people were undressing across the way, she could see the shadows they made on the blinds, a hand put out a candle with a quick flap, and a man and a woman went to bed – then they were whispering together, just as her parents were whispering. Fini could no longer feel the night air, she saw red rings before her eyes, a sudden trickle of blood ran down her thighs, and the tips of her breasts grew, extended towards the world outside, the locomotives, the whistles, the stars.

A new day grayly dawned; there was a white sheen at the back of the houses. It was Sunday. The morning spread, the room swiftly brightened, in the afternoon we're going to the studio with Tilly; we are to experience wondrous new things in an unfamiliar world, great new things, tiny little Fini.

VII

That afternoon in the studio kept its shining distinctness even years later, by which time Fini was living in a different world, and had put behind her and forgotten the sweet foolishness of her early days. Surrounded by great and clever people, she felt even lonelier than she did at home, and even more insignificant than in the big wide streets of the city, as life stretched its iron vault over her little head. There, ideas flowed from every part of the wonderful, unknown and barely guessed at world, ideas beautiful and subtle, soft and incomprehensible, music produced by innumerable, scattered and concealed instruments. She didn't understand the half of it, and she didn't know whom to ask; because Tilly was out of reach – grownup, accomplished Tilly, who was boldly at home wherever she was put, and from the radiant center that she fittingly occupied sent cool smiles into Fini's quiet corner, and coldly brilliant shafts. Fini sensed there was no help, and she felt as though, all untutored and unprepared as she was, she would be required to take an examination in the hour ahead. The people here were proud and courageous; they must have come from large, cool, well-protected houses and fine rooms, where all the walls had mirrors which kept the manners of the proprietors under constant supervision and trained them to perfection. Whereas anyone who, like us, has grown up in small places, and with blind mirrors on the walls, is condemned to remain fearful and inhibited all his life.

The men were speaking already, they had brown faces and courageous eyes, and they too had been in the war, like Father; but they had not returned from it small and crushed and deaf, and even in their wounds there was splendor. Men are from a different world than little girls like us; they are clever and strong and proud, they have learned many things and understand many things, they seek out dangers, and they walk imperiously through the streets, and they may have whatever they want, the buildings, the streets, the women, and the whole of the city.

A painter, Ernst was his name, was showing Fini his sketches, there was a dog, a naked girl, and swallows in flight, and you could tell he wanted to give her something because he felt sorry for Fini. "Say something," he asked her, but she didn't have anything to say, and what could she have said anyway but idiotic things, to a painter who could draw swallows in flight, and dogs and naked girls, and could commit to paper whatever his eye lit on, and whatever pleased him. He spoke, and Fini took in very little, because she was thinking she should say something herself. Once or twice, she opened her mouth, but she left the half thought-out word unsaid, she was too afraid of saying something embarrassing. She grew hot in her corner, she didn't dare get up, she felt she would like to walk up and down a little, but she couldn't; helpless as a bird with trimmed feathers she perched on the little round stool, with the whitewashed wall behind her which she couldn't lean against on account of her dark blue dress. Far away, she could hear the voice of the host, who was a musician whose name was Ludwig, and who wore a flowered waistcoat with mother-of-pearl buttons, and had a voice like a dark cello, and Tilly was on first name terms with him, that's how close to these people she was, and how happy in their company.

One of Ernst's sketches was of a woman, walking along a narrow path between fields and woods, and even though there was no very obvious connection between that woman and Fini, she accepted it gratefully, and it seemed to her that this beautiful gentle woman was herself, with the narrow path between the green fields that were fertile but still somehow sad, and the melancholy of pointless flowering. She wrapped the picture in brown paper, and for three days it rested against the side of her handbag, till once, when no one was home, it too went into the secret hiding place that no one knew about, on the bare tabletop, under the oilcloth cover that was pinned to it, where the lovely flat silver paper was spread out, inestimable wealth, buried treasure.

VIII

All our little secrets that we've managed to preserve over months and months from the crude assaults of others' hands, sweet little mother-of-pearl buttons and pressed tinfoil, pretty postcard views and gaudy silk samples, all these things that we've carefully tended like a warm brood and that we think about every day: in the office, when Dr. Finkelstein is giving dictation and we sit in bewilderment in front of the confusing brown telephone switchboard, on the street, when we deliver letters, the important letters in the green-bound book – our warm brood, our comfort and our secret – one day (they're tidying up at home) they're ferreted out of their safe hiding-place, shamelessly exposed to the shameless eye of Mother and her cruelly destroying hand. Like little birds, spilled from the protection of a nest by a heartless force, our precious objects are lost in the wasteland strewn with pieces of broken furniture.

One evening, Fini returned home to find the table stripped bare, without its oilcloth covering; there was a little glittering heap of drawing-pins, and the picture postcards and the sketch of the woman wandering on the path between melancholy blossoming fields, all in little pieces. It was a return to a devastated home, which the enemy had laid waste. A whole world that had been lovingly and carefully assembled now lay in ruins. There was a piece of it in every one of the miserable scraps, and Fini wept, even though she knew she was making herself ridiculous in front of her brother and her mocking Mother. No one in the world understood what Fini had lost: the wonderful sketch of the woman walking, the present she had been given in an hour when the gates of a fresh, new, wonderful life had been opened. Fini wept and felt ashamed that she was weeping over childish things, but she was also weeping because she was forced to deny the preciousness of what was lost.

There was only one person who might understand her, and that was her deaf Father, who was listening with his eyes; they were understanding and sympathetic, and with the last vestiges of his majesty, he was at pains to calm his son and his intemperate wife. Suddenly, Fini felt his heavy hand on her shoulder; he spoke sensible words, and he sat down with Fini in her corner, on the edge of the large, iron-bound trunk and both were embittered captives in the kingdom of Fini's Mother and her raging brother. Since that day, Fini loved her Father.

Her never assuaged longing flared up, the longing for a small secret box of her own, a warm home in the chill apartment, a place that offered sanctuary and that kept things safe. Her Father promised her just such a box; she didn't understand how he could be infirm: his deafness left him, and he understood her deepest wishes with a thousand sensitive ears. His callused fingers trembled as they grasped Fini's, and he said: "Let's go for a walk."

And Fini went with her Father through the noisy streets in the gloaming, and she was as maternal as if she were leading her child, and she gave her hobbling Father all the love that she had felt for the tinfoil, the silk ribbons, and the walking woman. They went for a walk, and they felt safe from the iron clutch of Mother's indefatigable cleaning and tidying.

IX

On the road once, between the First Provincial Court and the firm of Marcus & Sons, she met the painter Ernst, who greeted her with a deep bow, the way only great ladies from Dr. Finkelstein's clientèle were greeted. She couldn't conceal the green-bound book, or the fact that she was delivering important letters by hand in order to get the postage for them. "I'm on business errands," she said, and she left the painter waiting outside the various buildings. Then he directed her to the darkening park, where courting couples sat out and love blossomed, where white swans swam on blue lakes, and where Mother, mindful of morality and her own maternal obligations, had forbidden her to set foot.

For the first time, Fini found herself walking with a man, in the evening, through a park she'd only ever been in in the afternoon, when people dozed on benches in the sun; till now, it was only in the afternoons that, restraining her rushing feet, she had dared to walk down the gravel paths, astonished by the profusion of the flowerbeds. Then alarmed by the mighty tolling of the church clock, she sped her steps to fight her rising panic.

The park was different by night, dense and dark, warm and nurturing. Fini couldn't see what was behind the trees, what was happening in the stupefying light of the lamps, those stalled silver lightnings that plunged the distance to the next light in deeper darkness. Melodies dropping from the terrace filtered softly through the foliage, were distracted by the evening rustle of the wind, seemed to come and go in strangely crafted waves, and the strong rhythm of a familiar march was smoothed in the dark avenue to a supple waltz.

And by Fini's side walked the man, the victorious man with the sonorous low voice, smelling alien and animal, like bitter herb and forest root, and it didn't matter what he said. As under a beatific rain, she walked under the stream of his talk, and she lowered her head, and kept a lookout in all the other faces for a face that was familiar and that might betray her at home.

They climbed the majestic marble steps that led up not to a pair of thrones but to the terrace of the restaurant, and ate melting yellow vanilla icecream from rounded bowls. They sat in a little nook, knees pressed against the low marble table, and the silver chime of their little spoons against the glass was, for a fraction of a second, like a narcotic to them.

Then they saw the silent marble forms pressed against the blackish green of the rustling trees, saw the frozen limbs come to life in the flooding silence of the night. It was the first time Fini had seen such living monuments. She heard the pumping of her own heart in the dead, dead no more, in the resurrected things, and felt her own blood circulating through the stones, the benches, the lawns and trees, in the nocturnally closed waterlily on the inaudibly muttering surface of the lake, and in the gloomily obstructive reeds.

They quit the park via the white, light-garlanded bridge, and reached the silent market place, wandering along in sweet perplexity, in among empty stalls, drawn to the sparse shadows of low roofs and carriages, carts and piled up barrels. Like homeless children, they wandered, seeking a roof, a place for their love. They walked down endless streets, and each time they passed a hotel, they both stopped momentarily, and then went on.

Suddenly, in a deserted corner, there is her Father, resting for a moment, propped on his stick, under the light of an arc-lamp, with a one-legged comrade – presumably on their way back from the hospital. Slowly, Father lifted his listening eyes, and waved to her, and she left Ernst and gave the old man her hand, and Father patted her cheek and showed her off to his comrade. He said nothing, he sent her back with a soft motion of his finger. Fini ran to Ernst who had been patiently waiting, and then began talking, as though not to the man, with his victorious smell of earth and roots, but to an intimate girlfriend. Everything she poured into his listening ear, the pining of the children and their daily fear and the affliction of the office and the crush of home. She told him about the lost picture and her sadness and pain over the wandering woman on the narrow path, in between sadly and futilely blooming fields; about the breathless dictation of Dr. Finkelstein, glinting horribly through his spectacle lenses, always avid, always predatory, with his flapping hat brim and menacingly brandished briefcase. About the brown telephone equipment with the bewildering jacks and the tangled lines, green-striped, red-striped and blue, of shrilly domineering women's voices demanding to speak to Dr. Blum, the other partner. About the strange little shutters that strangely fell away with a soft, plaintive clap. About Mother's futile selling trips out to Purkersdorf on the Wéstern Railway, and Tilly's betrayal in the office, when she had sharpened pencils, and stuck stamps, and failed to reply to Fini's look as she implored her help. About the lost files that were under the wrong letters when they were needed. About her Father's sudden deafness, and the necessity to make a fresh start.

They didn't take the tram back, they went all the way on foot, through the rushing streets of the city, where an iron life arches, no longer so terribly, over our heads. We are not lost at the side of a protective brother who is in possession of our secrets; our fear of home, our fear of the world are now behind us; years have passed since the last time we went home alone, years have passed since yesterday, a few weeks ago is already dim and distant, the time of our terrible loneliness is in the mythic past. We are hungry but we feel no hunger, our feet are tired and we could go on for many miles, the night is drawing in and we feel no chill.

Ernst promised new sketches, and another meeting in the market place, where the barrels were stacked next to the illuminated bridge – a discreet spot, where no one would see them. It was late, the concierge would no longer be loitering maliciously behind the balustrade. But alarming in his well-intentioned quietness was Father, as he stepped out of the next door pub; he had been waiting, waiting for Fini, to rescue her and himself from Mother's inquisitive glances; he would claim that they had been on a late night walk together, and the opportunity of sampling a rare 48% schnapps had been too much to resist.

They stumbled up the unlit steps in a tight embrace, the two sinners, each knowing the other's secret, and boldly they stepped into the kitchen to confront Mother.

X

Life, which only yesterday had been stifled in the narrowness of streets, city, house and office – how it now spread over the walls and into the woods. They met every day in the greedy shadows of the barrels that were heaped up overnight, they walked through the empty wooden huts, smelling the aroma of sold fishes and leftover onionskins, devoutly they walked past the dead tables and the empty sacks, hand in hand, always ready to pitch lover's camp in the majestic bleakness of a hut, terrorized by the distant echoing stride of a policeman on his beat, the barking of a dog, the shuffling of a beggar.

Or they rode out on the tram, out under hanging branches, caressed by the dark blue shady lilac, past the green benedictions of farmyards and the gray curses of barracks, out on to the climbing country road.

On soft moss they laid them down, put their arms round each other on steep paths, their bodies many times in close proximity, and always ahead of them the joyful prospect of their ultimate union. At all times, Fini could feel the soft caress of his cupping hand on her small breast, his quick fingertips wandering over her cool round shoulders and upper arms, whenever she was alone and at home, dreaming and waking and in the office, where Dr. Finkelstein suddenly lost his terror and the brown telephone switchboard was no longer alarming.

They listened to music, sitting close together in the close rows, surrounded by people and alone. She shivered at a sudden soft piece of singing, a quiver on her bare skin, and she waited for the return of that one exquisite tone. A rushing wave came and enveloped her in the same way as faintness is enveloped by a great silence. The silken violin bows slipped up and down, and barely visible in a corner, the percussionist humbly leaned forward to elicit a silvery peal of laughter from his triangle. The synchronized movements produced a warm rush that was like nothing in nature, no song of human or animal larynx. Finer than birdsong was the velvet stream of the flute, and the nimble skip of a young note on the broad back of a venerably burbling bass. Stronger than the bass, though, and the indigo cello, more lyrical than the velvet stream of the young flute, more percussive than the great thunder of the kettle drum and the mocking little snare drum, casting its spell upon all that magic, shadowing the notes, putting its own gloss on all the colors and containing in itself all the instruments, was the great voice of the organ in the background, the voice of the Almighty, the Lord of the World, the Creator, the cruel, good, great God. The organ brought forth all the instruments out of itself, and in every note that it produced there slumbered the one after and the one after that, the one just fading and the one long since echoed away, the distant echo of the loudly bearing and re-bearing woods. On the trembling waves of air swam words of an unfamiliar, incomprehensible language, and the strife of days sank to the bottom. In the sounds of the city that they later emerged into she continued to hear the music of the orchestra. "Music," said Ernst, "contains all the sounds of the human world, held by certain fixed laws and proportions, and lifted into the eternal." But Fini didn't understand that.

She came home through the grimly yawning gate, no longer timid and cowed, no longer afraid as she passed the shrill concierge, no longer sad as she climbed the creaking steps with the broken balustrade, no longer attending to the stink of young tomcats – and she had no ears for the ugly inquisition of her Mother, and the lie came easily to her lips, the music helped her to lie. Trams might stop for hours, collisions occur, people be taken by sudden weakness – and how the threads of a story weave together when we want, effortlessly we think up a collapsed horse receiving an injection on the street, a lunatic, stark-naked, climbing up a scaffold, we accept the summons of an advertisement and present ourselves for an interview, where we are kept waiting for many hours and many applicants before our turn finally comes. We will be notified by post, in the event of our success.

Finally, she had her little box, loyally built for her by her Father. On Sunday, he produced it from a corner, a gleaming brown chest with a shiny nickel lock on it. New sketches of Ernst's, a new woman walking a lonely path between melancholy fields, found their way into it; with tender fingers, Fini smoothed out silver paper at night on the edge of her bed, silk ribbons and scraps, mother-of-pearl buttons and a tie-pin that she'd found, a colored paper Japanese umbrella, and a soft, much petted cock's feather glowing in russet and gold. It was a home from home, a secret home, sheltering and sheltered, loving and beloved, locked up and generous. The chest stood under the bed, waiting for the tender solitary hour of bedtime, the shiny steel key clicked twice in the snugly fitting lock, and easily as a joint, the lid moved on its hinges. Everything was preserved from the intrusions of questing fingers.

XI

It was during this time that Tilly became ill. That meant weeks without the inexhaustible confidante, the thirstily open ear, and the experiences of many days accumulated unconfessed in Fini.

She learned nothing of the nature of her girlfriend's illness, her worried questions met with evasions and suspicious smiles. Two weeks later, Fini went to the sanatorium, she havered for a long time, dreading the smell and the barred windows of hospitals.

The hospital lived on inside her, unforgotten, unforgettable, the place where she had lain with scarlet fever when she was six, the creeping, black-wrapped nurse, the bearded nun who used to pluck hairs out of her chin in the ward at night in front of the mirror beside her bed. The sister with the wart, like a creepy insect on her upper lip. The white-robed doctor still stalked her in her dreams, his spectacles pushed up on his forehead, the four-eyed man with warm, yellow, hairy, groping hands; Fini still remembered the visiting hours between three and five, when Mother came bringing cake, to which the sister helped herself; the corridor with the patients in blue-striped pajamas and parchment faces; and the big bath hall full of naked women with hammer toes and lumpy swellings on their feet.

The smell of iodine and camphor hung over the hospital lawn, like a bad premonition, and slowed her step. Fini sniffed the lilac she had brought with her. Up on the third floor lay Tilly, all alone in the small ward, pale and altered, with a downturned mouth. No longer the grownup friend, alert and assured and admired; no longer her confidante, strong and consoling in her counsels, proud and aloof; Tilly was sick and incurable. It wasn't death that threatened her, she had that behind her, was changed, was another.

"Little Fini," said Tilly, "if only you knew. A man is an animal when he comes to us, and when he leaves us. When we succumb to the iron pressure of his thighs, and when he gets up exhausted, and hooks us into our dress with casual fingers. No doctor will give you an abortion, and if you use soap, it makes you ill. It's over now – he didn't come when I wrote to him that I was about to die, and he won't come now, either. He'll never come. He begged me on bended knee, and made me drink sweet orange liqueur. Little Fini, if only you knew."

Who was it? It was Ludwig. Fini had forgotten him, just as one forgets an old object at the bottom of a box of precious things one has treasured. Ludwig with the dark cello voice, the violinist in the flowered waistcoat. Tilly talked about his secret force, to which other, cleverer women, had also succumbed. If he touched you like that, you can't describe it, you couldn't help falling for him. The man, Ludwig, is an evil, alien animal.

"It happens to everyone. It'll happen to you too," said Tilly, weeping. All at once, the evening was upon them, it ambushed the sun. A blackbird whistled in the garden. A shout echoed in the corridor, followed by the brisk footfall of a sister. A bell went off. From a faroff street, came the wailing of a carhorn. The lilac she'd brought was as fragrant as a hundred gardens.

Fini walked through the streets alone, not past the nocturnal market place, where the stack of barrels cast a small shadow, where Ernst, the man, was waiting, a cruel beast. Even so, she felt the mild curve of his palm caressing her small breast, whose peaks rose hard and urgent towards the evening, the street, and the cruel man. She fled home, fearful and oppressed by the weight of an iron life, often, in the crush of the pavements, brushed by the arm of a man. She fled away home, little Fini, into the dark gateway, up the perilous staircase; there was no one there, so she could cry to her heart's content.

Later, weeks later, Tilly returned: older, different, with a short haircut, because her hair had gotten thinner. It was as though she'd come from some other part of town. She was quiet and kind, no longer with her head down over the rustling papers when Dr. Finkelstein came by, no longer sharpening pencils, but with a slacker bosom and a longer nose and pursed lips, no longer laughing through the streets they walked together, and only once loquacious, her eyes full of tears, in the small cheap cakeshop, while it rained outside, rained all afternoon. Strange and terrible was everything that Tilly had had to say, about Ludwig, whom all the girls fell for, about the young doctors at the hospital, about the anesthetic that you sank into like a sea of forgetting, about waking up having thought you were dead, about the gloomy evenings at home, and Mother's continual sighing.

It was raining, and Tilly talked; they sat miserably in the darkening corner of the cakeshop.

XII

Tilly applied for and found new jobs for them both in the large export–import business, where they were paid bonuses, and it was fun. The floors were large and bright, there were lots of windows, and it was sunny and noisy, and full of the bustle of girls and young men.

The girls sat at typewriters, white and smiling, they were like white flowers blossoming beside their desks. There were many young men, sullen ones and smiling ones. Superiors you were afraid of, and whom it was hard to charm, and others you might bump into in the corridor, outside the boss's padded double doors.

Fini made friends with blonde Hedi, who accepted chocolates and gave them out from her well-stocked desk drawer.

Sometimes the young Baron turned up, who didn't have to do military service and was convivial. He chucked the girls under the chin, and brought them flowers.

Officers on home-leave cheerfully came along bringing miraculous things to eat that we haven't seen for two years.

Fini no longer sat in terror before the brown telephone switchboard, in perplexity before the striped wires.

The air no longer trembled with the shouts of Dr. Finkelstein, with his terrible glinting spectacles.

And late in the afternoon the girls ran out into the flat yellow sunlight, and for each one of them there was a man waiting.

XIII

One day, Ludwig was waiting outside. Fini had forgotten all about him, as one forgets all about an object at the bottom of a box of treasures.

He spoke softly, with a muffled voice that sounded like a cello, he was bareheaded, with his soft hat rolled up in his coat pocket.

Fini was alarmed, and looked for a side street she could flee into. She was clumsy, and wondered how she might flee, if she were better versed in the arts of lying and evasion.

There was Ludwig, the man; his voice was soft, she liked the sound of it. She looked aside once to spy his face, and she found herself looking into his striking triangular shaped eyes and his narrow receding brows, and she thought of Tilly.

"You're thinking of Tilly," said Ludwig eerily, the man, the wild beast from whom there was no deliverance.

"Tilly is a stupid woman," said Ludwig with a short laugh.

Fini had never heard him laugh, it made a sound like a small velvet thunder.

"Are you in love with the painter Ernst?" asked Ludwig.

"No!"

"I'm in love with you," announced Ludwig, and he steered them into a crowded street, where they could not fail to be pressed together.

"Tilly has told you bad things about me, and it's true I haven't always treated her well. But I have always treated you well. You are young and shy and a little stupid."

His arm gave off a great warmth, Fini could feel it through her thin dress.

"Let's walk in the park," said Ludwig.

It's too late, she wanted to say, I have to go home. And yet, she walked at Ludwig's side, and she thought about Tilly.

They walked through the park, and Fini was afraid of running into Ernst at any moment.

"You needn't worry," said Ludwig. "Ernst has a date today."

He could read everything in her stupid eyes, and her fear rose and swelled, and now she was trembling faintly in the gloom of the park.

She felt Ludwig's arm, and at the same time her eye lit on a concealed bench. There sat Tilly, with a man beside her.

Ludwig laughed curtly, as before.

They walked through dark unfamiliar avenues; no longer was it the kind, shady park of memory. The sounds of music were far off, they came from a different world. The park was different, and the pond, and the waterlilies adrift upon it. Ludwig didn't take his arm away, it pressed her like a fetter that didn't hurt.

Then they found themselves standing in front of a certain house, went up a flight of stairs, another, and another, and Fini got tired, and all the steps made her dizzy, the unusually tall steps that went endlessly round and round up some tower, she thought. If she looked back down through the balustrade, she saw a small section of corridor, a dark, unknown and tempting hole. Going up the stairs beside her was Ludwig, pressed against her, spreading his warmth. Each time she stopped, in the hope that he would pass her or stay behind, this failed to happen, instead he stopped on the same step, sensed her fatigue, and put his arm around her. They didn't speak, they met no one, no voice rang out on the staircase, or was audible behind the apartment doors they passed on their ascent. All Fini heard was her own, and Ludwig's louder, breathing. She didn't know where he was taking her, and she wasn't afraid any more either. Instead, she felt a great emptiness in her, and she rested for a while. As though stifling veils had been laid over her, she heard the muffled creak of a door, and she saw herself – as in a mirror – step into a bright white studio.

She saw sheet music scattered over tables and chairs, a whole bewildering world that enjoined respect from her. Ludwig lived high up under a glass roof, and it occurred to Fini that it must be a dreadful thing to experience a thunderstorm up here, so vulnerable and alone, thunder and lightning and crashing rain, separated but not shielded from heaven's rage by the thickness of a single pane of glass. Now she could see the sun doing its red fade behind the roofs, and things in the studio acquired a warm, golden tinge. The notes were like mysterious symbols on the large stiff sheets, some of them only half-filled, and the little black rounds sat on the thin lines like tiny birds on telegraph wires.

"What would you like me to play you?" asked Ludwig, gripping the violin under his chin, and with surprisingly deft fingers he stroked the narrow, gleaming bow over it, as though sharpening a sword with which to kill Fini. She was embarrassed at the question, and silent, as she racked her poor, forgetful brain for the image of a concert program that had the name of a piece on it that she liked. What did she know about music, little Fini, and finally she realized that it didn't really matter what he played anyway.

So he began with low, purplish notes that gradually made light, the music curved into arcs, softly swelling waves, rippling with silver. He stopped abruptly and laid the violin down on the table, the sudden silence quite as shocking as a sudden noise.

With an unutterably delicate jingle, he produced a slender liqueur bottle and two thin-stemmed glasses from the disorderliness of a glass fronted cabinet. For the first time in her life, Fini drank liqueur, it tasted sweet and bitter, like orange peel, she had once tried chocolates that were like this, but this liqueur was naked, not amiably filled into a sweet casing, and it left a numb sweetness in its wake, and a gentle swaying of violet lights in front of her sleepy eyes.

She could still hear the sound of the abruptly discontinued violin, and she saw the evening sky close over the glass ceiling of the studio. She did not hear Ludwig's subtle movements, all she knew was that she was locked up in here with the man, who was dangerous, but who was still letting her alone, and she enjoyed this period of grace as much as the condemned man enjoys the final hour before his execution.

Now he was standing beside her, speaking to her, staring into her eyes, and before she knew what had happened, he had fallen to his knees, his head was buried in her dress, and he was weeping. Ludwig, the man, the beast, was weeping; his body trembled, his broad shoulders shook. Little Fini did not understand how it had come about, and she felt sorry for his pain.

Because we are so small and insignificant, it hurts us doubly when a big man who lives up under the sky, close to God, and plays melting melodies, lies at our feet, still smaller and more insignificant than we ourselves – and yet only we can save him. The clothes fall from us, the withered useless husks, the buttons loosen and undo themselves. It is the blood that prevails within us, our head is heavy, in a fog we see the hairy chest of the man, we sniff the scent, the strange animal smell, see the stranger's face, even stranger from close to. Fini shut her eyes, felt her breast in the warm, enveloping bowl of his hand, a painful and loving pressure, felt his quivering fingers press harder in the secret hollow at the back of her knee. His hot breath came over her and covered her, he bit her lips hard, and like a great, deadening, painful and terrifying jubilation, the man entered her, she felt him inside her, as he merged and melted with her, the stranger, a guest of hers and at home in her.

Gradually, Fini returned to the world, to Ludwig's tired and gentle kisses. She felt as though he was licking her face with his hot dry tongue, Ludwig, the man, the grateful humble beast.

XIV

At night, secretly, at the edge of her bed, Fini smoothed out newly collected silver paper and from her carefully guarded treasures, got out the picture of the woman walking between the melancholy blossoming fields.

No longer did she listen excitedly to her parents' nocturnal whisperings, no longer did she spy on the hot secrets of the apartments opposite. The trains were still whistling through the night, the sky arced over the sleeping street, the cats slunk about in the lee of the walls. But none of it was miraculous any more, the lonesome cry of the locomotive was no longer a lure, the secrets of the creeping animals and of the neighbors silhouetted behind lace curtains were all exposed. The days ahead were all empty, days without fear, without hope, days like empty rooms that could give nothing but the hesitant echo of a timid footfall. The bustle of the streets was of no interest, life was no longer an iron vault, no longer did Fini walk stooped in fear under a painful yoke.

No longer was she the woman walking between flowering fields, and far off and lost was Ernst, who waited in vain in the protective shadow of the stacked barrels at night.

At the end of the day lurked the awful thing that had befallen Tilly, still distant but already visible.

By now, the one exciting hour in the studio had been joined by others, and she had heard as much of Ludwig's speech as of his violin. He didn't get the jingling glasses and the slim liqueur bottle out of the cupboard any more. They went to bed with inexorable regularity, and their waking up was as bitter as the culmination of any of their carefully metered joys. Ludwig was unrecognizable when he was at home in his slippers and shirtsleeves, relaxed, and no longer struggling for his conquest and possession. He no longer smelled strange, not like an animal or of bitter roots, no longer a cruel animal – a lonely man, aging, short-sighted, with thinning hair, anxious and humdrum, casual and forgetful, oppressed by petty anxieties and small debts. His voice lost its warm sonority of a cello, he didn't play any more, and he was like an extinguished volcano.

Once, he said he needed spectacles – and he bought a pair with black horn rims and thick buffed lenses. Suddenly, he was different, altered, just like Father with his ear trumpet, and when he took off his spectacles, he fumbled awkwardly for objects that were at hand and that were still out of reach.

Pupils from whom he made his living were sent packing, scores he had ordered he didn't look at. Often he would run panting up the stairs, and then he would hurry down again. He would forget his hat and umbrella. He would kiss Fini fleetingly on the neck, and while he was speaking to her, his eye would rove restlessly over the street, the square, the garden. Once, he came home with a stray dog, and the following day, its owner turned up to reclaim it. Ludwig spent two days grieving for it. An old kidney ailment returned because he had gone out in the rain without a coat, and he was sick in bed for a week. He didn't wash, he had a temperature, his beard sprouted, gray stubble ringed his face, his triangular eyes sank deep into their sockets. His linen was torn and clumsily patched, and yellow the sheet on which he lay. He received no visitors. He sent his friends away, he canceled an engagement in the provinces, he accused his old charwoman of pilfering, and she stopped coming. His hair thinned rapidly, his fingernails grew long, he went off cigarettes, drank black coffee to stay awake, and took bromides to get to sleep.

"I want to marry you," he said to Fini, and she took him back to her parents. Her fate was settled, it was the end of youth, girlhood, childhood. She had fallen for him, she would remain true to him, and didn't need to wait for Tilly's destiny to befall her. He was an ill old man, poor and abandoned, by life, by music, by his friends. "We will become young again together," he said to Fini. She took him back to her parents, there was a stifling silence in the room where they sat, Mother with her hurriedly thrown on dressing-gown, Father with the ear trumpet in front of him on the table. Fini in the middle, sitting between him and her parents, hung her head, and all of them were strangers one to another, imprisoned in a glass ball each one, unable to see or to touch the others.

At last, Father began to talk, he talked about the War, and Mother started up too, and began to talk about inconsequential things. Cannily, she began to pump Ludwig for information. Age, social position, family and address, birth and parents, and then Ludwig, briefly animated, talked about his childhood and his long-dead mother, his professional worries and his plans for the future.

He wanted to found a music academy, to go to a wealthy faroff country twice a year, and return laden with money. He wasn't yet old and ill, no, he felt rejuvenated, it was only bachelor living that took it out of him, and with a good appetite and wide grinding jaws, he ate the hurriedly prepared dishes that were set before him.

He left late in the evening, kissing Fini on the lips in front of her tearful Mother, while her Father lit his way down the stairs with a candle. Her Mother hugged Fini and kissed her, as she hadn't for some considerable time. Fini took Ernst's pictures out of her treasure chest and burned them, one at a time, over a crackling candle flame, sobbing quietly.

XV

There was as yet no talk of marriage, but it was palpably near, and Fini was reckoned among the grownups, she had a voice, a vote, she was no longer merely there to be scolded, she demanded and was offered kindness.

And for all that, nothing changed, and the days were full of the chattering of machines.

Tilly found a boyfriend, and no longer thought of Ludwig and the unhappiness she'd been through with him.

Fini no longer had anyone to talk to, and she would have liked to talk about what the world looked like now, a world without secrets, without fear or expectation.

Once – the tension of our pounding heart, the street we strode along, full of secrets, the adventures that waited for us at every corner! Now, our expectation is quenched. Where we walk there is a limitless silence, a landscape without hills obscuring the distances, we know it all, beginning and end, the inadequacy of the male and the bitter future awaiting us.

Gone was the sweet music of the unknown, the inviting song of incipient life, dimmed the luminous expanse of endless days ahead, and chilled the comforting warmth of youth. Our short path is over, and the man is a stranger to us; and stranger yet with every day.

Fini watched him talking to others, how he took casual poses and didn't listen to their replies, how he carved pipes, hunkered down on low stools for hours on end, how he hoarded chocolate from her greedy eye, high up under cardboard lids, on top of the dusty cupboard, small bars and large, yellow with age, how he collected tinfoil in dense balls for decorating his pipes with. In amongst the music stands that were stacked up in corners, he kept tobacco and cigars, which he neither smoked nor ever offered anyone else, watching them carefully as a guard-dog. Material was piled up in wardrobes, wrapped up in alertly rustling paper, under layers of yellowing sheet music.

It couldn't be a sin to steal from him, it was like stealing from oneself. And so, while he sat hunkered on his low stool whittling away at his pipes, Fini went prowling around, climbed nimbly up on creaking chairs and splintering music-stands, grabbing treasures. And if she sent a timid glance in the direction of Ludwig's crafts corner, she saw that his eyes had fallen shut, and his knife was whittling away at the heads by itself, while his other senses were asleep, and she woke him.

Suddenly woken, he came to consciousness, smoothed his waistcoat, scooped up shavings and fluff with his fingertips, and started talking about trips abroad and warmly shining suns. Sometimes they went out together in the streets for hours and hours at a time, cream-filled pastries beckoned to them from the windows of bakeries, sweet and brown. Fini was hungry, she craved smooth, yellow, yielding icecream in round bowls. She went hungrily through the city at Ludwig's side. A prey to asthma, he needed to sit down, and he wouldn't sit on the green chairs in the shady park, because you had to pay for those, but only on the dusty benches in the pitiless sun. Stretching out his legs, he made an unconscious display of gaping fly buttons and knotted and re-knotted bootlaces. Fini wept as she talked, she wept back into herself, her tears dried, dammed up rivers of tears gathered inside her and dried. She choked painfully on her collected suffering. When she saw women passing by, pushing crippled husbands on three-wheeled carts, each of the women seemed to have her face.

Once a week, or maybe twice, they had congress on the studio sofa, a miserable surrender, silent and accompanied by silent weeping, like the desperate birthday celebrations of a terminal patient.

At that time, a letter arrived from Ernst, he wanted to see her again. They met where they had weeks before, in the same nocturnal market place, the pressure of his hand felt strange to her, Fini no longer went around in the balmy rain of his kindly words. They rode out, as before, on the tram, under hanging boughs, silently they climbed the road together, and they lay down on the dewy roadside grass together, hymned by buzzing crickets.

It grew late, they took a room in an inn, with a bed and a straw mattress. Fini waited for the dawn with eyes wide, pressed to the wall, on the rustling straw.

XVI

The summer was sweet and hot, and then there was an autumn and a winter, the primulas appeared in the steamy woods, the War was over, and Fini walked past the great events, small and irrelevant. The worries of the big world are too weighty for the likes of us.

On her nineteenth birthday, in April, she had to weep, even though Ludwig had bought a rose for her, a heavy bloom beginning to cast aside its outer petals like burdensome garments.

Father's prospects improved, Uncle Arnold passed away, taken by a delayed typhoid fever; rich territories suddenly became available, his hearing improved, slowly his faraway eyes returned to the here and now, and his ear began to be attuned to Mother's tirades.

Fini went to the Prater, and she felt like a tardy convalescent from a long and exhausting illness, from which there could be no complete recovery. He must needs learn to live with an erratically beating heart and limbs that cry out for consideration. The young girls walk past us, not yet marked by a bitter taste, their future ahead of them like a fresh and shining lawn, unscarred by feet.

XVII

Once, she heard Rabold speaking, Rabold the orator, pressed between listening crowds, on a big square under the open canopy of sky. Some spoke before him, others followed him, and all their voices died in so much space, and were defeated by the chance sounds of the street. Only his voice, bold and singing, conquered space, as though the unattainable skies had moved closer to line the street, and protect it from the sounds of ill-mannered vehicles. All the speakers, Rabold included, stood on the roof of the same auto-mobile. But as soon as he stepped out on to it, it became a pedestal and a throne, for a King.

Little Fini stood pressed between the crowds of listeners. The voice sang on in her, sonorous and clear – as if a bell were chiming metal words. It remained with the audience for a long time, and was still with them when they went their ways, late, with the night wind. She should have gone upstairs, up the innumerable narrow stairs to the studio. But as though someone were pushing her, she turned up a side street instead, where there was only one person walking, tall and in a nimbus of thoughtfulness and silence, looking at her: Rabold.

And when, belatedly, she did encounter the miracle, she was already finished, her youth bitterly disposed of. Rabold stood in the middle of the street and waited for her to approach. She had the sense that, to reach him, she would have to break through the ring of silent thought first, there was one stride between them still, and she stopped. A word from him brought her closer. She didn't know what it was, she thought he might have called her name.

She guessed everything, that he is persecuted, and lives under assumed names, traveling from town to town. The servant of an unbending force, and remote from the machinery of this life.

Tomorrow, he was moving on, but an hour was sufficient, and she knew that from now on all her days and dreams would be filled with him.

She always had space and time for the stranger. Sometimes, he wrote her a letter poste restante. She went to the counter three times a day. Once there was a rushed word on a postcard. Sitting on her bedside at night, she hid the card in the bottom of her trunk between tissue-paper and the box of mother-of-pearl buttons.

XVIII

Under cover of darkness she crept to the station, Rabold didn't live far off, she could get there in six hours. In the waiting-room, she wrote letters home, and to Ludwig. The carefully swaddled cardboard box lay at her feet.

She reached him at night, and collapsed into his bed. Calmed was the whirling restlessness, stifled every wish, died the unhappy Fini, blissfully resurrected in Rabold's world.

They drove through small towns, walked along crooked lanes, summer returned with sunny evenings, walks, entwined, past ancient walls.

Their days and nights were dreams, as little Fini grew.

His name unknown, he lived anonymously in strange towns, pursued by bounty hunters, always on the run, always poor, eaters of dry bread.

In the autumn, the first snow had already fallen, they returned to the big city and spent a winter safely in a warm room, high up in the uncertain quarter of paupers, whores and murderers. The timid muddle of roofs, crooked gables, and shared cornices came into their room's only window, the wail of factory hooters came to them, and the incomprehensible cry of a neighborly world.

Friends came to see him, men without fear, wanted men, happy fugitives. Once, Fini received a letter, they had found her hiding-place, it said something about a Mother's and even a Father's tears. But the pain she read about was alien pain, what were her Mother's tears to her.

Rabold lived in her, Rabold whom she knew, but whose first name she didn't know, for whom she had invented a name, Rabold, who slept beside her, who came to her burning and strange, ever new in a thousand guises, a god to the mortal woman. She could feel his body as she fell asleep, his tired knee, his sweet shoulder, the warm hairy cave under the arm on which she laid her head. She bore the nightly imprint of his lips on her mouth, the loving bite of his teeth in the swelling flesh of her breast. Beside her, in her, all around her, was Rabold, her husband. In the dark of the night, she saw his glowing eyes, and thirstily she drank in the kindly words he poured out to her. Once, he went away and Fini had to stay behind. Emptiness, void, came from every corner, she didn't light the small, iron stove, and huddled on a chest, swaddled in her thin coat, with wild hair and eyes that reddened though they could not weep. She had no picture of him, and she was gripped by panic that she might forget this or that feature of his beloved face, the curve of his nose, the lofty brow over his eye, the quiet bend of his neck and his way of picking up an object, with an exact movement of the hand, and utter calm of his arm and body. She repeatedly closed her smarting eyes – full of unwept tears – and pictured his face. She went to bed late. The bed was cold, and she drifted off in the hesitantly spreading warmth, suddenly her knee thrust forward into emptiness, she started because there was no one beside her, and awoke. He's dead! she suddenly thought, and with trembling legs she got out of bed, lit a lamp, got out of the cupboard a postcard he had once written to her, looked long and avidly at every stroke of its rushed penmanship, just to convince herself that he had been alive once, at her side, with her, and to some extent, for her. Somewhere else she turned up his neckerchief, it was soft and kind, it was his, smelled of him still, his body, his life, – he couldn't have died, his necker-chief was still warm, she took it back to bed with her, pressed it to her cheek, and so, fell asleep.

By day, she listened to people's footfall outside, expecting the postman, and lamenting disappearing strides like lost happiness. A friend came, bringing news of Rabold, but no letter, only some money. Fini didn't need it, she threw the notes in her sewing-basket, and pondered. He must have died and left instructions for her to be given money, he wasn't alive any more, otherwise he would have written. She wanted nothing more than to see the dear curve of his letters, in fresh, convincing ink. Night came like the last, cold and empty, the last of the midnight steps died in the house. Fini wanted to die, she wanted to die tonight.

XIX

But she woke to the boisterous twittering of an early bird, and the plink of the ice melting on the metal windowsill. The sky was high and blue over the jagged roofs, and the noise of the neighbors' children came in through the open window. Quite early still, a hurdy-gurdy came into the yard, like a herald of spring in the city. It looked as though she would have news of Rabold today, or he would be there in person. When the postman's footsteps had retreated disappointingly, Fini decided to go out into the street to wait for her husband, and, who knows, perhaps catch him on the street. She went out, surrounded by hurrying people, greeted by the sun and the fresh air of the smiling March morning. She walked into the center of town, striding fleet-footed through the wide streets.

She left the city, reached the river and followed its course. The sun was high, sank lower, flowed from the sky into the river, reddening both. She sat down on the bank. An old fisherman stood there, waiting for a bite. She heard an evening flute, crickets chirped.

Fini sat, but felt she was walking on and up, up into the sky, into golden clouds, scarlet clouds, up stairs of purple. They led up to Rabold. He was standing and waiting for her, arms spread to receive her.

She wasn't aware of hunger, but it was eating her up, sat in her bowels, clutched at her heart – and still she didn't feel it. She didn't feel her tired legs, she lay on the soft bank and felt she was floating. The stairway of clouds bore her aloft, she didn't need to climb.

She saw the old fisherman like a shadow on the opposite bank. The old fellow grew and stood up like a servant, waiting respectfully at an entrance. Had Rabold sent him on ahead to receive her?

She nodded at him, she wanted to stroke him, and she reached into the damp grass, sank down, slipped, thought she had slipped on a cloud, and tried to catch herself, but it was beyond her. She was affected by a kind of fatigue, she would never reach Rabold. Why did he not come to help her?

She fell into the water, uttered a little cry, sank back, and was swept away by the river, which hid her too from the eyes of the world. Her body was picked up three miles downstream, swollen, with weeds and waterlilies in her hair, mouth half-open.

She was mentioned in the police report; identity, cause of death, unknown.

Her body lay in the morgue, and was then handed on to an anatomy department; there was a shortage of cadavers, so even drowned bodies were taken. No one knew that she had wanted to go to heaven, and had fallen into the water. She had broken on the soft steps of gold and purple clouds.

THE GRAND HOUSE OPPOSITE

At the time the following events took place, I was neither rich nor poor. I wasn't doing so badly as to be struck with envy – the consolation of the poor, they say – at the sight of grand houses or rich people. Then again, I wasn't doing so well that I could keep my equanimity at the sight of wealth. Rather, I found myself in the sort of situation where a man is impelled to seek out the proximity of wealth in a sort of secret and carefully unacknowledged hope that it might somehow rub off on him. I found myself in a situation where I thought of my poor surroundings with revulsion, the bad area, the wretched, narrow streets. I decided to move into an area whose very name was as magnificent as the power of its inhabitants. As soon as that name was pronounced or perused, it seemed to designate not a part of town, but an entire, remote empire, where it was impossible to find a person in distress. One easily forgot that the quarter also housed civil servants, domestics, shopkeepers and craftsmen. The name of the quarter eclipsed the poverty of its poor, and if I had happened to run into one of them, it would never have occurred to me that he might also live there, where the great news-paper editors, the bankers and the manufacturers had their proud mansions.

I found a small hotel that was only different from any of those I had patronized hitherto, by virtue of the fact that it was in a wealthy suburb. My neighbors were rich people fallen on hard times, unwilling to leave the proximity of money, because they evidently believed that, that way, when their fortunes finally changed, they would have less time and trouble. In the same way, a dog one has put out will stay close to the door by which it was made to leave. Opposite my small, narrow window was a large, broad house. Its brown gate was shut, and in the middle of it was a golden knob that caught and intensified and reflected the light, giving the illusion that it wasn't there in place of a humble handle, but to play a spotlight, sending its light directly to my window, so that by its kindly agency I was made acquainted with the sun, which neglected my hotel and was lavishing itself on the grand house opposite.

In the windows of the house were discreet blinds – drawn at all times. Sometimes I would spend two hours or more, watching the big, yellow-brown gates, in the hope of catching someone going in or out. It seemed to me something of the first importance to get to know my rich neighbors. I couldn't spend all day – much less, day after day – in the knowledge that there, staring me in the face, was a secret that seemed to have been put there deliberately to disquiet me. But the gate didn't open. Darkness fell, and I went to bed.

In the morning, I was awoken by joyful, bustling sounds. I looked out of my window. The grand house opposite had thrown open all its windows, and its gate as well. Men and women dressed in livery and white aprons were cleaning the windows and the furniture, beating rugs, airing bedding, and waxing and polishing floors. I saw windows, tall and wide as double doorways, sensed the silent depths of rich suites of rooms, the silent and reserved sheen of precious objects, I even thought I could smell the scent of wood from the furniture, and hear the brassy voice of a maid going about her work, belting out an old ballad.

An hour later, the windows and the gate were all shut up again, and the house once more abandoned. The servants must have left by some separate exit, somewhere at the back. The blinds hung in the windows, taciturn and proud.

The same thing happened every morning. For two months. The winter passed. The sun blazed ever more fiercely in the golden knob on the gate, at midday it was as if it were going to melt, I even thought I heard drops off it splash down on the paving stones, like sealing wax on an envelope. But the gate remained locked.

I asked my landlady. That house, she told me, is where an old gentleman lives, who spends just two months there every year. He was due to arrive soon.

One day, there he was. Slowly he glided through the open gate in a large black car. In the afternoon, he appeared on the verandah. He was propped on a stick, wearing a white waistcoat and a brown jacket, accompanied by a dog with an admirable sense of ceremony. The old gentleman's features were fine, gray, clean-shaven. His nose was as hard and sharp as the edge of a peculiar weapon. His eyes were narrow and gray, and they were looking straight across at me, without admitting it. It was as though they weren't there to transmit images of the outside world to the old gentleman's consciousness, but to project the images they had been hoarding within on to his retina. Every afternoon, the old gentleman appeared on the verandah. A servant came out and brought him his coat. And so the gentleman stood, looking across at me.

One day, perhaps a week after his arrival, I greeted the old gentleman. He replied, hesitantly, but clearly enough. We looked at one another. Before leaving the verandah, he nodded to me, briskly. And every day, for a week, the same scene was replayed. Ten days later, the old gentleman died. Suddenly. Overnight. My landlady told me. In the quiet street, the little people – a cobbler, a coal merchant, servants – talked about his passing. I watched the funeral from my window. For an instant, I wondered whether I shouldn't accompany it to the cemetery. But the formality and splendor of the cool, proud mourners put me off.

The house remained silent and locked. I was just thinking about the cruelty of the old man, who had come home so coolly, almost inhumanly, because his death had been waiting for him already, and who had probably lived without love, merely as the administrator of his wealth, when the famous notary M. — whom I had heard of — had himself announced to me. The notary handed me a letter and told me it was from my neighbor, whose will had been opened yesterday. In his will, the old gentleman had stipulated that the notary was to hand me the letter. "That'll be another one of his eccentricities!" said the notary, and he set off. The letter read:

Dear Sir,
As you see, I have learned your name. To what end? Because I have grown fond of you. You were the only one who might have become a friend to me. Because, even though you liked me, you kept your distance, and even though you were curious, you remained discreet. I leave only debts. Otherwise, you would have been my heir. Think of me with kindness.
                    Your I.B.

The next day, I moved to a different street.

STRAWBERRIES

The town I was born in was situated in Eastern Europe, on a great and sparsely inhabited plain. To the east, it stretched on for ever. To the west, it was bounded by a line of blue hills that were only visible on clear summer days.

My birthplace was home to about ten thousand people. Three thousand of them were insane, if not dangerously so. A mild insanity wafted around them like a golden cloud. They carried on their businesses and earned money. They married and had children. They read books and newspapers. They concerned themselves with the things of this world. They conversed with one another in all the languages that were used by the very diverse population of this part of the world.

My fellow-citizens were gifted people. Many of them now reside in the great cities of the old world and the new. All of them are important, and some of them are famous. It is from my homeland that the Paris doctor comes, who rejuvenates rich old men, and recovers the virginities of old ladies; the Amsterdam astronomer who discovered the comet Gallias; Cardinal P., who for the past two decades has been making policy for the Vatican; the Scottish Archbishop Lord L.; the Milan rabbi K., whose mother tongue was

Coptic; the great shipping-agent S., whose business sign may be read in every railway station in the world, and in every port on five continents. I will not give their names. Any of my readers who subscribe to a newspaper will be familiar with them. My own name is immaterial. No one knows it, as I live under an assumed one. For what it's worth, I'm called Naphtali Kroy.

I'm what's called a conman. That's what they call people in Europe who claim to be something other than what they really are. It's no different from what every Western European does. Only, they aren't conmen, because they have papers, passports, identity cards, birth certificates. Some even have family trees. Whereas I have a false passport, no birth certificate, and no family tree. So it's fair to say: Naphtali Kroy is a conman.

In my homeland I didn't need any papers. Everyone knew who I was. I cleaned the burgomaster's boots when I was six years old. When I was twelve, I was apprenticed to a barber. There I soaped the burgomaster's chops. At fifteen, I became a coachman, and I took the burgomaster for drives on Sundays. We had thirteen policemen. I drank schnapps with every one of them. What did I need papers for?

The countryside was run by the gendarmerie. Their sergeant slept with my aunt on Thursday afternoons. I sometimes smuggled schnapps from the country into the town – which was unlawful and liable for duty. The gendarmerie sergeant winked at the customs men, and they never bothered me.

In short, I was on a good footing with the authorities when I was young. Later on, things changed. Times changed, authorities changed.

I don't think anyone had papers where I came from. There was a law court, a prison, lawyers, tax offices – but there wasn't anywhere where you had to identify yourself. What did it matter who you were arrested as, if they arrested you? If you paid taxes or not – whom did it drive to ruin, and who derived any benefit from it?

The main thing was that the officials had to live. They lived off bribes. That's why no one went to prison. That's why no one paid taxes. That's why no one had papers.

Occasionally, there were grave crimes, trivial crimes were not investigated.

Fire-raising was overlooked, that was an act of personal retribution. Vagrancy, begging and hawking were all long-established local practices. Forest fires were dealt with by foresters. Affray and manslaughter were put down to excessive consumption of alcohol. Robbers and muggers were not pursued, on the grounds that they punished themselves sufficiently by renouncing ordinary human society, trade and conversation. Counterfeiters put in an appearance from time to time. They were left in peace, because they damaged the government more than they did their fellow-citizens. The courts and lawyers were kept busy, if only because they worked terribly slowly. They made it their business to settle conflicts and arbitrate in disagreements. Payments were invariably in arrears.

Where I came from, we lived at peace. Only near neighbors were enemies. People got drunk together and made it up. Commercial rivals did nothing to hurt one another. They took it out on the customer and the client. They all owed money to each other. None had anything to hold against any of the others.

There was no tolerance of political parties. No distinctions were drawn between people of different nationalities, because everyone spoke every language. Only the Jews stood out on account of their kaftans and their hats and their superiority. There were occasional little pogroms. In the general hurly-burly, they were soon forgotten. The murdered Jews were put in the ground, and the plundered ones denied that they had lost anything.

All my compatriots loved Nature, not for her own sake, but because they had a taste for certain of her fruits.

In the autumn, they went into the fields to roast potatoes. In the spring, they trekked into the forests to pick strawberries.

Our autumn consisted of molten gold and molten silver, of wind, swarms of ravens and mild frosts. Autumn lasted almost as long as winter. In August, the leaves turned yellow, in the first days of September already they lay on the ground. No one bothered to sweep them up. It wasn't until I came to Western Europe that I saw people sweeping up the autumn into a proper dungheap. No wind blew on our clear autumn days. The sun was still very hot, and already very slant and very yellow. It went down in a red west, and rose every morning from a bed of silver and mist. It took a long time for the sky to become a deep blue, but then it stayed like that for the whole of the short day.

The fields were yellow and rough and prickly and they hurt your feet. Their smell was stronger than it was in spring, more acrid and intractable. The forests at their edges remained green – they were conifers. In autumn, they got silver crests on their tops. We roasted potatoes. There was a smell of fire, coal, burnt potato skins and scorched earth. The swamps, which were all around, bore a light sparkling glaze of frost. They smelled as dank as fishermen's nets. In many places, smoke rose steeply and teasingly into the sky. From nearby and distant farmyards, came the crowing of cocks who had caught a whiff of the smoke.

In November, we had our first snow. It was thin, brittle and durable. It didn't melt. At that point we stopped roasting potatoes. We stayed at home. We had bad stoves, cracks in the doors, and gaps in the flooring. Our window frames were made of light, unseasoned fir, they had warped during the summer, and now they didn't close properly. We stuffed cotton wool into the joins. We laid newspaper under the doors. We chopped wood for the winter.

In March, when the icicles dripped from the eaves, we could already hear spring galloping up. We disregarded the snowdrops in the forests. We waited till May. We were going picking strawberries.

The woodpeckers were already hammering at the trees. It rained a lot. The rains were soft, water in its most velvety form. It might rain for a day, two days, a week. A wind blew, but the clouds didn't budge, they stood in the sky, immovable, like fixed stars. It rained diligently and thoroughly. The paths softened. The swamps encroached into the forests, frogs swam in the underbrush. The wheels of the peasants' carts no longer crunched. All vehicles moved as though on rubber tires. The hooves of the horses were silent. Everybody took off their boots, hung them over their shoulders, and waded barefoot.

It cleared overnight. One morning, the rain stopped. The sun came out, as though back from holiday.

That was the day we had been waiting for. On that day the strawberries had to be ripe.

So we passed down the road that led out of our town into the forest. Our town was predictable and basic in its layout. Its two main streets met in the middle. Around that center, there was a little square, where the market took place twice a week. One of the streets led from the station to the cemetery. The other from the prison to the forest.

The forest was to the west. We walked with the sun. The forest enjoyed the longest days. If you stood at its extreme western edge, you could see the sun disappear below the rim of the horizon, and you could taste its dying beams.

That was where the best strawberries grew. They didn't shyly hide themselves, as they tend to do otherwise. They showed themselves to whoever was looking for them. They teetered on the end of frail-looking but tough stalks. They were full in size, and they didn't grow out of the ground from humility, but from pride. We had to bend down to pick them. Whereas, to reach apples or cherries or pears, we had to get up on tiptoe or climb.

The strawberries had little clumps of dirt sticking to them, that you didn't readily see with the naked eye, so we popped them in our mouths too. The dirt crunched between our teeth, but then the juice of the strawberries washed it away, and their soft flesh soothed our gums.

Everyone picked strawberries, though it was forbidden. If the forester caught the women at it, he would confiscate their baskets, tip out the beautiful red strawberries, and trample them into the ground.

But what could he do to us, who ate them right away? He looked at us crossly, and whistled up his dog. The dog wore a brass placket round its neck. It had a greeny, steely shimmer to it, a rare metal object in a world of leaves, wood and earth.

The forester didn't frighten anyone. The more strawberries he trampled, the more grew in the forest.

Newspapers reached us late. The train stopped just three times a week at our station. It brought a few travelers, mainly hop-dealers, who did business in the area.

Lots of people made a living from hops. The coachmen, for instance. They drove the strangers out into the villages and the farms. My father was a coachman.

His name was Manes Kroy. We kept two horses, a cart for week-days, a cart for Sundays, and a sleigh for winter. I barely knew my father. He was a drinker. He only came home once a week, went to bed, and snored and talked in his sleep. He cursed us, his children.

We were eight sons. He got our names wrong. Our mother was dead. Our father had a flame-red beard that covered his face, and a big fur cap that he wore all the year round. It was made out of cat fur. I can't forget its smell. It smelled of sweat, dead animal, raw leather and tallow.

My father's beard didn't grow out in straight hairs, like ordinary beards did, but in tufts of red wool. All that could be seen of his face was his thick, fleshy nose, whose swollen skin was made up of little lumps, soft, juicy and uneven like orange peel. I can still remember my father's snow white eyebrows. They hung over the wilderness below like a couple of crescent moons over a tangled forest.

He didn't talk to us. He slept. Everything he said to us was unconscious and in his cups. It came out of him, both tender and terrible.

He treated his horses well. He had a hundred endearments for them, good, fresh oats and wellwater from clean buckets of yellow wood. He didn't beat them. He used a whip with a leather handle and eight knots. He used to crack it. It sounded like a gunshot when he cracked his whip.

One morning, in winter, the thermometer showed 35 degrees below, my father's frozen body was found by the side of the road. He had fallen off his sleigh in his drunkenness.

My seven brothers left home and country. One became a boxer in America, another a dock worker in Odessa, a third joined up – he died – a fourth was apprenticed to a village blacksmith, the fifth went to St. Petersburg, got involved in bomb-making and was probably blown up, the sixth was shot by a firing-squad in 1917, and the seventh is a dentist in Mexico. That's Gabriel, who's married and writes me letters twice a year.

I kept a horse, a cart, the sleigh and the beautiful whip, I went home to bed once a week like my father, and I wore his fur cap.

I wasn't any good with the horse. It ran into a fence, went lame and developed a limp. One day it died in our stable, with its thin legs all stretched out and its clever eyes burst.

For six months, I was a trainee barber, even though I didn't know how to use the razor properly. I had heavy hands that were always cold. Anyway, I didn't like the faces.

Then I was taken on by Petrusz the tailor. He was poor. My people didn't need many clothes. They didn't follow fashion either.

My master was unable to read or write, he couldn't even form numbers. He didn't use a tape measure, but a piece of string that he tied knots in. He kept little samples of every piece of cloth he was ever given. He looked after the family of his brother-in-law who lived with him, that was Schapak the glazier.

It was the fault of the glazier that I lost my job.

He despised tailors. I despised glaziers. He offered no reasons. Nowadays, I have no prejudice against any kind of worker. But back then, I believed that a glazier was inferior to a tailor.

What's so clever about glaziers? There's all the difference in the world between measuring up a window frame and a man.

Schapak was able to read and write. He made a lot of play with that. Maybe he assumed that no tailor can read or write. He despised not only his brother-in-law, who kept him, but the entire guild of tailors.

My master would probably not have minded the personal slights. What he couldn't stand was to have aspersions cast upon his work.

I can remember the tailor and the glazier arguing about the merits of their respective jobs. The quarrel, like all great catastrophes, arose out of an utterly trivial matter, the use of the other's crockery.

The glazier's children broke a couple of plates. The glazier's wife used my master's plates. They were gold-rimmed and had little landscapes painted on them. "Have you not yet told your wife," cried my master, "thou shalt not steal?"

"My wife doesn't steal," replied the glazier, "she's not a tailor's wife!"

That was an allusion to the scraps of material which Petrusz kept, and which were strictly speaking the property of his customers.

"I don't keep back little leftover pieces of window," said the glazier.

"Glaziers are beggars," replied the tailor.

"I refuse to talk to an uncultured man," said the glazier. "You can't even read numbers. You don't know what time it is."

"You sold my silver watch, you thief!" shouted Petrusz.

"What do you want with a silver watch, you donkey?" asked Schapak, the glazier.

The tailor Petrusz grabbed the iron and threw it at the box where the glazier kept his sheets of glass. He missed. He had a kind heart. He deliberately missed with the iron.

Then it was quiet.

The glazier sent me out for schnapps. I asked the tailor: "Master, should I go? Your brother-in-law asked me."

I was duty-bound to ask the tailor. The glazier was offended.

Like all glaziers, he had a diamond for cutting the panes of glass. It cuts through them like butter, he said. At the time, I was persuaded that any diamond – even one that was used for cutting glass – was worth a fortune. I couldn't understand why the glazier didn't sell his stone to become a wealthy man and live in a palace.

When I asked him: "Why don't you sell your diamond?" he would reply: "Then what would I live on?" Even though what he was living on all along was his brother-in-law.

One day, the diamond vanished.

"Kroy has stolen it!" said the glazier.

It was a winter evening, I was lying on the bench by the stove that I used for a bed. The oil lamp was almost out. It stank of smoke and grease and the piss of the children. You could hear the wind outside. It made a sound like steel being whetted on stone. That was how hard it blew over the frozen snow. It was whetting the houses. The fire in the stove began to go out. It was one of those sorry hours where a man feels warmth inevitably seeping away, and cold slipping down the chimney into the stove, a lump of ice. At times like that, you have the illusion that that last bit of warmth, in spite of everything, can survive. The cold will remain trapped in the chimney. You cling to the stove. You press yourself against it. To encourage it, you give it some of your own warmth. And all the time, you know it's useless.

The glazier went to get the oil can – it was kept under my bench – replenished the lamp, and it was as light as it was at six o'clock, and the tailor, my master, sat there and didn't stir. The movements of the glazier were slow and precise, controlled by a single thought, like the troops of a general. I knew what was coming, and I didn't budge. I was neither shocked nor offended. It wasn't the suspicion of the glazier that pained me, but the cowardice of the tailor.

Somehow, I was impressed by the glazier. His deliberateness was lit up by an inner joy. In his soft yellow face, that looked as though it was made from leftover putty, I saw a calm, quiet serenity. He didn't look at me once. But all the time he was thinking about me.

His thoughts wrapped themselves around me like soft, evil, implacable tendrils.

Carefully he carried the lamp over to my bench. "Get up!" he said.

He searched my rucksack and my sheet with silent, creeping fingers. His hands were like stockinged feet.

His serenity was at an end. His soft, broad, yellow face had put out a few blond hairs. There were forty-eight of them, I counted.

He didn't find anything on my bench or in my pockets. He turned them inside out, they flopped out of my jacket and my trousers, dirty, yellow, flaccid. All my belongings were on the table. I felt more ashamed of my legitimate possessions than I would have felt if he had found the diamond on me. In the light of the revived, replenished, reinvigorated lamp, there were my scissors, a couple of round pebbles, a flat green piece of chalk, a hand mirror, a heavy claspknife with a hook on the handle, and a smooth, brown piece of horn:

"A murder weapon!" exclaimed the glazier, weighing the knife in his hands.

Suddenly he shouted: "Out, out, out!" He shouted it maybe a dozen times. He had forgotten his entire vocabulary, and that was all that was left.

I looked at the tailor. He trapped a fly, a tired, gray winter fly, held it by its wings, and counted its feebly kicking legs.

Then I pulled on my father's short fur jacket, put all my things in my pockets, and left.

A few minutes later, I heard my name being called. It was the tailor. He was running after me, hunched and crooked, his coat-tails flapping in the wind. I was expecting him. He pressed a little bag into my hand. It was his purse of cold, wrinkled leather, with a rusty lock.

I think the tailor had tears in his eyes.

On winter nights, our town was a brutal place. The snow masked its meanness. It stifled the bickering voices that came out of the houses. Every one of the houses had locked brown shutters, with a narrow strip of yellow light creaming through them. A few street corners boasted flickering little red flames on yellow oil lamps. The snow shimmered both gently and painfully. The wind brushed the roofs, and a white powder flew up. The wind was like a cold hand in front of my mouth. Buried under the snow were the wooden boards that we had for pavements. I was up to my knees in snow.

It was still snowing. I couldn't see the sky. No gates were open. A couple of old men labored along in silence. They carried long sticks.

I took the street that led to the graveyard. I must have meant to go the other way, to the station. But I got my wires crossed. Maybe I was thinking that the station wouldn't open till the morning, whereas the cemetery had to be open at all hours of day and night.

There was a light on in the morgue. Old Pantaleimon slept in there. I knew him, he knew me too. It was the custom in our town to promenade in the cemetery. (Other towns might have their gardens and parks, we had our cemetery. The children played among the tombstones. The old folks sat on the stones, sniffing the soil which was made from our forefathers, and was like butter.)

I went into the morgue. There was the body of a beggar who was to be buried the next day. I woke Pantaleimon.

Like all nurses and gravediggers, he had a deep sleep. He thought it was the dead beggar waking him, and he said, still half-asleep: "Pipe down, Peter Onucha, I'll get around to you tomorrow!"

When he opened his eyes – he had these little small eyes submerged in a tangle of hair and eyebrows and eyelashes, so it was hard to tell – he recognized me.

"The tailor threw me out!" I said to Pantaleimon.

Pantaleimon sat up. His legs were wrapped in thick, raw cat fur. His fur waistcoat was open.

"You've stolen something!" said Pantaleimon.

I told him the story. I swore that I hadn't stolen any diamond.

Pantaleimon, though, whispered in my ear: "Where've you got it, you cunning fellow? You smart operator! Where've you hidden it? Go on, you can tell me!"

That night, I learned that there's no point in telling the truth, and that it's easier to sell God to an unbeliever than it is to explain robbery to an honest man, or honesty to a thief.

Pantaleimon, you see, was a thief.

I don't mind that he was a thief. Or not even a proper one, as he didn't even steal. Anyway, who wouldn't steal if he could?

I don't mind about his suspicion either. I owe it to him that I didn't freeze and starve to death. I stayed with him, and helped him dig holes and make sure the graves looked their best. On Sundays, we shared our tips and the money we got for candles.

I began to love the dead, and among the living, only Pantaleimon. I slept in his house, and once again, my bed was a bench by the stove. I was kept busy trying to make peace between Pantaleimon and his wife and his three children.

Pantaleimon's wife did not respect her husband. But neither would she leave him, even though she had been threatening to for ten years. Pantaleimon had no authority. His wife beat him. He let it happen.

Other people had also attempted to take a hand in Pantaleimon's marriage. The most exalted among them was our Count. That was our name for the gentleman who lived in a castle outside our town, who could be seen walking through the streets every day, as though he wasn't really a Count.

He was a good man, he got on with everyone, and most of all with Pantaleimon.

Pantaleimon had the run of the castle, he waited on the Count, he cleaned his floors and his suits, and he also performed more delicate missions.

The Count had other servants, but he had only one friend, and that was Pantaleimon.

Once a year, the Count left his castle. He traveled to Paris, and to Nice and to Monte Carlo. He was away for three months.

All that time, Pantaleimon would remain in the castle, spying on the lackeys, the estate manager, the maids, and with his short, broad hand that was like a shovel, he would write weekly reports on them all and send them to the Count.

If Pantaleimon had been a perfectly ordinary thief, he could have stolen the entire castle, but he was a thief who didn't steal. That was the peculiar thing about him.

Our Count was from a very old family that was related to several of the crowned heads of Europe. On his coat of arms were three lilies, with their heads pressed together. Above them, broad and flat, was a two-edged sword.

The Count was about sixty. He always wore dark blue suits and dark blue cloaks, patent leather shoes, galoshes, white gloves, and carried an umbrella. What did he need it for? If it was raining, he rode out in his shiny, dark blue carriage. The few steps he had to walk to get from the terrace of his house to the carriage, he was escorted by a servant with an umbrella. I often watched, as the lackey, who was a little shorter than his master, raised his arm so that the whole of the Count was protected, while he himself got wet. Yes, even in the short time that the Count was sitting in his carriage and before the horses started to pull and while the coachman was taking his whip out of its cover, the lackey stood there with furled umbrella, hatless and dripping, a few steps in front. Then he would slowly go back inside, unprotected, the umbrella over his arm, impervious to the wet, as though the sun were beaming down. There were times when the lackey seemed even more aristocratic than the Count.

On fine spring afternoons, the Count would sit out on the terrace of the only café in town, eating cake and chatting with our cavalry officers. He had connections with the army, his sons were officers, he himself was a connoisseur of horseflesh, he owned a dozen horses and occasionally rode out on a gray. The Count was on first name terms with the young officers. All gave him a military salute, as if he'd been a general. The Count saluted back, even though he was in mufti. He touched two fingers against the brim of his top hat.

Every Friday morning, the poor people of our town gathered outside the castle. The Count stepped out on to the verandah, and tossed coins in their direction. For about half an hour it rained money, and then the Count raised his hands. All the beggars cried three times: Long live the Count! – and then they dispersed.

There was no Countess. She had died long ago. But there was a lady living in the castle, who was almost a Countess, she was the widow of a major in the Dragoons who had been killed in a duel. The talk was that the Count would marry her. But his sons kept coming to visit him, whenever the marriage seemed imminent, and the major's widow never got to become a Countess.

Perhaps it's as well that she never got to be a Countess. I once saw her beating a servant because he was talking to me, and didn't hear her ring. The poor wouldn't have been asked to come up to the castle on Fridays any more. The Count wouldn't have been able to travel to Paris, Nice, and Monte Carlo on his own any more. Who knows what would have happened to Pantaleimon and me. I have a lot to be grateful to the Count for myself. I'll get on to that later.

The Count was a benefactor to us all. He made sure that only our very strongest young men were recruited by the army, and of those, only the ones who had nothing to lose. Every year when the examining commission came round, those young men liable for conscription went to the Count. He invited the members of the commission round, spoke to the major and the army doctor, and warned them. He gave them good, heavy wines and a list of those young men they were allowed to conscript.

His method didn't always work. There are some majors who are unimpressed by Counts, and tear up lists. That's why it seemed advisable to our young people to martyr themselves at conscription time, to take poisons, to weaken their hearts, to catch pneumonia, to give themselves terrible eye diseases, and all sorts of disabilities.

Yes, with some their aversion to the army was so powerful that they allowed their feet to be crippled, and their fingers to be hacked off. I knew a red-haired locksmith who had the tendons in his ankles severed. He was lame all his life. I knew a roofer who poured acids into his left eye till it was permanently blinded.

The commission came every March, they were like our föhn, our warm mountain wind that brings the spring. And then those young men who didn't put all their trust in the Count began drinking black coffee, sleeping around, or not going to bed at all. Some took cold baths, came down with pneumonia or tuberculosis, and died slowly or in short order. But they were never soldiers. The cleverest emigrated to America.

To get to America, you needed not only a lot of money, but also false papers. A few people got involved in the business of getting young men to America, and with the production of false papers. They made masses of money. They were not reliable. At the very last moment, when you were sitting in the train but hadn't yet crossed the border, they wired the authorities, and, instead of America, you landed in prison.

You had to be on good terms with the emigration agents. You could never prove that they had broken the law, and even if you had been able to, nothing would have happened to them. They lived in our town, and therefore they lived scot-free. Living among us we had the lunatics, the criminals, the innocent, the foolish, the wise, and all of them enjoyed the same liberty.

The police turned up on the doorstep of one deserter's parents, and asked if they had any letters from the missing man. The parents replied that their son had left home without their knowledge, that they had heard nothing from him, and that he was not their son any more. The police put all that in their protocol, and nothing more was said.

The people in our town had a craving for beauty and art. From time immemorial, we had had our little park where chestnuts flowered – very ancient, venerable, thick-stemmed trees whose crowns the magistrate sometimes had lopped, and in whose shadow people slept on hot summer days. The park was circular, as though measured by dividers, surrounded by a gray paling fence that was barely functional – really, not much of a fence. It was more like a wooden ring, soft, splintering, moldering in some places and broken in others, but broadly still extant, like a loose belt slung around the park's hips. It could keep out neither the dogs nor the mudlarks, who on principle never used the official entrances. It was only our love of order that had prompted us to draw a largely symbolic line between the park and the street.

In the middle of the park stood a little wooden booth with crooked gables, and a little weathercock on one end. The weathercock also served no purpose. No wind ever penetrated the thick canopy of chestnut leaves. The weathercock had nothing to do. Even so, some people went by it. Because it sometimes happened that for some inscrutable reason, it pointed west on one day, and north the next. I think someone probably went to the trouble to move our town weathercock in the direction of the prevailing wind. Probably one of the many lunatics who filled official functions in our town.

The true purpose of the wooden booth was another: it was a refreshment stand, serving icecream and soda water with syrup or without, and was run by a beautiful, statuesque, blonde woman, who initiated me and many others in matters of love. The soda water she served must have been of a special type, or else the local young men were.

Our pavilion was sometimes closed at times when one wouldn't have expected it to be. At midday, at a time when in all the other towns and cities of the world sodas are being drunk, our pavilion was shut, dumb, gray, taciturn. The birds twittered in the crowns of the trees overhead. It almost seemed as though there were a curse on it. No sound was heard from within. There was no lock to be seen on the door; it must have been bolted from within.

No one knew when it would open again. But an hour later, or two or three, it was bound to be open. And it was. It opened and shut by magic. Never did you see it happen. Not even the young men on whose account it was abruptly shut, could say why they had suddenly been locked in. They didn't get a chance to look at the door.

The pavilion was the only ornament of our park and our town. One day it struck our burgomaster as insufficient, and unworthy of the status of our town. Consequently, they erected a red-and-yellow brick tower, with a clock whose face was lit up every night. Then a little shop was installed in it, and a woman moved in, who sold flowers. She was another beautiful, statuesque blonde, but her flower shop was always open.

Our need for soda water was greater than our need for floral decorations. The flower woman, unable to adapt to our habits, remained unregarded, sickened and died young. Her shop was inherited by the husband of our blonde, the only peddler in our town to deal with old watches, a gaunt fellow with one eye. For ten years, he had dealt ambiently. There were never fewer than a dozen broken watches lying in his left hand. Their heavy chains of nickel and pinchbeck hung down like thongs of a metal whip. On Mondays, there was the pig market. The farmers came, made their sales, and wanted jewelry. Our peddler went from one farmer's cart to the next, shook his watches to make them tick, and offered them to the farmers.

Now he was become a proper shopkeeper, he settled into the flower shop, hung his watches in the window, and waited for the farmers to come to him. Our beautiful tower was desecrated. The farmers came, bringing their pigs with them, wearing their muddy boots, and our mayor had to think of a new amenity.

All the leading towns in the world have monuments. Our town didn't.

One could have gone through the entire history of the town without finding a personality worth commemorating.

Not that we were short of great men! I referred to a few of them at the beginning. But not one among them who had done his work at home, and remained a living memory! Not one among them who didn't have the worrying traits of a rebel, a malcontent, a revolutionary! All of them had hated the authorities. The authorities couldn't thank them by putting up a monument to them. All of them had left their birthplace. Their birthplace should not thank them for it.

They could have put up a monument to the Count, but the superstitious among us opposed that. They said a monument to a living man would hasten his death, and that a living Count was worth more than a stone one.

These superstitious voices might have been outvoted if we'd had enough money. We didn't have much. Our mayor needed support for the erection of a monument, and he was obliged to turn to the Count for a loan.

But how was it possible to ask the Count for money for a monument to the Count?

The town was in a quandary. They ransacked the chronicles for suitable great men. They found a celebrated rabbi. Regrettably, the Jewish faith forbids monuments, and besides, a rabbi is not a sufficiently emblematic figure.

A poet lived in our town. He wrote in none of the vernacular languages. His poems were in Latin.

His name was Raphael Stoklos, which has a Greek ring to it. In his youth, he wanted to be a university professor. But, if you're born in a town that is hundreds of miles from the nearest university, and if you have no money and not enough savvy, the lot that awaits you is that of Latin poet.

Stoklos gave lessons in ancient and modern languages. In return, he got a room and board. Money defeated him.

The council was on the point of conferring immortality upon their living poet. Then Stoklos himself came up with a let-out: a celebrated seventeenth century writer and scholar was born in a village no more than six miles away from our town.

At that time, our town had been no more than a village itself. But seeing as it had now become the only town in a ten mile radius – couldn't it lay claim to that village and its celebrated man?

He too had written in Latin, as was the fashion of his time. But he was now as dead as his language. He was in the encyclopedias and the literary histories. He was famous.

Our Count advanced the money, the stonemason was hired. Stoklos came up with an engraving of the famous man.

The stonemason created a big man with glasses, a flowing cloak, a book in his hand, and a quill tucked behind his ear. That was our memorial. It stood on an imitation marble pedestal. Round about it grew a green lawn. The lawn was surrounded by a wire fence. Later, they planted pansies on the lawn, beautiful big pansies with soft, clever faces.

And so we had our monument. We stood or sat in front of it and admired the features of our great countryman.

His book was always open at the same place.

In autumn, we worried about the effect of the damp and the frost on the expensive stone. We erected a lofty, wooden casing around the monument.

All winter long, up until April, our great scholar was behind planks. He hibernated, the way some animals do.

When spring arrived, there were sounds of hammering from the park, the protection was taken off the monument. For us it was one of the portents of spring.

The monument's out again! Spring must be just around the corner! – people said to one another in April.

[. . .]

Pantaleimon and I, we never forgot him.

One day, Pantaleimon found a hanged man in the graveyard. He was a tramp, and not one we knew. He caused quite a stir in the town, and even some way outside. Because, as you might think, it wasn't every day that someone killed themselves in a world that really wasn't difficult to live in.

Pantaleimon didn't cut him down immediately. He went and got me first. I was in the middle of peeling potatoes, and Pantaleimon came in and said: "Hey, there's a man hanging out there!"

"Why didn't you cut him down?" I asked.

Pantaleimon didn't reply.

We were walking along, side by side. It was all crosses and gravestones, and then suddenly there was this thin man dangling from the bough of a lonely fir tree. The tip of his tongue was blue. He had it sticking out of the corner of his mouth, the way some idiots do. His feet almost touched the ground. A bread-sack, which was full, and a tin plate, which rattled slightly each time a wind stirred the twigs, hung from his hips.

Why didn't he take off his bread-sack? I asked myself. Why didn't he take off his tin plate? Given that his bread-sack was full, why did he want to die? He could have lived another day at least! Two more days!

Why does someone quit this life, like quitting a room in winter when there's no stove in it? Shuts the door after him, and sticks his tongue out childishly and cussedly?

I had already seen lots of dead people who had died in their white and dirty beds – all the dead who came into the morgue, on their way underground. All of them were basically through with life, they were a part of the cemetery already, it was as though they'd been dead for years, before they were brought to us.

But here was a dead man hanging, as though he were still alive. His feet moved, as though they wanted to walk. He had a bread-sack and clothes. It was then I decided that suicide was not for me.

[. . .]

It was impossible to die and hang from a branch and be found by Pantaleimon.

In fact, it was a stroke of luck for him. Ropes that people have hanged themselves with are famously sought after. They're lucky, there's no argument about that.

Pantaleimon's first thought was to find a buyer for the rope. Who would buy it? Who would buy it for a lot of money?

Rich people are not normally superstitious. They buy gold chains and strings of pearls, but not hemp ropes. They are lucky without having to try.

We were left with our Count, who was rich, but certainly superstitious into the bargain. Only, this fell in that time of the year when the Count had set off on his travels to unknown parts.

"How about," I said to Pantaleimon, "if we cut up the rope, and sell the individual pieces!"

"What a clever fellow you are," said Pantaleimon. "I bet you did hide that diamond!"

We cut up the rope. The buyers came. We buried the suicide with ceremony, without a priest, under the tree he had hanged himself on. Our poet gave a talk on the unknown stranger, who had died far from home, who knows why, alone, perhaps ostracized. His fate was not merely tragic, it was more, it was unknown.

Straight after the burial, we had the sale. By evening, we had a lot of money in the drawer, and not one piece of rope left.

We said nothing to Pantaleimon's wife about our earnings.

We decided we would be rich, the rope had emboldened us, and the jingling coins we counted cheered us like schnapps.

"Where will I find another hanged man?" asked Pantaleimon. "People hang themselves so rarely!" he complained. "The priest scares them off. Tells them they won't get to Heaven. How does he know? It seems life is like prison, and we have to wait for God to let us out, and then we're free. But if someone hangs himself on a nice fir tree, and it's summer, and the birds are all twittering, and the sky is blue, and the flies are buzzing, then the devils will chase his poor soul to Hell.

But what if he's mistaken, and people wind up in Hell, whether they waited for death, or went and got it for themselves! Then none of it will have made any difference, except to me. I'll only have had to wait another hundred years for my next bit of rope!"

Suddenly, I felt as though someone had directed my attention to the stove. I saw the rope that we used to lower the cheap coffins into the graves.

I took a knife, cut up the rope, and laid the pieces before Pantaleimon. "We can sell this rope," I said.

"What if it's not lucky?" asked Pantaleimon.

"I think," I said, "that all ropes are lucky."

I was probably right. People kept coming, we sold teeny weeny bits, and we kept starting on new ropes.

I got myself a new fur cap and a pair of boots, Pantaleimon got himself a waistcoat. He gave his wife corals.

We were very rich.

I had enough to go out into the world I was dying to see.

"Wait for the Count," said Pantaleimon, "I'm sure he'll tell you where's a good place to go!"

The summer lay there, waiting to finish. Autumn was when the strangers were expected, the hop-merchants from Austria, Germany and England, the rich men off whom many people in our town made their livings.

The summer lay there, and it spawned various illnesses. People got belly aches and died from eating rotten fruit, the water ran out in the wells, a couple of pine forests burned down, and the dry grass on the steppes caught alight. At night, the horizon was red, and the air was full of acrid fumes.

We kept getting new visitors to the morgue. The authorities announced that the water was dangerous. We drank hot tea, and avoided cherries, even sour cherries. Apples and pears were not yet ripe.

A lot of people went to the steam baths, to sweat out the poisons. Frau Bardach, the owner of the baths, was kept so busy that she fell ill. Another two weeks, then she was dead, and she was buried in the Jewish cemetery, before her son could get there, her son out in the wide world who wrote to her a couple of times a year.

His uncle, Frau Bardach's brother, was a rich timber merchant in Vienna. Wolf, the nephew, had crossed the border to join him when still a boy.

It was said he had become a great lawyer, a celebrated man. Everyone was eager to see him.

He came. He really was worth seeing. Could that gentleman really be a son of our town?

Wolf Bardach was not merely wide and fat, with glinting spectacles in the middle of his face, with a stiff gray hat perched on his head, with shiny red cheeks – Bardach also wore light checked pants. They were the first such pants that had ever been seen in our town, not even the Count had such a pair.

Bardach inherited a large fortune. Steam baths are a good business. If Bardach had stayed to run his mother's business, he would have made millions within a few years.

He had no shortage of advisers, either. People who had known Wolf Bardach when he was a little boy came to him with propositions. Wolf Bardach was staying in a hotel, oh, what a hotel!

Because of course we had a hotel, it stood at the end of the street that led to the station. A simple little house, with a bar in the middle, and a ridiculous sign over the door. It showed a fat knight, holding a beer tankard aloft in his right hand, while his armor vainly strove to restrain his bulging belly.

The hotel had no more than three rooms. Each of the rooms was heated by a bad stove. None of the rooms had a bed with a mattress in it. All the beds had straw sacks.

There will have been vermin as well. It was known as The Cockroach Arms. In fact, the hotel was called The Drunken Bear. That was where the great lawyer Wolf Bardach stayed, the famous man, the man in light checked pants.

He took all three rooms for himself. There was nowhere left for any other visitors. Even rich people who came to our town were forced to stay with our two bakers, who let out their beds at night, while they did their baking.

It was probably the pitiful condition of the tourist facilities in our town that persuaded the attorney to build a new hotel.

He decided to build a hotel along American lines. He wanted a hotel such as you might have found in New York City.

Wolf Bardach sold the steam baths and his mother's house. He bought five little houses, and had them torn down.

It wasn't just the houses themselves that cost money. The demolition cost as well. Because on average three families lived in each of the five houses, and because each family had lots of children, Herr Bardach had to build tenements to rehouse all these homeless people.

So there was work in our town. The oldest men, men with white beards, men you would have called on at most to fix your stove in winter, now clambered up and down scaffolding poles. They were like bearded weasels.

I too found work. I had a notebook, and wrote down meters and centimeters and kept a tally of planks, posts and bricks.

I wasn't the only one either. There were other intelligent young men with notebooks with me.

We were indispensable.

The hotel was to be five storeys high. It was the tallest building anywhere within ten miles.

White, tall, lonely, it stuck out over the world. Our old people, who didn't think much of progress, were angry. They thought the hotel was a Tower of Babel.

But it kept growing.

One day, the engineer who was in charge of the building climbed up on the scaffolding, fell off, and was dead.

He was buried between the Christian and Jewish cemeteries because no one could remember his faith.

His death provoked a huge kerfuffle. But Bardach, a progressive chap, was undeterred, and he hired a new engineer, and he went on building.

Four months later, with the snow already in deep piles on the streets, he was forced to call a halt.

But when the first swallows arrived, so did Herr Bardach.

We carried on building.

On a hot July day, the work was finally finished. But the money was finished too.

Creditors came. Invoices came. Only no travelers came, and all two hundred rooms were empty.

To save his bacon, he set up a café on the ground floor, a café featuring classical music.

But no customers came.

The music played to empty tables. One or two wealthy officers went in, played a game of billiards, and went out again.

Instead of sitting in the café and enjoying life, the inhabitants of our town stood outside the windows, which were protected by thick green curtains.

The inhabitants of our town would drink their coffee at home, then walk up to the windows, and listen to the music, without having to pay anything.

That thrifty style of course did nothing for our hotel owner. One day, he quietly packed his bags and left.

At least, we had earned some money. We had a new hotel. When visitors came, they stayed there, and they sat in the café, and listened to the music.

But in summer, spring and winter, the great building remained empty. A porter stood in front of the door like a stone statue, perfectly immobile. He aged visibly, his gold buttons grew dull, his black tailcoat acquired a greenish patina.

Nothing more was heard of the fearless builder. The steam baths sent gay plumes of smoke into the sky every day. Unlike the hotel and the café, they were always busy.

Our town was poor. Our people had no regular income, they were sustained by miracles. There were many people who had no occupation at all. They borrowed money. But who gave them loans? Even the money-lenders didn't have any money. People lived off lucky breaks.

Things kept happening that gave us new hope. The building of the hotel had only led to disappointment. A winter followed, with hard early frosts, it fell upon us like a murderer, by the end of November it was already twenty-five below. The birds fell out of the trees, we could pick them up every morning. The snow groaned underfoot, the frost cut into our flesh with a thousand tiny lashes, our stoves were filled to bursting, the wind pushed the smoke back down the chimneys, so that we were almost asphyxiated in our rooms. We couldn't open the windows, because we had already wedged them shut with cotton wool and newspapers. The windowpanes acquired thick crusts of opaque crystal, the strange flora of winter.

The poor were fed by our Count. Those who couldn't beg, starved and died, people were for ever running through the streets with corpses, the black-clad coachmen whipped their black steeds to a gallop, and the mourners ran after the departed, it was as though there was a race between the quick and the dead, to see who would reach the overflowing graveyards first. No room! No room! – screamed the crows. Those ravenous birds hung heavy and black in the bare boughs, they were like winged fruits, they beat their wings at each other and squabbled noisily, they flew around the houses and pecked like sparrows at the frozen windows, they were at hand like bad news, they were remote like gloomy premonitions, they were black and menacing on the black boughs and the white snow.

How suddenly the evenings used to fall there, evenings that came with a keen wind, with remote glittering stars in a frozen blue sky, with short vehement darkening indoors, with howling devils in the stoves, with ghosts spun from nothing. The sun was visible for half an hour a day. It was pale and white, obscured by a frozen windowpane. Long heavy icicles hung off the low roofs, like tassels with rigor mortis. Narrow paths were trodden into deep snow, people walked between tall white walls of snow. The only cheerful thing was the jingling of the sleigh bells, a ringing almost like spring. The frost imparted a short, harsh, glassy echo to the sound, from a distance it was like the buzzing of alert young flies.

The pine forests were black slashes on a white field. Fog blanketed the distant hills, streams lay gurgling behind thick windows, and round the wells were circles of thick, honed, dangerous glass.

In that winter, which made our poor still poorer, we awaited, with more than usual impatience, the arrival from faraway Peking of the wealthy Herr Britz, the wealthy tea merchant whose trademark (a set of scales held by an angel) is known the world over as a guarantee of genuine China tea.

When Herr Britz arrived, things looked up for everyone. He spent two weeks in our midst, he visited the grave of his father, he visited his dead relatives and his living relatives, those he didn't know as well, he was invited by the rich, and he invited the poor.

He came every winter, in the middle of winter, when the frost had reached its sharpest intensity, he came like an envoy from God. Everyone blessed him, wherever he came and went.

I don't know how people learned of his coming. At any rate, one day everyone knew. The train only stopped in our station on Wednesdays. And every Wednesday people said to themselves: He'll be coming in two weeks! In a week!

The train got in at twenty-five past five in the evening. That was late evening in this part of the world, by rights the windows should have been shuttered, and people back in their homes. But not a bit of it. All the shutters were still open, the lights were on in all the houses; the windows looked illuminated, the lamps had all been cleaned, and gave out all the light they possessed. Sleighs, crowded with people, slid along the straight road to the station, dropped their dark cargo, curved elegantly to a stop, blue smoke came out of the horses' nostrils, their hooves cracked on the ice, impatiently they whinnied, the coachmen rubbed their hands and smacked their shoulders, people stood at the bar and warmed up with schnapps and stamped their feet just like the horses.

Then out came the porter, there was ice on his fair mustache, he announced the train, doors opened, there was a ringing on the platform, the train drew in, steam came hissing from the locomotive. And among the passengers who got off was Herr Britz.

The fine and stately figure he cut! The beaver and sealskin coat! The beautiful silk scarf thrown round his neck!

He wasn't tired, there wasn't a wrinkle on his clean-shaven face, his skin was rosy and brown, his dark eyes clear and kind, his large, slender hands slipped easily out of their heavy fur mittens, and reached out to greet everyone.

All the coachmen fought over him, all of them wanted to take him. If only he had brought his entire wardrobe with him, then he could have divided it among all the sleighs! It wasn't even as though he had a lot of luggage, just a single suitcase! He couldn't break himself up into pieces, he couldn't stand in ten sleighs with just two feet. He sat down in one of them, the first in line, and all the others set off after him, with bells chiming! When he got out of his sleigh, he had to pay all the coachmen. But that didn't matter! He had money!

We had a new hotel now, Herr Britz was delighted with the luxury. "We had it built for you," lied the mayor at the reception the town put on in Herr Britz's honor that evening. Maybe Herr Britz believed him.

He took five rooms on the first floor, he received the poor, he doled out money, every day he chartered a different sleigh, he took the edge off winter, he distributed wood and coal, bread and herrings, tea and lard, he bought Madeira for the sick, and in short he warmed the world like a hundred summers.

When he went away, he left a lot of happy people behind, but he didn't look as fresh as he had when he arrived, he was tired and stooped, his skin was pale, his kind eyes shone less brightly. That's what a strain charity can be.

That year, Herr Britz left us so much money that we could finally equip an expedition to the underground passages that had gripped our imagination for many years, and to which we looked for a solution for our perennial shortage of funds.

The underground passages, so they said, had been dug in the seventeenth century, and led from the church, which was right in the middle of town, as far as the Count's castle, past the cellars of many old houses, containing quantities of gold and silver that had been hidden in times of war from whatever enemies we were facing at the time.

Underground, then, we had a lot of gold, it was only on the surface that we were poor. Our excavations could make us all wealthy. Then we wouldn't have to work any more. Every inhabitant of our town would have so much money that he wouldn't have to worry for the rest of his life, and his children would have a future.

But we were short of money to reach the treasure. We needed equipment, gasmasks, various kinds of instruments, lamps. Above all, we needed courageous men, prepared to risk their lives. They would have to be well paid. The rich benefactors of our town (the Count, for instance) had always been skeptical about this undertaking. They didn't believe in the buried treasure, they didn't even believe in the historical existence of our old passages.

But now, at last, we had the money.

When the spring arrived, we walked around the streets all day long, discussing subterranean matters. What a sensation, every step you take, to believe there are quantities of gold and jewels underfoot! Every man who climbed down into his cellar in those days to fetch ladders, wine, vinegar or whatever else, could not fail to be awestruck. Everyone fancied doing some digging for themselves. Some did it on quiet nights, others tapped their walls, looking for hollow spots. It was already being said that so-and-so had unearthed treasures in his cellar. Everyone grew suspicious. There came a time when everyone began to complain how badly they were doing, so as not to be suspected of having discovered treasure. Of course, the more people complained, the more suspicious they made themselves. It was a time when people stopped giving to beggars, because they believed they were the ones who had struck gold and silver, and were just begging as a front. The shops were empty, because everyone was afraid that making a purchase would incur suspicion of a windfall. When people noticed that their complaints were met with suspicion and unbelief, they stopped speaking altogether. It was all they could do to exchange casual greetings. When two were seen talking together, people pointed at them and called them millionaires.

One day a history professor arrived, with assistants, lamps and gasmasks. Placards were put up on houses, saying the town council was looking for courageous workmen.

Pantaleimon came forward, taking me with him. We were experienced diggers, and well used to subterranean things from the graveyard. We were experts in matters subterranean.

We demanded to be paid in advance, because we were afraid we might meet our death tunneling, and die for nothing. We buried our wages next to the fourth grave in the oldest row, wrote our wills and put them in our pockets. Pantaleimon left his wage not to his own family, but to the Count. I had a long think about who I should bequeath my money to. I had the money I had saved for my great trip abroad. I left it to my brother in Mexico.

We got up at five in the morning, it was 10 May, the birds were twittering for all they were worth. There were ten of us, with shovels and mattocks. We were issued with rubber boots, descended into Herr Jampoller's cellar, broke down a nailed-up door, and found ourselves at the beginning of our subterranean journey.

Oh, the stink, I'll never forget it! It stank of old potatoes and rotten hay, of mushrooms and mold, and a little bit of autumn forests in the rain. We lit the tunnel and the walls with the scientific lamps. We found skeletons, chests, the professor wrote it all down, the stone walls were dripping, they were covered with whitish slime, we encountered stone coffins, inscriptions, but we found no gold, no silver, no jewels.

We worked all day. When we returned to the surface, it was evening, and we were near the castle.

We had earned our money, and we dug it up, and put it with our savings.

The town calmed down, people lost their suspiciousness, there was life in the streets again, and the beggars fared better once more.

But even so, Herr Brandes was mistaken.

He had emigrated to London twenty years previously, he had earned money, married a freckled English redhead, and put on a belly with a heavy watch-chain looped across it.

Now he was returning, he had money coming out of his ears, so people said. Why did he come back to our poor town? Why didn't he stay put in London?

But no, he was back, a missionary for English civilization. He wanted to show us how people did business in the world. He bought up some common land from the town, he bought up our "open space", where traveling fairs, menageries and magicians always used to pitch their tents, where sad gray grass and little yellow flowers sprouted, and which seemed to have been designated by God to be our open space, and nothing else besides.

Brandes built a house, not as tall as the hotel, but a two storey house all the same. Extraordinarily, it had no windows. People were not a little astonished. How would Brandes manage to do without windows? Did people in London live without natural light?

When the scaffolding came down, and the white walls stood there, blind, windowless, smooth, without stucco or ornamentation – we had expected there to be some, of course – no one had any doubts but that Herr Brandes was insane.

But Brandes turned out not to be as insane as we believed at the time. It wasn't a dwelling he had built, but a big store, a department store, perhaps they had them like that in London!

[. . .]

THIS MORNING, A
LETTER ARRIVED . . .

This morning, a letter arrived from my friend Naphtali Kroy in Buenos Aires. He's happy, he's enjoying life in the big and presumably very exotic foreign city. He's met people from home, acquaintances. They're dealing in tobacco or other goods, and they say hello to me. They haven't forgotten me, even though I was just a boy when I left them, to travel west, to my father's family in Vienna. The people of my town have a good memory, because they remember with their hearts. I for my part had almost forgotten them, because I've been living, and still live, in Western Europe, where the heart counts for nothing, the head for a little, and the fist for everything.

Who knows where I might not have landed up, had my friend Naphtali Kroy not also gone west. I was already in the process of losing my heart, my desire, and my capacity for love and pain, which is as strong as longing, love and death put together. Already I had forgotten my birthplace, the little town in Russia which no longer exists, which has died, which has fallen in the Great War, as if it had been an infantryman, a human being. Oh, it was so much more than a human being! It was a fertile womb, from which many

166

individuals, striking individuals, were cast out like seeds on the broad fields of the world.

The town no longer exists. It has been blown up by guns, burned down by fires, trampled upon by boots, and now the golden maize flowers where once were dirty lanes and houses, and the wind blows over the streets and pavements of my childhood. Other towns grow rich and powerful, or, if they are condemned to die, they die slowly, death torments them for a hundred years or a thousand. But our little town it abruptly mowed down with its big, sharp scythe.

Now I was born nowhere and belong nowhere. It's a strange and terrible thing, and I seem to myself like a dream, without roots and without purpose, with no beginning and no end, coming and going and not knowing whither or why. It's the same with my compatriots too. They have been scattered all over the wide world, they grip foreign soil with their frail roots, lie buried in foreign soil, have children who don't know their father's birthplace, and to whom their grandfather is a mythical figure. From time to time, I hear from one or other of them. I happen to know, for instance, that the baker Surokin now runs a restaurant in Tokyo, is married to a Japanese woman, and has six children, two of whom are studying in Europe somewhere. The wealthy Herr Kobritz stumbled upon Surokin in curious fashion. Herr Kobritz trades with half the world, and so in due course he found himself in Tokyo, sat down in a restaurant, and was served some excellent fish. The fish was completely according to his taste, and the wealthy Herr Kobritz was already beginning to philosophize, expounding his theory that the whole world was just a village, one big village, and that people were the same all over the world. How else was it possible that he could travel to the end of the world, to Tokyo, there to be served fish of the very sort that his cook at home prepared for him? Herr Kobritz was very pleased with his philosophy when the chef walked up to him, a Japanese man with thick glasses, saying: "Good evening, Herr Kobritz!" So the world really was just one big village, where everyone knew the wealthy Herr Kobritz. "Don't you recognize me?" asked the

Japanese man. "No!" replied Herr Kobritz, "I've never been to Tokyo before." "But I knew you right away," replied the Japanese man. "I used to be the baker Mendel Surokin, and now I've been Japanese for thirty years."

Herr Kobritz came to Vienna, so I had the story straight from the horse's mouth, and I told it to my friend Naphtali, who's now busy giving it currency all over Buenos Aires. Soon everyone will know what became of the baker Mendel Surokin. But I'm racked by curiosity. I want to know what happened to the others, to blind Turek, for example, to Pantaleimon the gravedigger, to Peisach the tailor, to Dr. Habich, to Jonathan Bruh, and to Mordechai the scribe. I can vividly remember every one of them. I can see Jonathan Bruh as if he were in front of me now, a Swabian from the German colony, a retired postman who went around in a shako and an old saber and a lot of tin medallions on his jacket. He thought he was a prince or a great general, related to kings and emperors all over the world, and sometimes he read out a letter from the Emperor of China. "Dear Cousin," wrote the Emperor of China, "I am surprised I haven't heard from you for so long. Under separate cover, I send you my latest order. Please write to confirm its safe arrival. Your Faithful Emperor." The letter was brushed on old parchment with Chinese characters. That's why no one was able to read it, and we were dependant on the truthfulness of Jonathan Bruh.

Even more important would be to discover what has become of Peisach the tailor. He was the nonpareil of tailors, you wouldn't find another like him anywhere in the world. He knew the measurements of all his customers by heart, because he couldn't write, not even figures. Often we stared through his windows, Naphtali Kroy and I, when we returned from roasting potatoes in the fields. There we saw the greasy yellow glow of the little lamp on the tailor's table, and himself as he sat on the kitchen bench, pondering. Certainly he was busy trying to picture the dimensions of his customers, to remember their bellies and chests and thighs. When he picked up his scissors, it was as though he had them standing in front of him, and he had no trouble cutting out their coats and trousers and waistcoats. But from time to time, he did make a little mistake, and so he was left with enough material to make the occasional suit for himself. Because it was only right and proper that a tailor who knows all his customers' measurements by heart, should be allowed to keep a little material for his own poor, scrawny, shivering body.

So what happened to our tailor? His son, I know, has been living in America for years, and is also a tailor, he always said in his letters that he was the owner of a fashion house. I suppose it's not impossible that the son got his father to come to America, and that tailor Peisach is sitting in a corner of his fashion house, old and short-sighted and hard of hearing, and still unable to write.

Mordechai, the scribe, didn't have any children. I think he died alone. He was a widower and he taught writing, and he always used to carry a pen and an ink bottle around with him when he went to his pupils. But his pockets were holey, and his wife was dead, and there wasn't anyone to patch his pockets. Therefore he used to wear a top hat on his head: he kept his writing gear in his top hat. Because of that, he wasn't able to greet anyone. He had to content himself with putting one finger to the brim of his hat. That was his greeting. There was only one person whom he couldn't greet like that, and that was our burgomaster. So he always avoided the burgomaster, and when he came to a corner, he would always stop and look around furtively, and not walk on until he had assured himself that the burgomaster wasn't coming.

Dr. Habich was a doctor who found anything and everything more interesting than patients and diseases. He had studied medicine in Vienna, and he would probably have liked to be a famous consultant in a big city. But just as he was finishing his studies, his father died. Dr. Habich had no money and returned home, even though his professor had told him that talented individuals were much sought after in Western Europe. There weren't any particular illnesses in our town. People had a hernia, or a catarrh, or an upset stomach, a broken leg, or a farmer cut himself on his scythe. These weren't the sort of things to keep a gifted and ambitious doctor interested. Year after year, with every new patient that came to him, Dr. Habich hoped to come across a grave and interesting condition. But all it was was a hernia or a catarrh or a late birth. Then Dr. Habich stopped writing prescriptions, and if you sent for him, he never came, and gave instructions without seeing the patient. A new young doctor arrived in town, who understood his business, and managed to treat a catarrh in such a way that it turned into a nice double pneumonia. People started dying in droves, and the young doctor was in constant demand, and no one ever sent for Dr. Habich.

He sometimes sat in the bar that Naphtali and I used to go to too. There were Pantaleimon and blind Turek, drinking and talking. Pantaleimon had cut a suicide off a tree, he'd kept the rope, and was looking for a buyer for it. Whoever had a hanged man's rope would get a lot of milk from his cows, his horses would thrive, the wheat would grow heavy on his fields, and he himself would be immune to the Evil Eye. A rope like that was worth a couple of hens among brothers, or at the very least a few dozen eggs. Pantaleimon didn't need money. Anyone who's been a gravedigger all his life, and has seen the rich having to leave behind their two large rooms and kitchen and a bag of money under their pillows – anyone who's seen that a hundred times over, doesn't want money. Think of the worms, says Pantaleimon each time he sees a big wedding procession. He always thinks of the worms.

But now he has his rope to sell. Who can fit us up with a purchaser? Who is familiar with everyone's requirements? Who gets to go everywhere? Who sees everything? – Blind Josef Turek, the brushmaker, who learned his handiwork at blind school in the big city and always talks about the beauty of the city, as though he'd had a proper sight of it. He knows it better than a sighted person. Because he is blind.

"I wouldn't sell the rope to one single purchaser," says Josef Turek.

"Fool," replies Pantaleimon, "it's only a single rope."

"Just a moment," says Turek. "Who's the fool? Why not turn one into many? You get a hen for each one. And you go on selling pieces of rope all your life."

"Now, unless I'm very mistaken," objects Pantaleimon, "I'm somewhere between sixty and sixty-five. And I want to live to be a hundred. So how many years have I got left?"

"Thirty-five or forty."

"You see! There's not so much rope that I can go on selling it for forty years."

"Who says it has to be the same rope? When the first one is finished, you just cut another one in little pieces."

"But a rope that hasn't hanged anyone isn't going to be a lucky rope!" said Pantaleimon.

"All ropes are lucky!" retorted Josef Turek. And he's right.

Such were the conversations you might catch in the bar at night. I drank schnapps there, even though I was barely ten years old, but Naphtali Kroy, who was eight years older, had honored me with his friendship, and so I just had to play at being older, and drink schnapps. It tasted not at all bad.

In fact, it tasted very good, and it kept me alive when I returned from potato roasting tired and chilled to the marrow. We set out early in the morning. The fogs were still hanging over the earth, and over the autumn morning, which looked like an old man, silent and dumb and all swaddled up. The crows sat on the swaying branches for minutes on end, till you thought they were grown on, like big, mournful autumnal fruit. They lifted into the air when we lit our fires and the smoke went up. We were the enemies of the crows. Sometimes we threw stones at them. Sometimes we brought one down, picked it up, and were invariably alarmed by the crooked sharp beak, which was like a little two-edged saber. Willows smelled bitter and narcotic, there was a reek of mold and putrescence. The damp passed through the soles of our boots up into our bodies, we flapped our arms to get warm, and stomped about on the stubble fields and breathed into our cupped hands. On the edge of the woods, lonely animals peeped out shyly and furtively. Exhausted late beetles crept over the furrows, black and gleaming like bits of coal. The clouds stood insistently in the sky like a curse in waiting. It was only afternoon, and the western horizon began to redden with the sun we couldn't see. We hadn't seen it rise in the morning, we didn't see it at the height of its powers at midday, we only saw its final decline, its flat beams and its painful red reflection in the evening clouds. The wind got up on tiptoe and set off on its nocturnal walkabout. At the same time, a few yellow lights started to flicker in distant hovels, like sparks struck by the wind. Naphtali whistled the song of the miller whose wheel turns, whose years pass. From our little plume of smoke, we could tell that the wind had changed, only yesterday it had been from the north, today it was from the northwest, and the first snow would be with us in a few days. Already, I longed for its small, hard, cutting stars, and its lashing, annealing sharpness in my face. The smell of our roasting potatoes was like a kind of home to us. The crows had gotten used to the smoke by now, and had returned to their boughs, where they spread their wings from time to time without taking off, maybe just to give us a fright, or because they themselves were frightened. And long, tall, lanky, red-haired Naphtali walked home with long steps. I scuttled after him, and couldn't keep up. I got back to town ten minutes after he did. He was standing in front of the bar, waiting for me.

It was the saddest autumn of my life, the autumn that Naphtali Kroy went to Vienna. The War and the Revolution were over, and the countries and peoples were still trembling, even though the storm that had shaken them was already moving off. I was a poor bastard. I had nothing but my rucksack. My rucksack had my coat in it. The shoes I wore at the time I owed to an embarrassing act of charity. They were patent leather boots. That happened to be the pair my benefactor could do without. The leather was cracked, and all the damp of the rainy autumnal world seeped through their thin soles. When I cleaned the mud off them, they glowed startlingly. They were a traumatic present.

Then Naphtali Kroy arrived, blown from east to west like everyone else, he arrived with the poor, the refugees, the prisoners of war. He was poor, and so was I, together we were even poorer than we were separately. But we were friends, and friendship is a great wealth.

If Naphtali had had a regular job, it wouldn't have been so bad. But he was just a coachman. At the age of twenty, he had married a widow, a widow with a couple of half-grown children. The widow was forty. She owned a cab with a horse. Her husband, the coachman, had been a drunkard, and died insane. Now the poor horse stood in its little stable, whinnying, and in the yard stood the cab with its broken windows, spattered with gray mud, with its sorry shaft that rested glumly on the ground. The sight broke Naphtali's heart. Every day he looked into the stable and the yard, till one morning, he impulsively hitched up the horse to the carriage, climbed up on the box, and trotted along to the station. Visitors arrived. Naphtali was in luck. He stayed up on his box. Every day that trains arrived, he rode to the station. He married the carriage and got the widow and her children thrown in. During the War, the town was occupied by the Austrians. They requisitioned the carriage, the horse and Naphtali Kroy. The horse died on the battlefield, Frau Kroy died at home. The children were taken off by typhoid fever. The carriage was a piece of junk abandoned somewhere. Only Naphtali was healthy. He went to Vienna.

On the way there, he stabbed a Hungarian who had attempted to rob him of his new yellow boots.

YOUTH

I loved to make myself invisible. I used to dream of a cap of invisibility. I wasn't a puny boy, who was afraid of a fight. Even so, a fight in which I was invisible to my enemy always struck me as the only one possible.

I had what they call a devious nature. I despised boys of my own age, who measured their equal or unequal strength. It seemed to me perfectly honorable to vanquish a foe by subterfuge, and assassination, if it was done for a good reason, didn't seem to me to be shameful.

I was capable of persuading myself that I was invisible, although really I knew that everyone could see me. I liked hiding. I was an expert at hide-and-seek, no one ever found me. I always felt a measure of contempt for the heroes I read about in fairy tales and story books. And even so, they impressed me, not on account of their actions, but because of the postures they struck, the splendid roles they were allowed to play. I liked to compare myself with them.

Because, obviously, I was ambitious as well. I was quite set on outstripping the run of mankind – how, I wasn't quite sure yet. I was determined to let nothing get in my way. Of the poverty that surrounded me in my youth I was not greatly aware. I saw it as one of the many obstacles that fate puts in a man's way. It was something to be overcome. I did not envy other, well-fed and smartly dressed boys. I had always known that to feel sorry for myself was just as reprehensible as feeling sorry for others. Joyfully, almost lustfully, I embraced poverty, and that set me apart from my peers.

I was always at pains to be on good terms with everyone else. I recognized quite early on that resentment and enmity – in particular the enmity of my inferiors – could hurt me. It wasn't that I lacked courage to confront a hostile world. But I preferred peace to conflict, because the latter would have flushed me out, and I wanted to live clandestinely. Equally, I was not short of rebellious feelings towards teachers and seniors. Only, I didn't show it. I was an excellent pupil, not by industry but by sheer superiority. It would have struck me as embarrassing to be caught out by the teacher reading something I shouldn't have been, or smoking a cigarette, or copying someone else's homework, to stumble over a recitation, or to require a prompt from a neighbor. I yielded to insurmountable odds, and because they couldn't touch me, I felt at liberty. The rebels, the daredevils and the incorruptibles, meanwhile, were on the run from the teachers, who hunted them down. It amused me to take no part in the chase, but merely to spectate at it.

It seemed unworthy to me to be caught lying, though lying itself was perfectly respectable. I made use of secret advantages, dishonestly come by. I soon saw that people took me for honest but smart, and that they were afraid of me, but didn't think me capable of anything underhand. They trusted me, in spite of their fear. They came to me for advice, and I helped them out. They were true to me, I was indifferent to them. I paid them for their trust, and owed them nothing. They envied me, I let them. I met with successes, and enjoyed the fruits of my successes, not the successes themselves.

Soon I saw that I was in danger of falling in love with myself. I sat up. I wanted to be as immune to myself as I was to everyone else. My vicious and immoral nature was very helpful to me in this. Every day I discovered new flaws in myself, because I was still convinced, then, that such things as egoism, malice, arrogance, cowardice and cunning are absolute vices. I contrived to like myself, and at the same time to think of myself as an outcast. I did not want to be noble. It was enough for me to have discovered that I was not noble. This recognition saved me from myself quite as much as my vices saved me from others.

I believed in the existence and the virtue, so to speak, of virtue, but I knew it wasn't for me. I believed in the high-mindedness of certain individuals, and the uselessness of low endeavors. I believed in positive forces, and hated negative forces. I hated the devil. But I only believed shyly in god. I knew for a fact that he did not exist, and yet I prayed to him.

For two years, from my fourteenth to my sixteenth year, I was an atheist. I looked up, and I knew there was only blue air. But I had completely failed to notice that god hadn't disappeared, so much as merely relocated, from the sky to some other place, I didn't know where, but probably quite close to me. That no one ruled the world was quite clear to me, but I had a sense that someone was looking out for me personally. I prayed often, and my prayers were very short. They consisted of a single thought, often just a single idea. The one to whom I was praying always helped, he never punished. Yes, and neither did I shrink from asking for his help with my low, almost criminal, but certainly sinful undertakings. He helped, too. I would have denied him for ever. But the more eagerly did I believe him. He was there like a reality.

It took two years for my personal god to turn into the god of the world and lord of the universe. I knew, from our old comradeship, that he was well-disposed to me. I wasn't scared of him. I trusted him. And if something bad happened to me, it wasn't punishment, but a sort of masked or dissembled form of grace.

I had nothing to be afraid of. I was on good terms with god, I knew myself, and I had other people well in hand. Spirits, ghosts and the dead I was able to reconcile. If I saw them in dreams, I wasn't alarmed, but had calm and objective conversations with them. I stood my ground with them, forcing them to see that there wasn't anything to be gained from me.

The only things I was afraid of were death and disease. I believed in some form of afterlife, but it was an unpleasant idea to me, suddenly to find myself in some alien and unexplorable environment. I steered clear of death, of burials, graveyards, and the sight of corpses. Once, I happened upon a burial — and was troubled for weeks afterwards. I felt I was near to death myself, and made myself ready to die.

When I saw that my life was still secure, I ceased to fear the infectiousness of death. I sought out an old cemetery, and spent many hours there. I made friends with an old cemetery attendant, who told me blood-curdling stories that I didn't believe. He talked about supernatural manifestations, and the living strength of the dead as they lay in the mortuary before their burial. Once I spent a whole night with the dead. They didn't move. I still somehow didn't believe in their deadness. But it seemed clear to me that no communication was possible between us.

I got used to the sight of corpses and the hysterics of the bereaved, sad chants, gruesome things, unspeakable things, and even ugly things. Once I saw a telegraph mast hitting a worker. He hit the ground without making a sound. I saw his smashed skull, my eyes took in the quickly drying blood. I heard the wailing of his wife and two daughters, and wasn't at all affected by any of it. From then on, the sufferings of others didn't touch me. Once, my mother scalded her hand. She was in agony. She cried. I remained cool. Another time, two carthorses shied, and a farrier was dragged along the ground for a long way. I watched it all coolly, while everyone else lost their heads. Nothing could fluster me. I would never have been able to save someone's life at a risk to my own. I wouldn't want to jump in after some drowning man, I never learned to swim, I don't want to swim. I despise the pathetic efforts of humans to ape fish, I believe in some absolute machinery that will one day enable us to walk on the water. And as long as this machinery hasn't been invented, I say let them drown, the lemmings! I doubt whether the world's any the better for their rescue anyway. But it would be a shame to lose me.

I don't put my trust in the body, I put my trust in the victorious human spirit. I'd sooner trust a revolver than a boxer, and it pleases me that the strongest muscles cannot withstand a bullet. I'm pleased that swords and armor are useless, and bravery in a man strikes me as being a pretty hopeless quality.

On the other hand, I was quick to appreciate that women are impressed by acts of heroism, and I despised them for it. Unfortunately, they seemed to be indispensable to me, and I enjoyed their nudity when they were clothed. I wanted to seduce them, possess them and leave them.

I never raved about any particular woman, I was never besotted. The whole female sex was like an individual to me. Once I saw a young female attendant at a public swimming baths. I was sitting in the waiting-room, waiting for a cubicle to become vacant, she was talking to a couple of old biddies, stretching both her arms up in the air, for no reason, just for the hell of it. Her breasts lifted, her blouse revealed a flash of white undergarment, her feet half slipped out of their sandals. She seemed fantastically desirable to me, I was practically swooning. She saw me, gestured to me, but I fled.

That night, I was afraid to undress. I was afraid of my own nakedness, my solitariness and masculinity. I wished with all my heart to be both man and woman, to enjoy and to be enjoyed, lover and beloved. I felt incomplete in myself, I got excited, I conjured up the girl, I magicked her into bed with me and had my way with her, but even in my ecstasy I never lost my mind. I knew all the time that she wasn't really there, that she was in another bed with some other man.

At last, I got up, went out, and saw my neighbor's fifteen-year-old daughter standing by her window. She was waiting for her parents to come back from some family wedding a long way off. I climbed up to her room, blew out her light, and we lay together for a couple of hours. When I left, she cried, but she didn't move. "You're going to marry me, aren't you?" she said, smiling through her tears. "Could be," I replied.

At about that time, I fell in love with poets and plays and poems. I retained everything in my memory, without trying to learn it by heart. I loved the beauty of it, the language, the images and sounds, and that led me to try to love the content too, more than I was really able to at the time. To have a better appreciation of the beauties of poetry, to really understand it properly, I thought I had to fall in love myself. I found a pretty girl whom a lot of my classmates adored, and pursued her in the street. I thought about her, I dreamed about her, but all the time I knew I wasn't capable of giving up anything for her; that I walked outside her window in the rain to get a sense of what it must be like to suffer, but not actually to suffer myself. Soon I decided to my satisfaction that I had experienced love. I turned to other matters.

I turned to the matters that the poems and plays dealt with, the so-called big subjects, like Nature, Morality, Fatherland, Freedom, Home and Language. All these concepts existed for me as only real things could, as distant but as apprehensible as bells, whose lofty, almost heavenly being one doesn't question, because one hears them ringing. At that time, I knew nothing of the relation between the sound and the instrument that makes it, of the tension that is created between the flow of time and the stability of things, and I was a little self-centered skeptic, who worshipped general truths without applying them.

If I read a poem, I didn't doubt that it was right. If someone hymned the beauty of a certain meadow, then the beauty of that meadow was as dear to me as it was to the poet. I respected anything printed. I worshipped tradition. I didn't love any particular thing among all these generalities. I didn't value the subjects of one more highly than those of the others. I reckoned them all equally.

I liked Faust and I liked William Tell. I learned Shakespeare by heart, and Hölderlin, and even though I found disagreements, the differences between these two great figures were masked by a blanket of loftiness, dignity and beauty. Never would I have conducted myself in the same way as one of their heroes. And yet I believed that the poets and their heroes were in the right. I didn't know why Nathan the Wise had to behave quite so nobly. I felt pity for the tragedy of Shylock. But I thought I was an exception, not enviable, not even estimable, perhaps even an outcast. Everything that was preached and sung and believed was perfectly right, and suited the world. If someone sang the pains of love, I didn't really understand why he suffered so, but I believed such sufferings were normal.

Proverbs that didn't fit my distinctive, personal version of life still seemed to me to be wise, or at least founded on wise experiences and conclusions. Quotations that have over the years attained a wide currency, seemed to me to be the expression of a universally acknowledged wisdom, fixed over time . . .

. . . I attended university with indifference, even disappointment, without application and with none of the respect with which I had sometimes looked forward to it at school. I studied German and philosophy. In other words, I attended boring lectures by various professors. From what I had been told at school, I had imagined that studying at a university would be something noble, free and exalted, without any of the pettiness of school. But now I saw the professors not exerting themselves, lecturing for half an hour, sometimes dropping their lectures altogether, and that in the examinations most of them still arrogated to themselves the right to be strict, pedantic, much more pedantic than high school teachers, and be governed by personal feelings, preferences and biases. I looked back on high school with a certain amount of tenderness.

The occasional seminars, exercises in Gothic and Middle High German grammar, were just like high school lessons, only you weren't compelled to attend, and could walk out of the class if you'd had enough. There were fools among the students, ambitious and deluded . . .

STATIONMASTER FALLMERAYER

I

The strange story of the Austrian stationmaster Adam Fallmerayer deserves, without a doubt, to be written down for posterity. He lost his life, which, let it be said, would never have been a glittering one – and perhaps not even a satisfying one – in the most extraordinary way. On all known form, he was not an obvious candidate for an unusual fate. And yet, it reached him, it took him – and he even seemed to give himself up to it with a certain pleasure.

He had been a stationmaster since 1908. Shortly after taking up his post in the station of L., two hours south of Vienna, he married the daughter of a Chancery Councillor from Brünn – a good woman, slightly dim, no longer in the first flush of her youth. It was a "love match", as people used to say in those days, when marriages of convenience were the norm. His parents were no longer alive. In marrying, Fallmerayer followed not the voice of common sense but the cool prompting of his cool heart. He became a father – to twin girls. He had expected a son. It was in his nature to expect a son, and therefore to view the simultaneous arrival of two girls as an embarrassment and a setback, if not as an outright prank on the part of the Almighty. But as he was comfortably off and had pension rights, he grew reconciled to the bounty of nature, and, some three months after the birth, he began to love his children. To love them, in other words: to care for them with the traditional diligence of a father and a loyal official.

One day in March, 1914, Adam Fallmerayer, as usual, was sitting in his office. The telegraph was ticking away incessantly. Outside it was raining. It was a premature rain. Only a week before, they had had to shovel the snow off the tracks, and the trains had arrived and departed with appalling delays. Then, overnight, it had started raining. The snow vanished. And, over the little station, where the dazzling, unattainable splendor of Alpine snow seemed to have guaranteed the everlasting dominion of winter, there had now been for some days a kind of nondescript gray-blue haze, compounded of clouds, sky, rain and granite.

It was raining, and the air was warm. Stationmaster Fallmerayer had never known such an early spring. The big express trains that went south, to Merano, to Trieste, to Italy, never stopped at his tiny station. Twice daily, the expresses swept past Fallmerayer, who stepped out on to the platform in his bright red cap to greet them; they almost demoted the stationmaster to a signalman. The faces of the passengers in the big windows blended into one indistinct gray-white mass. Stationmaster Fallmerayer had never really been able to see the face of a passenger heading south. And "the South" was more than just a geographical term for the stationmaster. "The South" was the sea, a sea of sun, freedom and happiness.

Free rail travel for all the family was one of the perks enjoyed by senior officials on the Southern Railway. When the twins were just three years old, he had taken them to Bolzano. They had had to ride on a local train for an hour to reach the station where the proud expresses stopped, and there they got out, got on, got out again – and they still weren't in the South by any manner of means. The holiday lasted for four weeks. He saw rich people from all over the world – and it was as though the ones he saw were the very richest of all. For them, it wasn't a holiday. Their lives were one long holiday. And as far as he could see – far and wide – the richest people in the world were not afflicted with twins, much less twin girls. In fact: It was the rich who brought Southernness into the South. An official of the Southern Railway lived in a permanent North.

So he went back, and went back to his work. The telegraph ticked away incessantly. And the rain rained down.

Fallmerayer looked up from his desk. It was five o'clock in the afternoon. Although the sun hadn't gone down yet, what with the rain, it was already starting to feel dark. On the sloping glass roof over the platform, the rain drummed away just as incessantly as the ticking of the telegraph – and there was a cosy, incessant dialogue between man and nature. The platform, with its big blue paving stones, was kept dry by the glass roof. But the rails, and between them, the tiny pieces of gravel ballast, glistened – in spite of the darkness – in the damp magic of the rain.

Even though Stationmaster Fallmerayer was hardly of a fanciful cast of mind, this day still struck him for some reason as a fateful day, and, as he looked out of the window, he felt himself beginning to tremble. In thirty-six minutes the express to Meran was due to pass through. In thirty-six minutes – so Fallmerayer thought – the night would be at hand – a dreadful night. Upstairs, the twins were rampaging as always; he heard their footfall overhead, tripping, toddlerish and yet somehow brutal. He threw open the window. It wasn't cold any more. The spring was coming over the Alps. He could hear the whistles of the shunting locomotives, as he could every day, and the shouts of the railwaymen, and the dull clattering buffetings of coupled wagons. Even so – Fallmerayer thought – there was something distinctive about the locomotives' whistles today. He was an utterly ordinary man. And the oddest thing of all was the fact that on that day, in all these familiar, routine sounds he thought he heard the inexplicable voice of an uncommon fate. But on that day there occurred the overwhelming catastrophe whose consequences were to transform Adam Fallmerayer's life.

II

The express was already running slightly late when it left the town of B. Two minutes before it was due in L., because of some incorrectly set points, it ran into the back of a waiting freight train. The catastrophe had happened.

Hastily picking up a perfectly useless lantern that had been left on the platform, Stationmaster Fallmerayer ran along the tracks towards the place of the accident. He had felt the need to pick up some object or other. It seemed to him unacceptable to run towards the catastrophe, with empty, as it were, weaponless hands. He ran for ten minutes, without a coat, feeling the steady lash of the rain on his neck and shoulders.

When he reached the site of the catastrophe, people had already begun carrying out the dead, the hurt, the trapped. The darkness was falling more rapidly now, as though night itself were in a hurry to be there for the initial impact, and to magnify the terror. The fire brigade from the little town arrived with torches that crackled and sputtered in protest at the rain. Thirteen carriages lay wrecked on the rails. The driver and boiler-plate man – both of them dead – had already been taken away. Railwaymen and firemen and passengers were pulling at the wreckage with any tools they could find. The screams of the injured were pitiful, the rain poured down, the torches crackled in the wet. The stationmaster shivered as he stood in the rain. His teeth were chattering. He had the sense that he ought to do something like everyone else, but at the same time he was afraid he might not be allowed to help, because he might be to blame for the accident himself. There were a few of the railwaymen who recognized him and greeted him hurriedly in the midst of their work, and Fallmerayer tried to address them in a toneless voice that might equally have been a command and an apology. But none of them listened to him. He had never seemed to himself so utterly superfluous in the world. He was on the point of feeling sorry that he was not among the victims, when his aimlessly wandering eye lit on a woman who had just been brought out on a stretcher. There she lay, abandoned by the volunteers who had rescued her, her huge dark eyes staring at the torches nearest to her, draped from shoulders to hips in a silvery gray fur, and quite evidently not able to move. The indefatigable rain fell on her large, pale, wide face, and the torchlight flickered over it. The face itself shone wet and silvery in the magical play of flame and shadow. Her slim white hands lay on the fur, unmoving as well, two beautiful corpses. The stationmaster had the impression that this woman on her stretcher was resting on a great white island of calm, in the midst of a deafening sea of noise and clatter, and that she even spread more calm. And indeed it was as though all the rushing, bustling people were doing everything in their power to avoid the stretcher on which the woman was lying. Was she perhaps already dead? Was there nothing more to be done for her? Stationmaster Fallmerayer slowly approached the stretcher.

The woman was alive. She was unhurt. When Fallmerayer bent down to her, she said, without awaiting his question – almost as though she was afraid of his question – that there was nothing the matter with her, and that she thought she could get up. At worst she had lost her luggage. She was sure she could get up. And she made an effort to do so. Fallmerayer helped her. He took her fur in his left hand, and with his right he took the woman by the shoulder, waited for her to get up, laid the fur over her shoulders, and then his arm over the fur, and so they walked the few paces over the gravel and the rails, neither of them saying anything, to the hut of a pointsman nearby, up a few steps, into the dry and the warm.

"Just rest here for a minute or two," said Fallmerayer. "I have things to attend to outside. I'll be back very soon."

Even as he spoke, he knew he was lying. It was probably the first time in his life that he had lied. And yet, he didn't think twice about lying. Even though he wanted nothing more than to stay with the woman, it was too terrible to stand before her as a useless idler, with nothing to do, while outside a thousand hands were assisting and rescuing. So he plunged outside – and, to his own astonishment, he found he now had the courage and strength to assist and to rescue, to give a command here and a bit of advice there, and even though all the time he was assisting and rescuing and working, he was thinking about the woman in the hut, and even though the possibility that he might not see her later was ghastly and terrible to him, still he continued to occupy himself at the scene of the crash, afraid to return to her too soon, and so demonstrate his uselessness to the strange woman. He imagined her watching him and urging him on, and he soon regained confidence in his word and his judgment, and he proved to be a swift, resourceful and courageous helper.

So for two hours he worked, thinking all the time about the waiting woman. After the doctor and the medical staffs had tended to the injured, Fallmerayer set off back to the pointsman's hut. In passing, he told the doctor, whom he knew, that there was one more victim of the catastrophe sheltering there. Not without pride, he looked down at his scraped and bloodied hands and soiled uniform. He took the doctor to the pointsman's front room, and greeted the woman, who seemed not to have stirred from the spot, with the cheerful confident smile with which one greets an old friend.

"Kindly examine the lady!" he said to the doctor. And he himself walked outside.

He waited for a few minutes. The doctor came out and said: "A minor shock, nothing worse. She should probably stay here for a while. Can you put her up in your apartment?"

"Certainly, certainly!" replied Fallmerayer. And together they brought the woman to the station, up the steps, to the stationmaster's apartment.

"She'll be completely recovered in three or four days," said the doctor.

At that moment, Fallmerayer wished it could be many more days.

III

Fallmerayer gave the woman his room and his bed. The stationmaster's wife was kept shuttling between her and the children. Twice a day Fallmerayer put in an appearance. The twins were under strict orders to keep quiet.

A day later, all traces of the accident had been removed, the usual investigation set up, Fallmerayer questioned, and the culpable signalman removed from duty. Twice a day, as before, the expresses rushed past the saluting stationmaster.

The evening after the disaster, Fallmerayer learned the name of the woman: she was a Countess Walevska, a Russian who came from the Kiev region, and had been on her way from Vienna to Merano. Part of her luggage was found and returned to her: black and brown leather suitcases. They smelled of leather and an unfamiliar perfume, the scent of which now dominated Fallmerayer's entire apartment.

He slept – since he had given his own bed to the woman – not in the bedroom, next to Frau Fallmerayer, but downstairs, in his office. Or rather: he didn't sleep. He lay awake. In the morning, at nine o'clock, he entered the room where the woman lay. He asked her how she'd slept and whether she'd breakfasted, how she was feeling. Took a bunch of fresh violets to the vase on the sideboard, where the old ones had stood, took the old ones out, stood the new ones in fresh water, and stopped for a moment at the foot of the bed. In front of him lay the woman, on his pillows, under his covers. He muttered indistinctly. With her large dark eyes, and strong white face, as wide as a strange, sweet landscape, on the pillows, under the covers of the stationmaster, lay the woman. "Won't you sit down?" she said to him, every day, twice. She spoke German with a harsh and strange Russian accent, in a strange, low voice. All the splendor of distance and the unknown were in her throat.

Fallmerayer would not sit. "Excuse me, I'm busy," he said, turned on his heel, and walked out.

For six days it was like that. On the seventh, the doctor told the woman she could travel. Her husband was waiting for her in Merano. So she went, leaving behind in every room, and most especially in Fallmerayer's bed, an inextinguishable smell of leather and an unfamiliar perfume.

IV

That strange scent remained in Fallmerayer's apartment, in his memory, yes, one could even say, in his heart, for much longer than the accident. And in the ensuing weeks, as the precise cause of the accident and a detailed account of the events were established in the course of the usual interminable public inquiry, before which Fallmerayer twice had to give evidence, he did not stop thinking about the woman, and, as if intoxicated by the scent she had left around him and on him, he gave almost incoherent answers to the most elementary questions. Had his duty not been comparatively straightforward, and had he not himself over the years become virtually a mechanical extension of that duty, he could not, in all conscience, have continued to perform it. Secretly, he was hoping for news of the woman with every post. He had no doubt that she would write, as was only proper, to thank him for his hospitality. And one day, a large dark blue letter arrived from Italy. Countess Walevska wrote that she and her husband had traveled further south. She was presently in Rome. She and her husband intended to go as far as Sicily. A day later, a pretty basket of fruit arrived for Fallmerayer's twins, and Countess Walevska's husband sent the stationmaster's wife a bunch of delicately scented pale pink roses. It had taken her a long time, wrote the Countess, to find time to thank her kind hosts, but even after her arrival in Merano she had still felt shaky, and in need of rest. Fallmerayer took the fruit and the flowers straight upstairs. The letter, though it had come the previous day, he kept back a little longer. The fruit and the roses carried a strong aroma of the South, but to Fallmerayer the Countess's letter was still more aromatic. It was a short letter. Fallmerayer quickly knew it by heart. He knew the exact position of each word. Written in purple ink, in beautiful, flowing strokes, the letters were like a beautiful swarm of exotic, slender, exquisitely plumed birds, soaring against a deep blue sky. The Countess had signed herself "Anya Walevska". He had long desired to know the first name of the woman, and had never dared to ask her, as though her first name were one of her hidden physical charms. And now that he knew it, he felt for a time as though she had made him privy to a sweet confidence. Out of jealousy, and to keep its possession for himself, he decided not to show his wife the letter for another two days. Ever since he'd found out Anya's first name, it seemed to him that that of his wife – it was Klara – was ugly. When he watched Klara's indifferent hands unfolding the letter, the memory of the writer's hands flooded back to him – as he had first seen them, motionless hands against her fur, two shimmering silver hands. I should have kissed them then and there, he thought. "What a nice note," said his wife, and laid it aside. Her eyes were steely blue and dutiful, she didn't even register any concern. Frau Klara Fallmerayer was able to transform even her concerns into duties, and to find a certain satisfaction in sorrow. All at once Fallmerayer – never previously given to such speculations or insights – thought he understood that. And that night he claimed some urgent official task, steered clear of their shared room, and lay down in his office downstairs, trying to convince himself that up above him the stranger was still sleeping in his own bed.

The days went by, the months. A couple of colorful postcards winged their way north from Sicily, with hurried greetings. Summer came, a hot summer. As the holiday season approached, Fallmerayer decided not to go anywhere. He sent his wife and children up for a holiday in the mountains. He stayed behind and worked. It was the first time he had been apart from his wife since their wedding. He had hoped for too much from this period of solitude. It wasn't until he found himself alone that he realized that that wasn't what he had wanted at all. He combed through all the drawers, searching for the woman's letter. But he couldn't find it anywhere. Frau Fallmerayer probably had thrown it away long ago.

His wife and children returned, July was almost over.

Then the general mobilization was at hand.

V

Fallmerayer was ensign in the reserves with the 21st Rifles. As his job had some strategic importance, it would have been possible for him to ask, as a number of his colleagues did, to stay in civilian life a while longer. Instead, Fallmerayer put on his uniform, packed his case, hugged his children, kissed his wife and joined his regiment. He handed over his duty to his deputy. Frau Fallmerayer wept, the twins cheered because they had never seen their father in army uniform before. Of course, Frau Fallmerayer did not fail to be proud of her husband as well – but only in the final hour of his departure. She kept back her tears. Her blue eyes shone with bitter conscientiousness.

As for the stationmaster himself, he didn't feel the grim finality of these hours until he found himself in a train compartment with a few of his comrades. And even then, he felt an unexpected cheerfulness set him apart from the others. They were all officers in the reserve. Each of them had left behind a home and loved ones. Each of them was, just then, a whole-hearted and committed soldier.

And at the same time, each of them was an inconsolable father, an inconsolable son. Only Fallmerayer had the sense that the mobilization had come along just in time to get him out of a hopeless situation. Of course, he felt sorry for the twins. And for his wife. Certainly, for his wife too. But while, when his comrades spoke of home, they revealed the deep tenderness they felt in every word and gesture, Fallmerayer felt that if he was to match them, he had, if not exactly to lie, then at least to put an exaggerated concern in his voice and eyes, when he spoke about his loved ones. Actually, he would rather have spoken about Countess Walevska than about his family. He forced himself to remain silent. And it seemed to him he was lying in a double sense: firstly, because he wasn't talking about what really moved him, and secondly, because when he did mention wife and children, they were much more remote from him then than Countess Walevska, a woman from a hostile nation. He began to feel a degree of contempt for himself.

VI

He joined the regiment. He was sent to the front. He saw action. He was a brave soldier. He wrote the usual matter-of-fact field postcards home. He was decorated, was promoted to lieutenant. He was wounded. He was put in a field-hospital. He was offered home-leave. He turned it down, and went back to the front. He fought in the East. In the free time left him in between battles, troop inspection, advances, he began to teach himself Russian from books he'd happened to pick up. He was passionate about it. Surrounded by the stink of gas and the smell of blood, in the rain, in the swamp, in the mud, in the sweat of the living, in the reek of the moldering dead, Fallmerayer pursued the strange scent of leather and the unfamiliar perfume of the woman who had once lain in his bed, on his pillows, under his covers. He learned the woman's mother-tongue, and he imagined he was speaking to her, in her language.

He learned endearments, sweet nothings, love-whisperings in Russian. He talked to her. Separated from her by the whole of the World War, he talked to her. He questioned Russian prisoners. With hearing sharpened hundred-fold, he took in the faintest nuances, and his fluent tongue reproduced them. With every new sound of the foreign language he was learning, he was coming closer to the strange woman. He knew nothing more about her than what he'd last seen: a dashed-off greeting and a dashed-off signature on a banal postcard. But he felt her living for him; waiting for him; before long he would speak to her.

When his battalion was transferred to the Southern Front, he found himself – because of his knowledge of Russian – seconded to one of the regiments that, shortly afterwards, were to make up the so-called Army of Occupation. First, Fallmerayer was employed as an interpreter at the divisional HQ, and then at "information and intelligence". Eventually, he found himself near Kiev.

VII

Of course, he had remembered the name Solovienki. More than remembered it: the name had become familiar, almost a part of himself.

It was easy enough to find out the name of the estate that belonged to the Walevski family. It was called Solovki, and it was some three versts south of Kiev. Fallmerayer felt a sweet and painful clutch of excitement. He felt endlessly grateful to fortune for taking him off to the War and now bringing him here, and at the same time he felt a nameless panic at whatever it might bring next. The war, the offensive, his wound, the chance of death: what wishy-washy experiences these were, compared to what he was facing now. Everything to date had been nothing more than a – who knows, inadequate – preparation for seeing the woman again. Was he really prepared for every eventuality? Would she be at home?

Wouldn't the invasion of the enemy army have driven her back to some more secure place? And if she was living at home, would her husband not be with her? There was nothing for it but to go there and see.

Fallmerayer had a carriage made ready, and he set off.

It was quite early one morning in May. He rolled along in a light two-wheeler, past flowering meadows, on a winding, sandy lane, through an almost uninhabited stretch of country. Troops were tramping and clattering around, doing their usual drills. Hidden up in the bright and lofty blue arc of heaven, the skylarks were trilling. Dense dark patches of pine forest alternated with the cheerful shimmer of silver birches. The fitful morning wind carried the sound of soldiers singing in their far-distant encampments. Fallmerayer thought of his childhood, of the nature he was used to in his own country. He had been born and raised not far from the station where he had served until the beginning of the war. His father before him had worked for the railways, as a junior official, a depot manager. All Fallmerayer's childhood, and his subsequent life as an adult, had been filled with as many of the sounds and smells of trains as of nature. The locomotives whistled duets with the birds. The heavy smell of anthracite overlaid the breathing of the fields in spring. The gray smoke of the locomotives blended with the blue clouds over the mountains to form a single fog of sweet melancholy and yearning. How different was this world here: it was at once cheerful and sad, no more gentle slopes with hidden bounty, the lilacs sparse, no full drooping clusters behind neatly painted fences. Low huts with low, wide roofs of straw like hoods over them, tiny villages, adrift in the huge distances, almost hidden on the vast plains. How different were all the different countries! Was it like that with human hearts too? Will she understand me? Fallmerayer asked himself. Will she understand me? – And the closer he came to the Walevski estate, the more brightly the question burned in his heart. The closer he came, the more certain he was that he would find the woman at home. Soon, he was quite convinced that he was only a matter of minutes away from seeing her again. Yes, she was at home.

At the beginning of the little avenue of birches that lined the final climb up to the house, Fallmerayer leaped down from his carriage. He wanted to take the last few steps on foot, to spin them out a little longer still. An old retainer asked him what he had come about. To see the Countess, replied Fallmerayer. Then he would go and tell his mistress there was someone to see her, said the man, and he went off slowly, and in a little while came back. Yes, the Countess was at home, and would receive him.

The Countess of course didn't recognize Fallmerayer. She supposed he was just the latest of a succession of military visitors she had had to receive of late. She asked him to sit. Her voice, low, dark and strange, at once shocked him and seemed deeply familiar, a familiar thrill, a well-known, rapturously welcome, yearningly overdue terror. "I'm Fallmerayer!" said the officer. – Of course the name meant nothing to her. "You don't remember," he began again, "I'm the stationmaster in L." She stepped nearer, took his hands, and there it was, he smelled it again, the scent that had followed him for time immemorial, surrounded him, cossetted him, hurt and comforted him. For an instant her hands lay in his.

"Oh, you must have so much to tell me!" exclaimed the Countess. He told her in the most cursory terms how he had got on. "And what about your wife, and your children?" asked the Countess. "I haven't seen them!" said Fallmerayer. "I didn't take any leave."

A silence ensued. They looked at one another. The rich, golden sun of early morning shone into the broad, low-ceilinged, white-washed, almost bare room. Flies buzzed around the windows. Fallmerayer contemplated the broad, pale face of the Countess. Perhaps she did understand him. She got up to draw a curtain in front of the middle of the three windows. "Too bright for you?" she asked. "I like it dark!" replied Fallmerayer. She returned to the low tea-table, shook a little bell, the old servant appeared; she ordered tea. The silence between them was undisturbed: in fact, it deepened, until the tea was brought. Fallmerayer smoked. She was pouring the tea, when he suddenly asked: "Where's your husband?"

She finished pouring the tea, as though she had to consider her reply very carefully. "Why, at the front, of course!" she said at last. "I haven't had any news of him for three months. Correspondence isn't possible any more, obviously!" "Are you very worried about him?" asked Fallmerayer. "Of course I am," she replied, "just as your wife is about you, I expect." "I'm so sorry, I wasn't thinking," said Fallmerayer. He stared into his teacup.

She had refused, the Countess continued, to leave the house. She was not about to flee, either from her own peasants, or from the enemy. She was living there with four servants, a couple of horses and a dog. Her money and her jewels were —. She groped for the word, she had forgotten how to say "buried" in German, and she pointed to the ground. Fallmerayer said it in Russian. "Do you speak Russian, then?" she asked. "Yes," he said, "I learned it, learned it in the army." And he added, in Russian: "It was for you, to be able to talk to you, that I learned Russian."

She told him he spoke it remarkably well, as though his last sentence had been nothing but a linguistic exercise. Thus she sought to defuse his declaration, turn it into a meaningless grammatical display. But her response showed him that she had taken his meaning.

I'll go now, he thought. And he promptly stood up. Without waiting for her invitation, and knowing that she would put the correct construction upon his unmannerliness, he said: "I'll be back!" — She said nothing. He kissed her hand and left.

VIII

He left — and he no longer had any doubt that his destiny was beginning to fulfill itself. It is a law, he said to himself. It is not possible for one person to be so irresistibly drawn to another, and for the other to remain indifferent. Her feelings are the same as mine. And if she doesn't love me yet, then she soon will.

Fallmerayer discharged his duties with the habitual unquestioning efficiency of an official and an army officer. He took the decision to ask for a couple of weeks off, for the first time since he had joined up. His promotion to first lieutenant was imminent. He decided to wait for that to take effect first.

Two days later, he drove out to Solovki again. He was told that Countess Walevska was out, and not expected to return till noon. "Well," he said, "I'll just wait in the garden." And because no one dared throw him out, he was let into the garden behind the house.

He looked up at the two rows of windows. He sensed that the Countess was at home, and had merely pretended to be out. And indeed, he thought he caught a flash of a pale dress, now in this window, now in that. He waited patiently, positively serenely.

When it struck twelve from the nearby clock tower, he went back up to the house. There was Countess Walevska. She was just coming down the stairs, in a tight, black, high-necked dress, with a necklace of baby seed pearls round her neck, and a silver bracelet over her tight left cuff. It looked to Fallmerayer as though she had put on a suit of armor on his account – and the fire that had always burned in his heart for her, now suddenly acquired an extra little flame. Love lit new lights. Fallmerayer smiled. "I waited a long time," he said, "but as you know, I was glad to wait. I looked up at your windows from the garden, and persuaded myself I was blessed with the occasional glimpse of you. The time passed."

Did he want some lunch, asked the Countess, seeing as it was midday. Yes, he replied, he was hungry. But then, of the three courses that were served, he took only the most ridiculously tiny amounts.

The Countess talked about the outbreak of war. How they had hurried back from Cairo. Of her husband's guards regiment. Of his comrades. Then about her childhood. Her father and mother. How she had grown up. It was as though she were desperately casting about for things to say, and didn't even care if some of it was made up – anything to keep the taciturn Fallmerayer from speaking. He stroked his little blond mustache, and gave every appearance of paying close attention. But in fact he was far more attentive to her fragrance than to what she was saying. His pores were listening. And anyway: her speech was scented too, the words she spoke. He could guess all she had to say. Nothing about her could remain concealed from him. What could she conceal from him? He could see right through her puritanical dress. He could feel his hands yearning for her, his hands felt homesick for the woman. When they got up, he said he thought he might stay awhile, he had the day off, and he would be taking a much longer furlough in a few days' time, once he'd been promoted to first lieutenant. Where was he thinking of going? asked the Countess. "Nowhere!" said Fallmerayer. "I'd stay here with you!" She invited him to stay as long as he liked, today, and in future. But now she had to excuse herself, he had some business about the house. If he cared to stay, there were plenty of rooms, they wouldn't get in each other's way.

He took his leave. As she couldn't stay with him, he said, he preferred to go back to town.

When he climbed into his carriage, she was standing on the porch, in her strict black dress, with her broad, white face above it – and as he picked up the whip, she lifted her hand a little way, in a half repressed gesture of farewell.

IX

Perhaps a week after this visit, the newly promoted First Lieutenant Adam Fallmerayer was given his furlough. He told all his comrades that he was going home. Then, he went to the house of the Walevskis, moved into a ground floor room that had been made ready for him, took his meals every day with the lady of the house, talked with her about this and that, indifferent, remote subjects, told her about the front, didn't care what he talked about, and in turn didn't listen to her when she spoke. At night, he didn't sleep, just as he hadn't slept those years before at home in the station building, during those six nights the Countess had spent in his room, overhead. Once more, he had a sense of her over him at night, over his head, over his heart.

One night – it was humid, and a good, relieving rain began to fall – Fallmerayer got up, dressed and went outside. A yellow oil lamp lit the wide staircase. The house was silent, the night was silent, the rain was silent, it came down as on soft sand, and its monotonous melody was the sound of the nocturnal silence. A step creaked. Fallmerayer heard it, even though he was outside the front door. He had left the heavy door open. And he saw Countess Walevska coming down the stairs. She was dressed as if for the day. He bowed silently. She came up to him. They remained in silence for a second or two. Fallmerayer could hear his heart beating. He thought he could hear her heart beating as loud as his own – and in time with it. The air seemed all of a sudden to have become heavy again, not a breath of wind came in through the door. Fallmerayer said: "Let's walk in the rain, I'll get you a coat!" And without waiting to hear what she would say, he plunged into his room, came out with his own coat, and laid it round the shoulders of the woman, just as he once had laid her fur, on that one, unforgettable night of the disaster, and then he laid his arm over the coat. And so they walked out into the night and the rain.

They walked down the avenue of birches. In spite of the darkness and the damp, the frail reedy stems glinted silver, as though lit up from within. And as though the silvery sheen of these tenderest of trees awoke a corresponding tenderness in Fallmerayer, he pressed his arm more tightly around the woman's shoulder, he felt, through the stiff, sodden material, the yielding kindness of her body, briefly he thought he could feel it inclining towards him, even press itself against him, but a second later, there was a wide space between them once more. His hand left her shoulder, moved up to her wet hair, brushed over her wet ear, touched her wet face. And a moment later, they both stopped as one, turned to one another, clasped each other, the coat slipped from her shoulders and fell heavily to the ground – and so, in the rain and the night, they pressed their faces together, their mouths together, and they kissed and kissed.

X

There was one occasion when First Lieutenant Fallmerayer was earmarked for transfer to Shmerinka, but, after a lot of trouble, he was able to stay where he was. He was absolutely determined that he wouldn't go anywhere. Every morning and evening, he blessed the war and the occupation. Nothing terrified him as much as a sudden return of peace. He thought of Count Walevski as long dead, either killed in action, or murdered by mutinous Communist troops. The war simply had to go on indefinitely, and Fallmerayer for his part would happily serve indefinitely in this place and in this capacity.

Never again peace on earth.

Fallmerayer had fallen prey to exuberance, as happens in the case of people in whom excess of passion dazzles the senses, stifles insight, fools the mind. He thought there was just himself in the world, himself and the object of his love. But of course, quite heedless of him, the great and inscrutable wheel of the world was rolling on. The Revolution came. Fallmerayer, the amorous first lieutenant, hadn't seen it coming.

Even so, as is often the way in situations of extreme peril, the sudden stroke of the hour of destiny roused his sleepy brain, and with renewed alertness he saw that he had to save the lives of his beloved and himself, and above all, to rescue their union. And since, what with the confusion brought on by the sudden turn of events, and thanks to his military rank and his specialist line of service, there were still a few means of assistance and even some vestiges of authority left to him, he wasted no time in deploying them; and so, in the space of the few days in which the Austrian Army collapsed, the Germans pulled out of the Ukraine, the Red Russians began their advance, and a resentful peasantry once again began to loot and burn the houses of the estate owners, he was able to organize two well-protected vehicles for the use of Countess Walevska, half a dozen loyal troops with guns and ammunition, and supplies to last about a week.

One evening – the Countess at this stage was still refusing to leave her house – Fallmerayer turned up with his cars and soldiers, and with rough words and almost brute force, compelled his lover to retrieve the jewels she had buried in the garden, and get ready to leave. It took all night. When the dull and rainy late autumn day finally dawned, they were finished, and their flight could begin. The soldiers traveled in the larger of the two vehicles under the canvas roof. A military driver chauffeured the other car, with the Countess and Fallmerayer in the back. They had decided not to head west, along with everyone else, but south. It was a safe bet that all the roads west would be choked with returning or fleeing troops. And who knew what further obstacles they would face when they reached the borders of the newly created states in the west of Russia! It was even possible – and this turned out later to be indeed the case – that new wars would erupt in the western successor states. And then there was the fact that Countess Walevska had wealthy and powerful relatives in the Crimea and in the Caucasus. Even under the changed circumstances, they could still turn to them for help, should that become necessary. And most important of all: a profound instinct told the two lovers that at a time when the whole of the earth was plunged into chaos, the eternal sea must be the only place that would guarantee them freedom. Therefore the sea became their first objective. They offered the men a sizable sum in pure gold to escort them to the Caucasus. And, in an excited but confident frame of mind, they drove off.

As Fallmerayer had prepared everything very thoroughly, and had allowed for all sorts of possible and unlikely chances and mischances as well, they were able to reach Tbilisi in very quick time – no more than four days. There, they paid off their escorts, keeping only the driver as far as Baku. A good number of Russians from the aristocratic and propertied classes had also thought to flee south to the Crimea. In spite of their original intentions, the couple avoided contact with the Countess's friends and relatives. Instead, Fallmerayer endeavored to find a ship that would take them out of Baku to the nearest safe country. Inevitably, they encountered other families, more or less acquainted with the Walevskis, also, like Fallmerayer, looking for a ship to carry them to safety – and, equally inevitably, the Countess found herself having to give false information about Fallmerayer, and about the nature of their relationship. In the end, they were forced to acknowledge that they could not effect their planned flight alone, but only in concert with others similarly placed to themselves. So they came to an understanding with a group of eight other people, who wanted to leave Russia by sea, finally they found a trustworthy captain, with a rather unreliable looking steamer, and made first for Constantinople, from where there were still regular sailings on to France and Italy.

Three weeks later, Fallmerayer and his beloved reached Monte Carlo, where the Walevskis had bought a small villa before the war. Now Fallmerayer thought he had reached the pinnacle of happiness and life. He was loved by the most beautiful woman in the world. More: he loved the most beautiful woman in the world. She, whose image had lived in him so powerfully for years, was always by his side. He himself lived in her. When they were together – and there was hardly an hour of the day in which they were apart – he saw himself hourly reflected in her eyes. The woman who, only a little while ago, had been too proud to listen to the voice of her heart and of her senses, this woman now had no other aim or desire in life than to be the mistress of Fallmerayer, a stationmaster of the

Austrian Southern Railway, his child, his adored, his world. Countess Walevska was as perfectly happy as Fallmerayer. The storm of passion that had begun to grow in Fallmerayer's heart from the fateful night of the accident at the station of L., now swept up the woman as well, bore her off, took her thousands of miles from home and habit, from the reality she had lived in to that point. She was transported to a wild and unknown land of feeling and thought. And this land was her new home. The things that went on in the big, disorderly world failed to concern them. The possessions she had with her were enough to absolve them of the need to work for several years. In any case, they were not interested in the future. If they visited a casino, then it was out of sheer exuberance. They could afford to lose money – and lose money they did, in accordance with the proverb that says lucky in love, unlucky with money. Their losses delighted them; as though they needed that old superstition to reinforce their love. But like all happy people, they were inclined to test their happiness, so that, if it held, they might find themselves even happier.

XI

Even though Countess Walevska had her Fallmerayer all to herself, she still was incapable – as many women are incapable – of loving for long, without fearing the loss of her beloved (for often it is a woman's fear of losing a man that heightens her love and her passion for him). So, one day, even though Fallmerayer had given her no cause for any anxiety on that score, she began to ask him to divorce his wife and renounce his children and his job. Straight away, Fallmerayer wrote a letter to his cousin Heinrich, who was a senior official in the Education Ministry in Vienna, saying that he had irrevocably broken with his past life. He had no desire to travel to Vienna in person, but was eager that a well-qualified lawyer be found to expedite the divorce in his absence.

By strange coincidence – came Heinrich's reply a few days later – two years had just elapsed since Fallmerayer had been listed as missing. Since he had at no time given any sign of life, his wife and few remaining relatives all supposed him to have died. Long ago, L. had had a new stationmaster. Long ago, Frau Fallmerayer had taken the twins to live with her parents in Brünn. It seemed simplest to remain silent, always assuming that Fallmerayer didn't run into difficulties over passport or the like at any of the Austrian representations abroad.

Fallmerayer thanked his cousin, promised he would continue to write to him from time to time, and enjoined him to silence. He showed the correspondence to his beloved. Her mind was set at rest. She no longer feared Fallmerayer might leave. But, once gripped by the mysterious fear that Nature sows in the hearts of such ardent and passionate women (perhaps, who knows, to guarantee the future of the world), Countess Walevska desired to have a child with her lover – and from the moment the wish arose in her, she began to give herself over to imagining the excellent qualities of the child they would have together; she was, in a sense, devoting herself to it already. Impulsive and gay and quick as she was, still she saw in her lover – whose infinite love it had taken her own charming impetuousness to awaken – the embodiment of reasoned and thoughtful superiority. And nothing seemed to her more important than to bring a child into the world, a child that would unite her own qualities with those admirable traits of his.

She fell pregnant. Fallmerayer, like most men in his situation, as grateful to fate as to the particular woman who helped to bring it about, was beside himself with joy. There were no bounds now to his tenderness. He saw his own character and his own love unopposably confirmed. Life hadn't yet begun. The baby was due in six months. Life would begin in six months.

In the meantime, Fallmerayer had turned forty-five.

XII

Then one day a stranger turned up at the villa of the Walevskis, a Caucasian by the name of Kirdzashvilli, who informed the Countess that by some providential chance, and probably with the help of the icon of St. Procopius in the monastery of Pokrozhni as well, the Count had managed to survive the dual perils of war and the Bolsheviks, and was even now on his way to Monte Carlo. He expected to be there in about fourteen days. He himself, the envoy, and erstwhile Ataman Kirdzashvilli, was on his way to Belgrade on behalf of the Czarist counter-revolution. He had now discharged his duty, and would go.

Countess Walevska presented Fallmerayer to the stranger as the faithful steward of the house. During the Caucasian's visit, Fallmerayer said not a word. He escorted the visitor out of the house for a short distance. When he returned, he felt for the first time in his life a sharp sudden stabbing in his chest.

His mistress was sitting at the window, reading.

"You can't let him find us here!" said Fallmerayer. "We have to run away!"

"I'm going to tell him everything," she replied. "We'll stay!"

"You're carrying my child!" said Fallmerayer. "It's an impossible situation."

"You'll stay here till he comes! I know him! He'll understand!" replied the woman.

From that time forth, they didn't exchange another word about Count Walevski. They waited.

They waited, till one day a telegram came from him. He was coming on such and such an evening. They went to meet him at the station.

Two guards lifted him out of the carriage, and a porter came along with a wheelchair. He was put in the wheelchair. He held out his long, bony, yellow face towards his wife, she bent down and kissed him. With long, bony hands that were blue with cold, he kept trying, unsuccessfully, to pull a couple of brown rugs over his knees. Fallmerayer came to his aid.

Fallmerayer looked at the Count's long, yellow, bony face, with its sharp nose and bright eyes and the thin lips under the drooping black mustache. The Count was wheeled along the platform like one of his many pieces of luggage. His wife followed the wheelchair, Fallmerayer walked in front.

He had to be lifted into the car – Fallmerayer and the chauffeur did it together. The wheelchair was made fast to the roof.

He had to be carried into the villa. Fallmerayer took him by the head and shoulders, a servant took his feet.

"I'm hungry," said Count Walevski.

When they laid the table, they learned that Walevski was unable to feed himself. His wife had to feed him. And when, following a grim silent dinner, it was time for bed, the Count said: "I'm tired. Put me to bed."

Countess Walevska, the servant and Fallmerayer bundled the Count up the stairs to his room on the first floor, where a bed had been made ready.

"Good night!" said Fallmerayer. He saw, out of the corner of his eye, his mistress plump up the pillows, and sit down on the side of the bed.

XIII

And then Fallmerayer left; nothing has ever been heard of him since.

THE TRIUMPH OF BEAUTY

I

I have a high regard for the insight and perspicacity of my old friend Dr. Skovronnek. For more than twenty-five years, he has been a doctor at a famous spa for women, where the miraculous waters are said to cure such conditions as infertility, hysteria and ailments of the womb. Or so my friend, Dr. Skovronnek, claims, at any rate. In fact, he then goes on to speak, with almost the same degree of conviction, of the equally miraculous, if more readily explicable, effect of the presence of numbers of young, healthy, and love-hungry men on the comfort-needing patients at the spa every year. With the punctuality of certain species of migrating birds, the young men appear in the spa at the "beginning of the season", to give the healing waters a run for their money. Over the course of a quarter of a century, my friend, Dr. Skovronnek, has had every opportunity to become acquainted with the physical and mental ailments of women. Let us allow he had just thirty patients per season. Over twenty-five years, that would still mean that he had become closely acquainted with no fewer than seven hundred and fifty women. Ample justification, in my view, for holding my friend's judgment in high esteem.

For which reason I am in the habit of sending all husbands who tell me of the (real or imaginary) sufferings of their wives to Dr. Skovronnek. He treats the husbands, who suffer more at the hands of their wives, than the wives do from their illnesses, as his patients too – and he is right to do so. Yes, I am inclined to view my friend as a doctor for husbands first, and a gynecologist second – although my friend will have none of it, and claims my saying so will harm his reputation. I know him, though. And I know that the father-confessorly gentleness with which he inspects the hearts and kidneys of his sick ladies, masks a concern for the gentlemen behind each of his lady patients. Anyone who has examined so many women must come to feel a compassionate solidarity with their husbands.

Anyway, it so happened that I advised a friend of mine, the engineer M., to go and see Dr. Skovronnek; on his own, to begin with, without his sick wife, whom the engineer had told me about in all possible detail. The engineer was a young man, married for just a couple of years, no children. After a year of happy marriage – so-called – his wife had begun to complain about pains in her head, her back, her belly, her throat, her nose, her eyes, her feet. I know one shouldn't generalize, but it is my experience that engi-neers – and in particular bridge-builders, like my friend – don't understand anything about women. But maybe there are excep-tions. However, the bridge-builder in question was utterly panic-stricken, as every good man must be when he sees a woman in pain, or even just in tears. (It is the panic of the healthy con-fronted by the sick, of the strong faced by weakness. There is nothing worse than the mixture of love, sympathy and concern for a woman you love and feel sorry for. I always say a man is better off with a healthy Xanthippe than an ailing Juliet.) And so I counseled the engineer to look up Dr. Skovronnek.

At the engineer's express wish, and my own to the contrary, I was present at the consultation. I found myself more or less in the position of someone hearing his neighbor saying things of an embarrassing private nature, just the other side of a flimsy hotel partition – and unable to do anything to prevent it. I tried to distract myself. I took a newspaper with me. However, the professional curiosity of the writer prevailed over any private efforts at private discretion, and, without wishing to listen, I listened, as it were with my professional ear, to all manner of things that I cannot possibly divulge here and now.

Dr. Skovronnek himself said little. He listened. Finally, he dismissed the engineer, telling him to have his wife make an appointment.

The engineer left us. And, not understanding my friend's taciturnity, I began to feel worried myself about the engineer's wife, and asked:

"I say, is it really as bad as all that, what he told you about his wife? Why didn't you say anything?" "It's neither bad nor good!" replied the doctor. "It is as it is. If I hadn't recently been through certain experiences, I wouldn't have been quite so taciturn. But ever since, I've stopped feeling sorry for the husbands of ailing wives. It's simply not possible to treat incurables. You cannot keep alive someone who is set on killing himself, and the husbands of certain women I view as incurable suicides. To show you what I mean, I'll tell you the story. You should write it down one day."

And Dr. Skovronnek began:

II

"Many years ago, when I was just an obscure general practitioner in a middle-sized town, a young man came to see me in my practice. I didn't have many patients. Some days I had none at all. I sat there, reading thrillers and waiting. You will say I would have been better employed reading medical textbooks, but my respect for science and for the discoveries of my distinguished colleagues has always lagged behind my interest in criminals and detective work. You will appreciate that an underemployed doctor is bound to find an unusual patient quite fascinating. Even so, I let him stay in the waiting-room, just as any other idle doctor would have done. I finally admitted the young man after a few minutes – (and, believe me, I suffered more from impatience than he did). Impatience, as you know, is a dangerous illness, which may even have fatal consequences, as suicide. Well, I mastered myself. The more delightedly I feasted my eyes on the patient when I did finally admit him. Quite automatically, I scanned his form and features for signs of visible affliction, and his clothing for signs of possible wealth. Straight away, I saw he was a soothing sort of patient. He evidently belonged not merely to a moneyed class, but even a little better – and nor did he have a dangerous illness that would probably have obliged me to pass him on to a specialist. He was healthy, well-made, sinewy, handsome and tanned, he had a lean, attractive face, bright eyes, a fine neck, an arched forehead, strong, slender hands, he was both shy and self-confident, all in all what you call well-bred. I took him to be a civil servant of good background and mediocre gifts, and probably afflicted with one of those illnesses that in our society are described as *galant*.

I wasn't far wrong. He was a young diplomat, on the staff of our embassy in London, the son of a well-known arms-manufacturer – a little better off, then, than I had thought, looking at him – and his affliction was indeed one of a *galant* nature. He had come to me at a peradventure. He had no wish to talk to his parents' doctor. He therefore got out a list of doctors, put a pin on a name – it happened to be mine – and came and looked me up right away. I treated him cheerfully and attentively. I liked him. I told him stories. When he was better, he admitted he was almost sorry not to have some other, harmless condition to take to me while he was on holiday. I examined him, unfortunately he was the picture of health. I asked him if he had any passions or hobbies. 'No, I don't,' he said, 'just music.' Music, as you know, is my passion as well. Well, to cut a long story short: music first gave us a common interest, then it made us friends."

Dr. Skovronnek paused. Then he said: "We remained good friends until his death."

"Oh. He must have died young, then? And suddenly?"

"Young and lingeringly and from the deadliest and (pardon me) commonest of all afflictions: he died of a woman, his own wife . . ."

III

"Our friendship didn't end with his holiday and subsequent return to London. On the contrary: distance strengthened our friendship. We wrote each other almost every week. My practice was dire; I often spent hours waiting for patients, and reading thrillers. One day, he wrote suggesting I come and stay with him in England for a week or two.

I traveled to London. I didn't speak a word of English, so I was forced to look to my friend for help. You can always identify an 'upper class' character, because he will make it impossible for you to feel gratitude for things that he does, let alone express it to him. You're almost never in a position to say 'Thank you very much!' to a real gentleman. Somehow, he makes it appear that his little kindnesses and services are for his own benefit, and that your helplessness is really to his advantage. That's the way it was with my friend. I have never known a more distinguished host. His discreet behavior towards me in time became such that I sometimes even had the sense that he felt himself under some obligation to me. Yes, he put me to shame. I thought of the way I'd left him sitting in my waiting-room, out of silly professional vanity, the first time he'd come to see me, and one day I confessed to him that I'd made him wait for no reason. He didn't understand what I was telling him, or affected not to understand. 'I expect,' he said, I remember it very well, 'I expect you did have something to do, only you've forgotten what it was.

The same thing happens with me, too. I leave people to wait a bit, even if I'm not really doing anything. I need to collect myself before I can receive a visitor. There's nothing unusual about that.'

If I'd previously thought of him as averagely gifted, over time I became convinced that his positively emphatic mediocrity was nothing more or less than modesty on the grandest scale, as is often the case with people of good breeding. He didn't have the faintest ambition. He would regularly afford me insights into his occupation. And time and again I saw that he always did his utmost not to distinguish himself at the expense of his colleagues. He was the opposite of the ambitious diplomat. He must have been aware of all the imbecilities that his colleagues got up to, but he fell over himself not to appear any cleverer than they were. It is the plebeian who is ambitious. The true gentleman is anonymous. There is a force in aristocracy which is greater than the light of fame, the glitter of success, the power of the victor. Ambition, as I say, is a quality of the plebeian. The plebeian is in a hurry. He can't wait to attain honor, power, fame, respect. The nobleman, though, can afford to wait, yes, even to let others go ahead of him.

And that's what my friend was like. Even though I was older than him, I started to feel in awe of him. I revered him and adored him.

A week before I left to go home, he told me he'd fallen in love.

Well, it's perfectly natural for a young man to fall in love. Even I, as you know, in the days before I became a 'hard-boiled' gynecologist, have been in love once or twice. But as he was my friend, I felt alarmed. I guessed that this refined character must be in the grip of a powerful passion, and that it was in his nature to endow whoever it was he thought he was in love with, with the finest of his own qualities. If, as the proverb says, love makes ordinary people blind, imagine what it does to distinguished and select people!

So I was alarmed. And I told my friend I wanted to meet his beloved.

'You'll fall in love with her yourself,' he replied – with all the naivety of lovers who believe the object of their own passion is irresistible to all.

Well, then! And so we all met up together one evening.

She was what they call a young society lady. Pretty, yes, I'll grant you! A blonde virgin with sky blue eyes, strong teeth, a long and rather unexciting chin, and a strikingly good figure. Of course she had pretty manners, as they say. She was from a good background. Of course she was in love with my friend – and why wouldn't she be? In love as only women from a good background can be, for whom being in love with a young gentleman is something like sin without danger, vice without any nasty or criminal consequences. Young ladies of this type aren't hungry, they merely like to snack. A hunger that demands to be assuaged can bring down the most terrible punishment. A little snacking, however, can't do any harm, only pleasure and a consciousness of having been a little risky. It's like the difference between visiting the zoo, and climbing in with the lions. Of course, my friend didn't know any of that. To him, the fact that a girl from a tiptop English home was secretly kissing him was sufficient proof of her deep passion for him. To him, it was as though she had trekked thousands of miles through some desert, merely to hold her lips to his. He thought she was valiant, intrepid, magnanimous and, on top of everything else, terribly judicious.

Well, she was terribly stupid! She still is. She brought him to an early grave. She has grown old and ugly, but she is still stupid! Unfair as Nature is in the wicked way she makes a man blind when he's in love, she makes up for it by causing the glory of a woman that once was sufficient to dazzle a man, to dim fairly quickly, and by forcing old ladies to have recourse to the dubious assistance of hairdressers, masseurs and surgeons, so that the slack breasts and bellies and cheeks and thighs briefly recover a vaguely acceptable form. What were formerly beautiful women go to their graves as botched plaster figurines. Whereas the men who were wise enough not to lose their lives over them are rewarded by Nature: given the dignity of silver, and the not lesser dignity of physical frailty, they return to the bosom of Abraham."

IV

"In the better circles, a wedding usually follows an engagement as a flash of lightning is followed by a thunderclap. My friend married shortly after I left him, he went on honeymoon, and on the way back he came through our town, and called on me with his new bride. They both looked healthy and attractive, they seemed made for one another. In the evening, I took them out to a restaurant where officers, senior officials, local nobility and one or two landowners made up the clientèle. In a middle-sized town, in the so-called better class of restaurant, people crane their necks at every guest, never mind a stranger they haven't clapped eyes on before. The stir that my friend caused when he turned up with his wife, though, was uncommon, and comparable only to the astonishment that some extraordinary freak of nature causes in ordinary people. It was like a fairy story. All conversation died. The waiters stood rooted to the spot. The maître d' forgot to bow. It was a warm evening in late summer, the windows were open, and a light breeze was ruffling the red curtains. But I had the impression that even these curtains now froze. It was as though the gods had come down on a visit. My friend felt it, and hurried to move into the nearest unoccupied booth. His wife, however, seemed not to have noticed the astonished, almost stricken silence. She had a lorgnette, at the time that was the fashion with certain people, whether they had weak eyes or not. She raised it to her eyes, just for an instant, less than a second. And she let it fall. But my friend observed it, and it must have pained him, as it did me. Because he involuntarily touched his wife's arm – it was the gentlest of rebukes.

Once we were sitting in our booth, my friend's wife raised the lorgnette to her eyes once or twice more. I am convinced she didn't have the slightest interest in what was going on in the restaurant. Probably she only used it to look at the chandelier. But my friend and I were irked by her way of raising the glass to her eyes. It's an arrogant motion, a lorgnette is a somewhat arrogant item at the best of times, and in using it, even the most modest of women runs the risk of seeming stuck-up. I have known some truly aristocratic and properly myopic ladies, who evolved a very particular, almost embarrassed way of using a lorgnette, just as they had a special way of lifting their skirts. Well now, it's not as though my friend's wife didn't have excellent manners! But she lacked true nobility, which, it seems to me, consists not so much in what one does, as what one does not do. In the main, it consists of an awareness of what might shock another; and grasping it, intuitively, even before doing anything.

With my friend's wife, it was the opposite. She was like a little shopkeeper's daughter from London, she made fun of what passed for elegance in our town, the sloppy posture of the officers, the raw eagerness of the staff, the unfashionable hats of the ladies. My friend, troubled, ashamed and in love all at the same time, smiled. Now and again, he attempted to protect us. Once, I remember, he became quite explicit, and said something to the effect of: 'I say, Gwendoline! That's a sharp little tongue you have. If you carry on like that, you'd better show it to the doctor here. Isn't that right, Doctor?' And then, feeling his little joke had rather misfired, he carried on, perfectly seriously: 'I'm afraid my wife hasn't liked it here. We're planning to leave tomorrow night.'

To hide from my friend the fact that I'd seen through his rather mediocre joke, I tried to act in his spirit, and said: 'Kindly show the doctor your tongue!' – She straightway stuck out her narrow, almost crimson little tongue, and, believe me, I do it for a living, I must have seen many thousands of women's tongues over the years: but here, at the sight of this particular tongue, I had the primitive, but unmistakable sensation: snake.

The following morning, my friend came to see me. 'We're leaving tonight,' he said, 'I wanted to say goodbye.' 'Will I not clap eyes on your lovely wife again, then?' 'By all means come to the station, tonight. But I've come to take leave of you properly, personally.'

I could see he wasn't very happy. I suggested going for a walk. I know that private matters are more easily aired while walking than sitting down. You're not face to face. The speaker and the listener both have their eyes on the ground. A noisy street can help you get things off your chest just as much as a drink, or, if you like, the little nook in a church where the confessional waits. So we went for a walk. And there he told me that even on their honeymoon there had been a couple of moments of dissension between himself and his Gwendoline. It began with music. She loved Wagner. He reviled him. Nothing could be as provocative to a musician of his kind – and my kind too – as a taste for Wagner. Admittedly, the advocates of Wagner are musical people too. But it is possible to divide musical people into two groups: Mozart lovers and Wagner fanatics. You see? I'm not even capable of calling them Wagner lovers. I call them fanatics. People either have ears for kettle drums and trombones – or for violins, cellos and flutes. It's easier for a couple of deaf-mutes to talk to each other than for two musical people, of whom one likes Mozart and the other Wagner. I don't think it's possible to like both. People who do must be deaf, I think; or, failing that, conductors.

Well, that's all I need to say, really. They got along like Mozart and Wagner. I knew immediately that the marriage was over. But instead I said: 'Play Mozart at home, make love, sleep with your wife, she should have a baby before long. It has been known for pregnancy to have an influence on musical taste. God be with you.'

We embraced, prematurely. I understood that he would never have been able to embrace me at the station, in front of his wife.

I went along there later. Gwendoline held out her hand to be kissed, and quickly climbed aboard the train, with a cheap smile on her pretty mouth. (It's a curious thing that when a lady smiles, she looks exactly like a poor whore; and when she says a well-bred goodbye, she smiles like a girl giving a man the glad eye.)

My friend would have liked to join me on the platform for a moment. But he was too afraid to, it was as though his wife had grabbed hold of his coat-tails. All he could do was lean out of the window, shake my hand once more – and I walked off, long before the train left."

V

"I am not completely familiar with the niceties of international diplomatic protocol. But I believe I'm right in thinking that it's rather unusual for a diplomat to marry a woman from the country in which he is a diplomatic representative. There are exceptions, I have heard of one or two. My friend was not among them. Our ambassador at the time must have been a stickler for the rules. Because he'd married an Englishwoman, my friend was forced to leave London. His new posting happened to be none other than Belgrade.

I forgot to tell you that my friend's wife was her parents' only daughter. You know how it is: the English are great globetrotters, they know the various countries better than any of the other Western Europeans do; but they don't like sending their daughters to inhospitable places. Every country, even the most inhospitable, merits a visit, whether lengthy or brief. But one keeps a permanent address in England, or, failing that, in one of the better English colonies. My friend's parents-in-law would probably have had no objection to his going to India, say. But Serbia appalled them. Gwendoline for her part was terrified of Belgrade, and refused point-blank to go there, while my friend insisted that his wife accompany him. To his Scripture-versed, Protestant parents-in-law, he quoted the familiar line that the wife's place is at the side of her husband: but in vain. They had their first serious quarrel. My friend went to Vienna. In the Foreign Ministry he moved heaven and earth to obtain his transfer to Paris, or at least to Madrid. In vain.

There were other people in the picture, as you know, there were a good many holders of grace-and-favor positions in the old Austria. Paris, Madrid, Lisbon, they were all spoken for and in safe hands. Plus they really did need an efficient First Secretary in the Belgrade Embassy. Baron S., the head of section in the Ministry, knew of my friend's qualities, and was even a little concerned for his career. In a word, it was impossible. It had to be Belgrade.

By chance – or rather, not by chance, because I don't believe in chance – I was supposed to start work as the spa consultant in April of that year. In February, I gave up my existing practice. From among twenty general practitioners, presumably all of them poor devils like myself, the spa management had selected me. I knew how lucky I was. I wrote to all my friends, including, of course, my friend in London. He wrote back to say how fortunate the development was for him. Since he had to go to Belgrade in March, his wife would be able to stay in London till April, then come to me, spend the season under my care, and move on to Belgrade in August. My job marked an upturn in his fortunes as much as mine.

The poor fellow! He had no idea of the effect of spas on certain young women!

In due course, he would find out."

VI

"His wife agreed to the plan. In March, my friend would go to Belgrade, in April, his wife would come to me in the spa. Under my treatment, and strengthened by the miracle-working waters of the spa, perhaps even transformed by them, she would then follow her husband – this was my friend's hope – to Belgrade, without any homesickness or upset.

However: there are not many women with whom one can enter into a firm arrangement. Not that they set out to deceive you, or break their word on purpose, not at all! But their constitution is incompatible with firm arrangements. And when they decide to stick to an agreed plan, their bodies mutiny, without their even knowing it. They simply become ill.

The wife of my friend was not among the few exceptions with whom one can enter into a firm arrangement. Rather, she was one of those who become ill, in other words: whose bodies rebel against their good intentions – and the day before my friend was to set out for Belgrade she did indeed become ill. Not, please understand, she herself! – it was her constitution that did not want to submit to the inevitable. – What was wrong with her? – God alone knows, He made Eve. A gynecologist rarely knows what ails a woman.

It began in her stomach, and then moved across to her womb. The superficial doctors in London decided, as they usually do in these cases, that it was the appendix. My friend asked for and was allowed a postponement of a couple of days. They operated on his wife. Her appendix was inflamed, of course, like every other appendix that gets taken out. (Your appendix and my appendix, they're inflamed too.) The doctors and my friend imagined the woman had been saved from terrible danger. Enchanted, like any other lover, by the saving of his beloved, my friend went off to Belgrade, to his new posting.

They stuck to the terms of their agreement. Around the middle of April, Frau Gwendoline came to me in my spa. Of course, I met her at the station. She looked like a goddess, a convalescent goddess, a goddess with an appendectomy. She was suffering and triumphant at the same time, and from her convalescence she drew strength for her triumph. Of course, it took me about half an hour to collect and load up all her luggage. She had about twelve trunks. I took Frau Gwendoline to her room at the Hotel Imperial, and asked her to come to my surgery the following day.

She came, and I examined her. I remember the examination, not just because Gwendoline was the wife of my friend, but also because she was one of my earliest patients. Her appendix was gone. You could see the scar, but the woman claimed that 'they'd left something behind in there'. She suffered from hunger, nausea, palpitations, stomach pains, cramps, and hunger again. All symptoms of pregnancy, as you know. But no, she wasn't pregnant! That's about the only thing a gynecologist can establish with a fair degree of certainty. She wasn't pregnant! After reflecting for a while, I hit upon the most banal of afflictions. This beautiful, elegant lady – nothing human is alien, etc. – was unfortunately harboring a tapeworm.

Now, how to tell her, without offending her? – I began by talking about parasites, first harmless ones, then dangerous ones, and I described the tapeworm as one of the most dangerous enemies of feminine beauty. When I'd finally got her to the point when surely she would be fascinated by her own tapeworm, I embarked on instructions, diets and prescriptions. Never, in the history of tapeworms, can one have been taken so seriously. As far as Frau Gwendoline was concerned, hers was a distinct personality. She attributed all her desires and weaknesses to its influence. She came to see me again in the morning, and said: 'Just imagine, it woke me in the night, and insisted on champagne!' – It – meaning the tapeworm, of course. Or another time: 'I wanted to stay in, as you advised, Doctor, but it wasn't having any, it was making me feel ill, and I had to go out and dance.' And so on and so forth. She attended to her tapeworm more than she can ever have done to her husband. It seduced her, indulged her, was her hero. It gave her everything a woman like her needed: suffering, weakness, desire, pleasure. It made her dance and drink and eat, that worm excused everything. It became her scapegoat. A week later, it had notched up its first proper sin.

Will you admit that I must be the only doctor in the world to have treated such a positively reptilian tapeworm?"

VII

"About a week later, my friend wrote to me from Belgrade, to remind me that his wife's birthday was coming up. It fell on 1 May, an easy enough date to remember. In the early afternoon, before I began my surgery, I took an enormous bunch of red roses to the Hotel Imperial to my charge. I had meant to leave them with the porter. I don't know if you're like me in this respect or not, but I know I'm not alone in this: I feel completely ridiculous with an armful of flowers. It's not possible for any self-respecting man to go around carrying flowers. But seeing as it was for the wife of my friend, my charge, my patient, and on top of everything a 'birthday girl' as well, I decided to jam the roses under my arm and get into the elevator. I had myself announced on the second floor. I saw the liveried waiter knock on Frau Gwendoline's door, once, twice, three times. No reply. 'Could madame be asleep or in her bath?' 'No,' replied the floor waiter, 'I've just taken some champagne up to her, with two glasses.' 'Is she entertaining, then?' 'Indeed she is,' said the waiter, 'the doctor from room 32.' 'Who's that?' 'That's the young lawyer from Budapest, Dr. Jenö Lakatos.'

Well, that was enough for me. It was my first season at the spa. But even so, I wasn't born yesterday; and I knew that young lawyers from Budapest shouldn't be hanging around ladies' spas. In general, in the abstract, so to speak, I had no objection. But this was the wife of my friend, and I owed him a duty of care. I even began to feel deceived myself, on his behalf. I have been a bachelor all my life. But I have learned that we don't need to get married ourselves, if we have married friends. It's as though one were married to all the wives of one's close friends too, and we got divorced from their wives along with our friends, and were deceived by their wives along with our friends – unless one happened to be the deceiver oneself.

So I stood there in perplexity, in the magnificent, dazzling white corridor of the hotel, on the dark red carpet, looking in perplexity at the waiter in his blue jacket, the flowers under my arm, completely ridiculous – wouldn't you agree?! I thought I could feel the lovely roses withering against my hip, already I was holding a bunch of dead roses. I decided to go back downstairs. Suddenly the door

opened in front of me. Lakatos from room 32 came out backwards.
My first view of him was from behind. It was sufficient. A small,
round little head with black, gleaming, oiled hair: it was as if Nature
made her own wigs. A large square torso, like a wardrobe wearing
a blazer. Below that the part of the body one doesn't mention, perhaps six times as voluminous as the head, light gray trousers, canary
yellow shoes. That was Lakatos. Through the half-open door, he
was kissing his hand to her within, giggling, bowing, finally he shut
the door, turned round – and found himself facing the waiter and
me. His face, which seemed to consist entirely of little black button
eyes, little nose, and little coal black mustache, looked as if it were
made of wax, a kind of tinted wax. He didn't have a complexion,
more a type of make-up. And then: he wasn't the least bit discom-
fited. He grinned at us. I felt like throwing the huge bouquet of
roses in his face. Then I would have known why, for the first and
only time in my life, I was carting flowers about with me. But
instead I had to see Frau Gwendoline and wish her many happy
returns of the day.

In my embarrassment, I remarked to the waiter, 'You must know,
madame isn't at all well! She has a tapeworm.'

'Had, doctor,' the wag replied. 'He's just stepped out.'"

VIII

Dr. Skovronnek paused, looked at his watch, ordered a cognac,
and said: "I see I've detained you for quite a long time already. I beg
you to be patient a while longer, we're just getting on to the story
I meant to tell you."

He knocked back the cognac, and went on:

"The events I have been telling you about took place in 1910.
You remember, I'm sure, the Balkans were in turmoil, my friend in
Belgrade had his hands full. His letters dried up, he went to see his
parents two or three times a year, I only saw him outside my season,

in other words, when he happened to visit during the winter – because I was still living in that middle-sized town where I had first begun to practice, and left every spring to go to my spa.

My friend's visits were so brief that we barely found time to go to concerts, much less to play music together. On the rare evenings that we managed to meet up, we wanted to talk. But all those years, we didn't have any proper conversations. Music had made us friends. Without music, I felt, my friend's naturally discreet heart froze over. We sat side by side, but it was as though there was a wall of ice between us. We avoided looking each other in the eye. And if we did, for a second or so, there was an almost physical tenderness about it. If only you knew the full extent of it, his eyes seemed to say. And my eyes inquired: So tell me about it? But there was nothing to be done. We missed our music. That was what had been the germinating fire of our friendship. My friend was ashamed – I knew that. Nothing keeps a sensitive man from speaking so much as shame. When a sensitive man feels ashamed, he keeps silent, he even keeps silent about important things – and shame is capable of leading him to the most vulgar of human weaknesses, to the point of lying. Yes, once or twice I had the feeling that my friend was lying to me. But you know me: I'm no moralist. In other words: I don't condemn people for what they do and say, but for their reasons for what they do and say. And so I pretended to take his lies for gospel. He, meanwhile, felt that I was lying as much as he was. They were embarrassing conversations. His face had changed. In spite of his youth, he was graying at the temples, and his healthy tanned complexion had turned pale and liverish. A gray veil shrouded his erstwhile bright fine eyes, the gray veil of deceitfulness. Following every visit he paid me in the course of these years, I thought his shoulders had become thinner and more sloped, his back more bowed, his arms slacker. I always asked after his wife. And then he began to talk about her; talk about her so profusely, that I couldn't help but suppose that he was keeping even more from me than he was telling me. It was as though someone with a great many clothes, with far too many clothes, was trying to cover up his nakedness. Frau Gwendoline – if my friend was to be believed – was good, cheerful, loyal, serious and exuberant, a firework and a good fairy, a housewife and a queen of the parquet, seductive and modest withal, a lady and a sweet little girl, in a word: the perfect wife for a diplomat.

'And how's the tapeworm?' I would ask occasionally, recalling the impertinent reply of the waiter at the Hotel Imperial.

'My wife is in perfect health,' said my friend.

I didn't doubt it. Her health was the very last thing I would have worried about."

IX

"Then the War came along.

My friend (he was a first Lieutenant of the reserve with the 9th Dragoons) presented himself on the first day of mobilization. His regiment was stationed on the Russian border. Frau Gwendoline came to our town, to the parents of my friend, carrying a letter for me. In it, my friend asked me to take his wife along with me when the season began and – this is what he wrote – 'keep an eye on her'.

As you know, it was generally thought that the campaign would be all over in a matter of months. I had a feeling myself that it would last rather longer. Also, I knew that I would not be in a position to 'keep an eye on' the woman. But I did as I was requested. When the season began, I took her up to the spa with me.

Well, unfortunately, no sooner had the season begun than I was immediately ordered to join the reserves as a medico. I left Frau Gwendoline in the charge of one of my colleagues who was unfit to serve on account of a physical disability – he had a hunchback.

It wasn't for another two years – I spent them in a typhoid hospital, and had a bout of it myself – that I was able to return to the hinterland. In the mornings, I was a uniformed doctor with the reserve, examining sick soldiers. In the afternoons, I treated rudely healthy ladies, whose husbands were generally at the front, and whom I could really have left quite confidently to the rougher care that was offered them by my other patients, the convalescent soldiers. It was a wonderful time to be a lady. A Lakatos of the type I had seen emerging from the room of my friend's wife was like a choirboy, compared to the robust peasants from Bosnia, Herzegovina, Croatia and Slovenia. Never did the miraculous waters of our ladies' spa take such wonderful curative effect as they did at that time, when our brave troops waited to be cured in what was never so aptly called the pump room.

Of course, Frau Gwendoline wasn't absent . . . She seemed to have forgotten all about England, her fatherland with which we were at war. The extremely colorful manhood of the Austro-Hungarian Army must have displaced every feeling for England that she might have harbored in her beautiful bosom. She had become an Austrian patriot, no wonder! Love alone determines a woman's allegiance.

When the War was over, my friend returned, still in love and convinced, like every loving man, that his wife had remained faithful to him. Well, I hardly need to tell you that Frau Gwendoline was pretty irritated about the end of the War, and perhaps also about her husband's return. She embraced him with the proficiency she had learned in the course of those wartime years, and which my friend, of course, mistook for passion.

There was no Austro-Hungarian Monarchy any more. My friend, who could have pursued his career in the new and much diminished republic (because basically he was an excellent diplomat), gave up his job. He had enough money. His wife's parents were wealthy. And he decided that henceforth he would devote his life to Gwendoline."

X

"They traveled through the neutral countries. My friend wanted to 'get back to peacetime', as he put it. He didn't succeed. He returned home. His father's factory was not allowed to produce weapons and munitions any more. The whole of the country's arsenal had to be destroyed or else handed over to the victorious powers. And then one day, my friend's father fell ill. It felt wrong just to let the factory collapse. Other munitions plants had been successfully converted: instead of grenades and gun-barrels, they were now turning out bicycles, machine parts, wagons, wheels and cars. My friend wanted to give that a go as well. With typical diligence, he threw himself into a study of industrial management. He inspected factories in England, Germany, and Switzerland. When he thought he'd acquired enough experience, he returned home: alone – he'd left his wife in London, with her parents. He was optimistic, and full of ideas. It almost appeared as though he welcomed the blows of fate that had cast him out of his noble career. It seemed he had entrepreneurial gifts as well, good instincts in relation to people and materials. We saw a lot of each other. Of course, we played music together too, and went to concerts.

Once he came to me at an unusual hour. He knew I was a late bird. It was one in the morning. He set his briefcase down on my table, stood in front of me, and said: 'I want the truth. Tell me straight: is my wife faithful to me? – Has she deceived me? How often? Who with?'

A tricky situation, you will concede. It is one of the rules of gallantry not to betray a woman. Moreover, I'd had occasion to observe that the wrath of husbands sometimes turns not against their cheating wives, but against their friends, for being the bearers of such news. Even today I don't know which is more important: to spare the wife, or to tell my friend the truth. In the course of many years as a gynecologist, it seems to me I have become more and more gallant, which is to say, I have had more and more practice in treating women with kid gloves; but at the same time I have become ever more implacable in my condemnation of the weaker sex, whose strengths will always be far beyond ours. He was my best friend, my only friend. I looked at him, I didn't get up, and I said quietly:

'Your wife has deceived you many times.'

He sat down, turned his briefcase upside down, and spilled its contents over my table: army ribbands, plumes, bunches of edelweiss, metal buttons, little hand mirrors, all the sort of knickknacks that soldiers liked to give girls during the War.

And then there were the love letters, little ones, big ones, plain ones, colored cards and blue field postcards. My friend stood there and stared at the colorful heap. Then he looked at me for a long time, and asked:

'Why didn't you tell me?'

'It wasn't my job,' I replied.

'Ha!' he suddenly roared, 'wasn't your job! Well, so much for your friendship, you hear, and so much for you!'

He swept all the stuff back into his briefcase, shut it, and walked out of the house without giving me another look.

'Looks like I've lost a friend!' I said to myself. – It's a worse thing, much worse, than losing a wife.

I had two weeks to go. But I left for the spa town the following morning.

There, an agitated telegram from Frau Gwendoline reached me. She too was in a hurry to hear the truth from me: was her husband ill? – she didn't know why she was supposed to see him right away.

I forwarded the telegram to my friend, with no comment."

XI

"Four weeks later, the two of them suddenly turned up on my doorstep. No, first my friend plunged into my room. Something

227

terrible had happened. In breathless sentences he told me: There had been one of the usual scenes between them. His wife tried to deny it. He referred to and then produced the so-called 'overwhelming evidence'. His wife, in tears of course, decided to go back to London for good. Her bags were packed, her ticket bought. An hour before the train was due to leave, she turned up in his factory. The famous 'last farewell'. Of course, she brought flowers. You have no idea how life loves to copy the most hackneyed fiction. Or even, as you will see in a moment: medical textbooks. She behaved strangely. She fell to her knees and kissed my friend's toecaps. He couldn't fight her off. She slapped him as well. Then, she collapsed on the floor, lifeless as a doll. It wasn't possible to lift her up. She seemed to be welded to the carpet. Then she began to twitch. She was taken home, they sent for doctors, she was taken to Vienna to see some specialist nerve doctor. Her condition remains poor, but with an interesting array of symptoms. Now it's an arm that's paralyzed, now it's a leg. Now it's her head that jerks, now it's just one eyelid. She is unable to eat for days on end, the sight of food makes her ill. A couple of times she had to be put on a stretcher and carried to church, because she wanted to pray. She's angry with her husband. To her way of seeing it, he's the cause of it all.

And my poor friend did indeed give himself the responsibility. 'I've destroyed her,' he said. 'It's all my fault! I was deaf and blind. You can't leave a young woman alone. What was she to do, for so many days and nights without me? And how cruelly I dealt with her afterwards. I wasn't really hurt by any of what she did! It's just my wretched pride. My silly male vanity. Now no doctor can do anything for her. Only you, my friend! Please forgive me for everything!'

'I can't do anything to help her either, my poor dear friend!' I said. 'The only one who can do anything is she herself, if she wanted to. But that's why she's sick, because she doesn't want to help herself. In medicine we refer to it as refuge into illness. This is a textbook case. There's only one thing to do: you must save your-self. Put your wife in a good sanatorium.'

'Never!' he cried. 'I will never leave her side!'

'Very well,' I said. 'As you please. Let's go and see your wife.'

She greeted me with a lovely smile, her husband with a glare. The greatest actress couldn't have brought it off so well. Her right eye beamed happily at me, her left sent black lightnings in the direction of my friend. Only the day before, her eyelids had been twitching uncontrollably. Today she could only offer me her left hand, because her right was stiff. What about her legs? – They felt fine today. – In the tone I used to adopt with soldiers when I was an army doctor, I ordered her: 'Get up!' She got up. 'Come to the piano! I want to try and play something with you!' She went up to the piano. We sat down. And now I made the most extraordinary sacrifice for the sake of my friend. Imagine: I played – well, what do you think I played? – Wagner! – And what piece by Wagner? – The Pilgrim's Chorus. – And her right hand played along. – 'Wagner is a great master!' she said, when we had finished. 'Indeed he is, Madam! As a specific for sick ladies I find him unequaled,' I replied.

'You are the only doctor in the world!' raved my friend. Imagine, he didn't even notice that I'd played Wagner for the first time in my life!

All that is within a woman's compass, and more! Because from then on, she permitted me one or two absences in a day, and my friend none at all. Day after day, night after night, we sat with her, or rather sat clustered round her. In the brief intervals when I was given back my liberty, so that I could attend to my other patients, my friend didn't have an easy time of it. I could feel how desper-ately he'd been waiting for me. When I came, he embraced me, and stayed with me in the anteroom a long time, I knew exactly how much he yearned to be alone with me for an hour or two, or an evening; and I could feel his heart beating, his poor, timorous heart, the heart of a slave whose mistress peremptorily awaits. Every time we stepped into the room, his wife asked: 'What have you been doing out there all this time? It's warm! The doctor didn't have a coat! What are you trying to hide from me? Oh God, I'm forever being deceived!'

One day, I was unable to bite back the retort: 'Wouldn't you agree it was your turn . . .'

That day, she had her revenge on me. Her left foot went rigid and froze, and I had to spend fully an hour rubbing it.

My friend stood by, stroking her hair. No one said a word.

When her left foot finally started getting warm, I asked my friend: 'By the way, what's happening with your factory?'

'Factory — what factory?' cried the patient.

'It's all right, darling,' said the husband. 'The doctor was referring to a factory I inherited. I sold it a long time ago, my friend, we're living off the proceeds.'

Every day there were such scenes. Sometimes we went out together, the three of us. Then we took, or rather we dragged the woman along between us. She hung on our arms like a dead weight. We would eat and drink in silence.

Once, I remember, we went to a dancehall. You know I'm not an enthusiastic dancer. I hate every kind of exhibitionism — which is what, since the War, dancing has become. But seeing as I had once for my friend's sake played a Wagner duet with his wife, I decided to dance with her as well. The sacrifices a gynecologist is called upon to make! So, we danced. In the middle of our shimmy, she whispered: 'Doctor, I love you, I love only you.' — Of course I didn't reply. When we returned to our table, I said to my friend: 'Your wife has just confessed her love to me. She loves no other doctor, only me.'

A day or two later, the season was almost over, I urged my friend to take his wife back to England, to her parents, and, if he liked, to come back to see me next year.

'By the time we come back next year, we'll be well,' he said. And they went to London."

XII

"They did indeed come back the next year, but they weren't well. And I mean both of them: because my friend was just as ill as his wife. Typhoid, you know, is less infectious than hysteria. What makes a madman dangerous isn't the physical threat he poses to a normal environment, but the way he comes gradually to erode its entire stock of common sense. In this world madness is stronger than healthy common sense, wickedness more powerful than goodness.

I hadn't had much news of my friend that winter. Maybe my advice was poor. In her parents' house, the woman's malice gained new strength, it was like a recruiting-ground for her. Doctors, hyp-notists, faith-healers, mesmerists, preachers, old women: none of them did any good. One day, she claimed she couldn't move her legs any more. Revealingly enough, it was shortly after the evening on which her husband had gone to some banquet or other – in the company of his father-in-law, if you please – for the first time since she had fallen ill. Her legs were indeed stiff. Crutches, wooden legs, artificial limbs are all more flexible. The unmoving, unmovable legs quickly shriveled up, while her upper body rapidly put on weight. She had to be pushed around in a wheelchair. And since she wouldn't suffer a stranger near her, it had to be her husband, my friend, who did her this service. When I saw him again, he had become old and gray. Worse: this aristocratic man had taken on the bearing and expression of a servant – or even of a menial. When his wife called for him, he jumped like a new recruit hearing himself called by the sergeant-major. Her voice was hoarse and piercing. It sliced through the air like a circular saw. And yet, she still had laughing, sparkling, merry eyes, a pleasing smile, rosy cheeks that were getting plumper all the time, a dimple in her chin that was getting fatter, she was like a stranded Christmas tree angel with no wings, on wretched, stick-thin, immobile legs. My friend, mean-while, looked like a lackey. Next to him, an old coachman would have looked like a duke. My friend slunk around with bowed shoulders, on bent legs, maybe that was the result of having to push his love through life on her chariot the whole time. Yes, he looked whipped – that was exactly the word for it: whipped! Maybe she knocked him about a bit as well.

I asked him about love, physical love, I mean. Well, imagine: the man had to undress his wife every night, carry her bodily to bed, and of course lie beside her. The poor fellow was afraid that his wife would deceive him again, if he didn't make love to her. So he raved about her beauty! He raved about her beauty, to me, who had seen her thickening upper body, and her stick-thin legs!

Even worse for him was her jealousy. She couldn't be left alone for a minute, she refused nurses – for fear that her husband would fall for one of them. But her jealousy extended to me as well, to the maid, the waiter, the hotel porter, the elevator-boy. We dragged her off to concerts and cafés and restaurants, like a couple of mules, tethered to the miserable handles of her miserable, creaking wheelchair, panting through the sultry evenings, or in wind and rain, holding an umbrella above her always fashionable hats, forever smoothing rugs over her stiff knees. Seamstresses, dressmakers, tailors fluttered like moths around the hotel where she lived. We stopped in front of every third shop window. She had us wheel her into jewelers' shops, she spent hours looking for suitable jewelry. Every morning the hairdresser came in to her. Every morning, my friend had to lift her into her bath. And while she sat there, playing with her rubber bath toys, he read her silly English magazines and romantic novels. My treatment accomplished nothing. There was, as we doctors say, no 'desire to get better' in the woman, the psychosis had put down roots in her. She laughed in my face. I had no more authority with her.

I never succeeded in being alone with my friend. She wouldn't leave us together for five minutes. I looked for a ruse. Finally, I thought I'd found one: seeing as she was too jealous to allow a female nurse, what about a male nurse? I knew a presentable young fellow from our hospital. I spoke to him, he agreed. I introduced him to Frau Gwendoline, she liked him. 'But not now,' she said, 'we'll take him with us when we go. I don't want the two of you alone.' And that's how it remained. Shortly before the season's end, they went back to London, and took the young fellow with them.

I felt a small measure of satisfaction: maybe the male nurse would give my friend the occasional breathing space in London.

But that's not the way it turned out! Scarcely two months later, I received a short letter from my friend.

I had been right all along, he wrote, now he could confirm that, but it was never too late, and now he was leaving his wife. He had caught her in an intimate embrace with the young orderly. He would be in touch again soon.

Two years passed, I wrote and received no reply, I never heard again from my dear friend."

XIII

"One day, I went to Paris, and, more from boredom than expectation, visited one of the many night clubs in Montmartre, with phoney Cossacks on the doors to try and lure real Americans. Tired and aghast at my own stupidity, I sat and watched the dancing couples. All at once, I caught sight of Frau Gwendoline. It was her, no doubt about it! She was on the arm of a swarthy slippery-haired gigolo, dancing a so-called Java. The man could only be Lakatos. I mean to say: the type, not the individual. It wasn't actually old Lakatos from room 32. Suddenly she spotted me. She left her partner, walked up to my table, healthy, happy, smiling, a goddess. I caught myself leaning across to get a sight of her legs. Healthy, perfect legs in pale gray silk stockings.

'Surprised, Doctor?' she asked. 'Do you mind if I sit down a moment?'

She sat down.

'Where's your husband?' I asked. 'Why hasn't he written?'

In the corners of her eyes two big, shiny tears appeared on order, two sentries of sorrow.

'He's dead!' she said. 'Unfortunately, he killed himself. Over some silly thing.'

From her little handbag she took out her handkerchief and also her pocket mirror.

'When?' I asked.

'Two years ago!'

'And how long is it since you've been well again?'

'A year and a half!'

'And is that your new husband who's squiring you?'

'My intended. One Herr Lakatos, a Hungarian, a wonderful dancer, as you may have noticed.'

Ah, the tapeworm! I thought and called for the bill and paid. I left her sitting there, I never even said goodbye.

Many, many women passed me in the street, and some of them smiled at me.

Go on, I thought, smile, smile, turn, look over your shoulders, swing your hips, buy yourselves new hats, new stockings, new bits and bobs! Old age will catch up with you! Give it another little year or two! No surgeon will be able to do anything about it, no wig-maker. You will be disfigured, embittered, disappointed, you will sink into your graves and then further, into Hell. But go on, smile, smile! . . ."

THE BUST OF THE EMPEROR

I

In what was once East Galicia and is now Poland, but in any case a long way from the one railway line which connects the towns of Przemysl and Brody, lies the village of Lopatyny, which is the setting for the following remarkable story.

I hope the reader will be kind enough to forgive the author for prefacing his account with a few words of geo-political explanation. I plead the recent unnatural excesses of world history, which compel me to offer such an explanation.

Younger readers may need to be reminded that some of the territory that today belongs to the Polish Republic, used, until the end of the Great War (sometimes called the World War), to be among the many Crown Lands of the old Dual Monarchy of Austria-Hungary.

Well now, in the village of Lopatyny lived a Count Franz Xaver Morstin, the scion of an old Polish family – a family which, by the way, had originally come from Italy, and moved to Poland in the course of the sixteenth century. As a young man, Count Morstin had served with the 9th Dragoons. He thought of himself neither as Polish nor Italian, neither as a member of the Polish aristocracy nor as an aristocrat of Italian descent. No: along with so many

235

others like him in the former Crown Lands of Austria-Hungary, he belonged to the noblest and purest type of Austrian there can be, which is to say: he was a man beyond nationality, and therefore an aristocrat in the true sense. If one had asked him, for instance – but who would have wanted to ask such a nonsensical question? – to which "nationality" or people he felt he belonged: the Count would have looked blankly and uncomprehendingly at the questioner, or perhaps even with a measure of irritation. By what criteria should he have had to nominate his allegiance to this nation, or that? – He spoke most of the European languages with equal fluency, he knew his way around most European countries, he had friends and relatives scattered all over the wide and colorful world. Now, the Dual Monarchy was like this colorful world in parvo, and that was why it was the only possible homeland for the Count. He had one brother-in-law who was a District Commander in Sarajevo, and another who was on the Governor's Council in Prague, a brother who was a first lieutenant with the artillery in Bosnia, a cousin who was Embassy Secretary in Paris, another who was a landowner in the Hungarian Banat, a third who was in the Italian Diplomatic Service, and a fourth who had taken his love of the Orient to the point of taking up residence in Peking. From time to time, Franz Xaver visited his relatives, concentrating, as might be expected, on those who lived in the Dual Monarchy. He liked to call these visits his personal *tours d'horizon*. He went not only to see his relatives, but also his friends, who, having (like himself) graduated from the Theresian Academy, had remained in Vienna. Count Morstin visited twice a year in the summer and winter (a fortnight and more). As he traveled around the center of his multitudinous fatherland, what he responded to most were certain specific and unmistakable manifestations that recurred, in their unvarying and still colorful fashion, on every railway station, every kiosk, every public building, every school and church in all the Crown Lands of the Empire. All over, the policemen wore the same feathered hats or ocher helmets with golden pompoms and glittering Habsburg double eagles; all over, the wooden doors of the K. and K. Trafik stores were painted in black and yellow diagonals; all over, tax inspectors wore the same green (burgeoning almost) sword-knot on their spotless sabers; in every garrison town, there were the same blue uniform tunics and black saloon pants of infantry officers strolling on the Corso, the same red trousers of cavalrymen, the same coffee-colored jackets of the artillery; all over this big and colorful Empire, when the church clocks struck nine, the same retreat was sounded, made up of cheerfully sounding questions and mournful replies. All over, there were the same coffee houses, with vaulted, smoky ceilings, with dark niches where chess players sat hunkered like alert fowls, with bars full of multi-colored bottles and sparkling glasses, presided over by bosomy, blonde barmaids. Almost all over, in all the coffee houses of the Empire, padded a waiter with Dundreary wipers, a little shaky at the knee, his toes turned up, a napkin over his forearm, like a remote, humble version of the ancient servitors of His Majesty, the great whiskered lord over all the Crown Lands, the policemen, the Trafik shops, the level-crossings, the railways, the peoples. And in every land, they sang different songs; in every land, the farmers wore different attire; and in every land they spoke a different tongue, and a different selection of other tongues. And the thing that so delighted the Count was the formal and at the same time gladsome black-and-yellow, that shone out shyly from the rest of the colors; the equally formal and gladsome "*Gott erhalte*", which was at home among all the different folk songs, the particular, sloppy, nasal, gentle German – reminiscent of medieval German – of Austria, that repeatedly made itself heard among the various idioms and dialects of the various peoples. Like every Austrian of that time, Morstin was in love with the constant in the midst of change, the familiar in the variable, the dependable in the midst of the unaccustomed. In this way, what was foreign came to be homely to him, without losing its timbre, and home had the reliable charm of the exotic.

Within his village of Lopatyny, the Count was more important than any of the branches of officialdom that were known and feared by the peasants and the Jews: more than the judges in the local town, more than the District Commander in the same town, more than any of the senior officers who commanded the troops during the annual maneuvers, requisitioned houses and huts for billets, and represented the military on maneuvers – always so much more exhilarating than the military in time of war. The people of Lopatyny took Count to be not just a rank of nobility, but also an exalted rank of officialdom. The facts seemed to bear them out. For by virtue of his natural authority, Count Morstin was able to secure tax reductions, to get the sickly sons of some Jews excused from military service, to forward petitions for clemency, to obtain reduced sentences for innocent or too harshly punished prisoners, to secure lower train fares for poor people, to force gendarmes, policemen and officials who had gone beyond the limits to account for themselves, to get trainee teachers promoted to Gymnasium posts, to find retired NCOs a niche in civilian life as managers of Trafik stores, postmen and telegraphists, and to obtain bursaries for the gifted sons of poor peasants and Jews. How happy he was to do all this! He was irregular and unconstitutional, but he was certainly kept busier than most of the officials whom he had to go and see. He engaged two secretaries and three stenographers in the discharging of his duties. Above and beyond that, he followed the family tradition of "largesse". For more than a hundred years, tramps and beggars were used to assemble every Friday below the balcony of the Morstin house, to receive copper coins wrapped in paper from lackeys. Generally, the Count turned out on the balcony in person to welcome the beggars. It was as though he were thanking the beggars, who were thanking him: reciprocal gratitude between giver and receiver.

By the way: It wasn't always kindness of heart that produced all this charity, but one of those unwritten laws that some noble families have. Centuries ago, their forebears might have practiced charity, help and support out of pure love of the common people. But by and by, over the generations, this kindness had gradually set and hardened in the form of duty and tradition. Moreover, his decided willingness to be of assistance was Count Morstin's only avocation and distraction. To the rather tedious life of an aristocrat, who, unlike his neighbors and fellow-noblemen, had no interest even in hunting, it gave some content, and a constant and agreeable reminder of his influence. If he had helped one person to a Trafik store, another to an official permit, a third to a job, and a fourth to a hearing, he felt his conscience appeased, and his pride as well. Equally, if his intercession on behalf of one of his protégés happened to fail, his conscience pricked him, and his pride was injured. And so he refused to give up, he appealed to every successive tribunal until he had got what he wanted, or rather what his protégé wanted. For this reason, the local people loved and honored him. Because the people has a rather imperfect understanding of the motives of a powerful man in helping the weak and needy. It can only see the "good master" – and in its childlike confidence in the powerful man it often displays considerably more selflessness than the man himself. It is the profoundest and noblest desire of the common people to know that the mighty are just and noble. This is why it takes such terrible vengeance when it is disappointed – like a child, smashing its toy train, if it has once failed to work. This is a reason to give the people – like the children – toys that are well-made, and powerful men that are just.

Such considerations were certainly not going through the mind of Count Morstin, when he practiced protection, kindness and justice. They might have led one or other of his forebears to the exercise of kindness, compassion and justice, now they were present in the blood – or, as they like to say nowadays, in the "subconscious" – of their descendant.

As much as he felt himself obliged to help the weak, so he felt respect, reverence and obedience towards people of higher rank than himself. The person of His Royal and Imperial Majesty, whom he had served, remained for him unlike any other. It would have been quite impossible for the Count to view the Emperor as a simple mortal. The belief in the traditional hierarchy was so powerfully rooted in the soul of Franz Xaver that he loved his Emperor, not for his human qualities, but because of his Imperial traits. If any acquaintance, friend, or even relative spoke disrespectfully about the Emperor in his hearing, he would break off all contact with them forthwith. Perhaps he already guessed, long before the end of the monarchy, that little witticisms can be more deleterious than the assassination attempts of criminals and the solemn harangues of rebels and dissidents. And if he did, world history would have borne him out. Because the old Austro-Hungarian monarchy did not die by the hollow pathos of revolutionaries, but by the ironical shafts of those who should have been its faithful supports.

II

One day, it was a few years before the Great War, which people now call the World War, Count Morstin was told "in confidence", that the next round of Imperial maneuvers would take place in and around Lopatyny. The Emperor would stay with him at his house for several days, as much as a week or more. Morstin, in a state of high excitement, drove out to the District Commander, primed the civil political authorities and the local government of the nearest town, had the police and nightwatchmen of the whole area kitted out with new uniforms and sabers, had conversations with the church leaders of all three faiths, the Russian Orthodox and the Roman Catholic priests and the Jewish rabbi, wrote a speech for the Ruthenian mayor of the little town, which the mayor was unable to read but had to learn by heart, with the help of the schoolmaster, bought white dresses for the little girls of the village, notified the commanders of the local regiments, and all "in confidence" − with the result that, by early spring, long before the maneuvers, it was common knowledge throughout the area that the Emperor would be attending. At that time, Count Morstin was no longer young, but prematurely gray and gaunt, a bachelor of the type sometimes known as "confirmed", something of an oddity in the eyes of his more robust peers and associates, a bit "peculiar", something "unworldly about him". No one had ever seen him in female company. Never had he made any efforts at matrimony. No one had ever seen him drink, or gamble, or make love. His only evident passion was his opposition on the "nationality question". At that time, the so-called "nationality question" began to be acute in the monarchy. Everyone aligned themselves − whether they wanted to, or merely pretended to want to − with one or other of the many peoples there used to be in the old monarchy. For it had been discovered in the course of the nineteenth century that every individual had to be a member of a particular race or nation, if he wanted to be a fully rounded bourgeois individual. "From humanity via nationality to bestiality", as the Austrian poet Grillparzer put it. Nationality, the precursor to the bestiality of today, was then in its infancy. As for national feeling: it was quite evident that here was the fitting expression of the meanest instincts of all those who constitute the meanest castes of a recently created nation. There were among them photographers who were volunteer firemen on the side; so-called artistic painters, insufficiently talented to be taken on at the Academy of Arts, and consequently forced into sign-painting or interior decorating; disgruntled elementary schoolteachers, who fancied themselves at secondary schools; assistant pharmacists who would have liked to be doctors; tooth-surgeons who never made it up to dentists; subordinates in the post office or the railways; foresters; and in short, all those who pressed fatuous claims to unlimited status within bourgeois society. By and by, the upper layers of society gave in to them. And all those people who had never been anything other than Austrians, in Tarnopol, in Sarajevo, in Vienna, in Brünn, in Prague, in Czernowitz, in Oderburg, in Troppau, never anything other than Austrians: they now began, in compliance with the "order of the day", to call themselves part of the Polish, the Czech, the Ukrainian, the German, the Romanian, the Slovenian, the Croatian "nation" – and so on and so forth.

At about this time too, "universal, secret, and direct suffrage" was introduced in the monarchy. Count Morstin hated it as much as he hated the modern idea of the "nation". He was in the habit of going to the Jewish publican Solomon Piniowsky, the only man far and wide who he thought showed a bit of common sense, and saying: "Listen to me, Solomon! That hateful Darwin fellow who says people are descended from apes, well, he seems to be right after all. They are no longer content to be divided into peoples, no! – it seems they're hell-bent on belonging to different nations. Nationalism – get this, Solomon?! – Not even monkeys could have come up with that one. The only thing wrong with Darwin's theory is that it's arsy-versy. In my book, it's the monkeys that are descended from the nationalists, because they're a step up from them. You know your Bible, Solomon, you know it's written there that on the sixth day God created man, but where did it say anything about the nationalist? Isn't that right, Solomon?"

"Quite right, Count!" replied the Jew, Solomon.

"Now," the Count went on, "next thing. We're expecting the Emperor this summer. I'm going to give you some money. You'll do up your bar, and light up your window. You will get the portrait of the Emperor cleaned up and put it in the window. I'll give you a black-and-yellow banner with the double eagle, and I want you to fly that on your roof. Understand?"

Yes, the Jew Solomon Piniowsky understood, just as everyone else with whom the Count had discussed the Emperor's visit, had also understood.

III

The Imperial maneuvers were held in summer, and His Royal and Imperial Apostolic Majesty took up residence in the house of Count Morstin. The Emperor was seen riding out every morning to inspect the troops, and the peasants and the Jewish traders in the area assembled to watch him, the old fellow who ruled them. And as soon as he appeared with his retinue, they cried out: *hurrah* and *vivat* and *niech zyje* – each in his own language.

A few days after the Emperor's departure, the son of a local peasant came to call on Count Morstin. The young fellow, who had the desire to become a sculptor, had made a sandstone bust of the Emperor. Count Morstin was delighted. He promised to find a free place for the young sculptor at the Academy of Arts in Vienna.

He had the bust set up at the entrance to his little castle.

There it remained for some years, until the outbreak of the Great War, which was later called the World War.

When he volunteered, old, lean, bald and hollow-eyed, as he had over the years become, Count Morstin ordered the bust of the Emperor to be taken down, packed in straw and hidden in the cellar.

There it rested, until the end of the War and of the Monarchy, when Count Morstin returned, and the new Polish Republic was founded.

IV

So Count Franz Xaver Morstin had returned. But where had he returned to? Granted, they were the same fields, the same woods, the same huts, the same kind of peasant – the same kind, mind you – because many of the individuals whom the Count had known had fallen.

It was winter, one could feel Christmas was not far off. Just as it always was at this time, as it had been long before the War, the Lopatinka was frozen, the rooks squatted motionless on the bare chestnuts, and the steady easterly gale blew over the fields, against the west-facing windows of his house. The village (a consequence of the War) was full of widows and orphans: enough material for the charity of the returning lord. But, instead of greeting Lopatyny as home once more, Count Morstin threw himself into difficult and unhelpful speculation on the question of what was home. Seeing as this village, he thought, now belongs to Poland and not Austria: can it still be said to be my home? What is home, anyway? Are not the particular uniforms of the customs men and the gendarmes that we were used to seeing in our childhood, are they not just as much home as the pines and firs, the swamp and the meadow, the cloud and the stream? If the excise men and the police are different, and the pine and the fir and the stream and the swamp are the same: is that still home to me? Was I not – the Count proceeded to interrogate himself – so much at home in this place because it belonged to a master who owned just as many different places that I loved as well? No doubt about it! The unnatural excess of world history has also ruined my personal pleasure in what I called home. Now everywhere around me they speak of their new fatherland. And they think of me as *déraciné*. I always have been. Oh, there once was a fatherland, a real one, the only possible fatherland for orphaned nationals. And that was the old Monarchy. Now I am a homeless man who has lost the true home of the eternal wanderer.

In the delusive hope that he might forget this condition elsewhere, the Count decided to leave right away, only to learn, to his bewilderment, that he required a passport and several so-called visas, to obtain admission to the countries he wanted to visit. He was of an age to consider passports and visas and the rest of the bureaucratic obstacles that impeded contact between peoples after the War, as childish dreams and phantasms. But submitting to the fate that condemned him to spend his remaining years in a dreadful nightmare – while also hoping to find elsewhere, abroad, some part of that old reality he had lived in before the War – he accepted the conditions imposed on him by this spectral world, got a passport, procured visas, and headed first for Switzerland, supposing that because that country had not participated in the War, he would find there some vestiges of the old peace.

Now, he had known the city of Zürich for many years. It was about twelve years since he had last been there. He supposed it had nothing particular to offer him, neither good nor ill. His impression matched the prevalent, not quite unfounded opinion among the faster, not to say adventure-hungry set, of the well-behaved cities of the well-behaved Swiss. What was there that could possibly happen in them? Even so: for a man who had come from the War and the eastern marches of the former Austrian Monarchy, the peaceableness of a city that had known only fugitives from the war, was already something of an adventure. In the ensuing days, Franz Xaver Morstin reveled in the peace he had long lived without. He ate, drank, and slept.

But one day, or rather, one night, there was that ugly incident in a Zürich bar that had the effect of forcing Count Morstin to leave the country forthwith.

At that time, the newspapers of many countries regularly referred to a certain rich banker who was said to have in his possession – as collateral for a loan extended to the Austrian royal family – not only the bulk of the Habsburg crown jewels, but even the old Habsburg crown itself. No doubt this story came from the mouths and pens of those mindless scribblers called reporters; and while part of the royal family's fortune might indeed have fallen into the hands of an unscrupulous banker, surely the old crown of the Habsburgs was not part of it, Franz Xaver Morstin was convinced of that.

Well, one night, he found himself in one of the bars, known only to a very few insiders, that are open all night in the oh-so-ethical city of Zürich, where, as everyone knows, prostitution is illegal, immorality is scorned, and sin is prohibitively boring as well as prohibitively expensive. Not that the Count was looking for such diversions! Not at all: but so much peace had begun to bore him and give him sleepless nights, and he had decided to get through the nights any way he could.

He sipped his wine. He sat in one of the few quiet corners that this bar had to offer. Admittedly, he was irritated by the new-fangled American reddish lighting, the hygienic white of the barman, who looked like a surgeon, the fake blonde hair of the girls that put one in mind of chemists' shops: but then, what hadn't he had to get used to, the poor old Austrian? But what caused him to start up out of his hard-won peace was the sound of a rasping voice calling out: "And here, ladies and gentlemen, is the crown of the Habsburgs!"

Franz Xaver got to his feet. In the middle of the longish bar he saw a large, convivial group. He saw at a glance that though he knew none of those at the table individually, there were among them representatives of all the types he abominated: dyed blonde women in short skirts that shamelessly exposed their (ugly) knees; slender, willowy youths with olive complexions, smiling with perfect teeth like the promotional figures in dentists' premises, pliable, light-footed, cowardly, elegant and lurking, like a kind of devious hairdresser; older gentlemen with carefully, but ineffectually dissembled bellies and bald pates, bonhomous, lecherous, jolly, and knock-kneed. In short: a selection of the type of persons who were temporarily put in charge of administering the inheritance of the lost world, only to deliver it a few years later – at a profit to themselves – to the still more progressive and murderous inheritors.

One of the elderly gentlemen at this table now rose, first waved a crown around, then set it on his bald head, stepped out into the middle of the bar, danced around, wobbled his head and the crown on it, and sang, to the tune of a popular song of the time:

You wear the holy crown this way!

To begin with, Franz Xaver failed to understand the point of this disgusting spectacle. He merely sensed that this group was made up of undignified oldsters (their heads turned by the presence of the short-skirted models), of chambermaids on their night off, of bar-girls, who shared their champagne money and no doubt their own bodies with the waiters, of worthless spivs, who traded in women and foreign currencies, wore suits with padded shoulders and wide trousers that resembled skirts, of loathsome middlemen who dealt in houses, shops, citizenships, passports, concessions, wealthy marriage-matches, birth-certificates, religious confirmation papers, titles of nobility, children for adoption, brothels, and contraband cigarettes. This was the very society that had established itself in every capital city of the defeated European world, determined to live off cadavers, and whose satiated, insatiable mouths never ceased to slander the past, exploit the present, and tout the future. These were the new lords of the world, in the wake of the World War. Count Morstin felt like his own corpse. These people were dancing on his grave. It was to prepare the ground for these people that hundreds of thousands had died in agony – and hundreds of well-intentioned orators had worked to undermine the old Monarchy, yearned for its collapse, and the freeing of the nations! So there it was: On the grave of the old world, and round the cradles of the newly formed successor states danced the ghosts in the nocturnal American bar.

Morstin moved closer for a better view. The shadowy quality of these fleshly, well-nourished phantoms aroused his curiosity. On the bald head of the knock-kneed dancing man he identified the copy – surely it was only a copy – of the crown of St. Stephen. The waiter, eager to put all his customers in the picture, came over to Franz Xaver, and said: "That's the Russian banker, Walakin. He claims to own the crowns of all the unseated monarchs of Europe. He comes along with a different one every night. Last night, it was the Tsars' crown. Tonight it's the crown of St. Stephen."

Count Morstin felt his heart turn over. In that instant – though it felt as if it had lasted for at least an hour – he experienced a complete transformation of himself. It was as though a strange and terrible new Morstin were growing inside him, growing and rising up and spreading, taking possession of the body of the old, familiar one, and going on to spread right through the American bar. Never, not since childhood, had Franz Xaver Morstin experienced rage. His was a mild nature, and the protection afforded him by his social position, his wealth, the renown of his name, and his prestige, had, as it were, sealed him from the rough-and-tumble of the world, from any encounter with its baseness. Had it been otherwise, he would certainly have known rage much sooner. It was as though he understood, in the same instant in which he himself was transformed, that long before himself, the world had also been transformed. It was as though he now learned that his own transformation was merely a consequence of some wider transformation. Far more, though, than the previously unknown feeling of rage that sprang up in him, and grew, and foamed out past the limits of his own person, the general baseness must have grown, the baseness of the world, the nastiness that had kept itself out of sight, and cast itself in the guise of flattering "loyalty" and slavish submissiveness. It was as though he, who had unquestioningly assumed that everyone, quite naturally, had decency, in that instant learned the great error of his life, the error of any noble heart: namely the granting of credit, limitless credit. And his sudden insight filled him with that fastidious embarrassment that is a true sister of fastidious rage. When he sights meanness, the fastidious man feels doubly embarrassed: first at the mere fact of its existence, and then because he straightway understands he has been taken in. He feels cheated – and his pride is stung by the susceptibility of his heart.

He was no longer capable of reason or thought or restraint. It seemed to him that practically no form of violence was brutal enough when it came to punishing and avenging the meanness of a man who danced about with crowns on his bald dealer's head, a different one every night. A gramophone was belting out the song:

"What's Hans up to with his knee"; the bar-girls were squealing; the young men clapped their hands; the barman, in his hospital whites, did things with glasses, spoons and bottles, poured and mixed, brewing and coaxing out of metal cups the elixirs of the new age, clattered and rattled and every so often looked up benignly at the banker's antics, re-calculating the consumption. The reddish lights trembled with every one of the bald fellow's stamping footfalls. The lights, the gramophone, the noises of the mixer, the cooings and squealings of the women, combined to put Count Morstin into an extraordinary rage. An unbelievable thing happened: For the first time in his life, he was childish and laughable. He armed himself with his half-empty champagne bottle and a blue soda siphon, and walked up to the strangers. Then, with his left hand he doused the company, as though extinguishing a nasty fire, and with his right he brought down the bottle against the dancer's head. The banker fell to the floor. The crown slipped from his head. And while the Count bent down to pick it up, quite as if it had been a real crown and he had to save it and everything it stood for, the waiters and the girls and the spivs all fell upon him. Numbed by the coarse perfume of the girls and the blows of the young men, Count Morstin was finally taken outside. There, in front of the door to the American bar, the diligent waiter presented him with his bill, on a silver tray, in the open air, in the presence, so to speak, of all the faroff indifferent stars: for it was a bright winter night.

The following day, the Count returned to Lopatyny.

V

Why shouldn't I – he asked himself en route – return to Lopatyny? Since my world seems to be finally defeated, I have no home any more. And then the best thing I can do is to seek out the ruins of my former home!

His thoughts were with the bust of the Emperor Franz Joseph that was resting in his cellar, and with the body of his Emperor, which long since had been consigned to the Kapuzinergruft.

I was always an oddity – he proceeded to think – both in my village, and beyond. I will remain an oddity.

He telegraphed ahead to his steward to let him know when he was coming.

When he arrived, there was a welcome for him, as always, as before, as if there hadn't been any war, any end of the Monarchy, any new Polish Republic.

For it is one of the great mistaken beliefs of the new – or, as they like to call themselves, the modern – statesmen, that the people (the "nation") is as passionately interested in world politics as they are themselves.

But the people – in agreeable contrast to the politicians – in no way lives off world politics. The people lives off the soil it tills, the trade it conducts, the crafts it has learned. (And yet it also votes in public elections, dies in wars, and pays its taxes to the revenue.) At least, that's how it was in Count Morstin's village of Lopatyny. And the entire World War and all the changes to the map of Europe hadn't affected the outlook of the people of Lopatyny. Why should it? – How could it? – The sound common sense of the Jewish publicans, of the Polish and Ruthenian peasants resisted the incomprehensible excesses of world history. Those excesses are abstract: the inclinations and disinclinations of the people are grounded in reality. For instance, the people of Lopatyny had known Count Morstin, the representative of the Emperor and of the House of Habsburg, for many years. New policemen arrived, and a tax inspector is a tax inspector, but Count Morstin remains Count Morstin. Under the rule of the Habsburgs, the people of Lopatyny had been happy or unhappy – according to God's will. Quite regardless of the comings and goings of history, monarchy or republic, so-called national self-determination or so-called national oppression, in the lives of men there are always such things as a good harvest or a bad harvest, sound or cankered fruit, healthy or sickly livestock, lush or thin pastures, timely or untimely rain, propitious sun or sun that causes drought and devastation; for the Jewish tradesman, the world was divided into good and bad customers; for the publican thirsty and abstemious drinkers; whereas for the craftsman what mattered was whether people needed new roofs, new boots, new trousers, new stoves, new chimneys, new barrels, or not. At least, as I've said before, that was the way things stood in Lopatyny. And it is our personal opinion, at any rate, that the wide world is not so very different from the little village of Lopatyny as the leaders and the demagogues would have us believe. After they have read the newspapers, listened to the speeches, elected the representatives, and discussed the news with their friends, the good peasants, craftsmen and traders – and in the cities, the workers – go back to their homes and workshops. And their misery or happiness is what awaits them there: sick or healthy children, quarrelsome or agreeable wives, prompt or dilatory customers, pressing or easy-going creditors, a good or a bad supper, a clean or a squalid bed. Yes, it is our conviction that ordinary people don't trouble their heads over politics, even though they may spend their Sundays discussing nothing else. But, as we've said before, that may be only a personal opinion. Our business is to report on the village of Lopatyny. And things there were as we've described.

When Count Morstin returned home, he straightway went to see Solomon Piniowsky, the clever Jew, in whom, as in no one else in Lopatyny, cleverness and simplicity dwelt together harmoniously, like sisters. And the Count asked the Jew: "Solomon, what's your opinion of this world of ours?" "Count," replied Piniowsky, "it has sunk. The world is broken, there is no longer an Emperor, people elect a President, it's as though I were to look for a good attorney if I am involved in a law case. The whole people elect a lawyer to defend them. But – my question, Count – before what court? – Before a court composed of other lawyers. And if the people has no case of its own, and no need to defend itself, well, we all know that the presence of lawyers will get us involved with the law. And so there will be continual cases. I still have the black-and-yellow banner you gave me, Count. What would you like me to do with it? It's up in my attic. I still have the painting of the old Emperor. What shall I do with it? I read the papers, I think about business, I think about the state of the world. I know, Count, what foolish things are happening. But our peasants have no idea. They simply believe the old Emperor has introduced a different color of uniform, and emancipated his Poles. And that he's living in Warsaw now, not Vienna."

"Oh, leave them be," said Count Morstin.

And he went home, and had the bust of the Emperor Franz Joseph fetched up out of the cellar, and he set it up at the entrance to his house.

And from the next day forth – as though there had been no war – as though there were no new Polish Republic – as though the old Emperor had not long ago been laid to rest in the Kapuzinergruft – as though this village of Lopatyny were still part of the territory of the old Monarchy: every peasant who went that way, took off his hat to the sandstone bust of the old Emperor, and every Jew who passed it with his bundle on his back, murmured the prayer that believing Jews are supposed to say when they see the Emperor. And the unlikely bust, cut from cheap sandstone by the clumsy hand of a farmer's boy, the bust of the late Emperor in his old uniform tunic, with its stars and its medals and its order of the Golden Fleece, captured in stone as the naive eye of the boy had seen and loved his Emperor, in time acquired a special, artistic quality all of its own – even in the eyes of Count Morstin. It was as though the exalted subject worked from within over time to improve and ennoble the work that represented it. Wind and weather got to work with artistic skill on the crude stone. It was as though reverence and recollection also worked on the memorial, and as though every peasant's acknowledgment and every devout

Jew's prayer, brought the crude work of the young peasant's hand to artistic perfection.

And so the statue stood outside the house of Count Morstin for years, the only monument there had ever been in the village of Lopatyny, something for all the inhabitants to take just pride in.

To Count Morstin, who never left the village any more, the monument was even more significant: when he left his house, it gave him the sense that nothing had changed. More and more – he grew old prematurely – he caught himself thinking foolish thoughts. For hours on end, he would persist in the delusion – even though he had personally taken part in the most bloody of all wars – that it had all been a terrible nightmare, and that the changes that had followed, were only more terrible nightmares. He was forced to see, on an almost weekly basis, that his intercession on behalf of his protégés at courts and offices was unavailing now, worse, that the new officials actually made fun of him. He was more appalled than offended. It was generally proclaimed about the town, and in the area, and on his neighbors' estates, that "old man Morstin" was "half bonkers". People told one another that when he was at home he went around in his old captain's uniform from the Dragoons, complete with his old medals and insignia. One day, a local landowner – a certain Count Walewski – asked him straight out if there was any truth in it.

"Not so far," replied Morstin, "but you've given me an idea. I will wear my uniform – and not just at home. I'll go out in it too."

And so he did.

Henceforth Count Morstin was seen in the uniform of an Austrian captain of Dragoons – and the villagers did not give it another thought. Each time the captain stepped out of his house, he saluted his Commander-in-Chief, the bust of the dead Emperor Franz Joseph. Then he went the usual way along the sandy road between two little stands of pine to the nearest town. The peasants he encountered on the way took off their hats and said: "Praise the Lord," and appended a "Your Grace" – as though they believed the

Count was a close relation of the Saviour's, and two titles were better than one. Oh! – it was a long time now since he had been able to help them, as he had once helped them! The little peasants were still helpless. But he, the Count, was no longer powerful to help them! – And, like everyone who has once been powerful, he now seemed even less than powerless: in the eyes of officialdom, he was ridiculous. But the people of Lopatyny and its environs still believed in him, as they believed in Emperor Franz Joseph, whose bust they habitually greeted. To the peasants and the Jews of Lopatyny and environs, Count Morstin seemed not at all ridiculous, but venerable. They venerated his lean, bony frame, his gray hair, his ashen, crumpled face, his eyes, that seemed to be fixed on a limitless distance, and no wonder: they were looking at a lost past.

Then one day it happened that the *voivode* of Lvov, which used to be called Lemberg, went on a tour of inspection, and for some reason found himself forced to stay in Lopatyny. He was shown the house of Count Morstin, and he directed his steps there. To his astonishment, he glimpsed in a shrubbery in front of the house, the bust of the Emperor Franz Joseph. He looked at it a long time, and finally decided to go in and ask the Count himself what the meaning of the memorial might be. He was still more astounded – yes, he was alarmed – at the sight of Count Morstin, stepping up to meet him in the uniform of a captain of the Austrian Dragoons. The *voivode* himself was a "Little Pole", in other words: he was a native of the former province of Galicia. He too had served in the Austrian Army. Count Morstin was like a ghost from a period of history that he, the *voivode*, had considered dead and buried.

He got a grip on himself, and asked no questions. But later, when they were sitting at table, he began to make cautious inquiries about the memorial to the Emperor. – "Yes," said the Count, as if the new world simply didn't exist, "the Emperor, of blessed memory, spent a week here with me. A highly gifted peasant lad made that bust of him. It's always stood there. As long as I live, it will remain there."

The *voivode* didn't voice the determination he had just made, and said, with a smile and every appearance of casualness: "I see you still wear the old uniform?"

"Indeed I do," replied Morstin, "it's too late in life for me to get used to a new one. And I don't feel quite at ease in civvies, since the change in circumstances. I'm afraid I might be mistaken for someone else. – Here's to you," the Count continued – raised his glass, and drank to his guest.

The *voivode* sat a while longer, then he left the Count and the village of Lopatyny, resumed his tour of inspection, returned to his residence, and gave instructions that the bust of the Emperor was to be removed from outside Count Morstin's house.

These instructions were ultimately handed down to the burgomaster (now called the *woit*) of the village of Lopatyny, and thence came to the attention of Count Morstin.

It was the first time that the Count found himself in open conflict with the new authorities, whose existence he had barely acknowledged previously. He saw that he was too weak to mount a personal rebellion against them. He remembered the nocturnal scene in the American Bar in Zürich. Oh, there was no point any more in shutting one's eyes to this new world of new-minted republics, new bankers and crown-wearers, new ladies and gentlemen, new rulers of the world. It was time to bury the old world. But it had to be buried with dignity.

So Count Franz Xaver Morstin summoned the ten eldest inhabitants of Lopatyny to his house – and among them was the clever and simple Jew Solomon Piniowsky. Also of the company were the Greek Orthodox and the Roman Catholic priests and the rabbi.

And when they were all assembled, Count Morstin addressed them as follows:

"My dear fellow-citizens, you have all of you known the old Monarchy, your old fatherland. It has been dead for years – and there is no sense in not admitting it. Perhaps one day it will be resurrected, but we old folks will not live to see the day. And now we have been ordered to remove the bust of the Emperor Franz Joseph the First, God rest his soul, forthwith.

My friends, let us do more than simply remove it!

If the old times are dead, let us do with them what is done with the dead: let us bury them.

Therefore I beg you, my dear friends, to help me to lay to rest the dead Emperor, or rather his bust, with all appropriate ceremony and dignity, three days from now."

VI

The Ukrainian joiner Nikita Kolohin carpentered a magnificent coffin from oak boards. It was spacious enough to have accommodated three dead emperors quite comfortably.

The Polish blacksmith Jaroslav Wojciechowski smelted a huge double eagle in brass, which was cleated on to the lid of the coffin.

The Jewish Torah scribe Nuchim Kapturak inscribed with a goose quill on parchment the blessing that pious Jews are supposed to speak when they behold a crowned head, rolled it up in a box of hammered tin, and laid it in the coffin.

Early in the morning – it was a warm summer's day – countless invisible larks were trilling up in the sky, and countless invisible crickets whispered their responses from the meadows – the inhabitants of the village of Lopatyny assembled before the memorial to Franz Joseph I. Count Morstin and the burgomaster settled the bust in the magnificent great coffin. At that moment, the bells began to chime in the church on the hill. The leaders of all three denominations of worshippers walked at the head of the procession. Four old, strong peasants took the coffin on their shoulders. Behind it, with drawn saber, in his Dragoon's helmet draped with field-gray, walked Count Franz Xaver Morstin, the closest being to the late Emperor, all alone in that vast solitude that mourning brings, and behind him, with his round black skullcap on his silvered head walked the Jew Solomon Piniowsky, with his round velvet hat in his left hand, and the great black-and-yellow banner with the double eagle upraised in his right. And behind him followed the entire village, men and women.

The church bells clanged, the larks trilled, and the crickets whispered without let-up.

The grave had been dug. The coffin was lowered into it, the flag spread over it – and Franz Xaver Morstin stood, sword aloft, and saluted his Emperor for the last time.

Thereupon a sobbing was heard in the crowd, as if this were indeed the burial of Emperor Franz Joseph, of the old Monarchy, and the old country. The three men of God all prayed.

And so the old Emperor was buried for the second time, in the village of Lopatyñy, in the erstwhile Galicia.

A few weeks later, news of these proceedings appeared in the newspapers. They wrote them up in a few light-hearted words, under the heading "Marginal Notes".

VII

Count Morstin left the country. He went to live in the South of France, a decayed old man who plays chess and skat with old Russian generals. He devotes a couple of hours a day to writing his memoirs. In all probability, they won't have any great literary significance, because Count Morstin had neither much practice nor ambition as a writer. But as he is a man possessed of a certain grace and distinction, he occasionally manages the odd striking passage, like the following, which, with his permission, I should like to quote:

"In my time," writes the Count, "I have known the clever become stupid, the wise foolish, true prophets false, and lovers of truth deceitful. No human virtue is of enduring worth in this world, save only true piety. Faith cannot disappoint us, as it promises us nothing on this earth. The true believer cannot disappoint us, because he seeks no personal advantage. What this means to ordinary people is this: their pursuit of so-called national virtues, which are still more dubious than personal values, is fatuous. That is why I hate nations and nation-states. My former home, the Monarchy, was different, it was a large house with many doors and many rooms for many different kinds of people. This house has been divided, broken up, ruined. I have no business with what is there now. I am used to living in a house, not in cabins."

So, with pride and sadness, writes the old Count. Calmly, and with dignity, he awaits death. Probably he yearns for it too. Because he has stipulated in his will that he is to be buried in the village of Lopatyny – not in the family vault, but next to the grave where the Emperor Franz Joseph lies buried, the bust of the Emperor.

THE LEVIATHAN

I

In the small town of Progrody there lived a coral merchant who was known far and wide for his honesty and the reliability and quality of his wares. The farmers' wives came to him from far-distant villages when they needed an ornament for some festive occasion. There were other coral merchants who were closer at hand, but they knew that from them they would only get cheap stuff and no-good tat. And so, in their rickety little carts they traveled many versts to Progrody and the renowned coral merchant Nissen Piczenik.

They tended to come on market days, which were Mondays and Thursdays for horses and pigs respectively. While their menfolk were busy sizing up the animals, the women would go off together in little groups, barefooted, their boots dangling over their shoulders, with their brightly colored scarves that shone even on rainy days, to the house of Nissen Piczenik. The tough bare soles of their feet pattered happily along the hollow-planked wooden pavement, and down the broad cool passage of the old building where the merchant lived. The arching passageway led into a quiet yard where soft moss sprouted among the uneven cobblestones, and the occasional blade of grass raised its head in summer. Here Nissen

Piczenik's flock of chickens came joyfully out to meet them, the cocks leading the way with their proud red combs as red as the reddest of the corals.

They would knock three times on the iron door with the iron knocker. At that, Piczenik would open a little grille cut into the door, see who was outside, and draw the bolt and allow the farmers' wives to come in. In the case of beggars, traveling musicians, gypsies and men with dancing bears, he would merely pass a coin out through the grille. He had to be very careful because on each of the tables in his large kitchen and his parlor he had fine corals in large, small and middle-sized heaps, various races and breeds of corals all mixed up, or already sorted according to color and type. He didn't have so many eyes in his head that he could see what every beggar was up to, and Piczenik knew how seductively poverty led to sin. Of course, some prosperous farmers' wives sometimes stole things, too; for women are always tempted to help themselves illicitly and clandestinely to an item of jewelry they can comfortably afford to buy. But where his customers were concerned, the merchant would tend to turn a blind eye, and he included a few thefts in the prices he charged for his wares anyway.

He employed no fewer than ten threaders, pretty girls with keen eyes and soft hands. The girls sat in two rows either side of a long table, and fished for the corals with their fine needles. They put together beautiful regular necklaces, with the smallest corals at either end, and the largest and most brilliant in the middle. As they worked, the girls sang. On the hot, blue, sunny days of summer, when the long table where the women sat threading was set up outside in the yard, you could hear their summery voices all over the little town, louder than the twittering skylarks and the chirruping of the crickets in the gardens.

Most people, who only know corals from seeing them in shop windows and displays would be surprised to learn how many different varieties of them there are. For a start, they can be polished or not; they can be trimmed in a straight line or rounded off; there are thorny and stick-like corals that look like barbed wire; corals that gleam with a yellowish, almost a whitish red, like the rims of tea-rose petals; pinkish-yellow, pink, brick-red, beet-red, cinnabar-red corals, and finally there are those corals that look like hard, round drops of blood. There are rounds and half-rounds; corals like little barrels and little cylinders; there are straight, crooked and even hunchbacked corals. They come as stars, spears, hooks and blossoms. For corals are the noblest plants in the oceanic under-world; they are like roses for the capricious goddesses of the sea, as inexhaustible in their variety as the caprices of the goddesses.

As you see then, Nissen Piczenik didn't have a shop as such. He ran his business from home, which meant that he lived among the corals night and day, summer and winter, and as all the windows in his parlor and kitchen opened on to the courtyard, and were pro-tected by thick iron bars, there was in his apartment a beautiful and mysterious twilight that was like the light under the sea, and it was as though corals were not merely traded here, but that this was where they actually grew. Furthermore, thanks to a strange and canny quirk of nature, the coral merchant Nissen Piczenik was a red-haired Jew with a copper-colored goatee that looked like a particular kind of reddish seaweed, which gave the man a striking resemblance to a sea god. It was as though he made his corals him-self, or maybe sowed and reaped them in some way. In fact, so strong was the association between his wares and his appearance that in the small town of Progrody he was known not by his name, which had gradually fallen into disuse, but by his calling. For instance, people would say: Here comes the coral merchant – as though there were none but him in all the world.

And in fact, Nissen Piczenik did feel a kind of affinity or kinship with corals. He had never been to school, couldn't read or write, and was only able to mark his name crudely – but he lived with the wholly unscientific conviction that corals were not plants at all, but living creatures, a kind of tiny reddish sea-animal – and no profes-sor of marine science could have convinced him otherwise. Yes, for

Nissen Piczenik corals remained alive, even when they had been sawn, cut, polished, sorted and threaded. And perhaps he was right. Because with his own eyes he had seen how on the breasts of sick or poorly women his reddish strings of corals would begin to fade, while on the breasts of healthy women they kept their luster. In the course of his long experience as a coral merchant, he had often observed how corals that − for all their redness − had grown pale from lying in cupboards, once they were put round the neck of a healthy and beautiful young peasant woman, would start to glow as if they drew nourishment from the woman's blood. Sometimes the merchant was offered corals to buy back, and he recognized the stones he had once threaded and cherished − and he could tell right away whether the woman who had worn them had been healthy or unhealthy.

He had a very particular theory of his own regarding corals. As already stated, he thought of them as sea creatures, who as it were, out of prudence and modesty, only imitated plants and trees so as to avoid being attacked and eaten by sharks. It was every coral's dream to be plucked by a diver and brought to the surface, to be cut, polished and threaded, so as finally to be able to serve the purpose for which it had been created: namely to be an ornament on a beautiful peasant woman. Only there, on the fine, firm white throat of a woman, in close proximity to the living artery − sister of the feminine heart − did they revive, acquire luster and beauty, and exercise their innate ability to charm men and awaken their ardor. Now, the ancient god Jehovah had created everything, the earth and the beasts who walked upon it, the sea and all its creatures. But for the time being − namely until the coming of the Messiah − he had left the supervision of all the animals and plants of the sea, and in particular of corals, to the care of the Leviathan, who lay curled on the sea bed.

It might be supposed that the trader Nissen Piczenik had a reputation as something of an eccentric. Nothing could be further from the truth. Piczenik lived quietly and unobtrusively in the small town of Progrody, and his tales of corals and the Leviathan were treated with complete seriousness, as befitting the opinion of an expert, a man who must know his business, just as the haberdasher knew his German percale from his corduroy, and the tea merchant could tell the Russian tea from the famous firm of Popov from the English tea supplied by the equally famous firm of Liptons of London. All the inhabitants of Progrody and its surroundings were convinced that corals are living creatures, and that the great fish Leviathan was responsible for their well-being under the sea. There could be no question of that, seeing as Nissen Piczenik said so himself.

In Nissen Piczenik's house, the beautiful threaders often worked far into the night, sometimes even past midnight. Once they had gone home, the trader himself sat down with his stones, or rather his animals. First, he examined the strings the girls had threaded, then he counted the heaps of corals that were as yet unsorted and the heaps of those that had been sorted according to type and size, then he began sorting them himself, and with his strong and deft and reddish-haired fingers, he felt and smoothed and stroked each individual coral. There were some corals that were worm-eaten. They had holes in places where no holes were required. The sloppy Leviathan couldn't have been paying attention. And reproachfully, Nissen Piczenik lit a candle, and held a piece of red wax over the flame until it melted, and then dipping a fine needle into the wax, he sealed the worm-holes in the stone, all the while shaking his head, as though not comprehending how such a powerful god as Jehovah could have left such an irresponsible fish as the Leviathan in charge of all the corals.

Sometimes, out of pure pleasure in the stones, he would thread corals himself until the sky grew light and it was time for him to say his morning prayers. The work didn't tire him at all, he felt strong and alert. His wife was still under the blankets, asleep. He gave her a curt, indifferent look. He didn't love her or hate her, she was merely one of the many threaders who worked for him, though she was less attractive now than most of the others. Ten years he had been married to her, and she had borne him no children – when that alone was her function. He wanted a fertile woman, fertile as the sea on whose bed so many corals grew. His wife, though, was like a dried-up lake. Let her sleep alone, as many nights as she wanted. According to the law, he could divorce her. But by now he had become indifferent to wives and children. Corals were what he loved. And there was in his heart a vague longing which he couldn't quite explain: Nissen Piczenik, born and having lived all his life in the middle of a great land mass, longed for the sea.

Yes, he longed for the sea on whose bed the corals grew – or rather, as he was convinced – disported themselves. Far and wide there was no one to whom he could speak of his longing, he had to carry it pent up in himself, as the sea carries its corals. He had heard about ships and divers, sailors and sea captains. His corals arrived, still smelling of the sea, in neatly packed crates from Odessa, Hamburg and Trieste. The public scribe in the post office did his correspondence for him. He carefully examined the colorful stamps on the letters from his suppliers abroad before throwing away the envelopes. He had never left Progrody. The town didn't have a river, not so much as a pond, only swamps on all sides, where you could hear the water gurgle far below the green surface, without being able to see it. Nissen Piczenik imagined some secret communication between the buried water in the swamps and the mighty waters of the sea – and that deep down at the bottom of the swamp, there might be corals, too. He knew that if he ever said as much, he would be a laughing-stock all over town. And so he kept his silence, and didn't talk about his theories. Sometimes he dreamed that the Great Sea – he didn't know which one, he had never seen a map, and so where he was concerned, all the world's seas were just the Great Sea – would one day flood Russia, the part of it where he lived himself. That way, the sea which he had no hope of reaching, would come to him, the strange and mighty sea, with the immeasurable Leviathan on the bottom, and all its sweet and bitter and salty secrets.

The road from the small town of Progrody to the little railway station where trains called just three times a week led through the swamps. And even when Nissen Piczenik wasn't expecting any packages of coral, even on days when there weren't any trains, he would walk to the station, or rather to the swamps. He would stand often for an hour or more at the edge of the swamp and listen reverently to the croaking of the frogs, as if they could tell him of life at the bottom of the swamp, and sometimes he felt he had taken their meaning. In winter, when the swamp froze over, he even dared to take a few steps on it, and that gave him a peculiar delight. The moldy swamp-smell seemed to convey something of the powerful briny aroma of the sea, and to his eager ears the miserable glugging of the buried waters was transformed into the roaring of enormous green-blue breakers.

In the whole small town of Progrody there was no one who knew what was going on in the soul of the coral merchant. All the Jews took him for just another one like themselves. This man dealt in cloth, and that one in kerosene; one sold prayer shawls, another soaps and wax candles, and a third, kerchiefs for farmers' wives and pocket knives; one taught the children how to pray, another how to count, and a third sold kvas and beans and roasted maize kernels. And to all of them Nissen Piczenik seemed one of themselves – with the only difference that he happened to deal in coral. And yet – you will see – he was altogether different.

II

His customers were both rich and poor, regular and occasional. Among his rich customers were two local farmers. One of them, Timon Semyonovitch, was a hop grower, and every year when the buyers came down from Nuremberg and Zatec and Judenburg, he made a number of profitable deals. The other farmer was Nikita Ivanovitch. He had no fewer than eight daughters, whom he was marrying off one after the other, and all needed corals. The married daughters – to date there were four of them – a month or two after their weddings gave birth to children of their own – more daughters – and these, too, required corals, though they were only infants, to ward off the Evil Eye. The members of these two families were the most esteemed guests in Nissen Piczenik's house. For the daughters of these farmers, their sons-in-law and their grandchildren, the merchant kept a supply of good brandy in reserve, home-made brandy flavored with ants, dried mushrooms, parsley and centaury. The ordinary customers had to be content with ordinary shop-bought vodka. For in that part of the world there was no purchasing anything without a drink. Buyer and seller drank to the transaction, that it might bring profit and blessing to both parties. There were also heaps of loose tobacco in the apartment of the coral merchant, lying by the window, wrapped in damp blotting paper to keep it fresh. For customers didn't come to Nissen Piczenik the way people go into a shop, merely to buy the goods, pay and leave. The majority of the customers had covered many versts, and to Nissen Piczenik they were more than customers, they were also his guests. They drank with him, smoked with him, and sometimes even ate with him. The merchant's wife prepared buckwheat kasha with onions, borscht with sour cream, she roasted apples and potatoes, and chestnuts in the autumn. And so the customers were not just customers, they were guests of Nissen Piczenik's house. Sometimes, while they were hunting for suitable corals, the farmers' wives would join in the singing of the threaders; then they all would sing together, and even Nissen Piczenik would hum to himself, and in the kitchen his wife would beat time with a wooden spoon. Then, when the farmers returned from the market or from the pub to pick up their wives and pay for their purchases, the coral merchant would be obliged to drink brandy or tea with them, and smoke a cigarette. And all the old customers would kiss the merchant on both cheeks like a brother.

Because once we have got a drink or two inside us, all good

honest men are our brothers, and all lovely women our sisters – and there is no difference between farmer and merchant, Jew and Christian; and woe to anyone who says otherwise!

III

With every year that passed, unbeknownst to anyone in the small town of Progrody, Nissen Piczenik grew more dissatisfied with his uneventful life. Like every other Jew, the coral merchant went to synagogue twice a day, morning and evening, he celebrated holidays, fasted on fast days, he put on his prayer shawl and his phylacteries, and swayed back and forth from the waist, he talked to people, he had conversations about politics, about the war with Japan, about what was printed in the newspapers and preoccupying the world. But deep in his heart, there was still the longing for the sea, home of the corals, and, not being able to read, he asked to have read out to him any items relating to the sea when the newspapers came to Progrody twice a week. Just as he did about corals, he had a very particular notion of the sea. He knew that strictly speaking the world had many seas, but the one true sea was the one you had to cross in order to reach America.

Now it happened one day that the son of the hessian seller Alexander Komrower, who three years previously had enlisted and joined the navy, returned home for a short leave. No sooner had the coral merchant got to hear of young Komrower's return than he appeared in his house and started asking the sailor about all the mysteries of ships, water and winds. Whereas the rest of Progrody was convinced that it had been sheer stupidity that had got young Komrower hauled off to the dangerous oceans, the coral merchant saw in the sailor a fortunate youth, who had been granted the favor and the distinction of being made, as it were, an intimate of the corals, yes, even a kind of relation. And so the forty-five-year-old Nissen Piczenik and the twenty-two-year-old Komrower were seen walking about arm in arm in the market place of the little town for hours on end. People asked themselves: What does he want with that Komrower? And the young fellow asked himself: What does he want with me?

During the whole period of the young man's leave in Progrody, the coral merchant hardly left his side. Their exchanges, like the following, were bewildering to the younger man:

"Can you see down to the bottom of the sea with a telescope?"

"No," replied the sailor, "with a telescope you only look into the distance, not into the deep."

"Can you," Nissen Piczenik went on, "as a sailor, go down to the bottom of the sea?"

"No," said young Komrower, "except if you drown, then you might well go down to the bottom."

"What about the captain?"

"The captain can't either."

"Have you ever seen a diver?"

"A few times," said the sailor.

"Do sea creatures and sea plants sometimes climb up to the surface?"

"Only some fish like whales that aren't really fish at all."

"Describe the sea to me!" said Nissen Piczenik.

"It's full of water —" said the sailor Komrower.

"And is it very wide and flat, like a great steppe with no houses on it?"

"It's as wide as that — and more!" said the young sailor. "And it's just like you say: a wide plain with the odd house dotted about on it, only not a house but a ship."

"Where did you see divers?"

"We in the navy," said the young man, "have got our own divers. But they don't dive for pearls or oysters or corals. It's for military purposes, for instance, in case a warship goes down, and then they can retrieve important instruments or weapons."

"How many seas are there?"

"I wouldn't know," replied the sailor. "We were told at navy school, but I didn't pay any attention. The only ones I know are the Baltic, the Black Sea and the Great Ocean."

"Which sea is the deepest?"

"Don't know."

"Where are the most corals found?"

"Don't know that, either."

"Hm, hm," said the coral merchant, "pity you don't know that."

At the edge of the small town, there where the little houses of Progrody grew ever more wretched until they finally petered out altogether, and the wide hump-backed road to the station began, stood Podgorzev's bar, a house of ill-repute in which peasants, farm laborers, soldiers, stray girls and layabouts congregated. One day, the coral merchant Piczenik was seen going in there with the sailor Komrower. They were served strong, dark-red mead and salted peas. "Drink, my boy! Eat and drink, my boy!" said Nissen Piczenik to the sailor in fatherly fashion. And he ate and drank for all he was worth, for young as he was, he had already learned a thing or two in ports, and after the mead he was given some bad sour wine, and after the wine a 90-proof brandy. He was so quiet over the mead that the coral merchant feared he had heard all he was going to hear from the sailor on the subject of the sea, and that his knowledge was simply exhausted. After the wine, however, young Komrower got into conversation with the barkeeper, and when the 90-proof brandy came, he fell to singing at the top of his voice, one song after another, just like a real sailor. "Do you hail from our beloved little town?" asked the barkeeper. "Of course, I'm a child of your – my – our little town," replied the sailor, as if he wasn't the son of the plump Jew Komrower, but a regular farmer's boy. A couple of tramps and ne'er-do-wells came over to join Nissen Piczenik and the sailor at their table, and when the boy saw he had an audience, he felt a keen sense of dignity, such dignity as he thought only ships' officers could possibly have. And he played up to them: "Go on, fellows, ask all you like. I've got answers to all your questions. You see this dear old uncle here, you all know who he is, he's the best coral seller in the whole province, and I've told him a lot of things already!" Nissen Piczenik nodded. And since he felt uneasy in this unfamiliar company, he drank a glass of mead, and then another. Gradually, all these dubious faces he'd previously only seen through the grille in his door became as human as his own. But as caution and suspicion were ingrained in his nature, he went out into the yard, and hid his purse in his cap, leaving only a few coins loose in his pocket. Satisfied with his idea, and soothed by the pressure of the money against his skull, he sat down at the table again.

And yet he had to admit to himself that he didn't really know what he was doing, sitting in the bar with the sailor and these criminal types. All his life he had kept himself to himself, and prior to the arrival of the sailor, his secret passion for corals and the ocean home of corals had not been made public in any way. And there was something else that alarmed Nissen Piczenik deeply. He suddenly saw his secret longing for waters and whatever lived in them and upon them as coming to the surface of his own life, like some rare and precious creature at home on the sea bed, shooting up to the surface for some unknown reason – and he had never had such vivid thoughts before. The sudden fancy must have been prompted by the mead and the stimulating effect of the sailor's stories. The fact that such crazy notions could come to him upset and alarmed him even more than suddenly finding himself sitting at a bar room table among vice-ridden associates.

But all his alarm and upset remained submerged, well below the surface of his mind. All the while, he was listening with keen enjoyment to the incredible tales of the sailor Komrower. "And what about your own ship?" his new friends were asking him. He thought about it for a while. His ship was named after a famous nineteenth century admiral, but that name seemed as banal as his own, and Komrower was determined to impress them all mightily – and so he said: "My cruiser is called the *Little Mother Catherine*. Do you know who she was? Of course, you don't. So I'll tell you.

Well then, Catherine was the richest and most beautiful woman in the whole of Russia, and so one day the Tsar married her in the Kremlin in Moscow, and then he took her away on a sleigh – it was forty below – drawn by six horses to Tsarskoye Selo. Behind them came their whole retinue on sleighs – and there were so many of them, the road was blocked for three days and three nights. Then, a week after the magnificent wedding, the wanton and aggressive King of Sweden arrived in Petersburg harbor with his ridiculous wooden barges, but with a lot of soldiers standing up on them because the Swedes are very brave fighters on land – and this king had a plan to conquer the whole of Russia. So the Tsarina Catherine straightway got on a ship, namely the very cruiser I'm serving on, and with her own hands she bombed the silly barges of the King of Sweden and sank the lot of them. And she tossed the King a lifebelt and took him prisoner. She had his eyes put out, and ate them, and that made her even cleverer than she was before. As for the blind King, he was packed off to Siberia."

"Is that so," said one of the layabouts, scratching his head. "I can't hardly believe it."

"You say that again," retorted the sailor Komrower, "and I'll be obliged to kill you for insulting the Imperial Russian Navy. I'll have you know I learned this whole story at our naval academy, and His Grace, our Captain Voroshenko told it to us in person."

They drank some more mead and one or two more brandies, and then the coral merchant Nissen Piczenik paid for everyone. He had had a few drinks himself, though not as many as the others. But when he stepped out on to the street, arm in arm with the young sailor Komrower, it seemed to him as though the middle of the road was a river with waves rippling up and down it, the occasional oil lanterns were lighthouses, and he had better stick to the side of the road if he wasn't to fall into the water. The young fellow was swaying all over the place. Now, from his childhood days Nissen Piczenik had said his prayers every evening, the one that you say when it starts to get dark, the other one at nightfall. Today, for the first time, he had missed them both. The stars were twinkling reproachfully at him up in the sky, he didn't dare look at them. At home his wife would be waiting with his usual evening meal, radish with cucumbers and onions, a piece of bread and dripping, a glass of kvas and hot tea. He felt more shame on his own behalf than in front of other people. He had the feeling, walking along arm in arm with the heavy, stumbling young man that he was continually running into himself, the coral merchant Nissen Piczenik was meeting the coral merchant Nissen Piczenik, and they were laughing at one another. However, he was able to avoid meeting anyone else. He brought young Komrower home, took him into the room where the old Komrowers were sitting, and said: "Don't be angry with him, I went to the bar with him, he's had a bit to drink."

"You, Nissen Piczenik, the coral merchant, have been drinking with him?" asked old Komrower.

"Yes, I have!" said Piczenik. "Now good night!" And he went home. His beautiful threaders were still all sitting at the four long tables singing and fishing up corals with their delicate needles in their fine hands.

"Just give me some tea," said Nissen Piczenik to his wife. "I have work to do."

And he drank his tea, and while his hot fingers scrabbled about in the large, still unsorted heaps of corals, and in their delicious rosy cool, his poor heart was wandering over the wide and roaring highways of the mighty ocean.

And there was a mighty burning and roaring in his skull. Sensibly, though, he remembered to take off his cap, pull out his purse and put it back in his shirt once more.

IV

The day drew nigh when the sailor Komrower was to report back to his cruiser in Odessa – and the coral merchant dreaded the prospect. In all Progrody, young Komrower is the only sailor, and God knows when he'll be given leave again. Once he goes, that'll be the last you hear of the waters of the world, apart from the odd item in the newspapers.

The summer was well-advanced, a fine summer by the way, cloudless and dry, cooled by the steady breeze across the Volhynian steppes. Another two weeks and it would be harvest time, and the peasants would no longer be coming in from their villages on market days to buy corals from Nissen Piczenik. These two weeks were the height of the coral season. In this fortnight the customers came in great bunches and clusters, the threaders could hardly keep up with the work, they stayed up all night sorting and threading. In the beautiful early evenings, when the declining sun sent its golden adieus through Piczenik's barred windows, and the heaps of coral of every type and hue, animated by its melancholy and bracing light, started to glow as though each little stone carried its own microscopic lantern in its delicate interior, the farmers would turn up, boisterous and a little merry, to collect their wives, with their red-and-blue handkerchiefs filled with silver and copper coins, in heavy hobnailed boots that clattered on the cobbles in the yard outside. The farmers greeted Nissen Piczenik with embraces and kisses, like a long-lost friend. They meant well by him, they were even fond of him, the lanky, taciturn, red-haired Jew with the honest, sometimes wistful china blue eyes, where decency lived and fair dealing, the savvy of the expert and the ignorance of the man who had never once left the small town of Progrody. It wasn't easy to get the better of the farmers. For although they recognized the coral merchant as one of the few honest tradesmen in the area, they wouldn't forget that he was a Jew. And they weren't averse to haggling themselves. First, they made themselves at home on the chairs, the settee, the two wide wooden double beds with plump bolsters on them. And some of them, their boots encrusted with silvery-gray mud, even lay down on the beds, the sofa or the floor. They took pinches of loose tobacco from the pockets of their burlap trousers, or from the supplies on the windowsill, tore off the edges of old newspapers that were lying around in Piczenik's room, and rolled themselves cigarettes – cigarette papers were considered a luxury, even by the well-off among them. Soon, the coral merchant's apartment was filled with the dense blue smoke of cheap tobacco and rough paper, blue smoke gilded by the last of the sunlight, gradually emptying itself out into the street in small clouds drifting through the squares of the barred open windows. In a couple of copper samovars on a table in the middle of the room – these too burnished by the setting sun – hot water was kept boiling, and no fewer than fifty cheap green double-bottomed glasses were passed from hand to hand, full of schnapps and steaming golden-brown tea. The prices of the coral necklaces had already been agreed on with the women in the course of several hours' bargaining in the morning. But now the husbands were unhappy with the price, and so the haggling began all over again. It was a hard struggle for the skinny Jew, all on his own against overwhelming numbers of tight-fisted and suspicious, strongly built and in their cups potentially violent men. The sweat ran down under the black silk cap he wore at home, down his freckled, thinly bearded cheeks into the red goatee, and the hairs of his beard grew matted together, so that in the evening, after the battle, he had to part them with a little fine-toothed steel comb. Finally, he won the day against his customers, in spite of his ignorance. For, in the whole wide world, there were only two things that he understood, which were corals and the farmers of the region – and he knew how to thread the former and outwit the latter. The implacably obstinate ones would be given a so-called "extra" – in other words, when they agreed to pay the price he had secretly been hoping for all along, he would give them a tiny coral chain made from stones of little value, to put round the necks or wrists of their children, where it was guaranteed to be effective against the Evil Eye or spiteful neighbors and wicked witches. And all the time he had to watch what the hands of his customers were up to, and to keep gauging the size of the various piles of coral. It really wasn't easy!

In this particular high summer, however, Nissen Piczenik's manner was distracted, almost apathetic. He seemed indifferent to his customers and to his business. His loyal wife, long accustomed to his peculiar silences, noticed the change in him and took him to task. He had sold a string of corals too cheaply here, he had failed to spot a little theft there, today he had given an old customer no "extras", while yesterday he'd given a new and insignificant buyer quite a valuable necklace. There had never been any strife in the Piczenik household. But over the course of these days, the coral merchant lost his calm, and he felt himself how his indifference, his habitual indifference towards his wife suddenly turned into violent dislike. Yes, he who was incapable of drowning a single one of the many mice that were caught in his traps every night – the way everyone in Progrody did – but instead paid Saul the water carrier to do it for him, on this day, he, the peaceable Nissen Piczenik threw a heavy string of corals in his wife's face as she was criticizing him as usual, slammed the door and walked out of the house to sit by the edge of the great swamp, the cousin many times removed of the great oceans.

Just two days before the sailor's departure there surfaced in the coral merchant the notion of accompanying young Komrower to Odessa. A notion like that arrives suddenly, lightning is slow by comparison, and it hits the very place from where it sprang, which is to say the human heart. If you like, it strikes its own birthplace. Such was Nissen Piczenik's notion. And from such a notion to a resolution is only a short distance.

On the morning of the departure of the young sailor Komrower, Nissen Piczenik said to his wife: "I have to go away for a few days."

His wife was still in bed. It was eight in the morning, the coral merchant had just returned from morning prayers in the synagogue.

She sat up. Without her wig on, her thin hair in disarray and yellow crusts of sleep in the corners of her eyes, she looked unfamiliar, even hostile to him. Her appearance, her alarm, her consternation all confirmed him in a decision which even to him had seemed rash.

"I'm going to Odessa!" he said with unconcealed venom. "I'll be back in a week, God willing!"

"Now? Now?" stammered his wife amongst the pillows. "Does it have to be now, when all the farmers are coming?" "Right now!" said the coral merchant. "I have important business. Pack my things!"

And with a vicious and spiteful delight he had never previously felt, he watched as his wife got out of bed, saw her ugly toes, her fat legs below the long flea-spotted nightgown, and he heard her all too familiar sigh, the inevitable morning song of this woman with whom nothing connected him beyond the distant memory of a few nocturnal tendernesses, and the usual fear of divorce.

But within Nissen Piczenik there was a jubilant voice, a strange and familiar voice inside him: Piczenik is off to the corals! He's off to the corals! Nissen Piczenik is going to the home of the corals! . . .

V

So he boarded the train with the sailor Komrower and went to Odessa. It was a long and complicated journey, with a change at Kiev. It was the first time the coral merchant had been on a train, but he didn't feel about it the way most people do when they ride on a train for the first time. The locomotive, the signals, the bells, the telegraph masts, the tracks, the conductors and the landscape flying by outside, none of it interested him. He was preoccupied with water and the harbor he was headed for, and if he registered any of the characteristic features of railway travel, it was only in order to speculate on the still unfamiliar features of travel on board ship. "Do you have bells, too?" he asked the sailor. "Do they ring three times before the ship leaves? Does the ship have to turn round, or can it just swim backwards?"

Of course, as inevitably happens on journeys, they met other passengers who wanted to get into conversation, and so he had to discuss this and that with them. "I'm a coral merchant," said Nissen Piczenik truthfully, when he was asked what it was he did. But when the next question came: "What brings you to Odessa?" he began to lie. "I have some important business there." "How interesting," said a fellow-passenger, who until that moment had said nothing, "I, too, have important business in Odessa, and the merchandise I deal in is not unrelated to coral, although it is of course far finer and dearer!" "Dearer it may be," said Nissen Piczenik, "but it can't possibly be finer!" "You want to bet it isn't?" cried the man, "I tell you it's impossible. There's no point in betting!" "Well then," crowed the man, "I deal in pearls." "Pearls aren't at all finer," said Piczenik. "And besides they're unlucky." "They are if you lose them," said the pearl trader. By now everyone was listening to this extraordinary dispute. Finally, the pearl merchant reached into his trousers and took out a bag full of gleaming, flawless pearls. He tipped a few into the palm of his hand, and showed them to the other travelers. "To find a single pearl," he said, "hundreds of oyster shells have to be opened. The divers command very high wages. Among all the merchants of the world, we pearl traders are the most highly regarded. You could say we're a special breed. Take me, for example. I'm a merchant of the first guild, I live in Petersburg, I have a distinguished clientèle, including two Grand Dukes whose names are a trade secret, I've traveled halfway round the world, every year I go to Paris, Brussels and Amsterdam. Ask anywhere for the pearl trader Gorodotzky, even little children will be able to direct you."

"And I," said Nissen Piczenik, "have never left our small town of Progrody, and all my customers are farmers. But you will agree that a simple farmer's wife, decked out in a couple of chains of fine, flawless corals is not outdone by a Grand Duchess. Corals are worn by high and low alike, they raise the low, and grace the high. You can wear corals morning, noon and night, wear them to ceremonial balls, in summer and in winter, on the Sabbath and on weekdays, to work and in the home, in times happy and sad. There are many different varieties of red, my dear fellow-passengers, and it is written that our Jewish King Solomon had a very special kind for his royal robes, because the Phoenicians who revered him had made him a present of a special kind of worm that excretes red dye in its urine. You can't get this color any more, the purple of the Tsars is not the same, because after Solomon's death the whole species of that worm became extinct. Nowadays it is only in the very reddest corals that the color still exists. Now whoever heard of such a thing as red pearls?"

Never had the quiet coral merchant held such a long and impassioned address in front of a lot of complete strangers. He put his cap back and mopped his brow. He smiled round at his fellow-passengers, and they all applauded him: "He's right, he's right!" they all exclaimed at once.

And even the pearl merchant had to admit that, whatever the facts of the case, Nissen Piczenik had been an excellent advocate of corals.

They finally reached the glittering port city of Odessa, with its blue water and its host of bridal-white ships. Here the armored cruiser was waiting for the sailor Komrower, as a father's house awaits his son. Nissen Piczenik wanted very much to have a closer look at the ship. He went with the young fellow to the man on watch and said, "I'm his uncle, can I see the ship?" His own temerity surprised him. Oh yes, this wasn't the old terrestrial Nissen Piczenik who was addressing an armed sailor, it wasn't Nissen Piczenik from landlocked Progrody, this was somebody else, a man transformed, a man whose insides were now proudly on the outside, an oceanic Nissen Piczenik. It seemed to him that he hadn't just got off the train, but that he had climbed out of the water, out of the depths of the Black Sea. He felt at home by the water, as he had never felt at home in Progrody, where he was born and had lived all his life. Wherever he looks, he sees nothing but ships and water, water and ships. There are the ships, the boats, the tugs, the yachts, the motor boats apple-blossom white, raven-black, coral-red, yes, coral-red – and there is the water washing against their sides, no, not washing but lapping and stroking, in thousands of little wavelets, like tongues and hands at once. The Black Sea isn't black at all. In the distance, it's bluer than the sky, close to, it's as green as grass. When you toss a piece of bread in the water, thousands and thousands of swift little fishes leap, skip, slip, slither, flit and flash to the spot. A cloudless blue sky arches over the harbor, pricked by the masts and chimneys of the ships. "What's this? What's the name of that?" asks Nissen Piczenik incessantly. This is a mast, that's a bow, these are the lifebelts, there is a difference between a boat and a barge, a sailing vessel and a steamship, a mast and a funnel, a battleship and a merchantman, deck and stern, bow and keel. Nissen Piczenik's poor undaunted brain is bombarded by hundreds of new terms. After a long wait – he is very lucky, says the first mate – he is given permission to accompany his nephew on board, and to inspect the cruiser. This ship's lieutenant appears in person to watch a Jewish merchant go on board a vessel of the Imperial Russian Fleet. His Honor the lieutenant is pleased to smile. The long black skirts of the lanky red-haired Jew flutter in the gentle breeze, his striped trousers show, worn and patched, tucked into scuffed boots. The Jew Nissen Piczenik even forgets the laws of his faith. He doffs his black cap in front of the brilliant white and gold glory of the officer, and his red curls fly in the wind. "Your nephew's a fine lad," says His Honor, the officer, and Nissen Piczenik can think of no suitable reply. He smiles, he doesn't laugh, he smiles silently. His mouth is open, revealing his big yellow horsey teeth and his pink gums, and the copper-colored goatee drops down almost to his chest. He inspects the wheel, the cannons, he's allowed to peer down the ship's telescope – and by God, the far is brought near, what is a long way off is made to seem close at hand, in that glass. God gave man eyes, but what are ordinary eyes, compared to eyes looking through a telescope? God gave man eyes, but He also gave him understanding that he might invent the telescope and improve the power of his eyesight! And the sun shines down on the top deck, it shines on Nissen Piczenik's back, and still he doesn't grow hot, for there is a cooling breeze blowing over the sea, yes, it's as though the wind came out of the sea itself, a wind out of the very depths of the sea.

Finally, the hour of parting came. Nissen Piczenik embraced young Komrower, he bowed to the lieutenant and then to the sailors and he left the battle cruiser.

He had intended to return to Progrody straight after saying goodbye to young Komrower. But he remained in Odessa. He watched the battleship sail off, the sailors waved back to him as he stood on the quayside, waving his red-and-blue striped handkerchief. And he watched a lot of other ships sailing away, and he waved to their passengers as well. He went to the harbor every day, and every day he saw something new. For instance, he learned what it means: "to lift anchor", "furl the sails", "unload a cargo", "tighten a sheet", and so forth.

Every day he saw young men in sailor suits working on ships, swarming up the masts, he saw young men walking through the streets of Odessa, arm in arm, a line of sailors walking abreast, taking up the whole street – and he felt sad that he had no children of his own. Just then he wished he had sons and grandsons and – no question – he would have sent them all to sea. He'd have made sailors of them. And all the while his ugly and infertile wife was lying at home in Progrody. She was selling corals in his place. Did she know how? Did she have any appreciation of what corals meant?

In the port of Odessa, Nissen Piczenik rapidly forgot the obligations of an ordinary Jew from Progrody. He didn't go to the synagogue in the morning to say the prescribed prayers, nor yet in the evening. Instead, he prayed at home, hurriedly, without proper thought of God, he prayed in the manner of a phonograph, his tongue mechanically repeating the sounds that were engraved in his brain. Had the world ever seen such a Jew?

At home in Progrody, it was the coral season. Nissen Piczenik knew it, but then he wasn't the old continental Nissen Piczenik any more, he was the new, reborn, oceanic one.

There's plenty of time to go back to Progrody! he told himself. I'm not missing anything! Think of what I still have to do here!

And he stayed in Odessa for three weeks, and every day he spent happy hours with the sea and the ships and the little fishes.

It was the first time in his life that Nissen Piczenik had had a holiday.

VI

When he returned home to Progrody, he discovered that he was no less than one hundred and sixty rubles out of pocket, with all the expenses for his journey. But to his wife and to all those who asked him what he had been doing so long away from home, he replied that he had concluded some "important business" in Odessa.

The harvest was just now getting underway, and so the farmers didn't come to town so frequently on market days. As happened every year at this time, it grew quiet in the house of the coral merchant. The threaders went home in the afternoon. And in the evening, when Nissen Piczenik returned from the synagogue, he was greeted not by the melodious voices of the beautiful girls, but only by his wife, his plate of radish and onion, and the copper samovar. However, guided by the memory of his days in Odessa – whose commercial insignificance he kept secret – the coral merchant Piczenik bowed to the habitual rules of his autumnal days. Already he was thinking of claiming some further piece of important business in a few months' time, and going to visit a different harbor town, for instance, Petersburg.

He had no financial problems. All the money he had earned in the course of many years of selling corals was deposited and earning steady interest with the money-lender Pinkas Warschawsky, a respected usurer in the community, who, though pitiless in collecting any outstanding debts owing to him, was also punctual in paying interest. Nissen Piczenik had no material anxieties; he was childless and had no heirs to think of, so why not travel to another of the many harbors there were?

And the coral dealer had already begun to make plans for the spring when something strange happened in the small neighboring town of Sutschky.

In this town, which was no bigger than the small town of Progrody, the home of Nissen Piczenik, a complete stranger one day opened a coral shop. The man's name was Jenö Lakatos, and, as was soon learned, he came from the distant land of Hungary. He spoke Russian, German, Ukrainian and Polish, and yes, if required, and if someone happened to ask for it, then Mr. Lakatos would equally have spoken in French, English or Chinese. He was a young man with slick, blue-black pomaded hair – and he was also the only man far and wide to wear a shiny stiff collar and tie, and to carry a walking stick with a gold knob. This young man had been in Sutschky for just a few weeks, had struck up a friendship with the butcher Nikita Kolchin, and had pestered him for so long that he agreed to set up a coral business jointly with this Lakatos. There was a brilliant red sign outside with the name: Nikita Kolchin & Co.

In its window this shop displayed perfect shining red corals, lighter in weight than the stones of Nissen Piczenik, but also cheaper. A whole large coral necklace cost one ruble fifty, and there were smaller chains for eighty, fifty and twenty kopecks. The prices were prominently displayed in the window. Finally, to prevent anyone still walking past the shop, there was a phonograph inside turning out merry tunes all day long. It could be heard all over town, and in the outlying villages, too. There was no large market in Sutschky as there was in Progrody. Nevertheless – and in spite of the fact that it was harvest time – the farmers flocked to the shop of Mr. Lakatos to hear the music and buy the cheap corals.

One day, after Mr. Lakatos had been running his business successfully for a few weeks, a prosperous farmer came to Nissen Piczenik and said: "Nissen Semyonovitch, I can't believe the way you've been cheating me and everybody else these past twenty years. But now there's a man in Sutschky who's selling the most beautiful coral chains for fifty kopecks apiece. My wife wanted to go over there right away, but I thought I'd see what you had to say about it first, Nissen Semyonovitch."

"That Lakatos," said Nissen Piczenik, "is a thief and a cheat. There's no other way to explain his prices. But I'll go over there if you give me a lift in your cart."

"Very well," said the farmer, "see for yourself."

And so the coral merchant went to Sutschky. He stood in front of the shop window for a while, listening to the music blaring from inside the shop, then finally he stepped inside, and addressed Mr. Lakatos.

"I'm a coral seller myself," said Nissen Piczenik. "My wares come from Hamburg, Odessa, Trieste and Amsterdam, and I can't understand how you are able to sell such fine corals so cheaply."

"You're from the old school," replied Lakatos, "and if you'll pardon the expression, you're a bit behind the times."

So saying, he emerged from behind the counter – and Nissen Piczenik saw that he had a slight limp. His left leg was obviously shorter, because the heel of his left boot was twice as high as the one on his right. Powerful and intoxicating scents emanated from him – and one wondered what part of his frail body could possibly be home to all these scents. His hair was blackish blue as night. And while his dark eyes appeared gentle enough, they glowed so powerfully that a strange redness appeared to flare up in the midst of all their blackness. Under his curled black mustaches, Lakatos had a set of dazzling white and smiling mouse teeth.

"Well?" said the coral merchant Nissen Piczenik.

"Well," said Lakatos, "we're not mad. We don't go diving to the bottom of the sea. We simply manufacture artificial corals. I work for the company of Lowncastle Brothers, in New York. I've just had two very good years in Budapest. It doesn't bother the farmers. It didn't bother them in Hungary, it'll never bother them in Russia. Fine red flawless corals are what they're after. And I've got them. Cheap, competitively priced, pretty and wearable. What more do they want? Real corals don't come any better!" "What are your corals made of?" asked Nissen Piczenik. "Celluloid, my dear fellow, celluloid!" cried a delighted Lakatos. "It's no good arguing with science! Anyway, rubber trees grow in Africa, and it's rubber that you make celluloid out of. What's unnatural about that? Are rubber trees any less part of nature than corals? How is a rubber tree in Africa any worse than a coral tree on the sea bed? – Well, so what do you say? – Do you want to do a deal with me? – Just say the word! – A year from now, all your customers will have gone over to me, and you can take all your fine real corals back to the sea bed they came from. So, will you come in with me or not?"

"Give me two days to think it over," said Nissen Piczenik, and he went home.

VII

And that was how the Devil first came to tempt the coral merchant Nissen Piczenik. The Devil was Jenö Lakatos from Budapest, who introduced artificial coral to Russia, celluloid coral that burns with a bluish flame, the same color as the ring of purgatorial fire that burns around Hell.

When Nissen Piczenik got home, he kissed his wife indifferently on both cheeks, he greeted his threaders, and, with confused eyes, eyes confused by the Devil, he started looking at his beloved corals, his living corals that didn't look nearly as flawless as the fake celluloid corals that his rival Jenö Lakatos had shown him. And so the Devil inspired the honest coral merchant Nissen Piczenik with the idea of mixing fake corals with real.

One day he went to the public clerk in the post office and dictated a letter to Jenö Lakatos in Sutschky, and a few days later he received no less than twenty *pud* of fake coral. Dazzled and led astray by the Devil, Nissen Piczenik mixed the fake and the real corals, and thereby he betrayed both himself and the real corals.

The harvest was in progress out in the countryside, and hardly any farmers were coming to buy corals. But from the few who did occasionally turn up, Nissen Piczenik now earned more than he had before, when he had had many customers, thanks to the fake corals. He mixed genuine and fake – which was even worse than selling only fake. Because that is what happens to people when they are led astray by the Devil – they come to outdo him in devilishness. And so Nissen Piczenik outdid Jenö Lakatos from Budapest. And all that Nissen Piczenik earned he took conscientiously to Pinkas Warschawsky. And so corrupted had the coral merchant been by the Devil that he took real pleasure in the thought of his money being fruitful and multiplying.

Then one day the usurer Pinkas Warschawsky suddenly died, and at that Nissen Piczenik panicked, and he went right away to the usurer's heirs, and he demanded his money back with interest. It was paid out on the spot, and the sum came to no less than five thousand four hundred and fifty rubles and sixty kopecks. With that money he paid Lakatos for his fake corals, and he ordered another twenty *pud*.

One day the rich hop farmer came to Nissen Piczenik and asked for a chain of corals for one of his grandchildren, to ward off the Evil Eye.

The coral merchant threaded a chain made up entirely of fake corals, and he said: "These are the most beautiful corals I have."

The farmer paid him the price for real corals, and returned to the village.

A week after the fake corals had been placed round her neck, his granddaughter came down with diphtheria, and died horribly of suffocation. And in the village of Solovetzk where the rich farmer lived (and also in the surrounding villages), the news spread that the corals of Nissen Piczenik from Progrody brought bad luck and illness – and not only to those who had bought from him. For diphtheria began to rage in the surrounding villages, it took away many children, and the rumor spread that Nissen Piczenik's corals brought sickness and death.

And so that winter no more customers came to Nissen Piczenik. It was a hard winter. Every day brought with it an iron frost, hardly any snow fell, and even the ravens seemed to freeze as they crouched on the bare boughs of the chestnut trees. It grew very still in Nissen Piczenik's house. He dismissed his threaders one by one. On market days he sometimes ran into one of his old customers, but they never greeted him.

Yes, the farmers who in the summer had embraced him, now behaved as if they no longer knew the coral merchant.

The temperature fell to forty degrees below. The water froze in the water carrier's cans. A thick sheet of ice covered Nissen Piczenik's windows, so that he could no longer see what was going on in the street. Great heavy icicles hung from the crossbars of the iron grilles, and blinded the windows still further. Nissen Piczenik had no customers, but he blamed the severe winter for it, rather than the fake corals. And yet Mr. Lakatos's shop in Sutschky was continually bursting at the seams. The farmers bought his perfect cheap celluloid corals in preference to Nissen Piczenik's real ones.

The streets of the small town of Progrody were icy and treacherous. All the inhabitants teetered along with iron-tipped canes. Even so, some of them fell and broke their legs or their necks.

One evening, Nissen Piczenik's wife took a fall. She lay there unconscious for a long time before kind neighbors had pity on her and took her home.

She began to vomit violently. The army doctor of Progrody said she had a concussion.

She was taken to the hospital, and the doctor there confirmed the diagnosis of his army colleague.

The coral merchant visited his wife every day in the hospital. He sat down at her bedside, listened for half an hour to her meaningless babble, looked at her fevered eyes, her thinning hair, remembered the few tender times he had given her, sniffed the acrid camphor and iodine, and went back home, stood in front of the stove and prepared borscht and kasha for himself, cut bread and grated radish and brewed tea and lit the fire, all for himself. Then he tipped all the corals from his many bags on to one of his four tables, and started to sort them. Mr. Lakatos's celluloid corals he stored separately in the chest. The genuine corals had long since ceased to be like living creatures to Nissen Piczenik. Ever since Lakatos had turned up in the area, and since he, the coral merchant Nissen Piczenik had begun mixing up the flimsy celluloid stuff with the heavy real stones, the corals in his house were dead. Corals nowadays were made from celluloid! A dead substance to make corals that looked like live ones, and even more beautiful and perfect than the real live ones! Compared to that, what was the concussion of his wife?

Eight days later she died, it must have been of the effects of the concussion. But Nissen Piczenik told himself that she had not died only from her concussion, but also because her life had not been linked to that of any other human being in this world. No one had wanted her to remain alive, and so she had died.

Now the coral merchant Nissen Piczenik was a widower. He mourned his wife in the customary fashion. He bought her a relatively durable gravestone and had some pious phrases chiseled into it. He spoke the kaddish for her morning and night. But he did not miss her at all. He could make his own meals and his own tea. With his corals, he didn't feel lonely. All that saddened him was the fact that he had betrayed them to their false sisters, the celluloid corals, and himself to the dealer Lakatos.

He longed for spring, but when it came Nissen Piczenik realized that his longing had been pointless. In former years before Easter, when the icicles started melting a little at noon, the customers had come in their creaking wagons or on their jingling sleighs. They needed corals for Easter. But now spring had come, the sun was growing warm, with every day the icicles on the roofs grew shorter and the melting piles of snow by the side of the road grew smaller – and no customers came to Nissen Piczenik. In his oaken coffer, in his wheeled trunk which stood iron-hooped and massive next to the stove, the finest corals lay in piles, bunches and chains. But no customers came. It grew ever warmer, the snow vanished, balmy rains fell. Violets sprang up in the woods, and frogs croaked in the swamps: no customers came.

At about this time, a certain striking transformation in the person of Nissen Piczenik was first observed in Progrody. Yes, for the first time the people of the town began to suspect that the coral seller was an eccentric, even a peculiar fellow – and some lost their former respect for him, and others laughed openly at him. Many of the good people of Progrody no longer said: "There goes the coral merchant," instead, they said: "There goes Nissen Piczenik, he used to be a great coral merchant."

He had only himself to blame. He failed to behave in the way that the law and the dignity of widowerhood prescribed. If his strange friendship with the sailor Komrower was forgiven him, and their visit to Podgorzev's notorious bar, then his own further visits to that establishment could not be taken so lightly. For almost every day since the death of his wife, Nissen Piczenik visited Podgorzev's bar. He acquired a taste for mead, and when in time it got to be too sweet for him, he started mixing it with vodka. Sometimes one of the girls would sit beside him. And he, who all his life had known no other woman than his now dead wife, who had taken no pleasure in anything but stroking, sorting and threading his true loves, the corals, suddenly in Podgorzev's dive he succumbed to the cheap white flesh of women, to the pulsing of his own blood which mocked the dignity of a respectable existence, and to the wonderful narcotizing heat that radiated from the girls' bodies. So he drank and he stroked the girls who sat next to him or occasionally even on his lap. He felt pleasure, the same pleasure he felt when playing with his corals. And with his tough, red-haired fingers he groped, less expertly – with laughable clumsiness, in fact – for the nipples of the girls, which were as rosy red as some corals. And, as they say, he let himself go more and more, practically by the day. He felt it himself. His face grew thin, his bony back grew crooked and he no longer brushed his coat or his boots, or combed his beard. He recited his prayers mechanically every morning and evening. He felt it himself. He was no longer the coral merchant, he was Nissen Piczenik, formerly a great coral merchant.

He sensed that within a year, or maybe only six months, he would be the laughing-stock of the town – but what did he care? Progrody wasn't his home, his home was the ocean.

And so one day he made the fateful decision of his life.

But before that he went back to Sutschky one day – and there in the shop of Jenö Lakatos from Budapest he saw all his old customers, and they were listening to the blaring music on the phonograph, and buying celluloid corals at fifty kopecks a chain.

"So what did I tell you last year?" Lakatos called out to Nissen Piczenik. "You want another ten *pud*, twenty, thirty?"

Nissen Piczenik said: "I don't want any more fake corals. I only want to deal in real ones."

VIII

And he went home, back to Progrody, and he discreetly looked up the travel agent Benjamin Broczyner, who sold boat tickets to people who wanted to emigrate. These were for the most part deserters from the army or else the very poorest Jews, who had to go to Canada and America, and who provided Broczyner with his livelihood. He represented a Hamburg shipping company in Progrody.

"I want to go to Canada!" said the coral seller Nissen Piczenik. "And as soon as possible."

"The next sailing is on the *Phoenix* which leaves Hamburg in two weeks. We can have your papers all ready by then," said Broczyner.

"Good. Good," replied Piczenik. "And I don't want anyone to know about it."

And he went home and packed all his corals, his real ones, in his wheeled suitcase.

As for the celluloid corals, he placed them on the copper tray of the samovar, and he set fire to them and watched them burning with a blue flame and a terrible stench. It took a long time, there were more than fifteen *pud* of fake corals. Indeed, all that was left of the celluloid was a gigantic heap of gray-black scrolled ashes, and a cloud of blue-gray smoke twisting round the oil lamp in the middle of the room.

That was Nissen Piczenik's farewell to his home.

On 21 April, he boarded the steamship *Phoenix* in Hamburg, as a steerage passenger.

The ship had been four days at sea when disaster struck: perhaps some still remember it.

More than two hundred passengers went down with the *Phoenix*. They were drowned, of course.

But as far as Nissen Piczenik was concerned, who went down at the same time, one cannot simply say that he was drowned along with the others. It is truer to say that he went home to the corals, to the bottom of the ocean where the huge Leviathan lies coiled.

And, if we're to believe the report of a man who escaped death – as they say – by a miracle, then it appears that long before the lifeboat was filled, Nissen Piczenik leaped overboard to join his corals, his real corals.

I, for my part, willingly believe it, because I knew Nissen Piczenik, and I am ready to swear that he belonged to the corals, and that his only true home was the bottom of the ocean.

May he rest in peace beside the Leviathan until the coming of the Messiah.